S.L. Scott

Speak of the Devil

**trigger warning: NOT detailed in book - The heroine references she knew she couldn't misbehave without consequences from her father.

PLAYLIST

If you love music, the *Speak of the Devil* playlist is available on Spotify under my profile: slscottauthor

1. Down the Line - Beach Fossils
2. Good Looking - Suki Waterhouse
3. Taste - Sabrina Carpenter
4. Carpop - Daydream Twins.
5. Forever Dumb - Surf Curse
6. feelslikeimfallinginlove - Coldplay
7. If I Could - ALEXSUCKS
8. Obsession - Babe Rainbow
9. The Worst Person Alive - G Flip
10. Saturn - SZA
11. you look like you love me - Ella Langley, Riley Green
12. Guilty as Sin? - Taylor Swift
13. Monsters - Hurricane Bells
14. August - Taylor Swift
15. Lover - Taylor Swift

FOLLOW ME

To keep up to date with her writing and more, visit S.L. Scott's website: **www.slscottauthor.com**

To receive the newsletter about all of her publishing adventures, free books, giveaways, steals and more:

https://geni.us/SLScottNL

Follow me on TikTok: https://geni.us/SLTikTok
Follow on IG: https://geni.us/IGSLS
Follow on Bookbub: https://geni.us/SLScottBB

ALSO BY S.L. SCOTT

To keep up to date with her writing and more, visit her website: www.slscottauthor.com

To receive the scoop about all of her publishing adventures, free books, giveaways, steals and more:

Visit www.slscottauthor.com

Join S.L.'s Facebook group: S.L. Scott Books

Read the Bestselling Book that's been called **"The Most Romantic Book Ever"** by readers and have them raving. We Were Once is now available and FREE in Kindle Unlimited.

We Were Once

You do not want to miss the international sensation, **Best I Ever Had**. This book has won readers over with its emotion and soul deep love. **Best I Ever Had** is now available in ebook, audio, and paperback, and is Free in Kindle Unlimited.

Best I Ever Had

Audiobooks on Audible - CLICK HERE

The Westcott Series (Stand-alones)

Swear on My Life

Never Saw You Coming

Forgot to Say Goodbye

When I Had You

Never Have I Ever

Speak of the Devil

Hard to Resist Series (Stand-Alones)

The Resistance

The Reckoning

The Redemption

The Revolution

The Rebellion

The Crow Brothers (Stand-Alones)

Spark

Tulsa

Rivers

Ridge

The Crow Brothers Box Set

DARE - A Rock Star Hero (Stand-Alone)

New York Love Stories (Stand-Alones)

Never Got Over You

The One I Want

Crazy in Love

Head Over Feels

It Started with a Kiss

The Everest Brothers (Stand-Alones)

Everest - Ethan Everest

Bad Reputation - Hutton Everest

Force of Nature - Bennett Everest

The Everest Brothers Box Set

The Kingwood Series

SAVAGE

SAVIOR

SACRED

FINDING SOLACE

The Kingwood Series Box Set

Playboy in Paradise Series

Falling for the Playboy

Redeeming the Playboy

Loving the Playboy

Playboy in Paradise Box Set

Stand-Alone Books

Best I Ever Had

We Were Once

Along Came Charlie

Missing Grace

Finding Solace

Until I Met You

Drunk on Love

Lost in Translation

Sleeping with Mr. Sexy

Morning Glory

SPEAK OF THE DEVIL

S.L. SCOTT

1

Catalina "Cate" Farin

TEN MINUTES . . .

I lower my phone to the desk in front of me, but this wait is keeping me on the edge of my seat. Staring at a "Top Mortgage Broker of the Year" award framed on the wall, I drag my sweating palms down the front of my jeans. Sage green is supposed to be calming, but I grow more anxious the longer I'm stuck staring at these walls.

Is this deal going to fall apart at the last minute?

Has a red flag popped up on my credit report?

Are the owners backing out of the sale?

I covered my bases, but I still worry that I missed some detail. *Stop. Nothing was missed.* Not an I was left undotted or T missing its cross. Just like getting into college, earning my master's degree, and pursuing a career in medicine in a new city on my own, I have this. Like I always do.

But I'm glad I wore my hair in a ponytail off my neck, or I'd be sweating.

"Sorry to keep you waiting, Cate," Ross says, his eyes

glued to the paper in his hand as he walks back into the office.

"No worries." I shouldn't have wasted my energy stressing. Now he's back and—why is his brow hanging heavy off his forehead? "Is everything okay?"

He sits behind his desk and glides forward with a tap of the papers to align them on the hardwood surface. "Everything looks to be in order except for one piece."

"Oh? What's that?" Though I shouldn't, I let concern twist my stomach into knots. Buying my first home was a huge step, especially as I was building my career from the ground up. Five years of saving every other penny for the earnest money and down payment, leaving just enough to spend on a good time every now and again, has paid off today. "Hope I'm not about to lose this house," I joke, which isn't the least bit funny.

Although he has the courtesy to smile, his gaze bounces from my left hand to my eyes. "Your husband's financials weren't in the file."

"Sorry, come again?" I lean in because, surely, I misheard. "What do you mean by husband?"

Chuckling, he sets down the paperwork and leans back in his chair so casually that I find the briefest of comfort in the posture, like everything will work out. "I would have requested the reports sooner, but I didn't realize you were married since your husband was never mentioned. Do you happen to have his financials in order so we can submit them?"

I have a solid grasp of the English language, but I can't seem to understand what he's saying. In a show of trying to prove my singlehood, I rest my ringless left hand on the desk between us. "Bring what with me? I only brought the check for the down payment, as instructed. Everything else was attached in the email, which you said you received."

"It was all there except your husband's assets, bank statements—"

"My husband? You keep saying that like one will appear." I laugh, but I've lost the humor in this situation. "If I have a husband, this is news to me. Obviously, there's been a mix-up, and I don't want to lose the house that I had to outbid eight others to win. Can't we just update that document and finish the closing?"

"Unfortunately, we're going to need all the same information you submitted from him as well to close this deal."

"There is no husband," I say as panic takes over. "No husband's assets or bank accounts, no rings, and no exchange of vows." I take a breath, trying to calm the frustration that's tipping over on this poor guy. "Ross, there's been a mistake. Can we correct it and move forward?"

"I can't until I have all the paperwork. If you had mentioned your husband sooner, we—"

"I don't have a husband," I snap, popping to my feet. "One never existed. I've never been engaged, married, nor have I been divorced. No man of importance has been in my life for a long time. I don't know how to make this clearer."

I don't think he blinks for a good twenty awkward seconds, and then he huffs under his breath and picks up the paperwork again to study. "We use state and local records, but I can verify this online." His voice is even despite basically calling me a liar.

I hold my tongue and sit back down, a little embarrassed by my outburst, but still annoyed that this got so royally screwed up that I'm proclaiming to a practical stranger that no guy has ever wanted to put a ring on my finger.

Ross starts tapping quickly across the keys with his gaze

directed on the monitor while I sit tight, my entire future feeling a lot like it's wrapped up in his research. I tuck my hair behind my right ear and take another breath, this time slower to let it settle the turmoil inside me.

I thought buying a house would be fun, not a judgment on my dating life . . .

Inhale.

Exhale.

A place to call my very own without the assistance of anyone, without needing to wait until I marry. Now this happens . . .

Inhale.

Exhale . . .

His fingers stop, still poised like he's ready to test his typing speed. Then he hums, reading just softer than a whisper to himself. This is torture. He glances at me, and I catch a little accusatory side-eye as if he's just proved I didn't tell the truth.

I feel the cute little two-bedroom, two-bath home with the updated kitchen and large soaking tub slipping through my fingers with every second that passes. Every one of his judgmental slow blinks, the purse of his lips, and the heavy breathing through his nostrils takes me further from purchasing my charming blue home with white trim, a red door, and the orange tree that grows in the front.

Thirty minutes to the beach on a good traffic day.

A lively coffee shop two blocks over.

Two indie bookstores within a five-minute drive.

The home where I planned to start a garden and raise a few kittens is about to be given to the next bidder on the list. I can't let that happen. "What does it say?"

Turning back to me, he steeples his fingers. "You're

legally married in the state of California, so we'll need your husband's financials to close this deal."

"There must be a different Catalina Farin in your system."

"It's not *my* system. This is public records for the state, so if you've been confused for someone else . . ." He's right, knowing he can't change what the state got wrong. "This Catalina Farin matches your current occupation of nurse practitioner. There can't be two, so you'll need to take this up with them."

My temper cools as reality sets in, my heart crashing to the pit of my stomach. "Them, as in the state? Go plead my case like I have something to hide. I've never been married, Ross. I swear I haven't."

"I believe you, but I've never had something like this happen." He looks back at the screen as if he'll get a different answer this time. "Only one Catalina Farin shows up in public records."

"It's a unique name," I say as if recounting a story from my childhood. I hated it growing up, so I became Cat back then. Switching my mind away from anything that will lead to me having to explain my life's journey, my emotions begin to well in my throat.

"I'm sorry, Cate, there's nothing I can do to change the records, and as long as you're married in the eyes of the state, I can't hide assets on this purchase."

Taking a sobering breath, I ask, "How do I clear this up? Where do I even begin, and please don't tell me to get my husband's financials again." The laugh comes easier, the tension slowly dissolving. "Considering I don't have one and have no idea who the state of California has legally bound me to, that's not a viable option."

Ross comes around the desk and sits in the chair next to

me. "I don't have a solution. This is a first for me as well." His tone is sympathetic, his eyes rounding at the edges as the smallest of smiles squeezes between his cheeks. "Start with the county office where marriage licenses are filed."

"The county. Got it." That's a start. "I'll leave now, but be honest with me. Am I going to lose this house?"

"There is no clause to protect a buyer in this circumstance, but I'm sure they'll give you a few more days to get it sorted. I'll send a message to the real estate agent."

I stand, taking my phone and bag in hand. "I appreciate it, Ross. Hopefully, I can get it corrected in the system and close on this house."

He moves back to his chair. "My guess is it's just a clerical error. Fixed in a jiff."

"Let's hope." I start for the door when a little laugh bubbles up. "If I had known I had a husband, I would have taken advantage of the benefits." I reach the door and open it, wishing I had thought twice before speaking. Nothing says loneliness like admitting I want to take advantage of someone who doesn't exist. *Real classy.* "Instead, I'm tracking down some imaginary man I'm attached to."

"He's not imaginary," he says, stopping me in my tracks. "So he'll need to fix this on his end as well."

"What do you mean? He exists in real life?" I close the door and return to the desk. "Not just on paper?"

"There are two names on the marriage license."

"Who's my husband?" The words rush out as if my life depends on it. It sort of does.

Tapping the screen, he says, "Shane Faris."

My head jerks back. "Shane Faris?" My past and present come together slowly in my mind and are quickly followed by images from high school peppering my memories, flashes of flirting, and the kiss we once shared.

Out of all the people in California, how did I end up married to someone I went to high school with? This isn't feeling so random after all. "Are you sure?"

As if his eyes still deceive him, he squints. Turning the monitor toward me, he draws a line across the screen. "That's what it says right here."

"I know him." I stare at his name, disbelieving what I'm seeing with my own eyes. My chest squeezes as I try to riddle through how this could have happened. "We went to high school together."

"That's interesting," He leans back, rocking in his chair. "If you're going to be mistakenly married to someone, it could be worse than someone rich and famous. Am I right?"

I can't even force a laugh, still stuck on marriage and Shane Faris being said in the same sentence as my name. I catch up quickly, Ross's words hitting me on the head. "What in the world?" I whisper, still staring at the name on the screen. "Shane Faris is my husband?"

"I saw his band Faris Wheel play last summer. . ." His words blur as my mind tumbles through what this means.

What does it mean? "I'm married to Shane Faris."

"Incredible drummer. Top five of all time . . ."

Oh.

My.

God.

According to the state of California . . . *I'm married to a rock star.*

2

Cate

"Sixty-six?"

I snap my compact closed, feeling better now that I've touched up my makeup and straightened my hair. The lighter strands of highlights against my medium brown make me look fresher. I stand, push my hair over my shoulders, and cross the dim, fluorescently lit room, every clack of my hard heels echoing across the linoleum.

"Sixty-six," the lady behind the counter yells even louder this time.

"Hi, I'm here. I'm here." I hustle quicker and note her name on the tag pinned to her green blouse. "Hi, how are you?"

I'm not welcomed with a smile, but I can almost understand. The lobby is depressing, and despite couples being here to get married, a cloud hangs over her tight gray curls. Her icy-blue eyes shift beside me like she's expecting someone else. "Only you?"

"It's just me," I say, keeping my voice low to not make a scene that there's been a massive error.

"What can I do for you?"

Without background to fill her in, I land the punchline of the scenario, "I don't have a husband—"

"Sorry to hear that. Better you find out now instead of on the wedding day."

"Huh?" I finally realize she thinks I've been stood up. "No. No. He's not a no-show to marry me. He doesn't exist. Not in my world—"

"Oh," she says, covering her mouth. "I'm so sorry for your loss." The hand falls away as quickly as the surface-level concern from her expression did. "Death certificates are on the third floor. Take the elevator at the other end of the lobby." Her eyes dart past me, and she calls out, "Sixty-seven."

"No. No. No. Wait, Roberta." I throw my hands up, ready to plead my case. "There's been a mistake. Catalina Farin. You can look it up in the system. It says I'm married, but I never have been. The state of California has a man listed as my husband, though."

I feel someone hovering behind me. Dealing with this nonsense, I won't be pressured out of line prematurely. I turn around with my hands up between us. "She'll be with you in a minute, Sixty-seven." I nod toward the chairs, short of telling him to scram.

He grumbles but backs up, giving us space.

When I turn back to Roberta, she says, "Mrs. Farin—"

"Ms."

"*Ms.* Farin," she starts again, resting her hands on top of one another in front of her keyboard. "If he's listed legally as your husband, you'll have to divorce him. We can't just click a button to remove him. If only we could be so lucky to rid a loser out of our lives by pushing a button." Her laughter slips in the lobby and echoes. "You'll need to file through the courts." She waves Sixty-seven back up. "Approach."

Whipping my head to the side, I give him the evil eye. "Don't approach. I'm going to need a minute."

"Roberta," I say in a syrupy-sweet tone when I turn back. "There must be something you can do to help me. It's not *my* mistake." I know those are the wrong words the moment they leave my mouth.

Her eyes ice over and narrow, making me feel like the bull's-eye she's aiming for. "It's not mine either," she protests, crossing her arms over her large chest.

We stare at each other, but I know I'm the one who will lose in the end.

I thought I'd be unlocking my new house and moving in today. Ordering pizza and unpacking. That's clearly not going to happen now because Roberta has no intention of helping me unless I can produce a man.

I'm left with no other choice but to stalk a celebrity and convince him to divorce me.

Unsuccessful in my first attempt, I return to my car to start on plan B.

Sitting in my eleven-year-old car, it's a hot box until the air finally kicks in. I pull out my phone to start the online search now that I'm cooling down.

SHANE FARIS PHONE NUMBER.
Nothing.

SHANE FARIS HOME ADDRESS.

Los Angeles. Not helpful in a way I need, but at least we're in the same city to deal with this mess.

SHANE FARIS RECORD LABEL.
Outlaw Records.

OUTLAW RECORDS PHONE NUMBER.

"Bingo."

Taking the wildest chance that I'll get to speak with him, I call.

"Outlaw Records, how may I direct your call?"

"Shane Faris, please." The pause is particularly long, making me double-check that I wasn't hung up on. I bite my tongue and wait a few more seconds before I break. "Hello?"

"I can take a message."

Disappointing but not surprising. Like I'd really get to talk to someone famous just because I'm married to him and took a stab at calling his record label on the slimmest of chances he's hanging around the office randomly on a Monday.

I haven't thought this through. What do I say? Hey, call your wife? Surprise! You're married? *Ugh.* Is there a way to make me sound less like the stalker I am? "Is there a better time to call?"

"We only take messages for our clients."

"Ah. Right. Okay. Can you have him call Cate. C. A.T. E. Farin. F. A. R. I. N." I give her my number, and we disconnect. If I used her tone as a marker, he won't ever receive that message. She probably thinks I'm just another fan. I wish it were that easy to explain away.

That's not my case. But trying to explain that my future

relies on having a conversation with one of the biggest stars in music, add in me claiming to be his wife, and I'd probably be reported to the FBI.

It was probably best to keep the message simple and direct. Whether he ever gets it is another issue entirely.

So now what?

WITH A BOUQUET IN HAND, my best friend double steps when she sees me. "This is how I like to be greeted." I get a tight Luna embrace before she slips in the booth across from me. "A margarita on the rocks already waiting? You do love me."

"No lime. Tajin on the rim." I fluff my napkin over my lap. "Do I know you or what?"

Luna takes a sip, closing her eyes and savoring the liquid like it's been years since she's had such delights. It's been two days since we last went out. When her eyes reopen, she grins. "Better than any man ever did. Did I ever tell you how my college boyfriend used to always bring me six-packs of Stella Artois?" She's not really asking because she'll answer herself in three, two, one. "He just refused to believe I didn't love exactly what he did. I've always been a margarita girl. I love coffee. He loved tea. I think he was just pretentious."

"For loving tea?"

"No, the tea wasn't the issue. It was his collection of bags that outnumbered mine. He had like thirty Prada backpacks." She shrugs. "I didn't even know they made that many."

"And I thought I needed a drink." I adore her, but I feel like I'm about three drinks behind her when she's only on her first.

"God, I needed this after the day I've had—Oh, here." She hands the bouquet over the table. "Congratulations on the new home. Why aren't we celebrating at the new place?"

"Thank you, but I didn't close on the house." I smell them before setting them on the table.

"Oh no. What happened?" Her drink is forgotten, but her fingers find the basket of chips.

"There's been a mix-up with the paperwork. I spent hours trying to fix it but couldn't."

Reaching across the table, she gives my hand a squeeze. "I'm sorry. How are you feeling?" As an actress, Luna fills every one of her stories with life, imagery, and big feelings. As my best friend, she's always there for me—quieter, ready to listen, never throwing judgment around, and caring.

The adrenaline I've been running on all day drained away the moment I sat down, knowing I'm in a safe place to be able to tell her anything. "I'm not sure how I feel—numb, nervous, or frustrated by the situation. Maybe all the above."

"Do you want to talk about it?"

"You want the long or short version?"

As she reaches for a chip, her eyes widen. "There's a long version? Is that why we're drinking at three in the afternoon?" she asks as if it's odd for us. It's not. But day drinking is not usually a workweek event since I have a full-time job. The chip crumbles under the bite, causing crumbs to fly everywhere.

"I'm still processing what happened, so let's talk about you first."

She's dusting off her shirt when she replies, "The audition was terrible. I had absolutely no chemistry with the guy they cast as the lead, though I had sex with him three years ago in the pool house after an after-after Oscar party."

We met at a Hollywood party and instantly clicked.

Birds of a feather and all that jazz. We lead two entirely different lives, but we found common ground in the things that matter—friendship, loyalty, having each other's backs, and dating mishaps.

But four years into this friendship, she still manages to blindside me with some of her wilder stories. "Yikes. That bad, huh?"

"Yes, he was horrible in bed. How am I supposed to overcome that tragedy?"

"Well," I start, my head bobbing side to side. "That's kind of the purpose of your job. Pretending."

She can level me with a look, but she can never hold it and starts laughing. "True.

I didn't really want the part anyway. I just went because my dad pulled some strings to get me in the door."

"But you made it past the first three rounds all on your own. It's a hard business."

Anchoring her head to the side, she grins, but it's lacking the joy she usually carries with her. "They were doing my dad a favor." She takes another sip and then shrugs. "I have a feeling that nepotism has struck again."

Her dad is one of the biggest producers in Hollywood. He adores two things: his job and his daughter. After floundering around a few careers, she said she wanted to try acting at twenty-five. He cast her as a lead in a major motion picture that immediately panned her skills as "self-indulgent acting."

Self-indulgent? Maybe a little, but they missed the spark she brought to the part. I quite enjoyed her performance.

Luna Daize is hard to deter. She scrapped her team and started acting classes. Years later, she still can't land a role unless her dad is behind it. She loves the lifestyle he affords her but wants to earn the roles she gets.

She picks up her drink. "Enough about me. Tell me what happened with the house. Give me the long version."

I've debated how to tell her or anyone else. It's not a secret since it's only a mistake, but should I keep this on the down-low until after it's fixed? I need to vent, and who better to listen to my woes than someone who has heard and seen it all in LA?

Waggling my ringless fingers, I say, "I'm married." Margarita spews from her lips. "Luna!" I jump up, but my arm has already received the bulk of the liquid.

"Oh, I'm so sorry." She rushes around to rub me down with her napkin.

Batting her away, I say, "I have it. I have it." This is hardly the first time she's spewed her drink on me. We've made some great memories. "Can you turn away from me next time?" I tease, patting my skin dry.

She turns her attention to wiping the booth but still cackles under her breath. "You can't just drop a bomb on me like that."

Already giggling, I reply, "Apparently."

"I thought we were opposed to marriage."

"*You* are opposed to marriage. I've always been open to the idea. What I'm opposed to are the toads I've had to date to find my Prince Charming." Settling back into the booth, I reach over and pull her drink closer to me while I finish the story. For my safety because if that got her going, the rock star detail will finish her off, and drench me in the process. "As I was saying—"

"You're married?"

I nod, acting like any part of this is normal. The mental gymnastics of wrapping my head around what happened has worn me out. "According to the state of California, I am."

"I'm so confused. I feel like I've missed the start of the story." Swirling her finger in the air, she adds, "Rewind."

So I dive into the story, not leaving out any details. ". . . And then Ross says, Shane Faris is my husband."

"Shane Faris?" Her head drops lower, along with her jaw. "The drummer of Faris Wheel, *Shane Faris*?"

Grinning like a fool, I reply, "The very one." All I can do is laugh about this situation now.

She works hard to rid herself of the lines between her brows, but right now, they are out in full force despite her best efforts. "The same Shane Faris who made the sexiest man alive edition?"

As if this is my burden to bear, I try for solemn, but I'm not the actress and can't keep a poker face for anything. I end up smiling like a jackpot winner. Why not embrace this technicality while it exists? "I'm married to a rock star."

"Oh my God, Cate. That means—"

"I deserve the perks of being his wife? Luxury yachts, spontaneous trips to Europe . . ." I fluff my hair. "Spa memberships to use anytime I want?"

She cracks up laughing. "I was going to say that you never signed a prenup, so it's kind of the same thing. And trust me on the luxury yachting. It's overrated." Luna would know, but I'd love to find out for myself one day.

"Technically, I never married him either, so I'm not getting carried away thinking I'm winning half his estate. I wouldn't do that to him anyway. I don't want his money. I want my house, and right now, he's the only thing standing between me and the biggest purchase of my life, my little garden, and the kittens I want to raise."

"Listen," she says, scoping out the restaurant as if we're surrounded by spies. "You need to play this just right." Her green eyes return to mine, and she quirks a brow. "Sexy.

Talented. Top of his game. He has everything going for him."

"Including a soon-to-be ex-wife." I hold up my glass. "Cheers to that."

I'm side-eyed instead. "Let's think big picture here—"

"I'm not asking him for anything other than my freedom."

"Have you seen him lately?" She grabs her phone, ready to prove a point.

"I don't need to see him except when he's at the county office sweet-talking Roberta into fixing this error."

Glancing up, she asks, "Who's Roberta?" Then she squeals with a bounce in her chair. "See? Look at him!" Between gritted teeth, she grinds, "He's gorgeous."

I stare at the photo on her phone, finding myself smiling just looking at him. He really is an attractive man. More than . . . He was back in school as well. I had such a crush but did not have the nerve to act on it.

He did.

I remember the bonfire after graduation, the moon hanging over the horizon, and taking a walk with Shane down the beach to get away from the ruckus of the party. I haven't thought about that night in so long that it feels more like a dream to me now. Pressing my hand over my chest, I can feel my heart beating faster the moment I recall his lips touching mine.

One kiss. That's all we shared.

Of all the men in the world, I end up accidentally tied to him. Go figure.

"What happens now?" she asks, picking up her menu like this is totally normal. That's Hollywood for you. While she decides between the guacamole salad and the chicken tacos, I'm back to spinning, unsure what to do. Or order.

"I'll wait to see if he returns my call."

"You called him?"

"Called. Multiple times, but I didn't want to sound desperate."

"I think we're past that point." Tugging the basket of chips closer, she adds,

"Why rush things? You should enjoy the title of Mrs. for a while."

"I'm glad you're enjoying the chaos of my life."

"It's quite exciting compared to your normal day-to-day."

"True, but I'd rather deal with bickering retirees at Parkdale than be caught up in this mess." I pluck a chip from the basket, already knowing it's going to be hard to return to my patients when I'm so close to losing it all. "I don't need this kind of excitement. I need this resolved, or the house will go to the next highest bidder."

"Only you would luck into accidentally marrying a rock star and not want to take advantage of the situation." She smiles from the heart, saying, "You're too good for LA, Cate."

"Then why do I always fall for jerks?"

"Because they were fun when you met them."

"And then they show me who they really are." The last one sent me an invoice for an Uber because I chose a restaurant in Pasadena, which was too far for him to travel to meet me. That's his version. My side is that he thought he'd get laid on the first date because he bought me a burger at Hal's Burger House. I never paid. *Asshole.* "I'm starting to think Prince Charming doesn't exist."

"I gave up on that fairy tale a long time ago, but for you, I hope it comes true. Maybe Shane Faris—"

"Shane Faris," I whisper, not meaning to say it out loud as I roll his name around my thoughts. The images of him at the bonfire are still blazed into my memories.

"What are the chances?"

I think about it, toying with the idea of a coincidence. "One in a billion based on his fame. The odds are better, I suppose, that I've met him. Still, what are the chances . . ."

Turning to the server, she orders, "I'll have the chicken tacos with a guacamole salad on the side."

When a fresh basket of chips is delivered, Luna immediately grabs one, and says, "I can't resist." I laugh, though my mind is still on the coincidence that Shane Faris and I were put on the same marriage certificate by accident. Tapping her glass, she pulls me from my thoughts. "We're having another, right? Because I need to tell you about this date I went on last night, and you need to tell me how you know Shane Faris. You kind of left that very important tidbit out."

"I took the day off. Might as well make the most of it." I catch the server's attention and order, "Another round, please."

3

Shane Faris

I FEEL like the center of the fucking universe on stage. I'm a rock god with twenty-two thousand disciples of Faris Wheel singing the lyrics back to us.

No drugs nor alcohol can beat the high of performing live for fans who can't get enough of you. I have no complaints, but the three months of touring with only a handful of breaks makes it hard on the mind and body.

My hands are blistered and bloody from giving my all every night on the drum kit. I lost a drumstick mid-song when pain shot through my wrist. But there's no better high than killing it on percussion during the solo to end the show.

I won't disappoint. *I never do.*

That's why the ladies love me. Well, that and my—

"Shane Faris on drums!" Nikki says, closing the concert. "Thank you, and good night!"

Grabbing the shirt I pulled off halfway through the show, I walk to the edge of the stage and toss it into the audience. Plenty of beauties vie for my attention, but they'll have to be satisfied with my sticks. I give them to security to choose whoever he wants to give them to. He'll probably get laid. It always works for me. With a wave, I leave the stage, traveling down the steps.

I ruffle my hand over my hair to shake off the sweat dripping from the ends and move into the dark, where a curtain is pushed aside for me.

"Great show," Nikki says before drinking water. Soaked strands of her hair stick to the sides of her face. "But I lost my hairband on stage." She lifts her hair and rolls the cold bottle of water along the back of her neck. She kills it on stage every time she walks out there, captivating the audience with her vocal range and the edge she's mastered to rock our songs.

No doubt she's been the key, but we all must hold up our part of the show, or it falls apart for the band.

"I sweat my ass off." I reach for a bottle of water. It won't be enough to replace the water I lost during the performance, but it's a start. "These summer tours are brutal."

Laird grabs ice from the cooler to run over his shoulder. "Especially in Arizona." His guitar was left on stage, but the strap left its mark across his body, his neck rubbed raw. My cousin slips on a shirt that a roadie tossed him, then grabs another bottle of water to finish off.

Nikki kicks the toe of her shoe against her brother's, and asks, "How many shirts have you guys gone through on this tour?"

"Too many," I joke, wondering why no one tossed me a replacement. "Laird's end up on auction sites while mine end up in bed with hot-as-fuck women. I consider it a service to sacrifice my garments for their sexual pleasure."

"Disturbing," she adds, laughing right after.

"And fucking lies. My shirts make it home with plenty of women. I just don't keep track anymore. Why would I when I have the best wife a guy could ask for waiting for me at hom—"

I shove him sideways. "What happened to you, man? You used to be fun."

"Now he's in love," Nikki says, turning just in time to end up in her husband's arms.

Where the fuck did Tulsa Crow come from?

Lifting our lead singer, he kisses her. He's a cocky and sneaky fucker, but we all get along, which is good since he's a part of the family now. She wraps herself around him, and they kiss again like they just met, though they've been married for years. He says, "You were amazing on that stage, darlin'."

I'm with Laird, looking anywhere but at the lovebirds. She is my cousin, and I have no interest in seeing her make out with her husband. I can imagine it's worse for Laird. Realizing he's also a traitor, leaving me wingman-less and kicking it with the honeys on my own these days, I don't know how to feel lately. I'm the band's third member, but I'm starting to feel like a fifth wheel in our lives.

The three other members of The Crow Brothers band saunter over to hang at the side of the stage with us before they're announced to go on. Thank fuck. This whole lovey-dovey scene was getting on my nerves.

"How is it out there?" Jet asks, trying to catch a glimpse of the audience.

When Tulsa sets my cousin down, she tugs at her skirt, and replies, "Considering the heat, they're fantastic. I'd keep an eye out for any heat-related situations. Medics are standing by."

"Okay, I will." Since he's front and center playing guitar

and singing, he'll have that same view she had on stage. We've toured the past three summers with them since they're practically family, with Nikki and Tulsa being married and having a kid. It brought the Faris family and Crows together. The two bands touring to support each other was a natural step. But we should step into the headliner spot in the lineup next time.

With an album sitting on the charts, we've earned the spotlight.

Laird hits my arm. "Let's go." Turning to his sister, he asks, "Are you flying home with Tulsa or us?"

"Are you leaving now?" she asks. Laird and Nikki can't be visually more different even though they're twins, but Laird and I have a few similarities in our coloring and build. It makes sense that we didn't fall far from the Faris family tree when it came to genes.

"I'm ready to go," I respond, flexing my fingers so they don't tighten up on me or scab over too quickly. "My hand is busted, and I barely have the energy to stand upright." Seeing red snake through my fingers, I try to find something to wipe the blood away. "We haven't had enough time between gigs to let it heal."

She looks at me, and sympathy creases the corners of her eyes. "You guys go ahead. Get back and get some rest. I'll fly back with Tulsa." She studies my hand, and her expression falls into concern weaving through her forehead. "You'll take care of this before you leave?"

"Yeah," I lie, the blatancy needed to get back home quicker.

Laird and Nikki exchange a look before he says, "We'll see you back in LA."

They lean in to hug but then stop. "Ew." She laughs,

pushing her brother away. "We're too sweaty for that. Safe travels."

Laird and I head to the dressing room to grab our stuff. He asks, "You're not bringing any chicks, right?"

Pulling a tee over my head, I then close my bag. "Nah, not in the mood." I clean my hands to prep for new bandages, but I might let the fresh air heal me instead and deal with the rest tomorrow.

He chuckles, grabbing hold of his bag. "There's a first for everything."

"You're rubbing off on me, asshole. I used to be fun, getting laid and then skipping town. Now I'm becoming as boring as you without the perks of going home to someone." I follow him out the door with my bag thrown over my shoulder. "Don't think I haven't noticed how fast you're ready to jet after each stretch of shows."

"Since Poppy is pregnant with twins, the doctor ruled out flying to our shows." Still walking toward the door, he looks back at me. "Not going to lie, I can't wait to see her. I missed years loving that woman. I'm not going miss more than I need to for work."

Work? If that's all our struggles, efforts, and hard work are to him now, where does that leave me? I was warned about this part of growing up when I was a teen. My dad once told me to enjoy it now because one day I'll look around and everything will have changed. I just never saw it coming.

The sun is finally setting, but the temperatures are still blazing hot. The desert is quite the sight at sunset. Shades of orange and yellow blend into the remaining blue skies as we head to the SUV waiting to take us to the airport. I toss my bag in the back. The driver dips in to straighten our bags while we take over the second and third rows. After we settle in, I say, "Can I ask you something without you giving me shit for it?"

"I can't make that deal with you," he says behind a laugh. When I look back at him, Laird throws his hand between us. I slap mine against his. He adds, "You know you can trust me, Shane. Family first, always."

"I know." I lower my arm, staying angled his way. "How'd you know Poppy was the one?"

"Is there a reason you're asking?"

I've started searching for answers for a while now, unsure if I was going to blame them for how I feel or if I'm ready to make changes, like having someone waiting for me at home like he does. Nah, I'll blame my cousins. "Curiosity is all."

He turns his gaze out the window, seeming to ponder the question. "It was just different with her." Looking back at me, he adds, "And I knew it inside."

"Inside where?" I know what he means, but he still sounds like a fucking sap. And since I never promised not to give him a hard time, I'm obliged to take the shot.

Shaking his head, he chuckles again. "You haven't met the one."

"I'm not trying to. I don't have any interest in what you and Nikki are doing_"

"You will." He plugs in his earbuds, closing his eyes. "Now, if we're done with this heart-to-heart—"

"Shut it." I face forward, too awake to sleep on a thirty-minute car ride. I have an hour and a half ahead of me on the flight. But I can't wait to sleep in my own bed tonight.

Three hours later, I'm dropping my bag on the floor. Finally home. I lock the front door and head straight for the bedroom. A constant throbbing has replaced the feeling in my hands and wrists. At this point, exhaustion is running through my veins. I'm too tired to fuck around. I grab some packs from the freezer to ice my wrists, then strip the shirt from my body, kick off my shoes, tug my jeans down, and fall into bed.

"Oh shit!" I jump toward the headboard the moment I open my eyes. When my groggy mind catches up to the day, I ask, "What the fuck, Tommy? Why are you here so early?"

"It's two in the afternoon. I hadn't heard from you. Answer your phone every once in a damn while, and I wouldn't have to show up here unannounced." His tone doesn't give anything away, so I have to determine whether he's joking or mad by if the raging vein in his neck comes out to play. It's nowhere to be seen, so I lie back down again.

Naturally, I can't sleep. Especially knowing Tommy's sitting out there twiddling his thumbs while waiting for me. Staring up at the ceiling, I debate if I want to kick his ass for breaking in or get dressed to hear what he has to say. *Fuck me.* I push off the bed and land on my feet, aiming for the bathroom. I had plans of doing nothing but catching up on sleep today, but here I am, getting up to entertain him. I'm going to need two things to function, though: coffee and a shower.

A morning fuck wouldn't be bad either, but since I decided not to bring a woman to LA with me—not my wisest decision—I'll settle for the shower. Even with the water pouring down on me, easing the tension in my shoulders, I can't remember the last time I hooked up with a groupie.

When was the last time I booked a hotel room? Because I know I wasn't bringing women back to my sanctuary to fuck. When I need to sleep or shut out the ringing of the crowds in my ears, I do it here. It's not where I entertain one-night stands.

Coffee wafts into the bedroom, seducing me to the kitchen to find Tommy's brewed a pot.

He looks up from his phone before tucking it away. He says, "You guys are killing it on the charts."

I scrub a hand over my face, determined to get caffeine in me before I have any deep conversations. He's already made himself at home, taking up space on my couch like he intends to stay. I pour a cup and then ask, "What's so important that you had to break into my house to wake me?"

"You're killing it on stage. You're playing the hell out of those drums, and the fans are loving it."

Holding up my battered hands, I say, "Tell me something I don't know."

"You were sent the new contracts. Take a look at them, and if you have any questions, Rochelle and legal can meet with you to explain the details."

"But?" Leaning against the counter, I drink while he tries to get out whatever it is he's not saying.

"No but. But—"

"I knew it." I laugh, moving into the living room to sit in a chair by the coffee table. He's still chuckling, but I'm not. He's not one to beat around the bush. Tommy tells it like it is, so I start to wonder if something's wrong. "Everything okay?"

He grins like a motherfucker. I should have known he was fucking around. He says, "The band hit the bonuses for the gold records, and we want to lock down the next album with a bigger cut to Faris Wheel. How do you like those apples?"

"I like dollar bills better."

Chuckling, he stands, leaving his mug on the coffee table. "Yeah, I wanted to stop by to let you know personally. Keep kicking ass."

"I intend to." Our hands come together, but he pulls me in for a pat on the back. "It comes natural."

"Musicians are such a humble bunch." Pushing me away, he moves toward the door, his laughter trailing him. "Give 'em a stage, and they'll—"

"Take advantage of it every time."

"We'll go with that version. Hey, I'm heading to Laird's place next to tell him the good news. We included the band's requests, but still take a look at the paperwork. As soon as it's signed, we need to sit down as a band to discuss the next album, schedule studio time, and plan the next tour." Before grabbing the doorknob, he pulls his phone from his pocket. Texting, he says, "Someone left a handful of messages for you at the offices over the past few days. Serie flagged it because there was mention of a carriage, but she was reading a book at the time, so I'm thinking it was lost in translation."

My phone vibrates on the counter. I assume with the messages he just sent. "Will do." Glancing down, I only get a sneak peek, but his explanation makes more sense. "What's this part about Savage?"

"That's the name of the book."

Didn't know I was going to be riddling through this puzzle today, or I would have saved it until after the second cup of coffee. Reading the last exposed line, I look up at him totally confused. "Carriage?"

"That's the part that none of us could figure out. Not even Serie. HR is working with her on being more present at work."

"Someone looks desperate to get ahold of you." He

opens the door and walks out the front. "Let us know if we need to intervene to file a restraining order. Figured we'd check with you first to see if you recognize the caller."

"I'm not worried. The house has plenty of security."

Turning around, he walks backward. "We weren't worried about the house. We need to protect our people."

"And here I thought you'd say investment, ya big softie." I close the door and grab my phone to read the full text messages over coffee.

Scanning the first few lines, the name pops out first.

Cate Farin?

Cate . . . huh . . . Oh wow. *No way!* Cat?

Damnnn, Catalina Farin. That blast from the past doesn't disappoint. I scroll through the other messages, but Tommy's right. I can't make sense of how a carriage plays into the rest of the messages. I got her name but what the fuck with this number. It's a few digits short.

Running my fingers through my hair, I track back to that brown-eyed beauty in high school. I came back from our first tour to track her down, but she was gone.

Tommy's mention of intervening comes to mind when I count how many messages Cat left. *Five does seem excessive . .*
.

Should I give her the benefit of the doubt that she is anxious to reconnect? I'm a fucking superstar, so it's plausible. Or maybe she's turned into a groupie looking for one night with a rock star? We had a connection, though too brief, and she was hot back then. Can't say I'm not intrigued to see what she looks like now.

I could pop by and check her out from a distance since I have nothing on my schedule.

Chuckling, I'm starting to think maybe someone needs to intervene on her behalf with me sounding like a fucking stalker. I do what anyone would do in this situation. I get Rochelle at Outlaw Records to track down an address for me.

I'll see if I can catch a glimpse of Cat. If not, I'll find other entertainment in the form of a blond who likes fast cars and partying in the Hills, or maybe I'm more in the mood for a sexy fucking redhead and heading to Sunset. Live music, drinks, and then fun back at her place.

The choices are endless.

The opportunities in LA, or any other city, for that matter, are plenty.

My not-so-little black book of contacts has all kinds of women I can call on a moment's notice when I'm in town. A quick scroll and text, and the lucky lady will drop everything to spend time with me.

My stomach rumbles, distracting me from later to the here and now. I need food before any good time. I place an order to be delivered ASAP.

I barely have time to order food to the house before I have Cat Farin's address sitting on my phone.

She was gorgeous in high school and hands down the best-looking girl in our class. But I also remember how she used to make everyone feel like they mattered. I always felt like a rock star around her. *And now I am one.* Wonder how she'll react to me if I show up?

I eat with speed, not sure why I'm suddenly on a mission like it's my life's work, but I slip on my shoes and grab my wallet and keys to my Ferrari to see what Cat Farin's been up to all these years.

I'll check her out, then decide what to do after that.

With nothing to do and less to lose, I drive to the Valley.

4

Cate

"When was your last orgasm, Cate?"

I've learned to control my reaction when my patients try to shock me, but I've barely had time to set my bag on the table. So I fail today and pick my jaw off the retirement home floor. Adjusting the lapel of my white coat, I stretch my neck and try to reason my way back to calm, cool, and collected. "I think you meant to ask me how my day is going. Right, Maggie?"

"Nope." She pops the p, digging her heels in deeper, and stares at me with her vibrant green eyes, still expecting an answer.

Pulling out a chair for her, I won't egg her on by smiling, but a straight face is hard to maintain. I love how curious she is about others. She's kept her mind sharp and her wit intact. I only wish her curiosity didn't extend into my personal life. I'm not looking to feel bad about my recent lack-of-orgasms streak because one of my eighty-seven-year-old patients is looking for entertainment. I ask, "Were you always such a firecracker?"

"Yes. Was it recently?" She sits in the chair, facing away from me. "Achieved solo or by a partner?"

"Maggie," I caution with care. Knowing her for two years now, I shouldn't be so surprised by the intrusive line of questioning, but I still find myself having to restrain the shock from shaping my face. "That's inappropriate to ask your nurse."

She waves her hand in front of a scoff. "I gave up on being appropriate after my seventy-fifth birthday. I should have given it up when I was young and had a long life ahead. I missed out on so much choosing to be appropriate instead." Nodding her head, she adds, "Who cares what others think."

Her gaze lengthens across the room, landing on Mr. Rigsby. Looking up at me, she smiles. "Marty Freedleman asked me to make out in the back of his parents' 1955 Chrysler when I was eighteen. It was green with a sporty white stripe that matched the roof. What a car. What a man." Her tone is dreamy as if she can see him now. "He looked like a movie star standing in front of it."

I imagine Maggie was quite the catch herself. She still is. After winning Ms. Parkdale last month, she's been wearing her sash daily. I rest my hand on her shoulder and place my stethoscope to her back. "Did you take him up on his offer?"

"That's inappropriate to ask your patient," she says with a devious side-grin that has me raising an eyebrow.

"Is that a yes?"

Her hand covers mine with reassuring pressure, and she glances up at me over her shoulder. "No, I didn't, but I should have. I could just tell Marty was a great kisser. Have you ever had that feeling about someone?"

It's been a while . . . Oh wow, I can't remember the last time. I tick through all the bad dates I've had this year, and not one person would fit that description. Should I be sad no one evokes that emotion? Or glad I didn't settle for less? "Maybe a long time ago."

She laughs. "Oh honey, you don't know what a long time is. Why do you think I asked about your org—"

"Follow my finger." I shine a light in her eyes and move it back and forth. When I lower it, I add, "Your lungs have cleared."

"Uh-huh. I see what you did there, Nurse Cate." I don't get much past her. "Want some advice?"

I give her all the time she needs. "Sure, I'd like that."

"I still love my husband dearly." Henry passed years ago, but the sadness still hangs on her expression when she mentions him. My heart clenches just as she pats my hand and then shifts; the lightness of her usual personality returns the smile to her face. "But I regret being appropriate before I met him." Releasing a deep breath, she hums. "And I suppose since he passed."

If I'd been drinking a margarita, this would have been spew-worthy. "Keep doing what you're doing. It's working. Great checkup. The candy is in the bowl by Nurse Sandra." I stand back up and redirect my attention to my e-pad to make notes, hoping she doesn't loop this back to orgasms again because, frankly, it's been too long. I know it, and I suspect she can tell just by looking at me. "You're good to go. Stay hydrated per my usual recommendation, plenty of rest, and less needling Mrs. Louis."

Standing abruptly, she glares across the room. She can start a fire with only a look. "Daphne Louis talked to you, didn't she?"

"I'm not getting in the middle of—"

"I knew it." She fists her hands and whips her gaze to me. "She's such a snitch."

"I don't think getting yourself worked up over—"

"You know what she told me at gardening club on Tuesday?" There's no stopping her, so I let her vent. And secretly, I love to hear the Parkdale gossip. It's incredible what riles the residents up. Last week, it was sweet peas. A whole faction will only eat sweet corn, not the peas.

"What did she say?" When she keeps staring, I grow concerned. "Maggie?"

She grabs my arm, and says, "Good gracious, Cate."

"What is it?"

Running her fingers along the underside of the sash, she perks up—wide eyes and a smile that probably won Henry's heart. "They didn't make men like that in my day."

"What?"

"You think he ever dated a beauty queen?"

"Who are you talking about?" I follow her gaze to the front doors. The bright afternoon sun sneaks in, keeping a man in the shadow of a silhouette. Sunglasses shield his eyes until he turns in our direction and tugs them off.

Oh God.

He's here.

At my job.

Inside Parkdale Retirement Community.

Shane Faris.

The most gorgeous man I've ever laid eyes on.

My husband.

I bite my lip to savor that for a hot second until I remember what I'm wearing. *Dammit.* Anything in my closet would have been better than an ill-fitting beige skirt and a matching blouse that ties in a droopy bow at the neck, making me look like I'm auditioning to play the part of a

Parkdale couch in this scenario. Absolutely nothing about this outfit is sexy while he's looking every bit the rock star.

Naturally.

"There's always a first if he hasn't," she whispers.

"Maggie, please behave," I beg under my breath as a kaleidoscope of fluttering fills my stomach.

Twisting her sash, she marches forward. It's at that moment I realize she has no intention of behaving, and worse, she's going to take me down with her. Clearly, we're meant to be best friends.

"Sir, could you help me with this?" she asks, suddenly sounding like a doting great-grandmother in a TV Christmas movie instead of the spitfire she is.

"Of course."

She turns, facing me with a smug smile, and I swear I detect a devious glint in her eyes. *Trouble.*

Shane's eyes find mine, and a slight smirk comes into play. Then he says, "You're good to go, Mrs.—?"

"Mrs. Winston but call me Maggie."

"Hi, I'm Shane."

Not letting an opportunity pass her by, she squeezes his bicep and then glances my way as if to tease me. *That little minx.* "You're so big and strong, Shane," she says, making me think maybe she lied and did make out with Marty Freedleman. I wouldn't put it past her after seeing her in action.

"Thanks, Maggie. I work out regularly."

"It's paying off."

Chuckling under his breath, he looks from her to me again and nods in my direction. "Would you mind escorting me to see—"

"Nurse Cate?" she asks, grabbing his arm and staring up at him like he's James Dean reincarnated. "She's single, and it's been a long time since she's had an orgasm."

I cease to exist, withering from the inside out from mortification.

"Is that right?" His Mediterranean Sea–blue eyes lock onto mine while the most roguish grin I ever did see escapes him.

Unfortunately, I still exist in this reality where my orgasm history is on display for everyone. I try to hide the humiliation inside, to act like the little lady is so funny and full of tall fables. "Ha. Ha. Ha." I laugh, but it sounds so fake that I start laughing for real.

Dragging him over to where I've set up for my appointments today, she presents me like an entry in a pie contest with her hands stretched forward, displaying her baked goods. "And here she is."

I'm too caught up in the way he's devouring me whole to care about Maggie's antics. I swear that look alone could do me in, and the way he drags the pad of his thumb over his bottom lip has me biting mine. With a smile tugging the corners right up, he says, "Hello, Nurse Cate."

And this is how I happily die . . .

Swooned to death right here on the cold tile. All that will remain of me will be a white coat and an e-pad.

Bringing me back to life by pinching my arm, Maggie says, "When I talk about being inappropriate, this is the type of man I'm talking about."

"I'll take him from here . . . I mean *it* . . . him. You know what I mean. Have a great day, Maggie."

"Have fun, you two." She gives his arm a little squeeze as she leaves.

We both watch her walk away, a hint of silence leaving just enough room for me to grow nervous.

When Shane turns back, he says, "It's been a while, huh?"

"It's not been *that* long. I mean, if I really think back to the last time—*Oh*, you mean since we've seen each other?" I nod, about to bob my head right off my neck. "Yes, so long. Anyway, she's only four-eleven, but Maggie's a total menace. You can't believe everything she says."

"How long has it been?" His voice is smooth like whiskey. It would be easy to get drunk off the tone alone.

"Well, we were eighteen at the—" I facepalm myself. "You mean since my last . . ." I shake my head. "Can we talk about something else?"

"Like how good it is to see you?"

"Yes, I approve of that topic." Feeling every bit the schoolgirl talking to her crush, I look down at my shoes quickly but can't stop myself from staring into his eyes again. "It's good to see you, too, Shane."

Standing so sure of himself in front of me, he seems to have his life together, unlike the mess I am in his presence. He says, "You haven't changed."

Oh great. I've always been like this? I lick my lips, but my throat goes dry. Trying to clear it, I briefly turn away also hoping to catch the breath that escaped. I clear my throat again. *Why am I so nervous?*

I graduated summa cum laude from the University of Michigan.

Scored a coveted position in gerontology while earning my master's degree.

Worked my ass off to save a downpayment plus earnest money for a house all on my own.

So how is it that a guy I knew from high school, who also happens to be famous, has managed to turn me into my eighteen-year-old self, hoping to be kissed next to a bonfire in a matter of minutes in his presence?

I clasp my hands in front of me and raise my chin. I

refuse to act like a fan in front of him, even if I am one. "What brings you to Parkdale?"

He looks behind him, then drags his chin over his shoulder when his eyes return to me. "I was in the area."

Why does he have to be so attractive? *Still.*

"Yeah?" I feel my cheeks heating just looking at him. Wearing a T-shirt faded to gray with the sleeves hugging his biceps and a pair of jeans that have seen the wash more than a few times are hanging just right on him. I swear his jaw is modeled after the cliffs of La Jolla, with a dusting of scruff covering it. Even his hair is giving a rolled-out-of-bed sexy mess vibe. But I remember his eyes looking into mine like he could see the future.

Or maybe that's just how he makes me feel inside.

"No." He chuckles. "I was nowhere near, but I got your message, so I took a chance and drove over."

"Ah." I didn't expect to feel different around him now that he's a rock star, but I'm almost starstruck enough to have forgotten I called, that I'm married to this man, and will have to explain the mess we're in when I don't even fully understand the situation.

It's disappointing we couldn't carry on like old friends for a little longer. I'm not sure how he'll take the news, but I think it probably won't go well. Shaken from the fairy tale, the reality of our predicament kicks back in, and I say, "I'll be off work soon. Do you want to wait?"

"I'll wait for you." Shoving his hands in his pockets, he says, "I'll be in my car."

"Alright. I'll be done soon."

He turns to leave, but I catch him looking back over his shoulder, giving me a smile with so much potential. Too bad I'm about to ruin this reunion for us both.

I find the next file and call, "Mrs. Louis?"

Looking pretty in yellow, she comes over and sits in the chair. "I heard Maggie is gossiping about me again."

It's incredible how Shane Faris walked right back into my life, consuming me whole, and five minutes later, I'm back to playing mediator between two retirees. "I think if you two tried to talk to each—"

"I've tried. The best thing she can do is stick to Tai Chi on Tuesdays and leave me and the gardening club alone."

My nerves subsided the moment he walked away, so I dig back into helping my patients. This is about to be the longest thirty minutes of my life.

Downside to having to finish work?

Shane Faris waiting for me.

Silver lining?

Shane Faris waiting for me.

5

Cate

SKIPPING IS PROBABLY TOO MUCH.

Running would be worse.

Shane is here, and my heart wants me to burst through those doors to see him and to hear him call me Nurse Cate again. But most importantly, to settle this husband-wife thing we're tangled up in. But I walk because I'm an adult, not a giraffe-limbed teen anymore.

I do my round of usual goodbyes and then head for the exit. My eagerness to see him wanes as dread sneaks in, reminding me this isn't a date or a reunion of two friends. I have news to break to him, news that will change his life like it did mine.

It's not good to be the messenger. I know how that usually turns out.

Tugging at my collar, I push through doors, then scan the visitor's lot out front. I'm not sure what he's driving or where he parked. *Hmm.* I shade my eyes with my hand and even stand on my tiptoes to look around once more before heading in the direction where I parked.

Surely, he didn't leave . . . I check my watch. It's only been just under thirty minutes. Maybe he changed his mind and left. I hope not.

"Have a good night, Cate," a familiar woman's voice pulls my attention to a car in the front of the building.

Raising my free hand, I wave. "You, too, Misty." Parkdale's bookkeeper has her window down and gives me a little wave before driving away.

When it rolls forward, I'm caught by blue eyes that steal the show even under a cloudless sky and a smile that makes me forget who I am. *Temporarily.* My feet don't leave the spot where I stopped, trapped in a net of Shane Faris's attention.

Him, *the rock star.*

Me, *a woman who decided it was a good idea to wear all beige today . . .*

Shane Faris is waiting for me.

Me.

In spite of my early morning fashion decision, my heart beats loud like his drums, my breaths come hard and heavy from my chest, and those butterflies start fluttering wildly inside my tummy again. I'm not sure I'm the luckiest woman in the world, but I imagine this feeling is pretty close.

Giving me a wink, he pushes off his sports car and starts the short walk to greet me. Stark gaze, determined shoulders, his shirt ruffling lightly in the wind. Shane should come with a warning, He is a performer, but damn, I was not prepared for this show.

With brazen disregard for discretion, he takes me in from top to bottom like I'm his chosen dessert before dinner. I'm not even mad about it. Latching his eyes onto mine, he says, "Hey there, Nurse Cate."

My entire body blushes under his gaze, especially when it travels to my mouth. "Hi," I somehow manage to reply, though I'm not sure if I'm even breathing right now. I force myself to take one before I pass out in his arms even though I'm not totally against the idea. "What *really* brings you to the Valley, Shane Faris?" I ask, my throat raw with nerves. "You could have just called."

"I think this is more fun. Don't you, Catalina Farin?"

He remembers my name, *my full name*, saying it like he never forgot. I try to smother the giggle threatening to burst. "It's all fun until someone gets hurt."

"Are you going to hurt me?" Judging by the smirk on his face, pain is the last thing on his mind. *Or mine.*

I shift my bag in front of me, needing something more to hold on to. "It's not what I had in mind."

Tilting his head, he glances away briefly, and then asks, "And how do you know I don't live in the Valley?"

"You're . . ." I'm not sure if I need to point out the obvious, but he seems to be waiting. "Figured you would live in the Hollywood Hills, not by choice, but for proximity. The location is great, but Manhattan Beach or even Malibu might be more your jam. Ocean waves over city or hill views."

He chuckles and leans in, lowering his voice. "How do you figure?" he asks as if this is the most interesting thing he's ever heard.

"You're from La Jolla and grew up in a house with an ocean view."

"That was my cousin's house. I take it you went to a party over there? They had a few."

"Once. I wasn't invited. Just showed up like I could blend in. I didn't."

"You never could."

"Wow, okay . . ." I turn away, letting the insult sink in.

"I didn't mean it that way. You were never like other girls. You were too pretty."

I turn back, giving him my attention. "Go on . . ." Might as well soak it in and feed the pride demon.

When he laughs, I do as well. The release feels too good to let the tension remain between us. He says, "Nice. Too nice. You were so damn nice, a target for assholes in high school." I hadn't noticed we'd moved closer, the invisible line keeping us apart, broached by a few steps on both our parts. "How long were you at that party? I don't remember seeing you." I don't think he meant it rudely, but the comment still stings.

He and his cousin Laird were the kings of everything, including every girl's admiration. There was no reason for him to go looking for anything else when it was served on a silver platter to him. "Long enough to know I didn't belong." Making small talk with Shane Faris is not something I expected to be doing, but it's easier than I thought, considering he was so popular in high school and even more so now that he's famous.

"That's too bad. We could have hung out prior to the bonfire and gotten to know each other better."

I'm not sure what to say to that. Sure, it would've been nice to spend time with Shane back then, but life didn't end at the after-graduation party, and we both moved on. So, although my stress lessens the longer we stand around, deep down, casual conversation only delays the inevitable. I rip the bandage off. "You said you got my message?"

"All five." He may be smiling, but I cringe, tightening my hold on the bag's handles.

"Yikes. Sorry about that."

"It's okay. I go after what I want as well."

"Trust me, it was the most awkward call I've ever had to make. But it's such a relief that you already know." That he's not mad takes the pressure off from having to deal with that aspect before I beg him for this favor.

"Looks heavy." Reaching over, he wraps his hands around the handles, the sides of our hands together sending heat through me from the briefest encounters. "May I?"

"Thanks." Realizing we're still standing for all of Parkdale to gawk at from inside, I nod toward the larger section of the lot. "My car is around the corner." We walk in that direction, him holding my bag like it's as light as air while I still struggle to comprehend that he's here in the flesh. "I didn't expect you to show up at my work. How'd you know where I was?"

"A stroke of luck?"

"Doubt it." I quirk a quick smile, but then playfully bump into him. "Did you hire a detective to track me down?"

"I'm not that cunning. Deciphering the messages was a challenge. The new hire didn't include a seven-digit number. To her credit, she got the area code and first five on there."

I'm not sure if he's joking or not, but I go with it. "That's promising."

He stops and looks at me by his side. "To be honest, I asked a friend to do a search, and Parkdale's address came up for you."

I look at him, still stunned to see a rock star of his magnitude walking with me like this is normal. Maybe for him, but it's not for me. "Well, you found me. What are you going to do with me?"

He studies me out of the corner of his eye before his gaze shifts to the sidewalk in front of him. Sucking in a harsh

breath between his teeth, he holds my undivided attention
with his hiss. "Don't tempt me."

I've never wanted to tempt someone more.

I bite my tongue instead, knowing we have other business to tend to first. *First?* I need to get my mind out of the
gutter. Just because Shane is stupidly handsome to the point
of making me want to poke him to see if he's real doesn't
mean I should be having thoughts about him shirtless on a
beach or naked on a—*stop, Cate.*

I need to stop worrying about what happens next with
this man on a personal level. There's time for that if he's still
speaking to me once we're divorced. "I'm not sure if you've
had time to think about what we should do, but I have some
ideas."

His brow rises, breaking the evenness of his expression
prior to a wry grin sliding right into home base. "I'm hoping
Nurse Cate makes an appearance."

"It's such a relief to hear you say that. I've been worried
you wouldn't include me, do it without me, or want to get
others involved." I breathe easier, the burden lifted from my
shoulders, knowing I'm not alone in this mess. "I'm glad it
will be just the two of us. Well, us and Roberta."

His brows are squeezed so tightly together he could juice
lemons between them. "Who's Roberta?"

"She's the one who can help us."

Chuckling, he says, "We won't need help, baby."

"Baby?" I giggle as if the word commanded it. I hate that
I kind of like the nickname. "Do you say that to all the
girls?"

"Just the ones I'm going to fuck." He starts walking, the
distance growing when my entire being refuses to take
another step.

I'm still choking on his words when he finally discovers I'm not there. "Hey, what's wrong?"

"What's wrong?" I take a few steps closer, not wanting a scene in front of my biggest job assignment, so I keep a couple of feet between us. *For his safety.* I cross my arms over my chest, trying to restrain my anger. "Everything about what you just said to me is wrong."

"Which part?"

"The fucking part, Shane. That's what part." I march past him to the corner and nod so hard for him to follow that I might have pulled a muscle.

Shane catches me in only a few strides, but he then lets me stomp my way into the lead. I stop in front of my vehicle, my anger still burning in my gut. I poke him in the chest. "You may be big stuff—" He catches my finger before I land another, taking me by surprise.

"We don't have to do anything," he says as if sex is so casual that we'll be discussing the finer points before hopping into bed. "We can just get to know each other again."

"We didn't know each other the first time around. We talked, what? A handful of times and—"

"Kissed." I hate that his eyes seemed to have softened, reminding me not to jump to conclusions. Although his voice comforts like hot chocolate on a winter's night, he doesn't hide what's on his mind. "I might not remember seeing you at a party, but I remember that kiss." Releasing me, he runs his hand over his head, then wraps his palm around the back of his neck. "My apologies, Cat. I misread the situation. I assumed you called me to hook up, but there's no rush to do anything."

Taking my bag from him, I set it down beside me. I'd

rather have it on the sidewalk than in this man's possession. "There actually is."

He shifts, confusion narrowing his eyes. "Help me out here," he says, "I'm getting whiplash." Keeping his eyes on me, he drops his chin. "You do want to fuck?"

"Stop saying that. Good God, you're worse than Maggie. There's no fucking involved." I wish I hadn't swung my hands low in front of me to highlight that region of my body. The point could have been made without me redirecting his eyes below my waist. My face flares, and the burn in my cheeks causes me to sweat under the collar. I tug the bow loose and undo the top button of my blouse to cool down, but my mind travels at warp speed, causing chaos to my typically responsible self. "Like, none, it's been so long that we don't need to keep going on about the sex I'm not having."

Please Lord, take me now. I'm done here on earth. Toast.

"I don't know what you want, Cat."

"Cate."

"Cate," he says so quickly that it's hard to determine whether it's a jab or an innocent correction. *Hmm.* "What do you want? Just say it."

"I want a divorce." Throwing my arms wide, I say, "I figured you didn't want to stay in this marriage either."

So many emotions roll through his features that I'm unsure which will win out. "What the fuck are you talking about?" Annoyance takes the gold. Though anger might be trying to squeak in for a second-place finish.

"You know what?" I plant my hands on my hips, my good mood now soured by him. "I didn't cause this mess, so I don't appreciate your tone."

"My tone?" He laughs, but it's filled with a lack of

patience instead of humor. Looking around, he asks, "Is this a prank?"

"A prank?" Now, he has me paranoid. "*Is* this a prank?" I poke him hard in the chest again, accomplishing two things.

1. He's real. And he's hard. So hard my finger hurts.
2. A prank makes so much more sense.

I don't spot any cameras when I scan the parking lot and beyond, but technology is so good these days. Dropping my head back, I exhale, closing my eyes and soaking in the relief this brings me. When I lift back up, I cover my heart. "Thank God I didn't lose the house."

Good, now I can drop my guard and enjoy the reunion instead of dealing with this difficult situation. It feels so good to laugh. Resting my hand on his chest, I use him for support as the tension fades away like a cloud on a breezy day. "This week has been pure hell. I'm going to need a margarita after this." Looking around once more, I try to see if I spy Ross hanging around the bushes. I don't see him. Or anyone . . .

Maybe it's the silence or the way Shane's staring at me like I have two heads, but my gut tells me something isn't quite right. I lower my hand, but Shane takes a step back.

Anxiety returns, and I look at him to make it go away. "This was all a prank, right? Me losing the house. The marriage. You showing up here instead of calling. Feel free to hop in at any time."

That's when he takes another step backward. "The marriage?" The sensual roll of his dulcet tone clips at the ending. "I'm not marrying you. No offense."

I throw my hands up in surrender, and a shaky laugh

escapes me. "None taken. This wasn't ideal for me either. *No offense back at ya.* I'm just glad this was a joke."

"I don't know what you mean. I'm not in on any joke and didn't set out to prank you." He's backing away with every word coming from his mouth. With a shake of his head, disappointment fills his irises. "I thought you were different, but this crosses a line I've never seen before."

"What line have I crossed?" I walk behind him, baffled as to why he's making me feel foolish when I thought we were on the same page.

His pace picks up, and he doesn't bother to look back. "Married, Cat, really?"

"So it's *not* a prank," I whisper as reality dawns, burying me back in the nightmare I've been dealing with all week. "I'm really losing the house?"

There's no reply, but I can't let him get away. "We only have forty-eight hours, Shane."

Turning back, he looks at me from the end of the sidewalk. "For what?"

"To get to the county clerk's regarding the marriage license."

"Marriage?" he says. "Carriage. Fuck me. Fucking messages."

I move closer but don't want to alarm him anymore since he appears in dire peril. "I need you to go with me."

"No, Cat, Cate, whoever you are. I'm out of here."

"No, you can't. Don't leave me."

With his hands in front of him, he isn't surrendering. He's preparing. *Why?* "I can. Watch me." He turns his back and cuts through parked cars, but I see how he looks back as if I'm stalking him . . . Hit all at once with reality, I gasp, covering my mouth in disbelief. He doesn't know.

"You don't know," I voice barely above a whisper as if he can hear me.

The messages messed up by the new hire.

Me talking about marriage licenses.

Him rushing to his car like I'm about to attack him.

"Shane? Wait!" I run after him. "I'm not a stalker. I promise."

"Sure you aren't." Turning around in the middle of the lot, he scoffs. "That's what they all say, sweetheart. It's been . . . interesting."

"We need to talk."

"See you at the reunion, then." He has the decency not to run while I'm left ticking through the math of when the last reunion was held and counting the years until the next.

I panic. "The reunion isn't for another eight years?"

Nodding, he calls back, "I know."

"The messages were messed up." Cupping my hand to the side of my mouth, I shout, "I can explain the misunderstanding—"

"I got your messages. That's why I'm here. But I'm receiving this one louder and clearer. I'm out of here." He reaches his car, glances back, then ducks inside his vehicle. I hear the locks latch in place.

The heaviness of the disappointment and embarrassment I feel weighs on me, but I still make an effort to try again. "I only have forty-eight hours left to close this deal. I need you, Shane."

But I already know it's too late. He's reversed and ready to take off. "Shane? I can explain," I say, running up to a rolled-up window. And then I realize this is my last chance. I run in front of his car, reminding myself that a responsible adult wouldn't do that. It's not safe, but it's my only shot at getting through to him. "There's been a massive mistake."

Cracking his window, he commands, "Move out of the way."

"No, you don't understand. I tried to warn you in the messages." I dare to put my hands on the hood of his—*Oh my God, is this a Ferrari?* Matte black with the emblem between my hands confirms that, yes, it is indeed a Ferrari, and as stunning as he is.

A horn blaring startles the crap out of me, and I jump to the side, my natural instincts kicking in. He pulls around me, but the window is still sealed shut. Throwing my arms wide, I yell, "We're already married." But then I realize that will only make him drive away faster. I'm about to shout something else, but there's nothing I can say that won't make me sound like the stalker he already thinks I am.

I can't blame him. I wouldn't believe me either. Nothing about this situation makes any sense to a logical person.

Defeat sinks in, and my shoulders fall, watching him pull onto the main road. I tried . . . Insult to injury, the car's horsepower kicks into gear like he can't get away fast enough.

Now what? Hire a divorce attorney I can't afford to draw up the papers and hope they get filed before he obtains a restraining order?

The emotional toll of the past fifteen minutes have made every minute feel like a year of hard labor. I walk back to my car, more confused than ever about what I should do.

The first will be adding this encounter to the list of most mortifying things I've ever done. It definitely earns the top spot.

I load my bag into the back seat, then yank open the driver's door, ready to take a long bath and pray I can forget this ever happened. Tomorrow is another day to untangle this web.

Just before I sink in, I hear, "Why did you say we're married?"

6

Shane

"BECAUSE WE ARE," she says, moving closer to my car. I keep my foot on the brake, but I'm ready to hit the gas, just in case.

In this business, I had to be a quick study on reading people or they'd take advantage of me. I've gotten pretty good at it, and her eyes don't seem to be telling lies.

"Good night, Cate," a woman calls from a few cars down.

She turns to look and smiles when she sees a coworker. Her smile is so genuine, so pure, like the one I remember from when she was eighteen and standing on that beach. How'd this girl manage to stay herself through life in the twelve years since then?

So much has changed in my life, including me.

Cynical? *Maybe.*

Burned? *Many times.*

Guarded? *Definitely.*

Now that I know she isn't stalking me, I wasn't wrong in my initial assessment. Cat Farin is fucking stunning.

Gold threads through her hair, making her eyes shine brighter, if that's possible. I have to force my eyes off the curve of her neck and the fantasies forming in my head of licking her from the base to the shell of her ear. But it's when she shifts and her coat exposes the shape of her waist to those hips, the brown fabric not doing the killer body underneath justice.

When we were eighteen, she stole my breath and never gave it back. Even now I struggle to capture air into my lungs just looking at her. Like her beauty, it can't be caught.

I'm struck by a glare when I reach her eyes again. "You finished there?" she asks as if she's assuming I was undressing her. I was checking her out and far from done. But I'm definitely finished for good now because when she's angry, she's fucking spectacular. I bet she's great in bed. It's a fucking mystery why she isn't having sex whenever she wants. Looking that good, I'd fuck her at least once, even if she was stalking me. I mean, come on. *How could I resist?*

"Not really," I reply, "but we have business to tend to, so I'm all ears."

"First point of business, you thought I was trying to sleep with you?" she asks as if the words are insulting on top of the accusation.

"I didn't say anything about sleeping, sweetheart."

She gasps. "Are you kidding me?"

"Why lie?"

"You are . . ." She turns away as if the very sight of me leaves her speechless. Wouldn't be the first time that's happened to a woman. It's a regular occurrence, so I'm used to it. "You're a real piece of work, you know that?"

"I do know that."

Her head jerks back so fast she might need to see a chiropractor to fix it. "It's not a compliment, Shane."

With her buttons easily accessible, I continue to push a few more. "It would be a first, then."

"I can't." And then she apparently can because she anchors her fisted hands on the swell of her hips and stares at me like she's about to snap back. I don't think she has it in her. She's a sweet little nurse, after all. But it's fun to watch her try. "You really thought I reached out, that I left all those messages because I was desperate for sex? God, that's so LA of you. And then you thought I was stalking you because I didn't want to have sex with you? Is that right?"

"Stalkers say all kinds of crazy shit to get to me. Lie to my security. Pose as food delivery. Pretend to be gardeners, stalk my house, beg my band manager to meet me, claim to be family through 23 and Me, and show up at my parents' place back in La Jolla proclaiming undying love for their son. So it's not out of the realm of possibility that a chick from high school would try to reconnect now that I'm famous. It sure as fuck wouldn't be the first time—"

"It would be for me." She punctuates her response with an arched brow as her arms unwind with fists still restraining her fingers.

"What would be a first for you? Stalking a celebrity or hitting up someone for sex?" A myriad of emotions stumble through her expression along with a few verbal starts and stops, but she can't seem to lie to save herself. So I corner her. "You've never texted someone late at—"

"No!" She waves her arms erratically in front of her. "Not ever."

"Maybe that's why you're not having orgasms." I shrug. "Or sex." It was that moment I realized I had royally fucked up. With her mouth gaping open, she blinks rapidly at me. *Shit.* "Look, Cat—"

"Cate!" she corrects, then sends me to hell with a glare that would incinerate a weaker man.

"Cate," I say evenly, and then take a breath to find my inner calm since I'm trapped in the middle of her chaos. "This has gotten out of hand. Let's forget about the fucking for now—"

"Do you have that word on speed dial? Can you please stop saying it so much?"

"Can I stop saying what?"

She looks around like the swear police are going to nab her, and then whispers, "Fucking," with a roll of her eyes.

"Such a dirty mouth for a geriatrics nurse."

By the way she angles her head away from me, she tries to act like I'm nothing more than a gnat annoying her, but I see the smile tugging on her lips. She can't resist me or, at minimum, my sense of humor. Laughter is the way to her heart. *Noted.*

Breaking the uptight character she's been portraying, her shoulders rattle with amusement as her smile flies free, giving me a hard-earned victory. "Where do you think I learned those words?" With a huff of grievance, her shoulders lower, and she comes a little closer. "You really have women you don't know contacting you for sex?"

"I know you, Cate." Tightening my grip on the steering wheel, I confess, "That's why I'm here."

I'm not sure how I managed to turn this around with her, but I won't take her better mood for granted. She's still trying so hard to be mad about something by how much she's containing herself. I should go easy on her since we're on the right track. "As fun as it is teasing you about sex, which was your first point, I can't wait to find out about point two."

It's as if she's been given permission to relax, her body

alleviated from the defenses burdening it before, her fingers flexing from the fist. She says, "It started earlier this week when I went to buy a house." I have no idea where she's going with this, but I'm riveted. "All the paperwork was in perfect order." Stripping off the white coat, she says, "It's hot."

"Sure is."

She tosses it in the back seat of her Toyota. Not a flashy ride, but dependable. "Anyway, so I show up, and Ross, my mortgage broker, starts asking me for my husband's financials. Needless to say, I had no idea what he was talking about since I'm not married."

"Have you ever been married?"

"No. Just like you."

"Engaged?"

A huff escapes her, and she replies, "No, Shane."

"Why not?" Selfishly, I just want to know.

"Because I've been busy." Shooting her right eyebrow up, she says, "I was focusing on my career like you, but for a lot less pay." She's right.

The millions I've made would support me for the rest of my life, even if I never stepped on another stage. It's ridiculous money at levels that even a kid like me, who grew up with wealthy parents, can't wrap my head around. Does she deserve more? *Fuck yeah.* She's helping people, giving them comfort, and saving lives. "Wait a minute. How do you know I've never been married?"

"Because you're legally married to me. That's how."

"How are we legally married?" Although I feel my heart starting to thunder in my chest as panic rises in my throat, I try to remain calm. Freaking out won't get me to the answers any quicker. If there's one thing I've learned about who Cat is now, it's that her stories take the scenic route.

"That's what I'm getting to." Closing the gap between her and the car, she undoes another button near her neck. *The tease.* "I know this sounds wild, but I have two days to do one of the following:

    A. Prove you're not my husband. Or . . .
    B. Get a divorce if you are."

If I'm going to believe her, which I'm leaning toward on instinct, I still need proof. Should I be indulging her before I get said proof? *Probably not.* But I never was one to miss out on an adventure. "If any of this is true—"

"It's all true," she says, conviction taking control of her tone.

"What kind of proof does one need to show they're not married? That's not usually the lie people would tell, right?"

"I agree, but that's not the situation we're in, so all I can think to do is bring you back to Roberta and get a correction made." There's a thrill to her voice that makes me think she's confident of this plan when I'm still trying to catch up. "It's too late today. They're already closed, but we can go tomorrow." Getting me one step closer to agreeing, she smiles like she taught the sun how to shine.

"Why would she fix it if I'm there?"

"I only have two plans, Shane. I'm starting with A. If that doesn't work, then we move on to plan B." She stares at me like I'm expected to agree when I'm not sure what I can do if she didn't get it done already.

"So I show up, and what? Try to convince Roberta to believe us?"

"Yes."

I finally cut my engine off. "Why would she believe me over you?"

"She might," she replies, waving her hand in my direction, "because you're you."

"Because I'm in a band—"

"And famous and attractive."

She knows how to get her way. I'll loop back to the attractive part. "What if it doesn't work?"

"I don't need the negativity. I'm hot. I'm tired. It's been a horrible week, and you sit there comfortably in your fancy Ferrari with air-conditioning while I'm frying in the sun." She turns her back to me as if the Toyota tempts her to get inside.

I worry about giving her false hope that will only lead to disappointment. "I don't see how I can contribute in a way to help solve the house issue. We need to worry about this marriage situation first."

Dipping into her car, she sits there as if her thoughts have run away from her. "I don't know what to say to make you understand other than to lay it all out there. No holding cards close to my chest, just the God's honest truth." She angles to face me, and says, "I won't just lose the house. I'll lose the earnest money, which was all my savings outside of the down payment." She glances over at me one last time while reaching for her door. "I know this isn't your problem, and you don't owe me anything. But we are married and . . ." She sucks in a staggering breath. "Forget I ever contacted you. I can handle this on my own." She closes her door and starts the vehicle.

I'm left staring at her through the window, wondering what the fuck just happened.

We sit in our cars. Me, wondering why she's given up so fast when she's been nothing but a live wire of emotion this entire time.

Nah, it doesn't end like this. I release my door and move beside her car.

Cat ignoring me, despite being three inches from her window, makes it hard to get those soulful eyes to return to mine. While she's busy digging through her purse on the passenger's seat, I knock, willing to pick up the baton where it lays.

Deciding this is the perfect time to reapply her lipstick, she flips down the visor and applies it, leaving me standing right here next to her. And then I clue in . . .

"I'm sorry, Cate." The name still doesn't taste right on my tongue, but for her, I say it.

As soon as she puts the cap back on, she glances up at me, then cracks the window open. "Sorry for what?"

"I'm sorry for being an asshole, but can you give me the benefit of the doubt for questioning this story? For not jumping just because someone tells me to?"

With her pretty eyes staring into mine, I smirk but then give her what she wants—a genuine apology. Not something I do much these days. "I'm sorry for being an asshole. I didn't realize the gravity of the situation for you."

"I didn't need an apology, but I appreciate it." The window rolls down the rest of the way, and she holds her phone screen for me to read. "I should have done this in the first place." She taps the screen with the tip of her nail. "Look at this."

"It's a dot gov website."

Pulling it back down, she scrolls, then raises the phone toward me again. "See the names at the top of the page?"

My head drops forward after seeing our two names entangled throughout the document. I pinch the bridge of my nose before looking up again and scrolling to the top to see the category our names are listed under. Marriage

Licenses. "Fuck," I mutter, my eyes pivoting back to her. "That's public record?"

I press my palms to the top of her car, staring up at the sky as if I'll find a solution there. She sets the phone on her lap and reaches up to hold my wrist. "It's a lot to take in. Do you need to sit down?"

She could have been an asshole right back to me, knocked me off the throne I'd been sitting on this whole time, but she wasn't. "No . . . maybe."

"You can sit in my car with me if you'd like. No pressure."

I have a two-hundred-and seventy-nine-thousand-dollar custom car, but there is no debate in my head. I take the invite, moving around to the other side. She's dropping her purse in the back when I open the door. I climb in, lean back, and rummage through everything she's said.

I come to one conclusion: helping her is helping myself. I have no choice but to decide between two plans. There are not a lot of options other than helping to change the outcome.

I'm married. *I'm fucking married.*

It's shocking this information hasn't gotten out. It's my job to make sure it doesn't before it's fixed.

I roll my head to the side to face her, feeling trapped, though it's not her fault. This is heavy stuff and not what I imagined I'd be dealing with when I decided to see her today. The situation is what it is, though. All we can do is deal with it head-on using any means necessary. "Tell me about this Roberta."

7

Cate

I'M MET with dull gray everything—from the chairs to the walls to the linoleum flooring. "Cate," Shane calls, my name bouncing off the walls of the county clerk's office like a ball.

Even with what feels like a football field away, Shane Faris is easy to find. Nothing about him blends into the boring government waiting room. It's his hair, that mop of sex appeal that he wears like a badge of honor and the way he stares at me, like *I'm* the celebrity, that has me ready to maul him with my mouth.

My dreams about him were bad enough, in the sense that they were so good, but now I can't stop thinking about what he did to me last night in bed. I've never had a dream feel more real in my life. I'm pretty sure self-induced orgasms don't count in the way Maggie meant yesterday. But I won't deny that I'm feeling fantastic today.

I should probably be ashamed of what we did, even if only in my imagination, but I'm struggling to feel bad. I can't explain what's come over me regarding this man. I'm usually so temperate when it comes to guys, happy to take my time and see if we click.

I click with Shane.

At the very least, my body definitely understands the connection. So dirty . . . a giggle erupts.

I'm here for a reason, and it doesn't include the way he spread my legs—*dammit, Cate.* Get it together. Shane has shown up out of the kindness of his heart, taking time out of his busy schedule for me. So I need to collect myself and clear last night out of my brain. *For now.* Really, it should be forever. I have no business fantasizing about a rock star who will be out of my life as soon as he can be.

The long walk across the room draws bored eyes my way, my flats clacking loud enough along the linoleum to distract people from whatever they're doing. I'm glad my top is breezy when I walk, keeping the airflow around my torso. I try to avoid being the center of attention, but my cheeks are already heating under the gaze of so many people waiting their turn.

I catch the way he looks me over when I get closer, but I'm sure he caught me doing the same to him. Jeans, again, and sneakers, another tee that's seen a lot of years but fits him so well, and hands shoved in his pockets. I hate that my mind starts to wander right back to the wee hours when he kissed my inner thighs, then went higher. I can only imagine the real thing is even better.

"Hi," he says, standing.

"Hi."

We both lean in. Me thinking we'll shake hands. Him opening his arms to embrace me. A jab to his stomach has him groaning. "Oh gosh, I'm sorry." I scramble to cover the area I stabbed, but I'm met with muscles that I wouldn't mind seeing closer. "You hide rocks under there?"

Oh my God, please stop, I beg of myself.

"Yeah, that was not appropriate," I say, the words vomiting from my mouth. "I thought we were going in for a handshake." Covering my forehead with my hand, I'm tempted to close my eyes to hide from him, but since he's already seen me, I don't think that will work in my favor.

I reach over to help with the pain, but he's already got it covered, literally, with his hand. Taking a breath, he grins, but it's not half as big as I hoped it would be when he saw me. I thought we had made great headway yesterday, and now I've gone and injured the man. "It's okay," he says, sitting down. "But I won't make that mistake again."

"No, don't say that. Please. I'm so sorry. Please don't not hug me."

Chuckling, he asks, "Do you need a hug, Cate?"

It's been a long time since I've been held in someone's arms, so I don't lie. "I kind of do."

He stands, his hands taking hold of my arms. To keep me from stabbing him in the stomach again or to prepare me for what's about to happen? I don't know, but I stand still, so still that I don't even breathe as he wraps his arms around me.

I didn't expect him to do the dirty deed, but I'm never willingly leaving the warm embrace of his body. Not ever. I close my eyes, and the clean scent of his cologne and the way I get hints of him mixed in is intoxicating. Just as I melt against him, he releases me. I stumble but catch myself before he notices. Sitting back down, he pats the seat next to him. "I saved you a seat."

I'm not eighteen, but he makes me feel just like I did at the bonfire after graduation—giddy and alive. He's a dangerous combination that won't last, so I can't get sucked into the euphoria that is Shane Faris.

Sitting next to him, I set my purse on my lap, gripping it between my hands and hoping he can't see me inwardly freaking out, or he'll be running away like he did yesterday. This time, I'm sure he'd keep going. "Thanks," I reply, playing it off with a sway of my wrist. When I look around, not one seat is available in the waiting area, making his gesture even sweeter.

Shane's knee bumps into mine. "You know you don't need to be nervous around me."

"Pfft." I wave him off. "I'm not. I'm always like this." *What am I saying?*

"Anxious?"

He has a talent for throwing me off-kilter with his comments. There was all that "*fucking*" yesterday, and now he's diagnosing me in the lobby of the Los Angeles County clerk's office. "Um, that was not what I was going to say. The word particular fits better, or even responsible."

His knee taps mine twice, willing me to watch the connection and hope it repeats. "Why not toss dependable in the mix?"

I start an eye roll but catch myself before giving him the satisfaction of reacting. "You say that like it's a bad thing. Dependable is a great adjective."

"I say that because I can't imagine life being so orderly." He rests his arms forward on his legs, cupping his hands in front of him. "I live in twenty-four seven chaos."

"I can't imagine *that*. Sounds exhausting."

He chuckles and scrubs his hands over his face, ending with a slide of his fingers through his hair. When he sits back, he spreads his legs like he intends to be here for a while. "It is."

"Maybe you could use some order in your life?"

He shifts again. I'm not surprised he can't get comfortable. He's a big guy, and these chairs were made for earthly beings, not otherworldly rock gods of his stature. Resting his head back on the wall, he slips a slow grin onto his face. It's not big and showy, but it feels personal. "You're probably right."

Neither of us rushes to look away, but I finally blink, breaking the connection, which allows me to breathe again. It was almost easy to forget why we're here in the first place, but when the next number is called, I'm reminded. "Did you get a number?"

Holding up a slip of paper, he replies, "Eighty-three."

I glance up at the lighted board on the wall, then sag into my chair again since it will be a while. "Thirteen?" Glancing back at him, I add, "We're going to be here all day."

"Fourteen?" someone calls out from a distance.

He says, "It won't be so bad. We have each other to keep us company."

I'm kept guessing when it comes to him. He's arrogant and impulsive with his words, pushes my buttons—I'm thinking on purpose—but also can be a total gentleman, a good listener, puts me first, especially when he goes and says the sweetest things like that. My heart stops guarding the gate around him. "We do."

Two hours later . . .

"Fifty-two?"

"Come *onnn*." I close my eyes and drop my head into my hands. "I can't take this."

Touching my arm with a little rub of the exposed skin of my elbow, he stands. "I'll be right back."

Fortunately, I had rearranged my days, moving my visit to Beacon's Point Retirement Center to Friday, but I still had hoped to catch up on some paperwork at the office today. It's not looking likely by how slow the line is moving.

I'd been staring at my shoes, bored out of my mind instead of watching where Shane had disappeared when he reappears. I look up, sitting straighter. "Where'd you go?"

"Working my magic." His composed tone reassures me even with the nonspecific answer. Stressing sure wasn't helping, so this is a nice change. Though it's interesting to find comfort in a man I barely know simply because we joined forces on the same mission. Life is fascinating like that.

One day, I'm working with my patients.

The next day, I'm sitting in a lobby with a world-famous musician, waiting to get a divorce. A lot of steps were skipped between the two, but here we are, working together.

His sunglasses hide his eyes, so when he sits, I lean in closer to ask, "Hiding so you don't get recognized?"

"Something like that." He chuckles. "Sometimes I feel . . . normal again, having forgotten myself for a bit."

"Forgotten you're famous?"

Shane seems to ponder the question, mulling it over as he scrapes his teeth across the top of his bottom lip. "Yes," he whispers as if there's shame built in that he's come to accept. "Maybe not so much forgotten than remembering what it's like to be in public and not have anyone give a shit about me." He pulls the glasses off and eyes me out of the corner of his eye. "I'd pay to feel normal for an entire day."

I'm not sure what to say to that; the sentiment is not something I comprehend, but I reach over and cover the top of his hand with mine. I don't hold it. I'm just here for him.

He doesn't move his hand or pull away like I've crossed a line. We sit quietly together in the silence of the statement until another few numbers are called. It's strange how content I feel. This doesn't feel awkward but natural with him.

I slide my hand back to my denim-clad legs with a quick swipe of my palms down my thighs. Not to keep us suspended in whatever that was, I ask, "Are you really not going to tell me where you were?"

The clerk calls out, "Fifty-three?"

Standing, he lifts my arm by the elbow and takes me with him. "That's us."

"No, we're—"

"Fifty-three," he says, flipping a piece of paper up with that number on it and grinning like he got away with something he shouldn't have.

"You got someone to trade with you?"

"I don't want to make you an accomplice, so let's just leave it at I worked my magic."

Laughing softly, I say, "This is one of those perks of being famous I've always heard about, and I'm not complaining."

His hand slips around my lower back, and he whispers from behind my ear, "It's showtime."

A laugh bellows from my gut, the release feeling too good to use my inside voice. We slide up to the window like Bonnie and Clyde, ready to sweet-talk a cashier into handing over the money. Despite what I prefer, I put some space between us, a little pocket of air so our body language isn't misinterpreted. He rests on his arm, and says, "Hello, Roberta."

If she doesn't die from that sensual greeting, I will, and it wasn't even my name.

She spins to face him, smiling with a gleam in her eyes that reflects the unflattering fluorescent light above our heads. I recognize that look, but my eyes have stars, while hers carry fluorescent light beams.

Since I'm the one with everything on the line, I feel responsible for telling the story repeatedly, as if she didn't hear it a few days ago. By the blank stare she's giving me, I don't think she remembers a word of it or me.

I end it by showing off Shane like Vanna White, as if his presence, his denial to marrying me, will be enough proof to annul this marriage or, better yet, pretend it never happened.

He gets her back in the game when he nods on cue and leans in closer to eye level with her. When his chin dips down but his eyes stay locked on hers, she practically falls right off her stool. "What can we do here, Roberta?" His question is drawn out, his voice deeply personal as if they're the only two in the place. "How can we clear this up quickly?"

Glancing at me, he continues with his smooth voice that has gone into sultry territory. To her, he says, "Catalina is a lovely woman, and maybe under different circumstances we would have traveled down this road together. But under real life circumstances, we barely know each other."

"I married my husband after knowing him a month," Roberta counters, showing her ring to us. "He got this for our twentieth anniversary. We've celebrated fifteen since then." She straightens her shoulders, and that's when I realize it's already going downhill from here. "Maybe this is meant to be," she adds, "and an opportunity to spend a few days together to get to know each other better. In some countries, the couple doesn't even meet until—"

"You chose your husband, Roberta. I'd like to choose mine instead of leaving it to California." I lean in, my arm bumping against Shane's. "I've been married for twelve years and just found out four days ago."

"She's a gorgeous woman," Shane adds, suddenly drawing both of our attention. The unexpected compliment is both flattering and confusing. I have no idea where he's going with this, but I can't wait to find out.

A few seconds tick by as we stare at him, unsure what he'll say next or if he's going to say anything at all. When time drags on, I tuck my hair behind my ear, moving my eyes to his neck so I don't drown in the oceans of his eyes. "Um, thank you." With my hand signaling toward him, I tell her, "He's a very attractive man—"

"He really is," she adds, smiling at him again. "He deserves better."

"Hey, wait a minute." Raising my finger, I'm lost on how this turned on me. "I'm not so bad."

She's back to business but shoots me a stare. "He deserves someone who loves him."

"She does, too," Shane interjects. "A guy could only be so fortunate to call her his bride. She's funny, and well, she deserves to be called wife by someone she loves instead of due to a clerical error."

"I understand your frustration, Mr. Faris, but it's not been an error on our part." She looks between us, and her eyes land hard on me this time. *Again.* "There's an attraction to build on. I suggest you explore it because I'm not sure what kind of game you're playing, but your energy should be spent trying to make your marriage work."

Draping myself on the counter, I plead, "You have to help us." I can already see the house slipping away from me. The yo-yo of the highs and lows are trauma-inducing. "Please, Roberta."

"Pick yourself up, Mrs. Faris."

My back stiffens, giving me flashbacks from my childhood. "It's Farin."

"Now that's a coincidence. There's only one letter separating you from him. How convenient."

The warmth of Shane's hand finds my lower back again and rubs gently. "That's how we met in homeroom junior year. Catalina had just moved to—"

"That's all well and good," she interrupts, "and I'm sure it has a romantic plot twist since you got married, but I need to make myself very clear, Mr. Faris and Mrs. Farin. This isn't an error made in our office. All the correct information is filled out." She angles the screen toward us and points at a line. "As you can see, it's not a slip of the fingers by one of our employees. Around twenty different lines would have been filled out to make this official with signatures attached."

"Shit," he mutters, leaning in to read the screen. "Can we see the signatures?"

Clicking around the keyboard, she says, "Give me a second to get to that page. These computers, I swear, are from two thousand and four."

Too eager to look away, I'm staring at the screen like my life depends on it. I hear him whisper, "My signature is all over the internet. Autographs are sold on eBay."

Not to shoot down his theory before it has a chance to be proven, but my head can't wrap around the idea that someone would purposely do this to us. *Why me, of all people, if they were going for him?*

Since the scroll is so slow on Roberta's side of the window, I glance up at him. "Why would a fan legally bind you to me?"

The devil is in his eyes. "Legally bound to me. Why does that sound so incredibly sexy?" His tone is more fitting for cocktails at a hideaway bar where we'd have privacy before retiring to a hotel room. But that's not where we are, leaving me incapable of a response because my throat goes dry.

"Here you go," Roberta announces, eyeing the screen like I wasn't just about to mount this man beside me.

Returning my eyes to the monitor, I scan quickly to find the lines where we supposedly once signed. My body stills as I try to make sense of this. But I eventually turn to him for guidance, to say something, to help me understand how this happened. When Shane's eyes turn to mine, and he shrugs, I know we're in trouble. "It looks like it could be mine."

I look back once more, my future hanging in the balance of my response. "That's not my signature," I whisper, mentally kissing my house goodbye as I eye Cat Farin on the screen. "But it *was* when I was eighteen."

8

Shane

I'M NOT sure what to say, but anything would be better than the silence between us. "So we're married?"

"Yes," she replies at the end of a sigh, her eyes closing and her head dropping back like a weight on her neck.

There's no way to save her house unless my financials are attached, and that couldn't be gathered in time to help her. I understand her upset, the defeat overcoming her. I feel somewhat deflated as well, but I'm not sure it's from the reality of us actually being married or her reaction to us *being* married. "I'll try not to take your reaction personally, but damn, is it that bad being married to me?" I joke, hoping it lands the way it's intended.

A small smile grows when she opens her eyes, but she's still arching her brow at me. With a nudge to my arm, she laughs. "It's not funny."

"No, it's not." I chuckle.

"For real," she whines with that smile still shining. "What are we going to do?"

Her big eyes search mine for the answers neither of us has. Sadness permeates the inner golds of her irises, coating them with tears threatening to fall if I don't do something to fix this once and for all. She deserves happiness, but I'm not sure we can save the house in time. Taking a risk that may not pay off, I waggle my brows. "We could take the honeymoon we never had."

With a whack of her hand, she shakes her head and belts out laughter that travels across the lobby. "Shane, you're the worst." But I see the way her tears disappear, and joy takes over. Even if it's only for a moment, I'll take that reaction over the other.

With eyes on us, I know I can't stand around for long before the paparazzi are called so someone can get a payday. "Hate to cut this short, but I need to get out of here before a scene is caused."

She glances over her shoulder, suddenly in protective mode with a stiffening posture and ready to give the evil eye to anyone watching us. She's fucking adorable but has no idea what she's up against when it comes to my life. "Okay." Turning back to me, she whispers, "Let's talk outside."

Pushing through the door, she slips in front of me when I stop to let her by. "I'll make some calls about the—*oh shit.*" I duck back inside the building.

Cat tugs the door and returns after me. "What's wrong?"

"Paparazzi." Stupidly, I didn't realize the implications and how the story could be twisted and sold for a premium. "Fuck. I'm going to be all over the internet before I get home."

"The county clerk's—oh no." The reality of how this looks dawns in her eyes like a sunrise on the horizon. "I'm sorry for dragging you down here. They're going to think you're getting married."

"Or it will inspire them to do a little research and find out I already am. To you." *Fuck.* I've made her a target. *What have I done?* "I need to get out of here, but I can't take my car. It's too obvious."

"You can drive mine," she offers without hesitation. "They'll never expect to see you in my car. And I'm parked in the back lot, three aisles from the lamp post."

"Alright. That's what we'll do." Without having time to work through a plan, I start across the lobby back to Roberta. Cat is in tow, and as soon as we reach the window, she hands me her keys.

"Excuse me," I say, cutting in front of a happy couple. Roberta does a double-take, but I have her attention. "I need to exit out the back."

The guy next to me points his finger, though I'm only three inches from the dude. "Hey, you're Shane . . . Um . . ." He snaps his fingers. "What's your name again?"

Roberta hops off her stool, so tiny I can barely see her. "Last door down on the right. I'll meet you there."

My eyes only connect with Cat's briefly before we're on the move again. The door is opened, and Roberta waves us inside. "So you're a celebrity?"

"He's an incredible musician," Cat says as if she's paid PR.

I pause, watching my wife in wonder. *She's listened to Faris Wheel?* A warmth stirs inside me as I look at her in a different way. "Thanks."

Bumping into me, she plays it off. "Anytime."

If I weren't in such a hurry to get out of here, I'd be taking my time with her. But in this fucking life, time is stolen out from under us. I look at her hair hanging over her shoulders as her eyes exude the innocence of someone not exposed to my lifestyle. She's too beautiful to be caught up in my life. The last thing I want to do is put her under the invasive microscope of the press. "Stay here. If I'm caught, it shouldn't be with you."

"I'm not sure how to take that."

I glance back, and though a smile still creases her cheeks, I can tell I've left her unsure of my intentions. I stop and turn back, whispering, "I don't want them chasing you, digging into your life, or harassing you. That's what they'll do if they catch us together." I almost touch her cheek, caress the innocence and trust she's giving me through her eyes. I lower my hand for both of our sakes because this isn't the time or place.

We reach the exit in the back of the office, and they stop while I push through the door, and then look back. "There's a convenience store at the corner. I'll wait for you there."

"What about your car?" Cat asks, concern marring her forehead.

"Don't worry about it. My manager will get it." I step outside into the sunshine, but the blue sky can't compete with the gorgeous golden browns of her irises. "I'll see you soon."

She waves as if it might be a final goodbye, that worry still dominant in her features. "Be careful."

I chuckle. "Don't worry. Your car is safe with me."

"I'm not worried about the car. I was talking about you, Shane."

If we were any other couple in LA, every green flag would be waving for me to kiss her, but we don't live in reality. We're stuck inside the madness of my life. And with that comes long lenses and no privacy. I'm not able to do what I want, so I leave, taking away any option I thought I had back there.

It's better not to act like we could be a thing anyway. My

steps pause as the thought cements in my brain. *What am I saying?* Tied down is the last thing I want to be, not even in the bedroom. Plus, her life is designed exactly how she planned and is quiet. I bet she lounges around on Sundays and reads or something peaceful like that. She seems happy, and I'm struggling with the surety that being tied to me will taint her joy.

I'm a pro when it comes to trying to blend in. I'm not always successful; my height draws attention for most, but the photographers in LA are used to celebrities trying to move around incognito and have their eyes peeled. When I reach the corner, though, they aren't looking anywhere but at the front doors of the building.

What would I say if they saw me? Why am I here? Excuses run as fast as I do between cars on the first row, keeping my eyes on the ground and hitting the second lineup of vehicles. I work through that lot and to the back without them even looking around.

I recognize Cat's Toyota in the vicinity of where she directed me, but also by the ding on the back of her car. I hop in, jamming my legs. *Fuck me.* Adjusting the seat all the way back, I slide lower, hoping to escape without anyone noticing.

Cracking the window, I listen for my name while cruising responsibly through the parking lot, which I know Cat will appreciate. And then someone yells, "Hey, there he is! Get him."

Oh fuck. I sit up and go faster, reaching the exit but stopping to look both ways. I'm not getting in an accident for them. When I check the rearview mirror, they're all over some poor fuck on the steps. As much as I'm relieved they weren't coming for me, it sucks for that guy. Is nothing sacred in this city?

I look back once more, realizing that guy is basking in the attention. Keep 'em occupied, asshole. I take the long way around, and when I finally pull into the convenience store lot, Cat is already waiting for me.

I don't have many rules in my life. One night is my specialty, but I'm checking her out like she's my wife. *Fuck.* I shake my head, aware this is a unique situation. My wife. *Damn.* I reach around and scratch the back of my neck, not liking how good that sounds.

That tells me everything I need to know. For her sake, we need to wrap this up and both move on with our lives because she deserves better than a guy who has no interest in settling down.

Rolling down the passenger window, I stop in front of her. "Going my way?"

She opens the door and dips her head in. "Seems so." She buckles up just as I start to pull onto the main road. "Where are we heading?"

The bottom line is that I like the time I've spent with her. I like the way she needs me. It's different from how most women do. It may be out of necessity, but I can tell it's not a burden she carries regarding me. We're a team. Fuck my rules and her responsibilities. I glance over at her and give her my best newsworthy smirk. "Anywhere you want to go."

She looks ahead as if the world is our playground, then turns back to ask, "You hungry?"

"Starving."

"THE BEACH, HUH?" I relax, taking the last bite of my sandwich.

"It's grounding," she declares, letting the wind gently

blow across her face. "The sand and sound of the ocean reminds me of my childhood when we would visit my grandma. Coming to the beach was my favorite thing to do." Looking at me, she holds the remainder of her sandwich in one hand, sitting with her legs crossed. "I come out here to forget about the rat race of LA and just breathe in the salty air." Studying my face, she asks, "You never get out to the beach anymore?"

I sneak a glimpse of her when she's not looking. Even with her hair trapped in a band, some strands refuse to be tamed and blow wildly around her face. She wasn't wearing much makeup, but the wind has stolen most of it away. She's just as pretty, if not more so. I turn my gaze to the ocean's choppy waters. "I could bury myself in what I'm missing out on or live the life I have to the fullest."

"Do you live your life to the fullest?"

"I live. I've had experiences most will never get, traveled the world, and met people from every walk of life."

"Sounds like a dream, but you don't."

"I don't what?"

Wrapping the ends of the sub sandwich in the paper, she tucks it into the bag, and replies, "All those things are amazing, but they don't sound like your dream."

"I didn't set out to get famous."

"What did you set out to do?"

"Get chicks," I reply, chuckling.

She laughs, bringing her knees to her chest. "That worked out."

"It sure did."

Resting her chin on her knees, she doodles in the sand, but her eyes stay on mine. "Would you ever move back to La Jolla?"

I look out at the horizon, tossing around that question a

few times in my head. "Probably not. Our producers, the record label, our manager, and team are all here. So are my cousins and their families."

"What about your parents?"

Chuckling, I think about a text my dad sent yesterday from . . . I don't know where they are. "They travel a lot. They always did. I think I spent more time at Laird and Nikki's house than I did at my own growing up."

"I'm sorry," she says, the words grave in her tone.

"Nothing to be sorry about. They were good parents. We get along well. They just had big careers that took them away a lot." Tempted by her, I drag my finger through the sand. "Grounding is a good word," I add as if it's part of our conversation.

She smiles, facing me as if I'm more interesting than that incredible ocean in front of us. "We should get you to the beach more."

When I end up touching Cat's hand, I almost move mine away. I look down instead. "We should." I'll be a "we" with her any day.

Sliding my gaze from our fingers to her leg, I weave my way over the curve of her hip and higher to her chest. Still traveling north on her body, her lips make me lick mine, then I reach those eyes that encourage me to dig for treasure, the gold shining in the sunlight.

A heavy sigh is expelled on the launch of her saying, "I should go." She's lifting to her feet and dusting the sand from her jeans before I have a say in the matter.

I'm not sure what just happened, but she's right. I'm not looking for another friend, and she's not looking for a distraction. I stand, wiping the sand from my jeans, then grab the trash. It's tempting to ask all the questions populating my mind.

Why the rush?

Other plans?

Can I see you again?

Keep your mouth shut, Faris.

We walk to the parking lot, and I dump the trash in the bin. Producing her car key, I hold it in the air. "Thanks for the car."

"Anytime." When she smiles again, it's as if there's more she wants to say or time she'd like to burn with me. Or maybe I'm reading her all wrong. She takes the keys and looks down at them in her hand, fidgeting through the few on the ring. "I can give you a ride home." Looking back up, she adds, "I don't mind."

"The offer is enticing, but—"

"I'm happy to give you a ride." She cuts through two cars to get to hers, then turns back, still moving to her car. "Unless you're worried that I'm going to stalk you." Shrugging with her arms out to the sides, she laughs. "You willing to take the risk?" She's damn cute and even more enticing. Stopping in the middle of the parking lot, she huffs. "I double-dog dare you, Shane Faris."

I start walking because I never could pass up a dare. "Since you double-dog dared me ..."

9

Cate

I CATCH Shane sneaking peeks at me when he thinks I'm not looking. I swear his gaze softens, and my heart softens along with it. A gentle pitter-patter that leaves me wondering where we go from here. *Other than the divorce attorney's office, that is.*

There's no arrogance tucked into the corners of his mouth when he smiles at me. His eyes don't seem to hide any agendas to keep me on guard. But I still need to be careful with him. He's someone who "lives life to the fullest" as he puts it. That's not a lifestyle that meshes well with the predictability of my comfort zone.

Responsible.

Dependable.

Beige and boring.

I can't seem to set aside that he basically insinuated my life is orderly, in those exact words, too. Just another reason to safeguard my heart and keep him solidly in the friend zone. No harm in having a good time for a few hours that doesn't include a bed. That will probably be new for him and a nice change of pace as well.

We're finally moving through traffic again, and I turn as directed. I have always loved the tree-lined streets of Hollywood Hills, but it still surprises me that he lives here. "Do you still surf?" I ask, glancing at him when I come to a stop sign.

"Not as much as I'd like."

"Living by the beach might help."

He nods. "When I'm home for longer periods, I'll hit the waves with Laird sometimes."

I take a left, driving higher into the hills. "I'm failing in my stalking duties. Hope you don't mind the questions." That earns me a smile.

"I don't."

"Do you tour a lot?" I try to keep my eyes on the road but prefer looking at him. He's a very attractive . . . *friend*, I remind myself once again.

"The band always tours during the summer months, but we've been going since April of this year."

"It's August."

His head drops back on the headrest. "Yeah, it was a world tour to support our new album," he replies, staring out the side window. "It ends next month."

"Now I understand why you're exhausted."

"I love what I do."

"I'm sure, but it doesn't mean you don't burn out." I pull in front of a gate and brake. "How long are you home?" I ask, sounding very stalkerish.

Maybe he felt the same way because of the grin leading to a soft chuckle. "I leave tomorrow morning." He still answered without hesitation.

Shifting into park, I angle toward him. "Am I reading

you all wrong? You said you love what you do, but you don't seem excited . . ." When his eyes connect with mine, I whisper, "Or happy."

He shifts a wry grin into place, but it isn't natural. Not when deeper emotions hide in the depths of his eyes. "I'm about to get a divorce. What's there to be happy about?" He chuckles, but it's kept under wraps before humor has a chance to amp it up. He looks at the iron gate, a wall of steel blocking the view of the property. "You know where I live now." He gives me a wink along with a click of his tongue. "Don't break in and murder me in my sleep, okay?"

"If I were breaking in, I wouldn't murder you."

"Oh yeah? What would you do to me?"

I raise a finger in the air, laughter getting the better of me. "I think this is when I should say goodbye. I have a busy day ahead."

He pops the door open. "That's too bad. I was about to invite you in." Shutting the door behind him, he crosses in front of the car and punches in a code on the keypad I'm parked next to.

I'm still trying to convince myself that us becoming friends is a nice consolation prize. *Screw it.* Rolling down the window, I say, "Funny enough, my schedule just cleared. Want a ride to your mansion's front door?"

His laugh is bold and hearty as he stands in front of the gates as they open. "I think I can manage. I'll see you up there."

I watch him start up the edge of the driveway. It's not particularly long compared to what I imagined, but the house does not disappoint. It's smaller than I pictured in my head. *I like that.* A lot. Like he didn't sell his soul to LA yet. I'd say give him time, but he's had twelve years, and he still chose a modest house compared to Hollywood standards. I park and get out just as he walks up a short sidewalk to the front door.

The home is the opposite of modern on the outside. Greenery climbs the grayish bricks; French blue accents trim the roofline and highlight the front door. I assume he purchased it as is, but I'm still curious. "I love the house."

"Thanks. I had nothing to do with it. It came this way." He opens the door and waits for me to enter. "I knew it was the one when I saw it, though."

"But you kept it this way, so some credit is due." Across the living area, I'm hit by an incredible view of the city, causing my breath to catch. "Wow, that's . . ." I keep walking as if drawn to the light. "That view is everything."

"The house is unassuming in the front, which was what drew me to it. And then you walk in, and it's updated and bright, has a pool, but that view." He nods, staring through the glass. "That's why I bought it."

I look around the living room and back toward the kitchen. White walls surround serene furniture. A wooden coffee table accents a neutral beige couch, and a plush leather chair rests on the hardwood floor nearby. The sterile aesthetic feels more akin to the nursing home than a rock star's crash pad. Sparse furniture and a painting on the wall don't make it a home. I glance at him, not feeling like this place represents him at all.

"My bedroom is down the hall on the left if you're taking notes."

"Good to know." I smirk, giving him the satisfaction. Tapping my temple, I reply, "It's all up here for future reference."

Grinning like he has a juicy secret, he asks, "What can I get you to drink?"

I like the time together without the pressures of trying to

save a house or convincing people to help us. I still feel sick over losing the earnest money, but there's relief found in the slowdown of knowing it's over. The fight, the battle, the war was lost. "I'm good right now. I guess we should talk about how to proceed from here, though?"

"Want to sit outside or—?"

I wouldn't mind staring at the view while I can. "We can go outside."

He opens a massive sliding glass door and leaves it, so a breeze reaches me before I even step out. The pool is modern in design but isn't huge. Perfect for a family or couple, or a single guy in his case, to cool off. I wonder how often he uses it.

Making myself at home on a lounge chair with a puffy black-and-white cushion, I lie back, close my eyes, and soak in the sunrays. "I'd spend all my time out here if I had this to come home to."

"What would you do?"

"Read. Catch up on social media. Nap." I don't know why I make that sound like I'm breaking a rule, but a nap sounds indulgent to me most days.

"I don't use it as much as I should. I come out more often at night and watch the lights as I hit my sticks against the cushion." I watch him settle at the table nearby. He picks the far chair and faces me.

"You practice on your days off? Seems like you'd be a pro by now." Just a little teasing before we delve deeper.

By the amusement on his face, he gets me. "Probably not considered practicing at this stage in my career, but I still hit when I'm not performing." As if he's in on a joke I'm not, his chuckle remains under his breath. "Believe it or not, it relaxes me."

"I can believe it. Gardening relaxes me. It's work, but something peaceful can be found in its simplicity."

"And a reward in the results." It's strange how different we are but can still manage to find something to relate to. He says, "I'm sorry about the house. How much money did you lose?" He sits forward, his words rushing out, "I shouldn't have asked something so personal. You don't have to answer that."

"It's nothing in the scheme of your life, but it was years of sacrifice for me." I shouldn't feel defensive. He's done nothing wrong and so much good to help me. "I'm sorry for. . . that."

"Money is a tricky topic probably best left untouched among friends."

Friends. A kind reminder slipping back into my heart.

"Well," I start, remembering how it played out a few months ago. "My agent advised me to bid higher if I really wanted the house. Someone already had a thirty-five-thou-sand-dollar earnest money offer on the table. I took a chance and won the house but lost in the end."

"The sellers won't give it back?"

"Legally, they don't have to since the issue was on my side." I crisscross my legs and pluck at a loose thread on the cushion. I glance over, trying not to stare even though he beats the view of the city hands down every time. "That was my signature on the license, and I can only reason that it was yours since it's from before your signature went to the highest bidder."

"Odd, right?"

"It makes no sense and leaves us no choice but to file for divorce." I watch his face to see if I can detect how he feels, but I've discovered he's good at keeping his expression shifted in neutral when he wants to. "It might go public."

Dropping his sunglasses over his eyes, he angles away from me, redirecting his gaze beyond the hills. "I have people who can control it if given a heads-up."

"So secretive."

"Best you're not involved." The scrunch of his nose is a nice touch and draws me right in, making me want to be a part of any plan he's concocting.

"I'm already pretty damn involved." Speaking of rewards, I'm given a quirk of his lips that wins hearts all over the world. *And now I see why. Not that I didn't know already.* That charming smile hasn't changed so much since high school.

He sits forward suddenly, angling my way. "The timing will be everything. We'll need to plan this carefully."

His energy is contagious. "I love to plan. It's my specialty."

The dropping of his mouth isn't necessary. "Planning is your specialty?"

If I hadn't already hit my quota of eye rolls for the day, he'd be gifted with my most epic version. "You know what?" I fail to keep a straight face. "Not all of us need the limelight to get off."

He doesn't bother with polite. Shane practically laughs in my face. "Nothing like spending a Friday night with a good planner. You know, the kind with the grids and the extra numbered spaces to check off your accomplishments that day."

I push up, but before I stand, he's coming around the table with his hands up in surrender. "I'm kidding, Cat. Just giving you a hard time." He drops into the chair next to me, kicking his legs out and crossing them at the ankle, looking more like a movie star than ever.

I finally relax again, bending my legs at the knee just in case I need to duck out quickly. "Not funny."

"Kind of funny?" Holding up his fingers just an inch apart, he asks, "Just a little?"

Going for a half inch myself, I hold up my fingers. "Microscopically entertaining."

It's not like he stopped grinning, but it cracks his expression wide open. "I'll take microscopic unless it's referring to—"

"Nope," I say, stopping him with my hand between us before he finishes that sentence. "I've made a grave mistake by joking with you."

He chuckles and lifts his sunglasses back to the top of his head. "What is it about sex that makes you so uncomfortable?"

"You sure do make a lot of assumptions about me."

"I'll assume you do the same."

"See?" I swerve out my hand like a server's tray. "There's a prime example."

If someone had asked me even a week ago if I would be hanging out with Shane Faris, a guy I had a crush on in high school, I wouldn't have believed them. *Yet here we are.*

Though he embodies the rock star in the sexy bad boy way, he's also just Shane from the bonfire having a good time. He sure is making it hard to remember we're just friends at best or still acquaintances getting to know each other.

"You have me all figured out, Cat Farin."

"I don't think I've scratched the surface, Shane Faris."

"Is scratching something you're into?"

"Stop it. We're not going there. Not ever."

"Mmm." I catch him with his eyes closed, shaking his

head. "That's too bad. Not ever is a *long* time." Peeking his eyes open, he asks, "You up for the challenge?"

Laying my head back on the cushion, I close my eyes, enjoying everything about this moment. "Guess we'll find out."

"We sure will." Every word from his mouth feels like an insinuation of me ending up in his bed. No matter how deliciously naughty that idea is, I need to be careful. He's a celebrity, and for him, notches on bedposts are a dime a dozen. I can be one of many, or I can safeguard my heart. But I have a strong feeling I can't do both with him.

Dropping his feet to either side of the chair, he gives me that billion-dollar smile, looking happier than I've seen him, and asks, "Want to order dinner?"

"Absolutely."

10

Shane

"I won't be able to drive home if I have another glass." She's had one glass of wine and swings the wineglass out by the stem before bringing it back in to take the last sip.

Setting the bottle on the table, I say, "You could always stay." *No harm in trying.* I'm lying to myself. There's harm in trying with Cat. I can't hurt her. I don't want to, and if she stays, that will inevitably happen when I take off in the morning.

The fact that I want her to stay in my sanctuary makes me question if I've had one too many to drink myself. But I drink more than two beers when I'm out, so the effects shouldn't be different at home. My bet is on her being the difference and not the alcohol consumption.

"I have such a long drive home, too," she groans, sitting up. She's taken ownership of that lounge chair since she arrived. She wasn't lying earlier when she said she'd spend all her time out here if she had this to come home to.

"I can call a car to drive you home. You can return tomorrow to pick up your car."

"You'll be gone tomorrow. How would I get in? Climb the gate?" She tries to bury her curiosity in humor, but I'm on to her. There's an attraction that she's clearly denying. It's written in how her eyes light up when they meet mine and linger on my body when she thinks I'm not looking.

"What if I gave you the code?" Testing the waters has never made me nervous until now.

She looks at me with disapproval written all over her face. "I'm worried about you, Shane."

"Oh yeah? Why?"

"You shouldn't be offering your code to every stalker you meet."

I'm starting to think she's testing the same waters I am. "I judged you too quickly."

"Can't be sure these days. It's best to take it slow and get to know someone first." She tips the glass back but receives a cruel reminder when not a drop falls out. Lowering it down, she says, "I should go."

Between her, the beer, and the full stomach, I'm getting too comfortable in her company, and my thoughts are all over the place. "I'm not a relationship guy." *What the fuck am I saying?*

She had just set her feet on the decking but doesn't get up. Instead, with an empty plate in one hand and a wineglass in the other, she says, "I know." She stands as if nothing was said at all and walks inside the house.

Maybe she's doing me a favor by not making it a big deal. It was stupid to say anything, so I don't know why I did.

I trail her inside and set my plate next to hers on the counter. Appearing to start washing them, she positions herself in front of the sink and turns on the water. I turn it off. "I can clean up after us. You're a guest."

"Are you sure?"

"Yeah," I reply with a grin and shake my head. "I'm sure." Staring at each other in the smaller space of the cooking area, I'm at a loss for words with her. I want to warn her to stay away from me but turn around that message and have her stay. Am I lonely?

It's not loneliness.

It's Cat Farin.

She has me feeling differently about being home.

"It's been fun to catch up," I say, still feeling like she'll believe the bad press if I don't confess first.

She grips the edge of the counter, leaning back against it. "Why is this so awkward, Shane?" Tilting her head, she asks, "It's been so easy between us—to talk, to spend time together, to deal with the marriage mess. And now . . . and now it's not. Is it because we have to get a divorce?" She crosses the space between us, invading mine with full intention. "It's just paperwork. I've said it before, but you don't have to worry about me. I'm not asking for anything. In return, you'll get your freedom back."

"I'm not free. I never will be again. You saw the paparazzi at the clerk's office."

With a soft laugh, she pats me on the chest. "Free from me, silly." She turns to walk away, but I catch her by the wrist.

"With you is the freest I've felt in years." Our eyes are latched, her browns to my blues. The long hair hanging over her shoulders doesn't hide the rise and fall of her chest from heavier breaths.

She licks her lips, captivating me to watch the sexiest of gestures. She doesn't even have to try, and I'm mesmerized by her. "Shane—" Her gaze drops to the phone on the counter, the vibration making it buzz. Her expression falls as disillusionment settles in. I've seen that face enough to recognize it. Pulling her wrist away, she exhales an exhaustive breath. "I have a long drive."

"What just happened?"

"Nothing." She walks around the counter and grabs the bottle of water she started before the wine. "Nothing at all."

The phone buzzes again. This time, I glance down at it to find a screen full of messages. Fuck.

"You should get it. It must be important for Teri with an I to send so many texts."

Teri was insistent that I spelled her name with an I on the end the first time we met. It became a running joke all two times we've hooked up. "It's not important."

Her eyebrows rise as if she thought I'd say something else. She grabs her keys off the coffee table, then levels me with a look. "That makes it worse."

She starts for the door before I catch up—with her meaning and her steps. "What's worse?"

"She was worth your time when you were sleeping with her but not after. I feel sorry for Teri with an I."

I stop at the entrance to the hallway and lean against the wall. "I'm not chasing you, Cat."

"Thank God."

"I won't apologize for how I live my life either."

She turns back. "No one says you need to, but you should be honest with her."

"With her . . . or you? I told you I don't do relationships. She knew that when we met, so I'd say that's pretty fucking honest."

Flipping her hair over her right shoulder as if the

language is too crass, she looks down at the floor between us. I bet if she had pearls, she'd be clutching them.

As if those texts didn't already cause enough damage, my phone buzzes on the counter where I left it.

I exhale my frustration with the damn phone adding to my issues and justifying myself to Cat like I need to. *I don't.* "I can't control the text messages I get from other women."

She looks up with a mission in her eyes. "No one says you need to, but you should be honest with her."

"It's my business, babe."

"So you can bring up *my* sex life whenever it suits you, but yours is off-limits? Got it, *babe.*"

"Whose sex life are we talking about again? I was only aware of one."

Red seeps up her neck and strikes her cheeks. "Screw you, Shane."

"Watch your language, sweetheart."

She tugs the door open with enough force to damage the sheetrock, but she doesn't release it. She stands there with her back to me, her hand holding the handle like she needs the support. "Why did you have to ruin it?" she asks, her voice much quieter.

"It's what I do."

Nodding slowly, she walks forward, closing the door behind her.

I stand in the wake of her disappointment, left alone in my righteous indignation. Closing my eyes, I condemn every thought I have telling me to go after her. Nothing good will come of it. I'll disappoint her now or hurt her later. Cat doesn't deserve either.

Fuck it.

I tug open the door, ready to chase her down the driveway like I said I wouldn't. "Whoa!" I catch myself before tripping over her sitting on the top step. "Fuck, give a guy a heart attack, why don't you. You almost got trampled." She glances up as I walk down the other two steps and turn to face her. "What are you doing?"

"Beating myself up." She looks at me. "I have no right to judge you." Standing, she adds, "To the world, even to you before a few days ago, you were single."

I probably shouldn't smile, but her staking claim over me because of some error is adorable. I knowingly acknowledge that's typically the last thing I want a girl to do to me. Again, Cat is different. Not sure why, but I'd like to find out. "So you don't consider yourself single?"

The question has her searching our surroundings for an answer, but she won't find it there. Just like I didn't. "I haven't thought about it, but I guess I am. A technicality doesn't change anything."

"Except in the state's view," I add.

"Or if we were dating other people—"

"Good thing we're not."

"Right," she replies eagerly. "It's one less knot we don't need to undo."

Propping my foot one step higher, I ask, "Where do we go from here? I can have my attorney draw up the papers. You won't need to spare the expense."

"I can pay for an attorney—"

"You said you don't want anything, so it shouldn't be complicated."

She steps down, bringing us closer. "We should look into annulments. It might be a time-saver, and I imagine that we'd qualify based on . . ."

"Based on what?"

"We haven't consummated the marriage."

She's staring at me like she won a prize, but I'm not

seeing that option as a positive. I refuse to lose this staring contest, though. She blinks first and says, "I'll do some research."

Coming down two more steps puts her right in front of me. "When will you be back from touring?"

"Um . . ." I rummage through the schedule in my head. "Maybe Monday. Could be Tuesday."

"Touch base when you're back, and I'll share the data I've collected." Seeing how excited she is, I start grinning like she is.

When I touch her hip this time, she stops and turns back. Question marks dangle in her eyes, but my mind's gone blank in the proximity of her beauty. She pokes my stomach, and whispers, "See you next week, Shane."

"Yes." That's all I manage before she goes to her car and opens the door. With a quick wave of her hand, she then disappears inside, taking my breath and heartbeats with her.

Who needs those anyway?

They come in handy as a drummer. Fuck it, I can survive a few days without.

11

Shane

"SAY it to my fucking face, asshole!"

Yanked backward, I'm dragged away before I can punch the fuck out of that face for blindsiding me with a knock to my head. My ears are ringing, but the shouting of the death metal fans penetrates all else. I'm pushed through an opening, and the door is slammed closed behind me.

Seeing my cousins, especially Nikki, are safe, I whip back to the bodyguards, throwing my arms out wide. "Why'd you have to ruin a good time, fellas? We could have taken 'em."

They're smart enough to keep their mouths shut. Except for Jeff, who always pokes the bear. "Our job was to get you out of there, not have your back."

"And here I thought they were one and the same."

"Shane," Nikki says, grabbing my arm. "Don't." Her voice is quiet, her hands trembling even while holding me. "Please."

Should I be grateful that we were just pulled from a

mob? *Probably.* It's been a few years since Laird and I have been in a good fight, so it's hard to walk away instead of finishing what we didn't start.

Laird bends down to cool off. "What the fuck just happened?" When he stands back up, there's a slash of blood across his chin. It's hard to tell if it's his or someone else's.

"You're bleeding." Nikki goes to him. Lifting on the toes of her sneakers, she tells him to be still while she analyzes the situation.

Holding her by the elbow, he studies her as well. "Are you okay, sis?"

"Every hair on my head is accounted for, but you two took the brunt of it." Popping the hem of his shirt, she adds, "Wipe it off. It's superficial, but you should get a bandage so you're not bleeding on stage."

"Fuck that. I'll bleed." A smirk lifts the right side of his face. "Bleed for my audience. Bleed for the fans. What's more rock and roll than that?"

I shouldn't chuckle. I really shouldn't, but if this were the old days, we'd be working this situation hard in our favor and have a couple of chicks, *each*, lined up to take care of our needs before we left the stadium. We've had some good and wild times.

When she rolls her eyes, reminding me of Cat, which is easy to do since I've been thinking about her too much to be considered healthy, Nikki asks, "Do you really want to worry Poppy in her last trimester? If she sees you with blood on your face—"

"She'll already be upset that my face was touched." He laughs with a grin so prominent I don't think it could be wiped off. "She likes it a lot." When I look over her head, though, a look of concern drops his expression. "You took a hit to the head?"

The throbbing had become a distraction to what happened, but I was hoping to keep it on the down-low. I reach up to where a pulse has situated in my forehead, knowing there's no hiding it. "Fuck. Not good."

"You need ice on that," he adds, "before it swells."

"More than it is," I say, practically feeling it grow under my fingers. "That's what I get for keeping my head down." I shoot a glare behind me, but the guys are already gone. "Their one fucking job was to get us from the car to backstage. Nikki should have never been taken from the SUV."

Laird inspects her once more as if he knows she hates to bother others, even at her own expense. "Anything could have happened."

"Stop worrying about me. I'm fine." Nikki eyes my head. "You might have a concussion. Let's get ahold of Tommy." A tremor in her tone has her dropping her gaze to the ground. "I'm not sure what to do about performing." Looking at us for answers, she asks, "Do we still go on?"

Laird wraps her in his arms before she has time to say more. "Clearly not fans of the band."

Her shoulders rattle with laughter, and she pushes him off. "Don't make me laugh."

"Can't help it," he says, grinning in reaction to hers.

She wipes under her eyes where tears had threatened to fall, then her gaze volleys between us. "We're taking the stage." As if catching herself, her gaze darts back to me. "If you're okay, that is."

"Fine and dandy." I grab a cold bottle of water from the cooler nearby and hold it to my head. "I'm ready to rock this arena."

Laird nods. "We're here for the fans."

We start for the doors leading backstage, leaving this

loading area and the scuffle outside behind us. Nikki stops before we push through the doors and says, "Don't tell Tulsa until after The Crow Brothers perform. He'll lose it on security."

Do I agree with her plan? No, not really. He should know what happened, but I also realize it will cause much damage if he finds out before performing. He probably won't play, leading to turmoil and legal issues as a no-show on stage. Like the rest of us, she shouldn't have been put in danger, and that back there was a fucking mess. I wouldn't want someone I loved caught in it.

We've chosen this life, good or bad. People either love us or want to rip us to shreds. I say, "We're not doing this festival next year."

"Agreed," they reply in unison as we push through the double doors and enter the hall like the professionals we are to do our jobs like nothing ever happened.

Sɪᴛᴛɪɴɢ in the blackness of the stage, I can barely make out the drum kit in front of me.

This is my moment.

My time to shine.

It's all about leading us from the dark into the light.

When I tap my sticks, the lights blast on, illuminating the arena as soon as I slam down on my drums. Cheering explodes, the sound blasting into us and giving us life. Kicking into the steady beat of the opening song, Nikki sings like an angel to a mesmerized crowd. Her voice silences the critics and pulls them into the next ninety minutes of our rock set.

It's too hot to keep my shirt on, but it's not until we've

covered six songs that I tug it off without missing a beat. Laird looks back when the fans go wild, clueing him into something I'm doing.

I won't call attention to the blood that's returned to streak across his chin or the drops that have fallen, staining the front of his shirt. It's not enough to worry, but the visual is a reminder of the pain pulsing in my head. As if drumming wasn't doing that already.

Dizziness has me anchoring myself to my chair, and I look down, checking the setlist to stay on track despite knowing it by heart. I push through. I have no other choice.

Nikki swings out in front of my platform, making eye contact, but I know she's checking on me. She doesn't miss a word of the song and keeps moving like all is as it was meant to be. I can play every song by heart, drumming on instinct, but she gives me something to focus on instead of getting lost in the crowd of faces in the distance and blacking out.

Closing out the show by ripping across the drums, I hit the last beat of our set and slam the sticks down. Done. I'm behind Laird as we trail Nikki off stage. I'm hot, and the pain has intensified. I catch a bottle tossed to me and finish the water before we reach the dressing room.

I slump onto the leather couch, waiting for the door to close. As soon as Nikki closes it, I concede to the pain. "I need a medic."

"YOU HAVE A MILD CONCUSSION," the doctor says. "I'm surprised you got through the set."

"The show must go on, right, Doc?"

"To your detriment." He starts packing his bag, then

looks at me before shifting to Tommy. "You have the instructions. When does he fly back to LA?"

"I'm right here, by the way. As much as Tommy will love babying me, he's not my keeper." I check my phone like I might have missed a message, but there's not one. Though I wish I'd heard from a certain nurse.

The doc replies, "I find musicians lean toward more stubborn when it comes to taking time off."

Tommy is older than us but not so much to pretend to have control. Though I should be touched by the worry creasing his forehead. "They have another show tomorrow night."

The doc heads for the door. "The level of intensity required from a drummer is too much for me to recommend performing again that soon. But I know you're not going to listen to me anyway. Watch him over the next twenty-four hours, limit sleep to bedtime, and stock up on ibuprofen. Hydrating is always a good idea, no alcohol is ideal, and then check on him every few hours." He hits me with a look that makes me think this is more serious than I thought. "If you feel dizzy or notice anything strange, you should go to the ER right away." He opens the door, and as he backs out, he adds, "It was a great show."

When it's only the band and Tommy left, I say, "We're not canceling the show tomorrow night."

Rubbing the bridge of his nose, Tommy stops and crosses his arms over his chest. "We'll see." His stance widens as if he's guarding the door so we can't leave . . . or us from intruders. "We had a serious breakdown in protocol. The breach in security is going to cost the venue. The outside was theirs to secure. We were guaranteed it was, or I wouldn't have had you go that way."

Nikki sits in a chair in front of the Hollywood mirrors. "We know."

He says, "We're putting our guys on the bands to get you out of here safely. There's a place where the SUV will pull in backstage to take you to the hotel."

He looks at Nikki. "I want you out of here with these guys, no waiting for Tulsa. Knowing you're secure makes it easier to focus on The Crow Brothers when they come off stage."

Laird looks at his phone and plugs his ear when he holds it up to the other. "Hey, I'm okay . . ."

Nikki turns back to Tommy. "Laird was cut, and Shane has a concussion—"

"Mild," I add.

It doesn't deter her. "What if Tulsa or I would have had my daughter with us? This is not safe."

"It's not common either," Tommy says, "so let's figure out what went wrong, why those fans of the other band were able to bust through the barricades, and how we can prevent it from happening again. I can't do that right now, though. I need to get you guys out of here and then do the same for the Crows."

Laird paces with his head down, and whispering, "I didn't feel it. At worst, a little mark . . . You don't need to worry. I'm safe. We all are." He glances over at me. "We're leaving now. I love you."

Nikki grabs her bag. "Let's go then."

LAIRD AND NIKKI take their job of babysitting me all night seriously, bugging the shit out of me on a rotation every two hours like clockwork. Nikki. Laird. Now I'm stuck awake at one a.m. on the East Coast, thinking about a woman three hours behind in a different time zone. Not that I wasn't already.

She's on my mind like a melody I've already memorized. Only she doesn't know it's my favorite song. Familiar. Comforting. Bringing me back to happier times. Is that what Cat does for me? Grounds me in some way that I haven't had in years?

Though time with her makes me feel new, like discovering a passion and wanting to spend all your free time with it. I look at the window where the heavy blackout drapes were kept open "for my benefit." There are too many lights to see the stars from bed, but I know they're there for me and hanging over her head as well.

Still not tired, I grab my phone, willing . . . wanting to make the next move with her. It's not like we said we couldn't contact each other. Wasn't exchanging numbers a given that we would?

"Fuck it." I run my fingers through my hair and then text her:

> I couldn't wait until the reunion to talk to you again.

Why'd I send that? It's not funny. Fuck—
Cat:

> Who is this?

I stare at the screen a good minute, questioning everything from the details of our conversations to my existence in the universe. Does she really not know who it is or is she fucking with me?
Me:

. . . 😏 For real? My ego is wounded.

Cat:

I have no doubt that your ego will be just
fine. 😊 Missing me already?

Do I tell her the truth or . . .
Me:

Is your ego feeling left out?

Cat:

My ego could use some stroking.

Holy fuck. Blood rushes from my swollen head, going
south. Nurse Cate coming out to play was unexpected. I
grin, rubbing my cock with images of her wearing nothing
but that white coat coming to mind.

It takes me a few seconds to know how to respond. Was
it an invitation? Only one way to find out.

Me:

Be right over.

Cat:

You're a wanted man. No hot dates to keep
you entertained?

Me:

I'm entertained. Let's go back to that
stroking.

Cat:

> LOL. How about we talk about you? How
> was the show?

She can't do anything from the West Coast, so no need to worry a nurse over a little concussion.

Me:

> It was good. The crowd was wild. I don't
> want to talk about me when you're much
> more interesting. How was your day?

Cat:

> Wild here, too. The retirees at River Elms are
> protesting this week. They had pudding
> removed from the dessert table due to
> budget concerns. It's now only available if
> someone is sick or needs softer food.
> Ginger snaps were broken in the kerfuffle.

Chuckling, I read her text several times, enjoying more each time. *She's so fucking cute.*

Me:

> Sounds dangerous. Stay safe out there.

I imagine her laughing, those pretty eyes of hers shining just for me while she texts.

Cat:

> I'm prepared for Monday. I bought boxes of
> pudding to make. I'll come bearing gifts to
> calm the residents. Nothing like getting high
> blood pressure readings because they didn't
> get their pudding.

I'm about to type, but another message pops up:

> It was good to hear from you, Shane. I'm
> exhausted from the day and heading to bed.
> Have a good night.

I get the hint, but I'm not sure how I feel about it. Maybe she's just tired like I am. I'm not going to lie here second-guessing what her intentions are and take it at face value. I type:

> You, too.

I'm close to calling her just to hear her say good night, but I set the phone down beside me instead. The door opens, and Laird looks in my general direction in the dark. "You alive, Shane?"

"Fuck off."

"Sounds like you're back to normal." He closes the door.

I'm left with scrambled thoughts of Cat. Why do I feel so good when she's around, even via text? This isn't normal. We just reconnected, barely know each other, and only came back together with the common goal of getting divorced.

But there's more to it, and Laird's words come to mind. *"It was just different with her."*

I bolt upright in bed, aggravating the knot on my head. Covering the pulse raging in my head, I try to quell the pain despite the epiphany that's now rocking my world.

Shit.

Do I have feelings for my wife?

12

Shane

I CHECK my watch like I haven't been checking it every couple of minutes already.

Why am I nervous?

I don't take Cat as the type who rushes out the door at five but more the kind of person who gives everyone the time they need with her. Leaning against the back of my car, I'm willing to wait however long it takes.

Thirty-seven minutes.

The doors slide open, and she walks out in her white coat, black pants, and a white shirt. I shouldn't have thoughts of her in that coat while fucking her, but the mind works in pretty obvious ways when I find someone attractive, and fuck me, I haven't stopped thinking about her.

"Need a ride?"

She glances over, a smile blooming across the delicate features of her face as soon as she sees me. The way she practically floats on air as she hurries over has me feeling like I'm king of the world. *And she's not even my girl.*

Though that's also crossed my mind a few times lately.

"What are you doing here?" she asks, just shy of jumping into my arms. I would have caught her. "When did you get back?"

I want to reach out. The temptation to help her cover the distance she left between us is strong. I don't, but I wonder if I'll kick myself for not doing it later. Cognizant of the bruising and welt on my head, I keep the right side tilted away from her and thumb behind me as if it relates to the story in any shape or form. "Two hours or so ago."

Her eyebrows shoot up, and her pretty eyes widen. Tucking hair that's fallen loose from the ponytail she's wearing, she then tilts her head. "And you came straight here?" Her eyes shift to the car, then her head wobbles. "I mean," she says, shrugging, "after you went home."

"Yeah. I went home first, though I'm regretting that now."

"Why is that?"

"Because of how happy you were when you thought I hadn't. I wouldn't have, but I needed my car to get here."

The apples of her cheeks pink, and the corners of her eyes soften just looking at me. "You don't owe me anything, Shane. You've done more than your share already."

"My share of what?"

"Favors. I owe you more than one."

"No, you don't. We're in this together, remember?"

"Yeah." She shifts, dipping her gaze between us. Shoving my hands in my front pockets, I take her in subtly. Or I thought I had until she laughs, looking away from me.

When she looks back, she asks, "Were you checking me out?"

"Yes."

Her mouth opens as if no man tells her the truth—she's fucking sexy. "Oh, um . . ." A shake of her head appears to remind her of what she was saying. "Anyway . . ."

"Are you done for the day?"

Shifting her bag as if the load is too heavy to bear for much longer, she holds it in front of her. I reach out, slipping my hand next to hers, my roughness against her softness. Neither of us moves, the connection making my heart thunder in my chest so loudly I wonder if she can hear it. I'd forgotten what this felt like while on tour. The way the simplest things with her—sandwiches at the beach, joking like old friends do, the thrill of spending time with someone who makes you feel alive again—are magnified to make life exciting.

"Shane!"

I'm startled from falling into her soulful eyes any deeper. "What?"

Releasing the bag, she reaches for my forehead. *Oh, that.* "What happened?"

"A run-in with a fist. It's nothing to worry about."

"That definitely sounds like something to worry about." With the tips of her fingers gently running over the bruised area, she lifts on her toes and looks me in the eyes. *Or tries to.* She's still a few inches short of her goal. "Yeeps."

"Yeeps? That's a new one."

She laughs, but it's light under the circumstances. "Have you iced the area?"

"More than I wanted."

Still studying the wound, she hums. "That's good." And then she looks at me, and asks, "Do you have a concussion?"

"I wouldn't say I'm *still* concussed."

When she drops onto her heels, the worry in her

medically trained eyes has me wondering if I fucked up. "You should be at home resting."

"I thought I wasn't supposed to rest."

"When did it happen?"

"Saturday."

"You're past the watch and worry stage, for the most part." Her gentle touch stroking my skin has me leaning closer to her. Her fingertips give comfort, and her concern for me makes me feel. It makes me feel something I haven't in a long time—cared for. Discomfort quickly shades the good, and I lean back again. "I'm fine."

I'm given a tight smile and a nod of reassurance. "You'll be okay, but you need to get home and rest. How long are you in LA?"

"Other than the shows, all I've been doing is resting. I was hoping you were free not to rest tonight."

"Like all night?" Her pink lips part into a smile again. "Free to do what?"

I thought about this woman every day I was away from her, so I'll take any time she spares me. "How about dinner?"

The smile falters, but her eyes never leave mine. "Are you asking me on a date, Shane?"

"No." *I'm a fucking liar.*

"Oh. That's right."

"What's right?"

She taps a finger to her head as if it's all coming back to her. "You're not a relationship guy."

Why'd I say that shit? Nothing like having your words used against you. "When I said that—"

"You don't have to hide who you are with me. We're friends. That's a good place to be and probably best for us," she says, sounding committed to the idea. Taking her bag from me, she then steps back. "If you're up for dinner, we can discuss my research on the divorce situation."

The tides turned quickly in my favor, but I'd forgotten about the divorcing her part. I don't like the taste of it, much less the sound of the words. I still won't say no. "Where should we go?"

"Based on your current condition, how about my place? I don't live too far from here. Beats sitting in traffic."

I hadn't thought about her place, her living somewhere, since I've only seen her here and a few other public locations. But now I can't wait to see where she lives. "Sure does."

She starts walking backward, I assume to her car. "Do you like Chinese food?"

"Love it."

"I'll text my address." She stops, strands blowing across her face, looking more beautiful in the sunshine than I've ever seen her. "It's not fancy, okay? Just a little apartment."

Like a gut punch, the shame hits hard. Is that what she thinks of me, that I would judge her by where she lives? Or is she lowering my expectations? Either way, I feel like shit that she felt the need to even say it. "I'm not judging, Cat."

"I'm only preparing you. There aren't the fancy accoutrements you're used to. No incredible views except of the parking lot. No great living spaces. We'll be cramped, especially you, big guy." *Big guy?* Why does that sound so seductive coming from her mouth?

She turns her back but throws me a wave in the air, walking to her car. I watch to make sure she gets in safely before returning to the Ferrari.

The address pops up in a text, and I map it out to meet her there. Deep down, I can't wait to see where she calls home. I bet it smells like her—the sweet vanilla mixed with a citrus twist. She reminds me of summers at the beach and some of my best days. I can only imagine being surrounded by her belongings and seeing what she chooses to display. Is she messy at home and only put together for work? What's in her fridge?

I've never been more fascinated by a woman, and I can't wait to snoop.

Half an hour later, I pull into a spot next to her and park. As soon as I open my door, she warns, "It's messy."

Girl speak for it's clean enough to eat off the floors, but I left a mug in the sink. "I swear I'm not judging you, Cat."

Pointing toward the apartment in front of us, she says, "This is me."

I don't like it. First floor? *Really?* For safety reasons alone, she should be on the second or third. The higher, the better.

She fumbles through her keys until she finds the right one. Dusting her feet off on the "You had me at meow" mat, she unlocks the door. I'm already having so many thoughts that will never leave my mouth.

Swinging the door open, she leans against it, and says, "Welcome to my humble abode."

I step in slowly, taking in the size—not much bigger than a shoebox full of the necessities, low ceilings, a dark green couch, and the artwork that hangs above it. I'm ushered in with tender pressure on my back to make way for the door to close. Her touching me has me doing the opposite, staying right where I am to feel her warmth for as long as I can.

She drops her bag beside the door and then tosses her white coat in a hamper on the other side before leaning against it.

I turn back to take in the overflowing wooden bookcase

by the sliding glass door where books are stacked high of varying heights. "You have your own library."

"I need to cull them soon. I don't have the room since I didn't get the house." The house . . . I still feel shitty for being a part, even unknowingly, of the reason she didn't get it.

The sound of the bolt latching has me turning back. "You going to murder me or keep me as your sex toy?"

A look of horror knits her brows together. "What?"

"Bad joke about the lock." That doesn't seem to ease her expression. "Forget it." I move in front of the painting, crossing my arms over my chest, and follow the colorful lines up and down, and then across to the black streak. "I like the painting."

"I did it to save money since I had this big blank wall. It turned out better than I expected."

"You painted this?"

"I did. Immodesty is a sin, but I'm damn proud of that painting."

Staring at her, I'm captivated by this beauty. "I'm impressed."

"Thanks." She comes to stand next to me on the far side of the coffee table.

With our attention focused on the painting again, I say, "It would look great at my place."

She doesn't say anything. We just stand there in the silence together.

My phone buzzing in my pocket makes me want to crush it for ruining this, and there's no way in fucking hell I'm checking it with her around. Fortunately, it stops before I force it.

She looks at me and asks, "Want the rest of the tour?"

"Do I get the VIP treatment?"

"Of course." She's laughing but detours away from the kitchen and leads me straight into the bedroom. "And this is—"

"Where the magic happens?" I stop in the doorway, taking in the space and then her right along with it. The lights are out, and she doesn't bother to turn them on, leaving the evening sun to sneak between the trees outside and the open blinds.

She sits on the end of the mattress, and says, "I was going to say this is where I sleep."

Nodding, I move inside, feeling more comfortable than I should in her bedroom. "Ah, that makes more sense."

"What do you mean by more sense?" She seems to know the answer already by how she rolls her eyes. Falling back with her arms wide, she releases a long breath as if she can finally breathe after the long day. "Am I ever going to live Maggie's comments down?"

Doing what I shouldn't, I sit next to her on the bed . . . in the dimly lit room . . . wanting so much to lie next to her. I find myself breathing easier too. The day of traveling has weighed down on me and made me drowsy. The head injury doesn't help.

The calming colors of the bedding and walls, the scent of her swirling in the air, the beat of her heart and mine mingling between us.

She hooks a finger in one of my back belt loops, and a gentle pull has me lying down next to her. I turn to find her eyes already finding mine, my breath deepening, hers wading through the shallows. The tips of her fingers run lightly over the injury, and she shifts, coming toward me.

My lips part when hers do. I caress her cheek, my gaze locked onto her mouth. And then she kisses me on the forehead. It's the most intimate thing I've ever felt. Her breaths are jagged, and her eyes shift away. With one hand on the bed, the other rests on her chest as if she's keeping her heart inside.

Sitting up, she catches her breath, and without looking back, she whispers, "We should order food."

When I sit up next to her, my heart still beats hard, but now my chest feels tight. I try swallowing down the mistake I just made and stand to leave the room. "Sounds good."

13

Cate

HE PUSHES his plate away from the edge of the coffee table and falls back on the couch with a groan. "I feel miserable." Only some sparse rice remains. He can eat, but I'm not surprised, considering the man in front of me seems nearly twice my height.

I'm still surprised he's here, though. Shane Faris sitting in my living room full of food we ordered together was not something I imagined when I started my day. But here he is, scrunched up on my couch that fits perfectly in this space, yet he's too tall to be comfortable for long. His presence takes up even more space than his large frame.

Seeing him was exhilarating, and he made the effort to see me after landing. But the bedroom incident . . . Every time I start to give a little, to yield some of the protection of my heart, I see him separate from the image I perceived and the one he gives off. I stumble past attraction into the feelings I'm developing for him. That connection I once felt has reignited, and that scares me. But then that damn phone buzzes again.

Never thinking I was the jealous type, I'm not sure I could handle his infamy with the ladies. The mayhem of his life would crash into this little life I've built. And when it's over, I'd be the one stuck cleaning up the wreckage to my heart while he moves on to someone else.

I touch my lips, still staring at him.

It would have been nice to share one kiss. *Just to know what I'm missing.*

Too late now.

"Me too. Why'd you let me eat that much?" I join in the misery, rubbing my stomach as if that will ease how stuffed I feel or the regret of what happened in the bedroom. Kicking my legs out, I prop my feet on the table in front of me.

"I wasn't coming between you and that last eggroll." Holding his hands up, he chuckles. "I need these babies."

"Ha." I try to giggle, but it kind of hurts to mix laughter with that much food in my belly and the remorse weighing me down. "Make it go away."

"Think about something else. Where do you go for your happy place?"

"Physically? Hawaii. When I'm getting a pap smear? I also take a trip to Hawaii in my thoughts."

"Hawaii and a pap smear are quite the image." His eyes are hard to read while staring at me indifferently. "That's a lot of information."

"Too much?" I ask, rolling my head to the side, too lazy to turn it. "I forget that other people don't talk about medical procedures so openly."

"I can handle you."

His referring to *me* over the *topic* has me reevaluating everything.

Does he want to kiss me? Or was that all me in the bedroom?

Why did he come to see me the same day he returned to LA?

He agreed to come over and let me feed him when he has all those text girls to tend to.

I'm so confused. He makes my heart and head twist the logic to what I want it to be instead of what it is, what we are, and maybe all we should be. Friends.

What if *we* were more?

What if we could make it work?

Is it right to play with my heart that way, to talk myself into what I know will be a disaster? Predictable and orderly are the furthest from what his life offers. It will only be a lose-lose for me once it's done.

I drag myself back to sitting in the chair like a proper human and then tuck my legs under me, needing to get to the business at hand instead of the ridiculous notion of me, Cate Farin, dating a rock star. "Want to talk about what I discovered in my research?"

"Do we have to?" His eyes don't even bother coming my way. His socked feet are suddenly way more interesting to him.

I laugh, but he doesn't. "Oh, you're being serious?" I'm now left guessing how to broach the topic. "We don't have to if you're too tired to talk tonight."

He sits up, looking at me like I'm dragging him to the dentist for a root canal. "It's fine," he says, releasing a long sigh. "We have to deal with it eventually, so we might as well get the options on the table."

I'm not exactly feeling the love, but I hope to turn it around. Or at least share a good laugh with him. "We have two," I say. When he just stares at me unamused, I continue,

"We can get an annulment, which would help us avoid a lot of other issues, like the press finding out and exposing you—"

"And you."

My throat thickens from the thought of having my life invaded. "Right. Another thing an annulment would do is erase the marriage from record like it never happened." Sitting forward, he rests his arms on his legs, life returning to his eyes. "And we won't need to involve attorneys."

"This sounds like the best option. How do we make it happen?"

"I couldn't agree more." I readjust in the chair, biting my lip. I already know how he's going to react, so I say it and hope for the best. "We'd have to appear in front of a judge together and make our appeal. Two options might apply to us in order to get the annulment granted. We need to figure out which one we're going with and be on the same page."

His brows pull together as he sits back again, looking so comfortable on my couch that I admire the trust in his eyes before I reveal the kicker. "You're really building the suspense. What are they?"

"Fraud, which sounds tricky. It's basically saying one of us defrauded the other into marriage."

"No." He glances away as the idea rolls around his expression. "That comes with legal issues tied to it, and if anyone ever got wind of it, it would ruin my career. What's the other?"

I take a deep breath and rush the words out. "We never consummated the marriage."

"Not a lie. This is our out." Still staring at me, hope comes in the widening of his eyes. "We don't have to prove it, do we?"

"No," I reply with that image now mortifying me. "We just have to agree it never happened."

"Easy," he says, brushing his hands together like this issue is done and dusted. "We can't have sex before we end the marriage, and we're golden."

Not a question, but a statement that leaves me narrowing my eyes to riddle through. Maybe it's not a riddle at all. "You make it sound like we will right after."

A shrug and a cocky smirk make themselves at home on his handsome face.

I'm not sure what to make of this, mainly because I'm not opposed to the idea. Sex is different from dating. Reason always sneaks in, though. "We didn't have sex when we were married, so why would we do it when we're not?" *And why am I pondering this as if it's a real possibility?* An opportunity even?

"Never say never."

Straightening my face, I lean in closer, and whisper, "Never, but I've always been ambitious."

I swear a growl rumbles around his chest before he takes a deep breath. "So the no sex thing seems to be our only option. For now."

"Forever. And yes, it's the best option we have." I weave my fingers together and hold my hands over my still full belly. "So when the judge asks us for the reason, we'll agree you couldn't perform your husbandly duties, and he'll grant the annulment."

Sitting forward again, he stares at me like I'm speaking another language. "What do you mean I couldn't perform?"

"Yeah," I say, hesitating. "That's part of the appeal."

"Doesn't sound appealing to me at all."

"No, but we must have a reason to annul, and for that specific option . . ." I use my hands to explain, but it's my nerves, knowing I have to go into detail. "To use the not consummating the marriage excuse, we'll need to go into why you haven't made love to me. Why you *can't* make love to me. It's strictly performance-based, so you'll swear that you have an incurable case of—"

"No fucking way." The horror on his face speaks volumes over his actual words. He's up and storming toward the kitchen. Turning, he paces to the sliding glass door, but the seven steps he takes to cover my apartment don't appear to satisfy the turmoil. Stopping on the other side of the coffee table, he clenches his jaw. "There's no fucking way I'm claiming I can't perform my duties. I can perform on stage and in the bedroom just fine, sweetheart."

"Prove it."

What the—I can't breathe until I realize I said that in my head. *Oh my God.* Thank goodness. I drop my head into my hands, needing a reprieve from the pressure cooker where we're trapped. "There are no other solutions."

"Except divorce," he replies, defeat tainting his tone.

We're here but apart. I hate feeling like this fight is between us instead of the situation we're in. He's been quiet for so long that I'm afraid to break the peace. I watch as he returns to the patio door to stare out like there's more than cars to look at. He crosses his arms over his chest in quiet contemplation, his breathing finally evening out again.

What can I say that won't upset him even more? But the silence is killing me. What is he thinking? I angle my body in his direction, and say, "I'm sorry."

"It's not you, Cat." When he glances back at me, I don't see the assurance I once did. No humor dances in his eyes. No flirty intentions in a smirk. All I see is the guy who said he's exhausted from his own life.

Lowering my feet, I pad across the short span of hardwood floors and stand next to him, staring ahead. Bold for me with him, but he's so different than I imagined. There's no chip on his shoulder when he's with me.

Friends can comfort each other, but I wonder why I keep justifying what feels right instead of leading with my heart when it comes to Shane. His status, his fame, his wealth has never been weaponized against me. I need to put down my own defenses and see him for who he really is.

I rest my cheek on his arm. "We don't have to decide tonight. We don't have to rush into anything either."

His arm comes around my waist, holding me in the nook of his body like I belong there. It feels so natural that I peek up at him in awe.

We stand together now, somehow an unlikely pair against the world that tricked us into a relationship, which is beginning to feel more like a match made in heaven with every day that passes.

The sun's almost down for the night. Since the other buildings are blocking the sunset, we catch the rays of light reflecting off the cars. It's magical in its own right . . . not a view of all of Los Angeles magical but quaint in its own way.

I'm finally willing to admit that this feels better than expected, making me glad to give whatever it is between us a chance to grow in its own direction. I wrap my arms around his middle, leaning against him, and whisper, "You can stay?"

I could have told him what I wanted a million other ways, but instead, I torture myself by tossing it out as a question. I close my eyes, hold my breath, and wait.

The tips of his fingers pull my chin up, and when I open my eyes, I'm staring into Shane's adoring gaze. "I'd like that."

"I DIDN'T BUY it for having company over," I explain, wriggling for more covers. "I bought the bed for me. A queen-sized bed for the queen of her own domain." I fall back on my fluffed pillow and turn to look at him.

Seeing him next to me in bed is a thrill I never thought I'd experience. I'll carry this to my deathbed, then spill the family secret that Grandma once shared a bed with Shane Faris.

He says, "It's just kind of . . . small."

Here I am, developing lifelong fantasies of this man, and he's still stuck on the size of the mattress. "I hear what you're saying, and I agree that it might be a bit small for a giant, but that's not what I'm working with over here. I'm five-five on a good posture day."

"A good posture day?" He chuckles, then gives me a wink. "Five-five is a stretch, don't you think?"

"Wow, thanks." I sit up, poking him in the bare chest that I can't get over. So tempting to rub all over his carved muscle and those abs. Hands or my tongue will do. I'm not picky when it comes to him, but I am turned on. "Fine. I'm five-four, the average height of an American woman. So tease me all you want, but this is all sixty-four inches of me."

I'm pulled into his arms; my body pressed to his athletic physique—hard in all the right places and growing against my leg. "I like every inch of you, Cat."

My heart races from the position, but his words have me swooning in his arms. He makes me feel so much and more than ready to cross lines we probably shouldn't. My nipples press against the thin cotton T-shirt I thought was a good choice when I put it on, but it practically puts my boobs on display, spotlights that draw his attention away from my face.

A large hand covers my ribs and moves higher until he's

cupping under my breast. With a stroke of his thumb, the pad brushes across my nipple, perking it even more. He tips his head and breathes across my neck, "Every inch."

The air is sucked from the room, leaving us to be consumed by sexual tension.

Did I expect a different outcome when I invited Shane into my bed?

I'm not innocent.

I knew what I was doing, and now I'll reap the benefits —*rewards*?

"I'm awful."

Tilting his head back, he finds my eyes again. "Why is that?" he asks, struggling to make the leap to where I've landed in my mindset.

I'm just as confused.

My body and deep desires I try to bury want a night of reckless abandon with him. My head, good old responsible Cate, wants me to deny myself. *Why?*

"I shouldn't take advantage of the situation with you."

His head falls back on the pillow, rubbing his eyes while a smile still sits prominently on his face. "*You* taking advantage of *me*?" He laughs, but when he turns back, the amusement is wiped clean from his face. "You're not kidding?" Quick to lean in again, he cups my face. "Listen to me. You're not taking advantage of me, Cat."

Wrapping my hands around his wrists, I hold on tight— to keep him there so I don't run away before telling him what's on my heart. "There are several reasons I asked you to stay. One was that I don't think you should be driving back to your house in the dark with a concussion."

He leans and kisses my forehead, his lips lingering against my skin before he whispers, "Because you're an amazing person."

"I wouldn't speak too soon. The second . . ." I scrunch my face, hoping I don't freak him out. "I also wanted you to stay. I know, it's selfish. I'm terrible—"

"You're not terrible. You knew what you wanted. Do you know what a fucking turn-on that is?" Lowering to look me in the eyes without distraction, he adds, "I stayed because I wanted to. Because I know what I want, too."

"What's that?" I'm breathy and desperate, but I don't care as I slip my leg between his, needing the pressure there as well.

His eyes track down, then he presses his mouth to mine, slow at first, gentle, but then our lips part as if a checkered flag has been waved. My breath is stolen, and my needs lit like dynamite. I rub my body against his, already on the edge of losing myself.

Grappling for purchase, I run my hands over the scruff of his jaw and upward over his temples, driving my fingers into his hair. But he flinches, causing me to stop and rip myself away from him. "I'm sorry."

"It's okay."

The knot is found easily, even in low light. "I got carried away."

"Carried away is a good thing." When he leans down to kiss me again, I push my hands to his chest, knowing I can't take advantage of this man when he's injured.

"I'm sorry. We shouldn't." I pull back to catch his gaze. "I don't want to hurt you. You need to be calm and rest to heal."

His hand drags up my bare leg, sliding under the hem of my pajama shorts. "It's so fucking sexy when you take care of me, Nurse Cate."

I laugh, but I shouldn't. "You're such a bad patient."

"Yes, babe. *So bad.*"

"No," I say, playfully pushing his shoulder. "I'm not role-playing, Shane. This is me saying this for real. We can't do this. You'll get worked up, and blood starts rushing to other places instead of where it needs to send the white blood cells so you can heal."

"I love listening to you talk about my dick."

"Well, it wasn't specifically about your—"

"*Shh.* Just keep going on about blood rushing to other parts, Nurse."

"And here I thought I was the terrible one." I laugh, but as soon as he starts kissing along my jaw, I go quiet. When he tugs the lobe of my ear into his mouth, the scrape of his teeth has my body squirming and reconsidering my stance altogether.

"We can't." I close my eyes, relishing his mouth on me.

I'm licked along my jawline, causing me to forget myself.

"Hear me out. What if we," he whispers in my ear, "take care of you instead?"

When he slips his hand over my shoulder, I know where he's headed. I could stop him, but I don't want to. *I want this.* I want this man and his big hands all over and inside me. I want him so badly that I can't think straight. "Okay." I'm not even sure what I'm agreeing to, but I'm more than happy to find out.

He kisses my mouth once more. I stop him before he goes lower and kiss him with as much passion right back. Our mouths take ownership of each other's, and our tongues embrace into a slow dance to match the pace of our bodies. A grind here and rubbing there.

I lean back, grasping for air and needing to see him. Look at the way his eyes drink me in so deeply that there's nothing left of me but desire. Breaking all my rules never felt so good.

Shane starts down my body, kissing over my shirt and my peaking nipples, over my ribs and swirls his tongue in my belly button. But when he shifts his entire body under the covers, and his hands are on either side of my hips, tugging my shorts down, I lie there staring up at the ceiling, ready to beg for mercy and fist pump in celebration equally.

Before my shorts reach my ankles, he's kissing and then licking the bend of my leg and going south from there. Pushing my legs farther apart, he shoulders his way to where he wants to be. Without warning, his nose dips, then his tongue licks through my lips. My mind goes blank when he stops, the bridge of his nose pressing against me. I close my eyes and enjoy the sweet torture of him inhaling me into his lungs.

Seconds. Minutes. Hours. I lose track of time when he begins ravaging with his tongue. It's been too long and feels too good. I buck my hips, taking on his chaos as he consumes me whole.

Fingers replace his tongue, and he fucks me with little foreplay. Other than a few kisses, he left me wanton for more. I push against his hand, getting closer to the edge with every thrust. But it's when his tongue flattens against my clit, claiming me as his through whispers and licks, that I fall so fast I fumble into ecstasy.

The stars shine before I land and bounce back to reality. I should be embarrassed for how little that took—a look, a kiss, so much connecting us that I lost myself in him.

He flips the covers up, and our eyes find each other in the dark. I find myself, the girl who used to dream, is now the woman who went after what she wanted.

I feel too good to worry about how this looks to the outside world. Instead, in this bed, what Shane thinks is all that matters to me.

Looking at me as he climbs up my body, his blue eyes shine like the devil escaped Alcatraz. He holds himself above me, his penis hard and prominent against my leg, then dips down to kiss me again. "You taste fucking amazing, babe."

My soul was pilfered for safekeeping with his, and a bag of bones is all that's left of me. Sliding my hands on either side of his head, I encourage him to let me bear the weight and to kiss him of my own accord as if we have all the time in the world.

Left breathless once more, I fall back, my head hitting the soft pillow and my body feeling like it's returning to life.

I reach down, wanting him to feel as good as I do, but my hand is caught and brought to his mouth. He kisses my fingers and my palm. "When I come, it will be inside you." The words are firm, but his tone dances between a command and the deep tone that makes me weak in the knees.

He kisses me once more and then turns us, me spinning around with swiftness. He curls me in his arms from behind, my back to the strong beat of his heart pumping in his chest. Every breath of his brushes across my skin, leaving goose bumps in the wake.

I want to talk to him and ask a million questions about what happens next, but I listen to his breathing even as sleep sets in. There's no rush for tomorrow when there's so much to enjoy about the here and now. We have time for the heavier conversations in daylight.

I almost fall asleep as well, but I force myself to stay awake a little longer—not only to check on him to make sure he's safe with the concussion but because I want to savor everything about this night with him.

While he's still my husband.

14

Cate

I WAKE before the alarm goes off and rip myself away from the only place I want to be—*Shane's arms.*

After contorting my body to slip out of bed without waking him, I'm confident that counts for my morning yoga routine. That, or an audition for Cirque de Soleil. As the shower spray rains down on my head, I close my eyes, remembering how he kissed my mouth and down my body. There's a sense of mourning as the water cleanses his touch from my skin. But that leaves me wondering what happens now.

Do we pretend nothing happened between us?

Go about our lives and never speak to each other again?

Date?

Dating seems like the obvious answer, but how do I even broach the topic? I shut the shower off and grab a towel. "Hey, Shane, so remember how you did that thing with your tongue last night? I'd like more of that along with spending all my waking minutes with you. Too much?"

"No. I have time now."

"Aah!" I jump, startled to see Shane filling the doorway. Twisting the towel tighter around me, I try to keep my heart from escaping my body. "Don't do that!" I say, still panicked. "You scared the hell out of me, Faris."

He's busy laughing, but at least he comes over to wrap me in his arms. "Sorry. I didn't think I'd scare you."

I knock my fist against his chest, though I'm comforted by his warm, hard body. "I'll never be able to step out of the shower without worrying someone will be there again."

"I wasn't trying to sneak in. I just happen to have perfect timing, but I am a drummer, so that's a given," he says, kissing the top of my head. "But I am sorry, babe."

Babe. I hated it the first time he said it to me, and now I gobble it up every time like it's little pieces of chocolate left by the Easter bunny. "I'll live. This time."

"That's good because I'd hate for you to miss out on the other tricks I can do with my tongue—"

I burrow myself into the nook of his shoulder, refusing to ever be seen by him again as mortification heats my face and chest and every other part of me. "So you heard that, huh?"

"Glad you enjoyed last night."

"That's a yes, then."

Stroking his hand over my back, he dips to kiss droplets of water off my shoulder. "It sure is."

"*M'kay.* Soooo . . ." I gulp and finally face the music, a.k.a. him, by walking to the mirror and gripping the edge of the faux marble countertop.

He leans against the doorframe, crossing his arms over his chest, and grins like the cat who ate the canary. What a terrible metaphor. "So?"

Is he going to force me to say it again? "Any thoughts on what was said?"

Checking a wrist where his watch typically is, he says, "Like I said, I have time now. I can have you coming within a few—"

"I meant the other part. About . . . well," I say, rolling my wrist and tossing it back to him. "You know."

"You mean the part about wanting to spend every waking minute of your day with me?" He gives me a wink, and his smirk arrives on time, right behind it.

"When you put it like that, maybe not every waking minute, but some minutes most days." And then I remember his words like he just said them. "What was I thinking?" I turn, facing the mirror and avoiding eye contact in the reflection. I tighten the hair clip holding my hair in place so it didn't get wet in the shower. Grabbing my vitamin serum, I squirt it onto my hand, hoping to distract from his rapt attention and the silence which is an answer as well. "I shouldn't have said anything. You made yourself very clear that you're not a relationship kind of guy." I mistakenly look into his eyes. His usually brighter blue eyes have darkened. It's hard to tell from here, and I'm too worried I've already crossed the million lines he drew between us.

I reach for my moisturizer just as he wraps me in his warmth again. I still, not sure if I'm even breathing when he kisses my jaw, then turns me toward him. Cupping my face, he kisses me once, and with our lips barely apart, he says, "I leave tomorrow. I want to see you tonight."

"You're asking me out?"

I shouldn't *act* surprised, but this man doesn't do relationships. It's a date, Cate. Not marriage . . . *oh wait*. That major life event was crossed off my list a long time ago.

Never thought that would be reality, or Shane Faris asking me out twelve years after graduation. I still shouldn't get ahead of myself when it comes to dates with him. One does not necessarily lead to more.

Releasing me, he turns to lean against the counter, facing me with a grin so big that you'd think he was the one who scored and not me. "Yes, I'm asking you on a date, Cat."

My gaze deviates to his bruise. It's healing, but fortunately, I can keep an eye on it without him being the wiser. "It doesn't have to be a production. It can be something easy, relaxing like watching a movie, a nice change from your busy schedule."

He sweeps hair from my face and tucks it behind my ear. "You deserve the big production—dates in public sharing Italian food or going to the Santa Monica Pier and holding hands at sunset." He takes a sobering breath as his smile falters. "I can't give that to you now, but one day I will."

Now he has me grinning. "Are you making long-term plans with me? The guy who doesn't believe in relationships?" I only tease to let him off the hook he's lodged himself on by thinking I need more. "I don't need all that. But I am thinking pizza tonight."

He kisses me again. "Pizza it is, then." Walking away, he adds, "And if you have time before work, I'm up for the job this morning."

"What job is that?" It hits me as soon as he walks out. "Oh!" Giddiness shoots through me, and I jump. But then I check the time. "Dammit."

He calls from the bed, "Don't worry, babe. It's not a one-time offer."

It's also something I won't be able to stop thinking about all day. I already wish it was over so I could climb back into bed with him.

"HOW HAVE you not done the deed yet?" Luna says over speaker for all of Pasadena to hear.

My office isn't much bigger than a matchbox, but I'm not here enough to worry. Her voice, on the other hand, is loud enough to reach reception. "Well, there are several reasons. One, he's been out of town except for two nights."

"Two's enough to get it on, Cate." *She's not wrong.* "Please don't ruin the fantasy and tell me he's been a perfect gentleman." *Right again.*

I know most have fantasies of how spending a night with a celebrity, especially one who looks like Shane, would go. I'm no exception. But we talk on the phone, even if just a quick hello, and text each day. He asks about my day and how I'm doing. It's so normal that I've started to forget he's famous, touring with his band and performing concerts each night that he's gone.

The divorce barely crosses our minds since I lost the house. Now that we don't have to worry about it, we can focus on him wrapping the tour and dealing with loose ends afterward.

I get Luna's interest, though. We share everything. I'm also fascinated when she dates recognizable names. But saying we watched *Gladiator* because it just happened to be on and we were too tired to search for something else won't quell her thirst for details.

It was a perfect night if she asked, though, especially falling asleep in his arms.

"He has, for the record. I get that you expected us to be

swinging from chandeliers and breaking beds several times over, but neither of us feels the need to rush into it."

"You do remember you're married, right? Like that's the headliner. Sex is the opening act." I get up to close the door just in case anyone else is hanging around this afternoon. "You've seen him, right? Tall, handsome, sexy as fu—"

"Ms. Farin, I was hoping to catch you."

Dammit. I cringe, but right my face as fast as I can. "Mr. Goodman, I didn't know you were in the office today." I rush around my desk and hang up on Luna. She'll understand. "Last update I received, you were in Mykonos for a few weeks."

"We were, but we cut the trip short. Too crowded to enjoy."

"Ah. Well, at least you enjoyed it three months ago when you docked your yacht." I sit down, pretending to be professional, considering I was acting anything but a few minutes earlier.

"True," he says, not catching the little jealousy I slipped in.

"How can I help you, Bob?"

He stands in the doorway with his white coat on, though he hasn't seen patients in years. He's barely seen this office, which he pays for monthly. He's busy making millions and running the firm from vacation spots around the world. "I have a lot of work to catch up on and will be working late."

I nod, understanding since I have a stack of files I'm working on tonight as well. And I come to work every day.

"We have a new account I wanted to discuss."

"Alright. Do you want to talk here or move into the conference room?"

Sitting in a chair on the other side of my desk, he looks around as if this is a whole new perspective. It is for him. His office is a palace full of wood furniture, leather chairs, and awards from the Chamber of Commerce and Better Business Bureau. I have a plastic chair with a broken swivel and a desk we acquired when the yoga studio moved out last year.

He picks at the rubber coming off the arm of the chair, and replies, "Here is fine, but you should look into replacing this chair."

"Will do, Bob."

"Let's discuss your future with our company." I wait for him to lead the discussion. "You may not know that we don't give promotions here." I most certainly do know this, but it's not something I need to quibble with my boss about. "We get more assignments with increased pay or lose locations, which means less money."

He has me on the edge of my seat in suspense of where he's going with this. He continues, "Flexibility is key to our business."

"I thought care was at the center of our business?"

"That's the business we're in. Not Endeavor Personal Healthcare's mission." I need to reread that mission to see if our values still align if that's not a priority. "We've had a banner year with record profits. You need to expand your mind beyond the basic duties of your job if you want to continue climbing the corporate ladder to have a career."

Corporate ladders are one of the reasons I went into healthcare. I have no interest in that rat race when I can focus on helping others live better lives. I'm not sure why this conversation depresses me, but hearing about his goals has me wondering when he lost his humanity.

Wasn't that what I thought about Shane initially? That his stardom made him lose touch with reality. He's real and present with me as if I'm the most important way he could spend his time. The corner of my mouth rises as recent memories collide, and I shake my head, hoping not to give them away through my expression.

Needing to focus on the conversation at hand, I remind myself that seeing patients is a highlight of my week.

"So you have a new account?" I ask, unsure why he doesn't just come out and say it.

"Yes, and I've been impressed with your performance. The surveys I sent out came back with only glowing reviews from both River Elms and Parkdale. We have Dally Point coming on board next month. It would be a good account to add to your schedule."

Okay, this is good. Really good. I should get a nice raise, too. "I'm honored."

"Don't be honored. You've worked hard, and you have happy patients and administrators. We're not just a facility that provides nurses for retirement homes. We're in the business of care. You care about your patients." Wasn't he just saying the opposite? I want to roll my eyes but stop myself, proving it can be done if I wanted. He leans in as if he's going to share a secret. "That's who we are as a company. Now about your pay."

"I'm all ears."

"You'll work at the facility on a trial basis for a week. You'll get a feel for it and write a report on whether you'd like to continue and why. The administrator will send their feedback to me. If you're approved to stay after the trial, the new pay increase will start three weeks from that point."

I'm mathing, but something is missing in the formula because it's not adding up. "You want me to add an entirely new facility into my schedule, donate two days of my week for one full month for free?"

"It's a trial."

"And then it's not for the other three weeks."

He stands and taps his fingers along the edge of my desk. "If you're not interested, I know Ryan is."

Fuck him and fuck Ryan. My insides seethe from the threat. "I'm more interested to know if you would have asked him to donate a month of his time."

"I'm looking for team players, Ms. Farin."

"You'll never find someone more dedicated than I am, but I also deserve to be paid fairly."

He heads for the door. "A discussion for another day. They're expecting you at Dally Point on Monday. Bright and early." Closing the door behind him, he saves me the trouble.

What a joke. I wish I could laugh about it.

I call Luna back, feeling a little sick to my stomach about the confrontation I just had with my boss. I vent to her, hoping to feel better.

She says, "Maybe it's a good thing the house didn't go through, or you'd be stuck with paying a mortgage."

"Thanks for the vote of confidence. I'm not losing my job, Luna." At least I don't think I am. I lift my chair and turn it so I can look out the window at the strip center parking lot.

"You're probably right, so let's get back to the important stuff. When are you going to have sex with Shane?" Never deterred from a mission, my friend is unwavering in her pursuits of gossip.

I reply, "Three nights. He doesn't return until Monday."

"Gives you time to plan. New lingerie. *Oh!* We should go shopping this weekend."

That's not a bad idea. I'm not plotting sex with Shane, but I'm also not opposed to it either. *I meannnn*, he's already gone downtown with his mouth, so it wouldn't hurt to look my absolute sexiest. "I'd be up for that. Now let's talk about your love life."

"God, I've been dying to." She dives right into the deep end. "Remember Adam? He does this thing with his . . ."

As much as work calls my name, I sit back and enjoy talking to my best friend for a few minutes instead.

15

Shane

"DID you add a show onto the schedule, Tommy?" I hold the phone with the new updated schedule in front of his face.

"It's a small gig," he replies, pushing my hand out of the way. "A pop-in at Continental Club. All the greats have played there when passing through Austin. Short set. Five songs. Laird and Nikki said they thought it was a fun idea. Though the pay reflects when you played gigs at the beach."

Hotel staff load trays of food onto the large dining table. It's noisy even in the vastness of the presidential suite. It smells good and causes my stomach to growl. "I was going to fly back to LA."

"Save the trip and enjoy a night in Austin." He stands when the hotel staff starts leaving. "What's the rush to get back anyway? There are plenty of hot chicks here."

"I didn't say anything about other women."

"Other women? What women are we talking about?"

The door to the far bedroom opens, and Laird emerges,

stretching like he's waking from hibernation. "Is the food here?"

Tommy walks to inspect the selection. "It's here."

Laird returns to the bedroom, peeking in and talking to Poppy. He flew his wife out for a few days since we're in the same city for three nights. I should have flown my wife out as well. I grin, looking down at my phone and the last message she sent: *Break a leg. Just not yours.* Her nurse humor is top-notch.

I click the screen off and tuck the phone in my back pocket. "Why am I the last to know about gigs being added?" When Poppy walks out of the bedroom, that's when it hits me. Laird has Poppy. Nikki has Tulsa and her daughter, Autumn. I look at Tommy and then at Laird. "Because I don't have anyone who cares about me?"

"We care about you, man," Laird says from the other side of the buffet. "What are you hungry for?" he whispers to Poppy.

"You know what I mean."

Tommy's digging into the pasta at the far end of the table. "Of course we care. We know your schedule is flexible."

"Maybe it's fucking not. Maybe I had plans."

"Come on, Shane." Tommy stops eating to look at me over his plate. "I'm the last guy to judge how you spend your time, but the band voted to add the gig."

"The band didn't vote. The twins did."

"Either way, you would have been outvoted."

"Would have been nice to be fucking asked."

Laird hands the plate to his wife and looks up. "What's going on, Shane? Why are you so upset? Missing out on a hot date?"

I'm about to lose my shit, but Poppy is a good reminder

to take a breath as she comes around with one arm around her pregnant belly and her plate in her free hand. She stops beside me and says, "I agree. You should have been asked."

Fuck. Now I feel bad. She shouldn't have to listen to this shit. "Thanks, Pop."

She nods, her mouth pressed together as sympathy tugs the corners down. Turning to the guys, she adds, "Shane has a life, too. It's different from ours but not any less important. He should always be included in decisions."

Tommy finally sets his plate down. He takes a beer from the ice bucket, and says, "Our bad. It's not happened before. It won't happen again." He tosses me the beer.

We have a few hours before we go on, so I crack it open and return to the buffet. "Thanks."

Patting me on the back, Laird says, "Sorry, brother."

"It's fine." It's not fine at all, but I know they didn't do anything with ill intention. It does mean another night without seeing Cat, and I'm missing her so fucking much that I'm getting cranky. And we haven't even had sex.

What have I gotten myself into?

I fill my plate and return to the living room. Tommy and Laird stand around the buffet, picking at it, but I sit across from Poppy. "How are you feeling?"

"Ready to live up to my name and pop."

"I heard Nikki say you're in your last trimester. I don't even know what that really means."

She laughs behind her hand to hide a mouth full of food. When she finally finishes, she replies, "It means I'm in the home stretch. Twins usually come early, though, so we'll see."

I eat some broccoli before tucking into the chicken. When I look up from the plate on my lap, Poppy whispers,

"I'm good at keeping secrets if you ever want to talk about the woman in your life."

My eyes dart to Laird and Tommy, who seemed wrapped up in their own conversation and oblivious to ours. "What woman?" I play dumb, but I can tell by the small smile forming that she's on to me.

"Just offering an ear with no judgment attached."

I glance back at the guys once more before saying, "I wanted to see her." What am I doing? I exhale long and slow before my hand starts for my head. I lower it and try to calm the nerves that have come over me.

With the cat out of the bag, her smile is too big to hide. "I don't think I've ever seen you smile like that."

"I didn't realize I was."

She nods, all-knowing with a raised brow. "You sure were. I bet you make her smile as well."

"Cat's smile is one of my favorite things."

Her hand rests on her chest. "Shane, that's so sweet." Being a good friend, Poppy glances over her shoulder to make sure no one's listening, and then whispers, "Do you have a picture of her?"

I wish I did. There hasn't been a good time to ask if I can have one for the personal library of photos I'm creating of her. Yeah, totally creepy. I can never say that to her, or she'll be out the door. "Not of her face." Her mouth falls open. "No. No. I didn't mean it like that. I don't have naked photos either." I mentally note to ask for those as well for the collection. The road gets lonely.

Poppy's laughing hard enough to make her belly bounce up and down. She's beautiful, so it's a given that Laird was attracted to her, but that beauty runs deeper than the surface with her. She genuinely cares about others. I'm reminded of Cat again. I think they'd really like each other.

It's important for a band this small, that spends this much time together, to get along. It's just as important for our partners to as well.

Laird asks, "What's so funny?"

"Nothing really," she replies, still laughing. "Shane and I were talking about photography." *She's not lying.*

"Sounds like a riot," he says, scooping more food onto his plate.

Setting my plate on the coffee table, I pull my phone from my pocket and tap to light up the screen to show her.

The smile ceases to exist as awe sets in. Her eyes go from the screen to mine, and she asks, "Did you take that?"

"Yeah." I turned my phone back to look at it again. I've stared at it more than would be considered healthy, and I never get enough. "I was holding her, fascinated by the gentle slope of her neck, the hair that tumbled over it, and her back bare and calling to me. I've kissed her there, right at the curve, that freckle my North Star in the middle of the night." I blink, then realize I've revealed every thought I've had staring at this photo. "Just took it because I liked it."

I took it because my wife is a goddamn goddess, and I needed something of her with me. If only I could tell her the full story. If only I could tell them the truth—that I'm married, and even though it was a mistake, I'm not in a rush to get a divorce.

When Poppy smiles this time, I know she sees right through me playing it off like it's nothing. It's fucking everything to me, and now it was even longer until I see her and my North Star again.

"That's got to be one of the most romantic things I've ever heard, and my husband is a swoony guy." She tries to sit forward but looks trapped in the cushions of the couch.

I move around the table, taking her by both hands to

help her up. When she's standing, she says, "Thank you for sharing with me. I can't wait to meet her." Nodding, I do feel lighter and better for talking to her. Before she walks away, she whispers, "I hope that one day you tell her everything you just said. That's the kind of stuff girls dream of hearing."

My phone buzzes with a message, but it's not from Cat. Dallas Jenny. I delete her message offering to drive to Austin to hook up like we did last year and block her number altogether.

There's only one person I want to hear from, so I go back to my bedroom and call her. As I'm standing at the window, the phone rings once, twice, and then I hear, "Hello?" mixed with laughter in the background.

"Hey, babe, I've been thinking about you."

"I've been thinking about you, too, babe." I grin, hearing Cat call me that. I know a part of her doesn't feel natural saying it, but the other part takes ownership like I was hers to begin with. Maybe I always have been. According to California, I was. "I can't really hear that well. I'm in a restaurant with Luna."

"Early day? Everything okay?"

"Yeah, we can talk about it when you return." There's a shuffle of noise on the other end, and she says, "I need to go outside to talk. I can barely hear you."

Staring out the window onto the water below, I say, "It's okay. Have fun with your friend. I was just calling to let you know that you have freckles—"

"Did you just say I have wrinkles?" she shouts to overcome the noise in the background.

Fuck. "No, that's not what I said. We'll catch up tomorrow."

"I'm sorry. I can't hear you."

I sigh. I was ready to talk about how I've been feeling

about her, but now is not the time. "Don't be, Cat. Have a good night."

"Break a leg, but not yours, okay?" She's going to run that one into the ground, yet I'm not bothered by it because she makes me smile every time.

"I won't. Talk soon."

I lie down on the bed with a stomach full of food, hoping to get a nap in before we have to leave for the stadium. But I can't stop thinking about the conversation I had with Poppy.

She's here for Laird. Maybe I should bring Cat with me next time. I pull up the schedule once more and scroll to see where we play next week. Grinning, I say, "Perfect."

The next thing to figure out is how I'm going to break it to the band that I'm bringing my wife on tour next week.

It kind of changes everything once it's out in the open.

First things first, though. *Ask Cat to join me in Seattle.*

16

Cate

As soon as I shut the door, I let the tears fall that I'd been holding back for the past hour. Telling patients their health hasn't gotten better is awful. Some retirees come to me with acceptance of their fates. They don't deny their age or the process of dying. Some even welcome the end so they can join their loved ones again.

They are braver than I am.

I barely know him. I opened an outdated chart as a baseline, scheduled his doctor's appointments, then met him for the first time and broke the news. It's not fair to be put in this position. It's not fair to him to have been ignored for so long. He knew.

He already knew it was coming. For him to comfort me gave me the strength to be there for his family, who will live in the pain of their loss for years to come.

I start the car and buckle in after wiping away my tears with a discarded Coffee Bean & Tea Leaf napkin from this morning. When I check the visor mirror, my eyes are as red and swollen as they feel.

My head is swimming in a day of heavy emotions. I'm drained after the rough day stole my energy away. I feel guilty for even considering not going to yoga class. It will be good to clear my head and relieve some of the pent-up stress I've carried around from the intensity of adding this new retirement home to my rotation.

I shouldn't have agreed to take it. I should have let Ryan take it. But he's an ass and wouldn't have delivered the news with any thought to their feelings once he walked out of the room.

I stayed. I stayed for hours after work to support them along with a nurse who works there full time. I don't regret a minute, but it's taken a toll.

It's okay if I miss a yoga class. I need to stop carrying guilt for stupid shit. My ass will be fine if I only miss one class. It's past eight o'clock, and I don't think I'd make it on time anyway. A hot bath and white wine are in my future instead.

The traffic isn't bad this evening, but I still can't get home quick enough. The remaining tears have dried, and my makeup is nonexistent. I finally pull past the gate into my apartment complex, breathing a sigh of relief to be almost there, and weave through the parking lot to my building in the back.

When I turn into my spot, my headlights stream across a sight that has me doing a double take. Am I imagining things? My heart knows, leaping from the vision of Shane waiting for me. Sitting on the base of the stairs that leads to the apartments above mine, he stands when he sees me— one hand shoved in his pocket, the other giving in a shy wave that pulls at my heartstrings. This man . . . *Gah!* Can he be any more perfect than he is? Not possible.

I cut the engine and hop out. I don't collect my stuff. I don't shut the door. I run right into that man's arms and cling to him with my entire being—soul, arms, legs, all of me.

"Miss me?" he whispers, kissing my neck as he holds me like he never wants to let go.

Please never let go.

"So much," I reply, my head snug against his neck as the tears return from joy this time. "You don't even know."

He chuckles, the sound just what I needed after this week. "I'm getting an idea and currently losing oxygen."

Loosening my arms, I lean back to see his eyes. "Oh gosh, I'm sorry."

"Don't be. I'd happily go to heaven if this is how I died." A tear slips down from his sweet words before I can stop it. His brows pinch together in the center as he reaches up to caress my face, the pad of his thumb wiping the tear away. "Why are you crying, babe?"

"I just . . ." Closing my eyes, I rest my head on his shoulder, wanting to disappear into his warmth for a while. "I'm just happy to see you."

Kissing my cheek, he says, "It's so good to see you." When he sets me down, he kisses the side of my head. "That was a better welcome than I expected."

I grin. "And what exactly were you expecting?"

"I don't know." His voice matches that shy wave he gave earlier. Despite the fame, the money, and adulation from around the world, I'm the one who makes him nervous. How is that possible? "I don't know where things stand with us."

I didn't realize confessions from his heart would be the balm that soothed my aching heart until he shared his fears with me. Now, I look up at him in a whole new light. He's in as deep as I am.

My heart squeezes, knowing he's wearing his heart on his sleeve for me. "We should talk about it before you leave." I hate that he must leave, already knowing it's going to be sooner than I'd like. Not that I ever like him leaving, but it would be nice to have more than a night together.

His hand slides against mine, our fingers folding together. "It's not a conversation I've ever had before."

"New doesn't mean bad. There's no pressure from me, though." I hug him again, resting my head on him and listening to his strong heartbeat in his chest. "I'm just happy to have you here."

A kiss to the head leads to him rubbing my back like we have all the time in the world or even more than a night. I don't get my hopes up. Stepping back, I ask, "Why didn't you tell me you were coming? I could have prepared."

"You don't need to prepare for me. I only came here for you." With two fingers under my chin, he lifts to stare into my eyes, which evokes a smile so genuine I could die a happy woman. "I seized an opportunity of a pocket of time and caught a flight. God, you're fucking beautiful."

Remembering the swollen lids, the red rim of my eyes, and the makeup that washed away with my tears, I lower my head and lean against him. "You're just saying that."

"I'm saying that because it's true. I don't need to lie to you." His sweet words and his being here have my emotions overwhelming me. Tears fall again, my body rattling against him. The release feels good. His being here is even better. Whispering in my ear, he says, "I don't want you to cry."

"I'm so happy to see you." I look up, not caring about the tears streaking my face.

"You definitely look happy to see me," he teases, kissing my cheeks and wiping the apples with his thumbs.

"I've had a long day, but you've made it so much better." I lift on my toes and kiss his mouth, missing those lips so much. Missing him. Missing his embrace so much, too.

Pushing his fingers into my hair, he holds the back of my head as our lips part for each other, and our tongues caress, deepening the kiss.

"Hey?" A stranger's voice has us jumping apart like we were just caught making out by our parents. Carrying a pizza in one hand, he asks, "Aren't you—"

"Nope," Shane replies, tightening his lips and shaking his head. Taking my hand, he moves closer, a slight posturing has his body protecting me.

He snaps his fingers and points. "You look so much like—"

"I get that all the time. I think it's the hair." Shane ruffles his hair as if it will somehow make him look less like himself . . . or maybe more. I'm not sure what he's trying to do, but it seems to be working.

The guy eyes his hair. "I can see that." He takes the stairs by two and disappears. "Have a good one."

"You, too," Shane replies.

I say, "We should get inside."

"Probably best. We've overstayed our welcome outside where the public has access." Access to him. *I'm not the draw here.* He is, and he's well aware.

After I retrieve my stuff and lock the car, Shane returns to the stairs to grab a huge bouquet that I hadn't even noticed. "You brought me flowers?"

"You deserve more, but this is all I could get on short notice."

My heart pitters faster as I take them in my arms. "Thank you." I dip to smell the pretty scent. "They're beautiful." Once we're settled in the apartment, I grab a vase from above my fridge and fill it with water. "I must say, for someone who doesn't do relationships, you sure are a romantic, Shane Faris."

"What can I say? I'm a multifaceted guy." He comes into the kitchen, making my ceilings feel lower because of how tall he is. I knew my apartment was small in square footage, but it always fit me. With Shane spending time in this place, maybe I'll eventually look for somewhere new and bigger. Just to rent. I'm not quite ready to jump into the real estate game again. And I can't without that divorce financially separating me from him.

Is it the flowers? Him surprising me, again? The hard day? I'm not sure, but I feel tender and raw from the heavy emotions. Dreaming of a future with him is a welcome escape. I start arranging the flowers, glancing at him leaning against the counter. "You are. Tell me how you're here. Pocket of time? I thought I wouldn't see you until Tuesday after that schedule change. Did the concert get canceled?"

"No," he says, coming around behind me to hold my hips and kiss my neck. I tilt to the side, giving him easier access. He hums, his tongue dipping out and tasting me. When his breath blows across my skin, the gentle foreplay is already making me want him. He replies, "We go on at nine. If I land by seven tomorrow night, I'm golden. They'll kick my ass for missing sound check, but we have a crew who can test the equipment."

I tuck the last flower, a pale pink ranunculus, into the vase, then turn in his arms. Wrapping mine around his neck. "Wait, you . . ." I can't seem to get a read on the situation. "You flew back for one night just to see me?"

"Yes." Kissing my temple, he says, "Trust me, it was self-serving." I feel what he means against my leg.

Tonight is the night, and I'm not prepared.

No new lingerie to wear for him.

No dinner waiting for us or even ordered, and it's almost nine o'clock.

I don't remember if I even made my bed.

It doesn't matter. It doesn't because he wants me as I am. I still plan to take that bath and wash the day away so we can enjoy tonight together.

My heart beats faster, but I'm pretty sure it never stopped racing from the moment we met back in high school. "You say the sweetest things," I joke, needing the laugh after the earlier sadness.

Chuckling, he says, "I try." His tone turns when his grin levels. "Cat?"

"Hmm?"

"You make me feel."

I wait patiently, knowing he isn't used to sharing his emotions. When he doesn't say anything else, I ask, "I make you feel what, babe?"

"Everything. You just make me feel anything and alive for the first time in forever." Stroking the side of my neck, he says, "Thank you."

"I . . ." I close my eyes, absorbing every word his heart just spoke to mine. I catch a breath and hold him a little tighter. "Careful, or you're going to make me fall in love." I tilt my head back enough to watch his reaction. I might be mistaken, but that might be love already reflecting in his blues. I fold myself into his arms again, needing to keep my heart from floating away.

In his arms, drifting in his words, I realize this is what was always missing from my life.

The magic.

The feeling that anything is possible.

Love blooming in my chest.

"There are worse things that could happen to a married couple than falling in love with each other."

Tightening my hold on him, I reply, "There sure are."

17

Cate

MY STRESSES DISAPPEARED when Shane arrived, but the hot water of the bubble bath helps relieve my muscles. I take a sip of wine, then set the glass back on the edge of the tub. Splashing the water, I rest back, making eye contact. "I'm happy to make room for you."

He laughs, sizing it up by giving it a once-over from his seat on the floor. "It's miniature."

"It fits me," I reply as if I've proven my point just by saying it. "Well, not entirely since only half my body can be underwater at a time."

"Next time I'm in town, come bathe in mine. You'll never leave after being so spoiled. It's deep, and your feet wouldn't be hanging out."

"Don't tempt me."

"I'm tempting you." He takes my hand, holding it between both of his. "Come stay with me."

"It won't take a lot of convincing, but it will take planning for me to get to work the next day since we live so far apart."

He brings my hand to his mouth and kisses the top. "I don't have weekends off until the tour is over. We can stay here until then."

"I've never been so sad about missing out on a tub."

"It will still be there. Or," he says, sitting back against the tiled wall, "I'll give you a key to enjoy it while I'm away."

Just when I think I'm safe from swooning over this man, he goes and offers me not just what I imagine to be an incredible tub, but his whole house. For Shane, that's the same as him giving me his heart. "You don't have to do that," I say. "I know we're moving fast, probably too fast for—"

"I want you at my house, Cat. I want you with me. I just . . . I want you. All the time."

I wasn't prepared earlier. *I'm definitely not now.*
How could I be?

I barely know this man in the greater sense but have been slowly falling in love with him since we reunited. We'd pushed the marriage and the divorce aside and started to get to know each other without the weight of those impending issues.

He doesn't do relationships but is breaking his rules for me. How can I not fall madly in love with him for that reason alone? Add in the other thousands of reasons and all eight of those rock-hard abs of his, and I'm sunk. I never stood a chance with him. Deep down, though, I've always known it.

"What are you saying?" I ask without remembering until now that we'd left this discussion for later. It's later, but I still didn't expect it to come so naturally.

"I want you with me, Cat. I want you in my life."

I sit forward through the water, where most of the bubbles have dissipated. "You do?"

He chuckles, moving closer to run his hand up my soapy arm and over my neck. "I do. Fuck." He rubs the back of his neck with his free hand. "Those are two words I never thought I'd say."

"According to the state of California, you've already said them to me." I laugh, and his cheeks tint the slightest shade of pink. But it's his glittering eyes, a pride for the young man he would have been, that make me say, "My, how the mighty have fallen."

Leaning forward, he kisses my arm, then higher. "For you." He slips a hand into the water, runs it between my breasts and then cups one, teasing the nipple and kneading. "I want to make love to you."

He hasn't even seen me fully naked, nor have I seen him without boxer briefs. I know he doesn't care about lace or sheer material when it all comes off anyway, but I'd still like to put something nice on for him.

"I want that, too." I do. The breathiness of my voice is a dead giveaway on its own. This is it. My thrill of nerves and excitement runs through me. Who cares if I ate my feels and a full lunch today, if my stomach isn't perfectly flat, or I'm not as toned from skipping my workout? He wants me, and that's all that matters.

Shane reaches for the towel and holds it open for me. I push up from the tub, careful when I stand, but I don't rush to cover myself. I feel good about my body, so I push through any fears of judgment and stand before him.

He looks me up and down twice before saying, "You're so fucking gorgeous." Kissing me, he urges me back against the wall where he was initially leaning. He drops the towel and dives in for my neck, his mouth taking claim as kisses are staked like he's marking his territory.

With my eyes closed, I feel every urgent grappling of hands to the kisses that extend from my mouth to my fingertips. Never one to get lost in foreplay, he slips his hand between my legs and slides higher. The bath was the warm-up, the lead-in, as two fingers slide through my desire for him. I moan, unable to stay quiet when feeling this good, this much of everything.

I plant my hands on his shoulders when my body becomes a live wire of nerve endings. Our chemistry is too much to keep my eyes open, the heat between us too hot to deny. I kiss him, wanting him as much as he wants me.

When he swipes through my lower lips, my breath catches, but he's quick to swallow when his mouth collides with mine. We're tongues and hands, moans, slippery soaped skin, legs with a pressure that feels so good, and water from my wet body soaking through his shirt.

The back of my head hits the tile, and his lips immediately find my neck, kissing, sucking, drowning me in his affection. Dragging his tongue under my jaw, he slides the bridge of his nose the rest of the way to my ear. My heart beats so loud in my ears that I wonder if he can hear it as well.

His fingers find purchase inside me, eliciting another moan I can't restrain. I start to lose my balance when my grip loosens under the intensity of sensations. "You feel that?" he asks through harsh breaths. "You feel so good, but I'm going to make you feel so much better when I'm inside you."

I want to speak, but words escape me. Every thrust of his fingers has me pushing back for more. *Begging.* When his thumb toys with my clitoris, I sink down, desperate for more pressure. "God yes, I want that. I need you. Right there."

"That's right, baby. Tell me everything you need, everything you want me to do to you." Pressing his large erection against my leg, he seeks to satisfy his own cravings by rocking against me.

I barely manage to crack my eyes open to find his already fixed on me. I run the tips of my fingers over his temple. "You, Shane. That's all I want."

He thrusts, his other hand gripping my hip to keep me steady. "You got me." The scrape of his teeth over my shoulder teases until I'm pleading for more. Faster. Harder. "Yes, Shane. Yes." Lightning strikes, sending little earthquakes to shock every part of my body. I go with the pleasure, flowing into the darkness of this ecstasy.

It takes years, seconds, moments stolen in time for my body to calm and the tremors to subside. My eyes are closed, and I need longer just to breathe my way back home. Quick and shallow, then deeper and peaceful. I open my eyes, too tired to hold myself up any longer. I sag, but he catches me, holding me so I won't fall.

Too late. I'm already long gone for this man.

His lips appreciate every millimeter of my mouth as he slides to the side and kisses each corner as well. Tipping his healed head against mine, he whispers, "Come to Seattle with me."

I smile, but it takes too much effort to hold on to after recovering from what we just did. "What do you mean, come to Seattle?"

His hands return to my face, the scent of our desire still mingling in the air. "We leave on Wednesday for Seattle. The show's on Thursday. I want you there. I want to see you watching me perform. I want to fuck you backstage. I want nights with you in my bed. Making love, watching movies, ordering food to be delivered. I want that with you, Cat."

The image is so clear that I can see it as well. I feel that same need to be with him. "Sounds like a dream." But it's not rational.

The blue of his eyes is electric, like we are together. His smile so big that I can't stop smiling for him. "It will be. I promise. I'll get the biggest suite they have and treat you to—"

"It sounds like a dream because it is." I steady myself after readjusting to stand on my own two feet. I cup his face, running the tips of my fingers over the sharper scruff of a few days' worth of growth. "I work next week and only have a few vacation days left because of the house issue."

Handing me the towel, he leaves too much space to dry off when he moves toward the door. I already miss his warmth. He stops across the small bathroom. "You won't come to Seattle, not even for me?"

"I can't. I'm sorry. Not next week."

"I need you with me." The admission makes me pause. What does he want me to do? Quit? *Not possible.*

"I need to work."

Looking past me, he stares at something over my head as if in disbelief. When his gaze meets mine again, he asks, "So you won't go? Not even for me?"

"I can't."

"You *won't.* There's a difference."

"You're twisting my words to fit a narrative you seem set on creating. I *would* go if I could, Shane. I can't because I don't have the time off earned this year. Those days were spent trying to buy a house and finding out I'm married."

"*We* are married. To each other."

"You say that like I don't know." Dumbfounded by a fight

that sprouted from nowhere, I say, "A piece of paper doesn't change anything. We didn't get married because we wanted to. It's only a mis—"

"Don't say it."

I secure the towel on my chest and cautiously walk closer to him. "You're not being fair. You can't toss our marriage around like we ever exchanged vows. We didn't. We didn't choose each other. The state did." We stand at an impasse, righteous in our own minds.

He steps away, letting cold air breeze between us, covering me in goose bumps. I say, "I added a new retirement home this week to my already busy portfolio. I'm sorry, babe. It's just not a good time."

"Fuck the job and just be with me." The sincerity in his voice and the plea to his tone have me wanting to comfort him in ways I don't think he'll let me. He only wants a yes because that's all he ever hears.

But I can't give it to him. Not this time. "I love what I do. I love the routine, the patients, and even the bad food they serve in the homes."

"You love beige. You love boring—"

"I love my life and did before you re-entered it like a storm on a mission to destroy it."

A visible change starts with his expression, hardening until it's not the same as Shane's usual handsome face. "You love your career, but you don't love me." Pain and anger merge in his eyes, his breathing coming hard. "Or not enough to sacrifice it."

"How can you say that when we haven't even said the words to each other?"

The fight leaves his body, his shoulders lowering with his tone when he says, "Because we felt it. I know you did, too."

He's right. I did feel it. I *do* feel it . . . I love him, and he's destroying everything in his path. He warned me he would. I can't let him. I can't let him destroy me. "Please," I whisper, another wave of the tears I thought I had cried returning to drown me this time. "Shane, please. We can talk instead of shout—"

"This was a mistake."

"You coming to see me wasn't a mistake."

His walls rise as if triggered by a thief who broke in to steal his heart. He stares at me with blue eyes iced over. "That's not what I was referring to."

I thought as much, but I don't want to confirm it.

This is not the man I know, the one whose world seemed to brighten just because I walked back into it. I don't recognize him in this form, but I need to acknowledge this is who he is—a rock star with an ego bigger than our flourishing love could ever be.

He sighs, and I can see the love leaving his eyes, the exhaustion returning to snuff out the ember I had lit. I know he wants to fight his rage to soften the blow, but I don't think he'll be able to save himself, much less the bystander he claims to love.

At a loss for words or words he doesn't want to voice, he leaves the bathroom and me still standing in a towel. I put on my armor the best I can and follow him, knowing I would have followed him anywhere a few hours before unless it keeps me from paying my bills. That's something that he doesn't have to think twice about. One of many troubles he'll never experience, if he ever did.

There's no point in fighting because the battle has already been lost. I swallow my pride and walk around him to the door. Opening it wide, I lean against the edge holding the knob behind me. "How did it all go wrong so quickly?"

I'm not really asking. The signs have been there all along. But he still feels the need to respond. "It was never supposed to. It was supposed to be one night."

"Another fuck to add to your scorecard, and then you'd be gone." I nod, looking down. I can't bear to hold my head higher with a knife stabbing my heart. "Got it."

His feet don't move, and he doesn't fill the gap of silence with more hurtful words. All that exists between us now is the pain we've caused each other. It's torture, but I won't throw him out. When he leaves, I'll know there's no coming back from this. Though I'm pretty sure we're already there.

I watch his feet step closer to me, stopping before he reaches the threshold of our ending. "Cat?" It's only a breath of a whisper filled with the same turmoil I feel inside.

And then his phone buzzes in his pocket.

I release a long-held breath, disappointment wrapping itself around my aching heart. I don't bother looking into his eyes. I don't need to carry his pain with mine. "You should get that . . . outside my apartment."

I start counting in my head, silently begging him to go so he doesn't have to witness more tears of mine, especially the ones I cry over him. He leaves just before I reach nine, standing on the doormat for a few seconds longer, and then he's gone.

I'm not sure how long I remain with the slight breeze slipping in, the air turning cooler with the later hour, or even when there are no more headlights to reinforce the hope that we could have a second chance.

He's gone.

Shane Faris never looked back.

I won't either.

18

Cate

Ten months later . . .

"Cate?" the receptionist calls from the front desk.

I look up from Mr. Rosen's back and lower my stethoscope. "I'll be right there, Misty." With a quick nod, she returns to answering other calls.

Coming around Mr. Rosen, I sit down. "What were the changes you wanted to make this past week?"

"I was cutting out sodas."

"How did that go?" I can already tell by his expression that things went off the rails. *My life can relate.*

His face, from his spikey gray brows to his jowls, hang with his frown. "I drank two more than usual and snuck one into my room after dinner service."

"There's something to be said about your honesty." I pat his shoulder. "These are lifestyle changes. Maybe instead of cutting them out, you start with drinking a few less this week."

"I'll try. Anything else, doc?"

"Nurse." I make a note in his file about what we discussed. "Yes. I'd like you to join the walking club."

He stands up like he's ready to take off. "I hate running." He could have fooled me.

"That's okay," I say, standing as well. "It's the walking club, not the running club. They do four laps on the track across the street four times a week and walk the parking lot twice in the morning and after dinner. You don't have to do both, but I would like you to build exercise into your daily routine."

"I have no choice if it's the doctor's orders," he groans.

"Nurse's orders." The white coat and stethoscope throw everybody off.

Walking away, he tugs his pants up by the belt. That leather decided a long time ago that it wasn't doing any heavy lifting, especially since he missed the loops when he threaded it this morning. "I better get out of here before you tell me to cut down on the fries."

"We do need to discuss the fries."

He waves me off without even looking back. "Next time."

He's ornery on his good days. On his bad, he's in one terrible mood. "Baby steps."

I head to the front desk and rest against the counter. "Hi, what's up?"

Misty looks up. "Mrs. Callender is taking meals in her room today."

"Do I have her scheduled this afternoon? I don't think I do." I glance back at my e-pad as if I can read it from here to verify.

"Nurse Lucy said she's not up for it and to reschedule for next week."

"Should I check on her?"

Leaning forward, she looks around conspiratorially, and whispers, "Mr. Rosen yelled at her for turning the TV channel last night after dinner. She's had her feelings hurt ever since. We've been working with him to apologize but haven't been successful yet."

I glance over at Mr. Rosen sitting on the beige couch staring at the twenty-four-hour news channel. I've thrown out a lot of beige in my life this past year. It wasn't serving me anymore. I've decided to stick to more color. Not playing it as safe has been a nice change, though like my advice to Mr. Rosen, baby steps. "Have we thought about putting something more uplifting on TV? Maybe have a movie day to break up the news cycle?"

Comparatively, my job is easy. I do the checkups and write progress and regressions if they need to follow up with their doctor or if all is well. The full-time nurses working in the homes deserve medals for handling their moods and personalities.

"Lucy plans to sit with him over lunch to discuss his moods."

"Let me know if she needs support or if he does."

"Will do."

I return to the desk in the corner they assigned me, sitting down to make more notes. I never quite settled in here at Dally Point. Maybe it was the timing of when it was added to my schedule or because every time I leave from my visits, I don't feel any difference has been made.

As a private facility, they need to hire a full-time patient advocate so I can do my job more effectively. I'm not a doctor, as they all assume, but I do think one needs to come more than once a month. I love the residents, but there's more than I can take on, and no small raise changes the facts.

My phone vibrates in the bag, the buzzing enough to catch my attention. I have a few minutes before my next patient, so I reach down to grab it and do a quick check to see who's texting.

I hate that my heart reacts so easily to something I should have seen coming since last August. Ten months is a long time, but not long enough by how my chest squeezes from the reminder. Everything still feels raw, exposed emotions left to wilt in the bad weather of winter months.

But the text isn't from Shane. It's from my attorney.

Attorney Whittier:

> We received divorce papers today.

I'd almost forgotten about the papers that were coming, but time plays tricks on the mind and the heart, if I'm being honest. I'd fooled myself into thinking it could wait, so I never bothered filing. There wasn't a rush on my side. Is there on his? Did he meet someone? Fall in lust with another notch on his post?

Neither my head nor my heart is tricked by the facts. He moved on while I rebuilt my life after his storm.

Another message appears:

> I didn't know you got married. I would have advised a meeting prior to the ceremony.

I laugh, but I shouldn't. It keeps me from crying, so I'll take the ridiculous reaction over the other, and type:

> It was a mistake.

No need to go into details about who made the first error and the whirlwind that led to this outcome.

Me:

> What happens now?

Attorney Whittier:

> Mr. Faris's attorney requested a meeting to work through the details.

Me:

> There's nothing to work through. I'll sign. When do I come in?

Attorney Whittier:

> May 17th at four p.m.

Next week. I look up my schedule. I'll be at River Elms that day. It's not too far from his office, so that works out.

Me:

> I'll be there.

Attorney Whittier:

> Divorce law is not my specialty, so I'm pulling in a colleague I work with at the office. They'll review everything before the meeting and consult if needed.

Me:

> Thank you.

I dread the bill I'm about to be hit with, but Shane and I should have done this last year. He's making it clear he's moving on. I've tried, but maybe this is the one thing that will force me to do it. Anyway, this is no big deal. I knew it was coming.

***

"MEN ARE THE WORST," I sob, blowing my nose into the last tissue from the box.

Patting my back, Luna hugs me to her shoulder. "Let it all out."

"Was I delusional? Why'd I let my guard down? He's a freaking rock star!" I point at the TV as Faris Wheel takes the stage of a late-night talk show to promote their upcoming album. "What did I possibly expect? Him to fall in love with a geriatric nurse from the Valley?" I blow my nose again, too stuffed up to say anything more.

Brokenhearted.

Mad.

Full of regret.

I'm all the things all over again.

I thought I was over him. I guess avoiding the topic of Shane Faris only put off the inevitable. It didn't help me to recover. I say, "I regret opening myself up to be hurt." Covering my face with my hands, I sink lower into the couch, embarrassed. "I hate that I was nothing but a groupie to him in the end." I peek over at her. There's no judgment on Luna's face. She's been where I am now. "I thought college was for dating bad boys. I'm thirty-one. Shouldn't I have outgrown that bad habit?"

"To give a little credit, you were only thirty when you met him."

"Seventeen. I was in eleventh grade." I toss the gross tissue to the floor with the rest of them, even more frustrated with my poor choices. My grandmother wouldn't be proud of my behavior. "I was thirty when I decided dating someone who literally told me he doesn't do relationships was a good idea." I roll to the side, wanting to hide under a pillow, but I can't escape myself, my harshest critic.

"Now he's getting married to someone else," I spout, sniffling between the tears he caused last August and the ones that fall because the end is near. This part of our lives will be put to bed with a simple signature. "Why?" I ask, watching Shane on drums kick off the song.

Luna rubs my blanket-covered leg from the other side of the couch. "Why what, hon?"

"Why would I let myself fall for someone who doesn't give a damn about . . . about . . ." I grab the remote and turn up the volume. "He's moved on. Maybe it's time for me to date again?" I glance at her, wanting permission, backup, anything that tells me this is how it's supposed to be.

"Um," she says, eyeing me and waffling her head. "Mmm . . . no, you're not ready. But when you are truly open to love, you'll find the love of your life."

Staring at the TV, unable to take my eyes off Shane, I ask, "You think?"

"Yes. I know." She settles in on the other side of the couch and watches with me.

"Why does he have to look so good?" Squinting my eyes, I study the inside of his left forearm. "Is that a new tattoo?"

Did he get it for her? His soon-to-be wife? Or is it to commemorate something special from his life?

Do I want to know? *Probably not.*

"I hate to tell you this," she says, watching the band perform, her eyes glued to the screen when I peek up at her.

"Is this a 'kick me when I'm down' comment, or an 'aren't you glad you got out of it' type deal?"

Her foot nudges my leg. "I'll never kick you when you're down."

"You literally just kicked me," I deadpan while smiling.

"It wasn't a kick. It was an I love you, you will get through, but I'm also loving this song, please don't hate me nudge."

I raise the volume a little louder. I was already tapping to the beat because it's catchy. "The song is really good, but is it awful of me to want to dwell in my feels a little longer?"

"Not at all. Dwell away."

I nudge her this time. "Thanks for coming over, Luna."

"Everything is going to be exactly how it's intended. I promise. Your soulmate awaits you." Soulmate is nothing I've given much credence to before, but it feels hopeful to have it enter the conversation at this time.

Until I find my soulmate, why does it hurt so much in the meantime?

"How are you holding up?" Luna asks over the speaker in my car a week later.

"I'm fine." My heart squeezes. "It's nothing really. There's nothing to negotiate, so the meeting should be quick. I'll go in, sign, and get out. Easy peasy."

"Cate? Talk to me." Her voice is somber despite me trying my best to make it sound like today is any other day of my life. It's not. I had it on my calendar—not just to remind me of the appointment but to prepare me for seeing Shane. Yet nothing could prepare me for walking into his storm again.

"What if he brings her with him?"

"It's a divorce. I don't think he'll be that cruel. Would he? Do you want me to drive over and go in with you?"

"You'd never make it in time, but I appreciate the offer." I honk, shaking my head at the jerk who just cut across two lanes for an exit he missed. "Asshole! Not you, Luna."

"I say this with love for my best friend. You have some anger to get out."

"I went to kickboxing last week. Yoga wasn't cutting it anymore."

She laughs softly this time. "It's always best to face it head-on."

"I'm assuming that's why they're demanding a face-to-face to review the details."

She hums and then releases a heavy breath. "I've dealt with his type all my life. He's a celebrity, Cate. I wouldn't be surprised if they try to force an NDA on you. Just remember, you don't have to do anything you don't want to. He doesn't hold all the cards. You both do equally."

I nod as if she can see me. "Equals."

"Exactly," she says, "I'm wrapping up at the studio, and then I'll see you at Margarita Cantina at five?"

"I'll be there, hopefully on my second by the time you arrive."

"That's my girl. Hold your chin up, friend. And tonight, drinks are on me."

"I'd prefer them in a glass, but okay. I'm up for anything as long as it has nothing to do with this divorce or my soon-to-be ex-husband."

Her laughter fills my car, causing me to laugh at my own stupid joke. She says, "See you at the restaurant."

"See you then." I disconnect the call from my car as I pull into my attorney's parking lot. I lock the doors, using the last few seconds of this sham of a married life to take a few deep breaths before heading inside. I can't say they help, but they sure don't hurt.

Heat hits as I enter the lobby. Great, now I'll be sweaty when I see Shane for the first time in ten months. Plucking my shirt to cool down, I step into the elevator, praying the air isn't broken in there, or I'm doomed to be a mess. Just as I punch the button for the ninth floor, a hand stops the doors from closing. I want to roll my eyes, but I've been trying to break the habit. It's been a daily struggle living in LA.

"Thanks," a familiar voice zips inside the hot steel box. The butterflies that had been dormant for so long awaken in a flurry in my belly.

It's too late to escape, but I go for it, running right into a chest of steel and arms of hard muscle catching me by the elbows. "Whoa," Shane says, probably before he realizes who is trapped in his arms. The doors try to close, but he stops it with his shoulder and then backs in. "I think we're going to the same place."

"I left something in my car," I lie, unable to look into his sea-blue eyes for fear of the loss I'll drown in all over again.

Without a word, he moves to the side, holding the door for me to exit. *Well, crap.* What do I do? Get off and catch the next? Go rummage through my car and bring some random thing back to corroborate my story? I step off the elevator, hating to play games and letting lies be the decision-maker because he makes me feel insecure.

Did he do that? Or is that me putting it on him?

I stop and turn around, finally looking at his face that's aged in all the right ways over the time I've not been around to notice. He's even more handsome, if possible. Those eyes that I was afraid to dive into don't hold anything but what they shouldn't any longer—reverence. He smiles just enough to throw me off balance. "Want a ride?"

I roll my eyes out of sheer frustration because I can tell he knows I was lying. "Try that line on someone who will fall for it." I add, "Twice," since I was fooled into falling the first time.

"Figured since we're going in the same direction—"

"Sure. Why not?" I step back on and turn my back to him. The button for the fourth floor is already lit up, so I stare straight ahead until the doors close. And then my eyes meet his in the reflection. Like the first time we saw each other after twelve years, my heart beats faster despite the long talk I had with it last night not to be such a traitor. *It didn't listen.* My breath stops hard in my chest. But at least the nerves I've carried around all day like a burden I can't shake have vanished.

Should I be nervous?

It's fine. I'll be fine, just like Luna said. But then I look at him and see the man I once did—fun and spontaneous, romantic, and so attractive that it should be illegal and probably is in several states.

My heart doesn't leap, but it tugs toward him from the connection we once shared. If I were being honest with myself, it's more a yank into his arms, but that's not my place anymore, and it would be wise for me to remember that.

We weren't together long enough to have core memories other than the ones that already existed between us—the bonfire, a few classes together like government and English in twelfth grade, and casual exchanges that didn't mean anything to him at the time but meant everything to me as the new kid.

Those memories alone have me staring at him now to see how he's changed. Shane's tall, like he always was, the clothes he's chosen flattering him in ways that should annoy me since it seems he dressed for the occasion of our divorce. A dark button-down has replaced his usual T-shirt with pants instead of jeans. A nice pair of leather shoes accents the large silver watch wrapped around his wrist. He looks good, looking every bit the celebrity. He also looks different. I can't put my finger on it, but something feels off.

He carries a magnetism without regard for anyone who falls for him.

Therein lies the problem.

I still care.

I'm still drawn to him.

It's just me, standing in front of Shane Faris again, feeling like I did at that party all those years ago in high school. But I'm older now, wiser, and can manage the pain. Time has benefited me in that way, or maybe the kickboxing helps temper my reaction. Either way, it's not as bad as I thought it would be in his presence.

Until the elevator jolts to a stop.

19

Cate

"HOW ARE YOU?" Shane asks from the far corner of the elevator. His eyes still stare at me like he always did, like we didn't crash and burn last August but walked away best friends.

I should be bothered that he makes me feel like a girl with a crush because he shined his attention on me. However, there are more pressing issues, like the elevator stuck somewhere between the third and fourth floors.

"Never better," I reply like my life isn't flashing before my eyes as I cling to the railing behind me. "Who'd you piss off?"

He chuckles. "Who haven't I pissed off might be easier to answer."

"You're not wrong." I try to smile, but it's too hard not to notice this metal box's lack of airflow. "You even managed to get on my bad side, and that's not easy to do."

Lowering his voice as if we're besties sharing a secret, he

says, "Between you and me, I don't think this is a hit job to take me out despite your prayers for it to happen."

"I didn't pray for any harm to come to you. That's not the karma I want to put into the universe. Though I might have wished for impotence on a few eleven-elevens over the past however months it's been."

"Ten."

"Ten what?" I hold his stare, each second that passes making it easier to see him again.

"It's been ten months since we lost each other." His jaw ticks as he looks away for a moment. Annoyance seemingly steals his cooler composure. When his gaze treks across the elevator to me, clearer skies have returned to his blue eyes. "I meant *last* saw each other."

"Lost each other works. Tomato, tomahto."

"Yeah, I suppose," he replies, not an ounce of him sounding convinced. Is the great rock star not on top of his game? He seems thrown. Of course, we are stuck in an elevator, so that might play a small part of it. I'm curious.

Forcing myself to stand straighter despite the fear I have of plummeting to my death in this elevator, I grip the railing and raise my chin as I right myself. "I didn't know we were dressing for the occasion. I would have chosen all black as well."

He can't stop the lopsided grin that makes him even more charming as he tries to hide it from me. "You look lovely. As always."

The sweetness of his words causes my chest to tighten. How can he say such things when he never saw me looking my best? He saw me after long days at work or in comfy couch-rotting clothes. He saw me fully naked the last night we had together. I glance down at the silky skirt that blows like Marilyn Monroe's in the wind if I'm not careful—

colorful stripes against a white background—the yellow Mary Janes remind me of sunshine, and the fitted white top I was dumb enough to wear when ordering a hot dog for lunch. However, most of the mustard stain came out when I scrubbed it with the hospital-grade soap. I felt good in this outfit and might have even worn it on purpose to appear more carefree than he remembers me. "Thank you," I say even though I'm a little choked up.

"Did you change your hair?"

I reach for a section and slide my hand down self-consciously. "It's a little shorter. Not much."

"The color." His eyes are set, reminding me how good it feels to be the center of his attention. "It's darker."

I glance into the shiny steel wall across from me to spot the difference from last August. "Oh, I've not been in the sun as much. It will lighten by the end of summer."

"The end of summer. That's what we were. Almost sounds like a song."

"Maybe you should write it."

"I already have. I just didn't have the words until now."

An alarm sounds, and the elevator lurches again, scaring me into holding the railing even tighter. "I think I need to sit down. My stomach doesn't react well to sudden movements. Or dying in elevators."

The alarm quietens, causing us both to look up. He says, "I didn't know that about you."

"Most people don't want to die in elevators."

A roguish grin slides onto his face, and it's so obvious why he made the sexiest man edition again this year. "I've forgotten how funny you are."

"A riot a minute. Anywho, I hate those rides that take you high in the air and then drop you. You bounce and go back up and then down and then up. It's torture." I slide down the wall, but he crosses the invisible barrier we had between us, dividing our safe spaces, rehearsing for when we're in the office divorcing.

"You'll get dirty on the floor. Would you like to sit on my lap?"

I'm both taken by his thoughtfulness and questioning his motive. Can they both exist equally? Or are they mutually exclusive? "You'll get dirty as well."

"I don't mind. It's for a good cause."

I shouldn't even be toying with this idea. Yet I can't seem to stop myself when it comes to Shane. "My skirt?"

"And what's in it."

"If I didn't know better, I'd think you were flirting." Just because you think it, Cate, doesn't mean you need to say it. My goal was not to embarrass myself, yet I'm failing.

He doesn't let more than two heartbeats go by before he says, "Sometimes we struggle to see what's right in front of us."

I hadn't noticed how close he'd gotten or how our hands touched on the railing. I didn't notice that his pupils had dilated or his breathing deepened. But now I do. I see it all right in front of me. I just don't know what to think of it. Or him.

"Are you going to sit, or are we standing here all day?"

Shane chuckles, maneuvering to the floor and settling against the wall. He pats his lap, and says, "Bring 'er in."

I start to bend, wondering if I should flop onto his legs or get to my knees and crawl on top of him. "Bring what in?"

"Your ass. Park it right here, babe."

Babe. It came so naturally that I swear the air got sucked right out of the elevator when we stopped breathing. As I fell onto his lap, we pretended it was never said. My ears heard it. My heart felt it. My soul clung to it, though it's always favored romance over rationale, so I no longer trust it.

The elevator jumps, the lights flash above our heads, and the alarm starts again. I bury my head against his, closing my eyes and holding his neck. I don't know what's worse—an elevator on the fritz threatening our lives or being held by Shane like he still loves me when I reasonably know that's not the case.

The elevator shifts, the lights now steady, and the alarm goes quiet as it starts moving again. There's no time to pull apart before we reach the fourth floor, though there is a delay in the doors sliding open for us.

He asks, "Is this part of that karma you mentioned putting out into the universe?"

"I have no doubt." He makes it hard to hate him when he has me smiling like we're still friends. "I didn't plan on being a part of the vengeance."

Chuckling, he tips his head against the wall of the elevator. "I think you're safe. And there's still time for it to take me down."

"I'm counting on it," I reply with a gentle roll of laughter. "Preferably when I'm not in the vicinity."

With a grin seated squarely on his face, Shane anchors his hand on the railing, pulling us both to our feet in one swift action. His other hand lingers on my hip. I look up, not sure what to say. I don't care about his hand. I like his touch and his warmth. I remember it all so vividly, which makes me hate myself for being so easily manipulated.

He's so tall in front of me. So tempting to cling to. . . I don't because what's the point? And because I got distracted enough to forget he has someone special in his life. This divorce isn't coming out of nowhere.

I had fun . . . I'm still having fun.

Damn him.

Why did he go and ruin a good thing?

Feeling sick to my stomach from the thought of Shane with another woman, I move away from him, pressing a palm to the wall to steady myself. "Why can't these stupid doors just open?"

"How are you, Cat?" *Cate* . . . We've come full circle as if everything between the question he asked earlier and then again just now has been erased. "Are you okay?"

"I'm . . . good." I'm not at all, but we're here for one thing, and that's to get a divorce. My feelings don't matter anymore and shouldn't to him. This is just a formality before we return to our own lives again. "You?" No need to be rude when he so chivalrously let me sit on him.

"We're about to find out."

I stare at him, wondering what the hell that means. "Don't worry, your bank account is safe from me." I don't bother to laugh. It wasn't a joke anyway.

Willing the doors to open for us, I'm so close to banging and yelling, but I'm positive that won't help in this situation. So I chant it inwardly instead of out loud.

"Money is the least of my concerns." His voice is so smooth, so confident that I'm trying to read between the lines as if I'm missing something.

Why am I suddenly feeling paranoid? I'm sure he wants to get this over with and back to his fantastical life as much as I want to get to drinking margaritas with Luna. "*Okaaay.*" I glance up at the floor indicator, noting that we are forever stuck on the fourth floor. "That feels showy, but you are an entertainer."

Offense narrows his eyes as he stares at me. "I'm a musician."

"You're an entertainer, though." I shrug, missing his point. "Comme ci comme ça."

"What?"

"It's French."

"Oui, parlez-vous français?"

"Non." I waggle my finger. "I took Spanish in high school."

Running his hand over his head, he looks up at the stalled number like he's ready to escape as well. "I don't even know how this conversation started."

"I was basically saying it must be nice to never want for anything." I dare to look his way again, catching him studying me like prey.

Should I be worried or—I pluck at my shirt again, hoping to cool off in the hot elevator. *Damn.* Why do I react so easily to him? He knows I do, too. I can just tell by the wry grin resting on his face.

He says, "I want—"

The doors open. I throw myself into the lobby of the law offices just in case it decides to trap us inside for another round of battering my heart.

Shane's exit is much cooler. He swaggers off like he owns the place. According to him, money flows like water right into his bank account, so I guess he could buy the place. I can't get caught up in his chaos again. We didn't have a great ending the last time. This meeting will make it final.

No use in delaying our destiny.

20

Cate

"I'm here to see Mr. Whittier," I say, whispering to the receptionist. "I have a meeting scheduled. We were caught on the elevator. Long story short, we're late."

She checks us in, and we follow her down the hall to the conference room. I stay close, needing to get my head off Shane and into the divorce game we're about to play. The proximity of his presence caresses my backside, which I swear I didn't imagine until my feet falter, and his hand keeps him from running into me.

When I peek over my shoulder, his eyes are still set on mine, but the smile he used back in the elevator is nowhere to be found. It hits me like a ton of bricks. He's the hunter. *I'm the prey.* The receptionist opens the door to the lion's den.

I thought I was ready, but I'm immensely unprepared for what I assumed was a simple meeting. It's not. Files and envelopes are lined up on the table, each side guarding theirs like secrets will be revealed. I look back at Shane once more, and whisper, "You're not asking for anything, right?"

He stops shy of pressing against my arm, but the high-quality fabric of his shirt is soft against my skin. "I never said that."

"But I did, so I assumed you wouldn't."

The blue of his eyes pierces me, and under his breath, he says, "We're already late." The hint is taken, so I lean against the door to let him by.

A million things run through my mind. I shared that I had lost the earnest money with the house but never spent the down payment. Shane saw my apartment. It's not exactly the lap of luxury, though I love it. He knows my car is older than Galileo, so what could he possibly want of mine?

I sit next to my attorney across from Shane and his attorney, who really looks like an asshole ready to take me to the cleaners. Max Whittier is jovial by nature, which is one of the reasons I've worked with him on little matters like a fender bender where the guy didn't want to pay up. Divorce is no joke. I need a viper to take on this snake.

Max introduces his colleague, Sheila Rick, and Shane's attorneys. Looking at me, he says, "This is highly unusual."

"That's not a good start." I shoot Shane a look that pins him to the chair he's relaxing in.

"It doesn't mean bad, but this is not a way my firm typically operates." Planting the tips of his fingers on the large manila envelope, he drags it across the table closer to him. "We've been asked to unseal the requests in the presence of everyone. We'll negotiate here at the table. If at any time we need a mediator, we can pause to bring one in to hopefully reach a successful conclusion to this marriage agreement."

Funny how neither of us ever agreed to this marriage, but here we are on opposing sides of a large wooden conference table suddenly fighting for . . . what? Assets I don't have? Motherfu—

"We weren't aware of any prior requests," Sheila says, directing her attention across the table. "Are these terms and conditions?"

"We didn't have any," I add. "No terms, and we definitely didn't discuss any conditions." I look back at Max. "I'm only requesting the divorce. I'm not after his money."

"This is highly unorthodox," he says, shifting a glare to the opposing attorney. When he turns back to me, he pats my arm. "We do not have to accept any offers, Cate, and we can fight any claims. If, at any point, you're uncomfortable, we can consult in my office. But let's see what they're claiming as their share of the marital property."

"Marital property?" My jaw hits the table as I try to burn Shane alive with one hard glare. *How dare he!*

Shane says, "I'm not asking for any property."

"Good, because you know I don't have any. I lost the house—"

"I know, Cat." He's too restrained, leaving me no emotions to riffle through. He's not like the man I spent time falling for and nothing like the boy I once knew. There's no familiarity with the person in front of me now except the exterior, and he has his parents to thank for that.

"Then what could you possibly want from me? My 2012 Toyota with dodgy air-conditioning? Spousal support off *my* salary? What? What is it?"

His attorney whispers, and they both go quiet.

I roll my eyes. Screw this whole situation. I'm done, and we've barely started.

Max opens the file and immediately shifts it between him and his colleague, studying it like they're about to be tested. I cross my arms over my chest to keep my anger at bay and my heart contained as it tries to escape. I knew it couldn't be trusted around him.

As my attorneys consult each other, I can't stop myself from replaying everything Shane said in the elevator, landing back on the ending that was never finished. Lowering my arms to my sides, I lean closer to the table, my eyes locked on his, and ask, "What were you going to say in the elevator? What do you want?"

His expression breaks, the man I knew last August returning, even if only for the briefest of seconds. "I want more time—"

"You're requesting time with my client?" Max asks, holding the paperwork in his hands. He flattens it on the table and points midway down. "Seventy-two hours. Is that correct?"

Shane's attorney states, "Everything is listed on page two. No other requests or obligations will be required."

I turn to Max. "What does that mean, he's requesting time?"

He blows out a long breath, his eyes still analyzing the text. When he turns to me, he replies, "The divorce will be granted after the agreed upon seventy-two hours." Shooting a look at Shane's attorney, he adds, "This is bordering on extortion, which is illegal in every state in the U.S."

I can't stop from looking at Shane as if he'll explain instead of being interrupted. When he doesn't continue, I ask Max, "I have to spend seventy-two hours with him to get cut loose from this sham of a marriage?"

"He has requested your company for . . ." He swivels his chair in my direction and speaks slower like I can't keep up, which I can't, it seems. "A period of three days or seventy-two hours, whichever works best for your schedules."

"*Our* schedules?" I sound like an idiot, but surely, I'm

hearing this wrong or not understanding the legal jargon or something because this sounds a lot like . . . *can't be.* I hold my hand up between us. "I hate to go in circles, but what do you mean by my company?"

Max looks across the table at Shane and his attorney, and says, "Again, this is highly unusual and barely legal, but I do have to advise you that an effort to work on the marriage looks better when you go before the judge to ask for the divorce. Most want to know that the parties made every attempt to stay together in cases of irreconcilable differences."

"And many have been saved," his attorney says, "by spending time together."

"I . . . um . . ." Still struggling to understand why Shane would even want this when he's moving on with someone else, I close my gaping mouth since my throat is going dry, clear it, and say, "We're not really married—"

"You are, Mrs. Faris," his attorney states so boldly.

"Farin. My last name is Farin."

"My apologies, Mrs. Farin—"

"Ms." The gall of this man . . . *and the one beside him.* I shoot Shane a glare I hope rattles his bones.

The attorney, undeterred as if the name game was planned from the beginning, continues, "Are you prepared to stand before a court under oath and declare you made every effort to save your marriage, Ms. Farin?"

"Yes," I say without a second thought. No debate. No doubt at all. I don't know Shane from Mr. Rosen, and I'm not marrying him. Okay, I can admit I know him better than my patients—the real him he showed in the privacy of my apartment right before he revealed his true self in that heated argument. Shifting my eyes to the man himself, I take a breath, then ask, "Why are you doing this? Please just sign the papers."

"I'll take forty-eight," he says, his interest shifting into a higher gear. Oh now he's all hands on deck instead of leaving it to his weaselly attorney to do his dirty work.

"So now you want less time with me?" I cross my arms over my chest, utterly offended that I'm being negotiated like a cow on the sale block.

Shane leans forward. "Forget everyone else, Cat. I want time with you."

"You had it and blew it."

"Give me another chance. I'll take anything you'll give me. I want a chance to get to know you, a chance to know my wife before we divorce."

I scoff. "Wife? That's rich, like you, yet I didn't make one request of you despite all that." I was softening until he threw that out like he did our relationship.

He says, "Make one. Right now. I'll give you anything you want."

Enticing, but I can't be bribed. "Unlike you, Shane, I didn't come here with any intention of making demands. That's all anyone ever does of you. I was giving you the opposite—your freedom."

"You don't have to be such a saint." My head jerks from the audacity of this man while he continues, "If you want something, just ask."

"I'm not *something*. I'm a person who you're requesting." Resting my hands calmly on the table in front of me, I push through the shock and gather myself back together. "I have a life, a career, friends who are waiting to have margaritas with me to celebrate my divorce—"

"Celebrate?" He looks away, his gaze distancing through

the window as the reality of what we are hits him like it did me last August when he walked out my door.

The tension in the room is so thick that the attorneys appear uncomfortable. The squeak of a chair across from me pulls my eyes back to Shane. I once saw sadness in his blue eyes, but this is deeper, causing my own heart to squeeze. Vulnerability is rare for a man of his stature, fame, and wealth. Shane Faris wears his heart on his sleeve for me, but why? "I'm asking for one chance to show you who I am."

"No, you're asking for two days."

"I'll take a day, a lunch, an hour. Fuck, another elevator ride—"

"I'll pass on the last part." My heart starts thumping in my chest again, my throat tightening as my emotions well in my eyes. I hate the unknown clouding truth with fiction, so I ask, "Are you marrying someone?"

"No," he replies without hesitation. "I'm already married."

Is it the words he said or the emotions he's showing me? It's both, and I believe him. I look down at the papers once more, not knowing why I'm even considering this. "If I give you the forty-eight hours, you'll sign the papers?"

"I already have. So even if you change your mind on the time together, all it will take is your signature to file."

He gave me the power before we walked in here. What do I do with that information? I keep my eyes on the documents, needing to be clear with my understanding before making a final decision. Will spending time together really make it easier to walk away from each other?

Maybe this is what we both need. Proof in real time that we'd be terrible together. His chance to say what he needs to get off his chest. Closure for me.

I don't know what the hell I'm doing. One of the worst ideas I've ever had comes to mind. I ask myself, what would Luna do? What do I want to do? I look up, doubting the words even as they come out of my mouth. "You have forty-eight hours. That's it. You better make the most of it."

"I won't disappoint you."

"This isn't about me, Shane. This is about you." I turn to my attorneys and say, "I'll agree to the amended terms on one condition of my own."

"Anything." Shane's winning smile makes quite the appearance, then it stumbles. "What is it?"

21

Shane

"What do you mean it's sealed?" I ask, walking toward the elevators with Stuart.

My attorney says, "She doesn't play ball. She hits back. Ms. Farin just flipped the script on us."

"How?"

We both go silent when the door to the offices is pushed open.

My. My. My. What have we here?

The little vixen herself. I don't think I've ever been more attracted to her than I am after she reverse-played me with her own secret weapon.

Shoving my hands in my pockets, I shift back on my heels and give her a wink. "Well played, Cat."

"Touché."

The elevator doors open, so I step aside so she can get on first. "Want a ride?" I tease, the line never getting old.

"You're wearing it out, Faris, and nice try. I'll be taking

the stairs." She pushes into the stairwell, and I can hear the soles of her shoes clacking as she gallops down.

I jump on the elevator and hit the lobby button repeatedly to get the doors to close. "Get on, Stuart."

He steps on, not fast enough for my liking, and the doors close behind him. "You got your forty-eight hours," he says, knowing exactly what I'm up to.

"I'll take anything I can get."

"This isn't like you, Shane. If she's that special, why aren't you staying married?"

I've never had to answer for the sins of my past, but I need to get used to it if I'm going to win Cat back. "I was an asshole. Right woman, wrong time. And a whole other slew of fuckups that led us here." I get ready as the elevator is about to land on the bottom floor. "I'll meet you in the parking lot."

The doors open, and I rush to the stairwell exit, tugging it open and leaning against it.

Cat slows as she comes down the last flight of stairs, a slow smile growing before my eyes. "That's quite the party trick." She passes in front of me, tapping my nose as she goes. "Thanks."

"You're welcome," I reply, watching that ass as she shakes it walking away. I release the door and double-time to catch up to her. "You're all mine for forty-eight hours."

"Don't make it sound so lascivious." She glances at me out of the corners of her eyes. "There will be no sex involved." Suddenly stopping before walking out the front doors of the building, she squares her shoulders to me. "You get *access* to me for forty-eight hours. You don't 'get' me." She uses finger quotes for emphasis, but as stern as she's trying to be, I don't believe she's as upset as she's pretending.

The way the edges of her mouth turn upward is a dead giveaway, but there are plenty of other signs. Her eyes are bright, the gold shining even in the bad lighting of the lobby. But the way she's happy to stop and talk about it makes me glad I made the effort. For me. For us. For her, though she may not realize it yet.

I'm not the man she once knew, and I intend to show her I've changed.

"I have no intentions of forcing you to do anything you don't want to. Remember, the papers are signed. Our fate is in your hands." I leave her standing there with her lips parted in shock. But I didn't miss the fire I lit in her eyes.

Stuart waits by my car when I head in that direction. From behind, my little Cat calls, "What do you mean our fate?"

I glance back over my shoulder, and reply, "I'll be in contact soon about our date."

"Forced proximity, you mean."

"Tomato tomahto." Something is so satisfying about using her words against her. Not that I find it a thrill to win, although I typically do, but that she knows I was paying attention.

When I reach Stuart, I turn around to see her scrambling to keep her skirt from blowing in the wind. I grin from watching her, from feeling like I just won the lottery with this second chance, and because she's fucking more spectacular than ever.

As soon as she slips into her car, I ask Stuart, "Tell me again what she requested. I missed it."

"You didn't miss anything," he says. "It's a sealed document. We won't know what it is until after the forty-eight hours."

"I don't like surprises."

"Neither do I, but you already agreed to it, so it's a done deal."

"Well, fuck."

He opens the door to the Lamborghini parked next to my Ferrari, making me realize I pay him way too much. He tosses his briefcase in the passenger's seat, then says, "She guaranteed us it's not financially motivated, and it won't give her ownership of any part of your personal property or business. If you ask me, she wanted control." He slips inside the red sports car. "I wouldn't worry about it. What could she possibly want from you if it doesn't pertain to getting a share of something you own or a piece of your fame?"

"I don't know."

"It's a mystery, but you'll know soon enough." I shut his door for him, not liking how wide it opens near my car anyway. He rolls down the window. "Let me know when you're done with the forty-eight hours, and I'll retrieve the envelope for you to open."

"Will do. Thanks for coming out here." You'd think I was asking him to travel to Barstow. It's just not Beverly Hills.

"That's my job."

Slipping inside my car, I can't help but replay what happened inside. Not the negotiations. That went as planned, except for the surprise Cat threw in at the end. The elevator was an unexpected development in the story. I chuckle, a smile working its way out from the memories. She probably thinks I paid someone to make that happen.

I shift into reverse and pull onto the main road with so much spinning through my thoughts. I got the days I wanted with her, but she twisted the plot right out from under me. *What game is she playing?*

The same one I am. I just wonder if her end goals are the same.

The ten months without her were brutal, but that's what it took for me to realize what I lost. I came here on a mission because of the time apart. I'm also a better man for it. But can I be the man she needs?

I fucking hope so.

I'm still uneasy about the unknown, and she's packing a punch with her comeback request. It doesn't seem to pertain to financial gain. That makes it worse. Unpredictable. I would have given her anything she wanted—my pride and joy Ferrari, a million dollars to get the house she lost back, or my fucking house. She could have had whatever she wanted.

Instead, she's going to hit me where it hurts. It only makes sense since I broke her heart first. And there's a strong possibility that she won't forgive me even though I'm destroyed. That won't stop me from trying. Her forgiveness matters more to me.

Forty-eight hours. That's all I have to prove I'm a changed man.

ME:

Hi, it's me.

It took me all damn day plus the week and a half I let pass to get the courage to text Cat, and that's what I go with? I'm even cringing. Sitting on the deck, I drop my head into my hand and rub my temple. *C'mon, babe, text me back.*

The sun is setting, so I look out to enjoy its beauty, but my hands are sweating, so I drag my palms down my jeans-clad legs. I used to be able to enjoy the sunrise or sunset on a surfboard in the ocean—starting my day and leading into a night of trouble once I got off the water. I've gotten away from surfing but can't shake my past. *Specifically, Cat.*

She saw me for who I was and wasn't putting up with that shit. I don't blame her. I respect her more for it. She should never settle for less. I take another shot of courage, the beer talking me into sending another text. Logic tells me to wait a few minutes. I'm on my first lager, so I don't fall for the tricks beer plays on its victims.

A message pops up and relief washes through that I didn't jump the shark on this situation. I look at my phone on the table.

Cat:

> I thought I blocked this number.

Grinning like an idiot, I laugh before I question whether she's joking. *Shit.* What do I say to that? I reply:

> Guess you forgot. I'll wait while you block it now.

Cat:

> Too late. You've already found me.

I drove by Parkdale twice and saw her once when she was leaving for the day. I didn't dare approach, figuring we were long past having a civil discussion. Though, I'm not sure that spying on her was any better. I sit back in the iron chair, and type:

Want to hear something really creepy?

Cat:

No.

I text to cajole her:

Come on . . .

Cat:

Fine. What?

Me:

I knew where you were all along.

Why the fuck did I think telling her that was a good idea? Fucking hell. I roll my eyes, another reminder of her. She's cute when she's annoyed. When wasn't she adorable, though? Not one memory comes to mind.

Cat:

It's so creepy you were stalking me like a celebrity.

I'm stuck on how to read between the lines. Is she fucking with me, being funny, or playing along. I type:

I'm not sure I know how to do it differently. I thought I was special.

Three dots roll across the bubble, then die. *Fuck.* I

thought she'd find the play on words charming. The three dots return, and another message pops up:

> You were.

If she wanted to gut me, she did it in two words. Scraping my fingers through my hair, I stare at the screen. There isn't anything clever I can say to make the words taste better.

She has a right to be mad. I was hurt and took it out on the one who felt in control of my pain. No excuses. Just facts. So it's not surprising she'd strike when she can. Unknowingly, I gave her the perfect setup for that reaction.

Another message pops onto the screen from her:

> You didn't have to spy on me. You could have stopped by to say hi instead.

Sobering. I remind myself that I didn't stay away because I wanted to. I kept my distance because she needed me to. She needed neat and orderly, a life she could fit in a little garden home plot. So why am I fucking it up for her? I know why.

Am I ready to admit it?

Not out loud. Not to her. Not even to me fully. I'm still grappling with who I was then and who I want to be, and I'm currently stuck between the two.

I text:

> I thought you'd refuse to see me or, at the very least, throw me out.

Cat:

> I would have because it was too soon for me. It still might be, Shane. But at least I would have known you cared.

I was a fool for what I did, but I know she'll value action more than words. I start to type when her next message pops up first:

> Maggie misses you. Specially, and I quote, "his big strong arms." She also mentioned your ass, but I don't want to feed that ego of yours. You have plenty of others up for the task.

I laugh to myself. If there's one thing she's protective of, besides her own heart, it's her patients. I text:

> If you like my ass, just come out and say it.

Cat:

> I like your ass, but you know what I like better?

Did I open a can of worms when all I was trying to do was sync our calendars for forty-eight hours? My fingers have been hovering over the letters. *Do I pretend she never asked or—*

Cat:

> Don't overthink it. It's burritos from El Fuego's.

She has me laughing, but I'm grateful she didn't slam the proverbial door in my face when I texted. She's done the opposite. She's kicked it open and invited me in. If she can crack jokes, I still have an inkling of a chance. It may be too late to get the girl, but I can make it up to her. She can move on and live her life. I'll move on with mine. At least she'll know I made the effort.

Me:

> I'm not sure how I feel about a burrito being better than my ass, but obviously, I need to amp up leg day.

Cat:

> Don't stress. Your ass is pretty great. But those burritos . . .

I'll take pretty great. As much as I'd like this to continue, I know she's probably got better things to do like saving lives or spending time with a boyfriend who is smart enough not to fuck it up.

That's something I hadn't considered prior to her assuming I wanted the divorce so I could marry someone else. I've failed her. But I'm not letting another guy win her heart before I have a chance to show her how I feel. I need to lock this down, so I text:

> What's your schedule look like for our time together?

Cat:

> Is it really time together, or we just need to spend time in the same zip code? I need details. All of them. I need to make plans for this hostage situation. Where are we going? What do I pack? Do I need to get a tracker inserted into my body so Luna can find me? You know, those kinds of things.

There's no trust left, but I don't blame her. I deserve it and don't mind earning it back. I'm surprised it's so far gone after the casualness of our text exchange leading me to believe otherwise. And she's not lost her sense of humor. A positive in this complicated situation. Me:

> Time together. You'll have your own room, if that alleviates your concerns. Pack for the lake. You can swim, right?

Cat:

> I can swim. It's all so fascinating.

I down my beer, needing every ounce of bravery I haven't mustered in ten months. *Tell her.* Me:

> You always were the most fascinating girl in school.

Cat:

> Thought you didn't notice?

Me:

> I never said that.

There's a pause in the conversation, and then a message from her pops up again:

> It almost sounds like you've been planning this for at least a few hours.

Me:

> Months, but who's counting?

Cat:

> You are, but . . .

Damn, she's fast with the comebacks. I don't know if anger or entertainment drives her, but she doesn't let a thing I say slide. The pause is killing me, though. I reply:

> But what?

Cat:

> How's Memorial Day weekend? I have a long weekend from work. After I serve my time at the lake, I'll still have a day to enjoy the time off.

Hit me where it hurts indeed.

She shouldn't make this easy, but I didn't know how my emotions would feel either. They're a scratchy, ill-fitting wool sweater. This is the path I chose, so I have to walk it. I reply:

> Memorial Day weekend is set. Thank you.

Cat:

> I didn't have a choice.

I stare at the message for probably too long, trying to read between the lines. Does she mean it, or is she teasing me? Although I struggle to read the meaning she's intended through text, she's not entirely wrong.

Feeling heavier after reading that finale of a line, I stand and go inside. I've caused enough damage already. I text:

> You always have a choice with me, Cat. I'll send you the details. You can decide what you want to do from there.

I stare at the screen for a few minutes before I add:

> Good night.

She replies:

> Good night.

I got what I wished for. *Don't fuck it up, Faris.*

22

Shane

"Fucking hell."

"Language," Poppy calls from the kitchen.

"Mack just spit up again." I hold the plump baby in front of me. He giggles as if this is part of his evil plan. "Even vomiting on one of my favorite T-shirts can't make me dislike you, kid." He got the Faris blue eyes, bright and jolly, and is the happiest baby. He likes to be held all the time and has taken to me since we met at the hospital last November. That's fair. I am pretty fucking awesome. I kiss his head because he's pretty awesome, too.

Laird comes with a package of wipes and swipes Mack out of my hands. Holding him up so they're face-to-face, he wipes the remains from his chin. "You're a messy little thing." Sitting on the couch, he says, "See how neat your sister is? She doesn't spit up on her favorite cousin." He looks at me. "It's weird that you're cousins with my kids. Maybe we should go with uncle?"

"We don't make the rules, but I'm cool with whatever."

Mack flaps his arms and blows raspberries when he looks at me. Reaching out for me, I can't say no to these kids, so I take him into my arms again.

Laird sits on the floor with his daughter. "How's my Posey Rosie? She's so good at sitting."

And there's that look of pure joy when she sees him. Her eyes widen, her dad the sun in her world, making her shine, and that smile, the laugh. The reward of being a dad. Having someone love you so much that they don't see your flaws. They only know that you hung the stars for them. That trust. The love.

Mack squeals, not appreciating my attention elsewhere. I squeeze one of my eyes closed until he's done. "Look, kid. I need my eardrums to play in this band. Don't go wrecking them." But yeah, he gets me with that two-teeth grin of his. Every time. He may not look at me like I hung the moon, but I can tell he knows I'll always have his back. I hug him to me and kiss his head again.

Poppy comes in and says, "It's nap time."

"For you or the kids?" Laird teases.

"Probably both. I'm exhausted."

He stands with Posey in his arms and wraps his arm around his wife. "You go lie down. I'll put the kids in their cribs and take it from here." He kisses her forehead, then gives her ass a little smack when she turns around.

Poppy's an amazing wife, mom, and friend to me. Hearing her giggle like she's getting away with something is fun to see. But I notice how Laird watches her. They don't get time alone anymore, so I say, "Hey, if you want to take a break, I'm here. I can hang out for a few hours."

He seems surprised when he turns back, his forehead doing the heavy lifting. "Really?" he asks, unsure if I'm serious by his tone. Then he sets Posey on the floor where she had been happy to sit—a new skill she's learned. Mack hasn't, but we all do things in our own time.

Don't I know it?

"Really," I reply.

"Are you sure, Shane?"

"I'm sure. Is it okay if they fall asleep here in the living room?"

"Yeah, it's fine, but if you want, you can put them in their cribs. They love it in there and usually fall asleep quickly." He checks his watch. "They'll both be zonked out in about twenty minutes anyway."

"Got it," I say. "Go. I can handle this."

Rubbing his hand over his head, a familiar Faris tic of mine as well, he grins. "Okay. Great. Knock if you need anything."

"I won't need anything." No fucking way am I disturbing them. I don't know if they'll be asleep or taking advantage of the time in other ways. I'm not going to be the one to interrupt either. "No worries."

"I appreciate it." He walks toward the hall and disappears down it. The sound of a door opening travels the short distance and closes right after.

I look at Mack, still grinning at me as he reaches for my nose, giggling when he runs his tiny fingers over my unshaven face. I rub my chin. "Yeah, I know. I need to shave." Slipping down to the floor, I put Mack on his tummy beside his sister. "Maybe you two can help me out. I need some advice." Posey looks at me, her dimples revealed when she smiles.

They have the cutest kids that ever existed. No surprise since the Faris genes held strong.

Poppy comes into the living room with a baby on each hip. "Hey," she greets me with a smile as she passes.

I sit up from the couch and click the game off. "Hey. I didn't hear them cry."

"They weren't. I was up, so I checked in on them." She laughs. "They were in their cribs but playing with each other across the room. Making faces. Humming. Happy."

Getting up, I go into the kitchen and take Posey while she sets Mack in his highchair and fastens him in. She reaches for Posey and latches her in next to him. "They're hungry when they get up from a nap."

"I am, too, so I get it."

Her ponytail swings when she laughs. "There's food in the fridge if you want something."

I stretch, feeling bent after lounging on the couch for so long. "No, I'm going to take off. There are a few things I need to do."

"Thanks for staying. That was sweet, Shane."

Leaning against the marble island, I say, "You guys have been through a lot, but if you ever need anyone or need help, you can call me."

"I appreciate that." She pauses while she adjusts the kids. "I can't imagine a better life. Truly. I feel like I'm living in a dream all because Laird gave me the opposite of what I grew up with. Love and being actively present in my and the babies' lives. He wants to spend time with me . . ." She runs a finger under Mack's chin, then tickles Posey. They are more than happy to hit the trays with their fists from excitement. "I love the twins more than anything. They keep me busy and tired, so my alone time with Laird is limited. It helps that the band isn't on the road this summer. Not all summer, that is."

Nikki and Tulsa went through something similar. I probably won't be unique when I have a family one day. "I know it's not easy to trust others when fame and money are involved, but I mean it. If you need a night out or a nap, let me know, and I'll be here."

She pulls their food out and lifts the lid. "You really mean that, don't you?" Sitting on a stool between them, she glances at me before feeding them.

"Of course."

"Can I ask you something personal?"

Poppy has a way of digging deep with me but making me feel . . . Safe? I can talk to her and know I won't get shit for it. "Sure."

"What happened to the girl we talked about when we were in Austin?" She's let that conversation slide for almost a year, though I'm sure she's been curious. Or maybe my becoming an utter asshole on the road once we got back gave her all the information she needed to know.

Do I tell her the story? Too much to share when I'm about to walk out the door. "My life blew up after that."

She stops with a spoonful of mush in front of Mack's mouth and looks at me. "It blew up, or you detonated the bomb?" When I don't answer right away, she feeds the babies, and says, "Ah. I see."

Pushing off the counter, I need to get going, but I don't rush. Not yet. I have the strongest urge to confide in her. Taking a breath, I stop myself, but having someone to talk to about the situation with Cat would be nice. A woman's perspective would be even better. I could speak to Nikki, but she has no patience for antics when it comes to relationships. How she ended up with Tulsa is still a mystery.

Guess they balance each other out.

Poppy says, "You've always supported our family. You were at the hospital when I thought things were going wrong with my pregnancy. You showed up without Laird even asking." Holding her hand to her chest, she takes a staggered breath. "That will always mean so much to me, Shane."

"I'm glad everything turned out okay."

"Me too. As for you, please let us be there for you when you need someone to talk to, or to listen. Though with me, you know I tend to give my opinion without being asked."

"I trust your opinion." I tap the counter, the urge growing stronger. "If you wanted . . ." *What do I want to say here?* "Fictitiously speaking, would you—" Fuck. Just say it, Faris. "That girl, the woman we talked about in Vegas . . .I want her back." I stare, waiting for her to react in any way. Good or bad.

She doesn't. She feeds each kid another bite, seeming to think about my problem. "How bad was the ending?"

"Not my greatest moment."

Her mouth dips down in the corner. "I see. Detonation."

"Yeah." I can't explain it away, so I don't try.

"Well," she starts, swiveling on the stool to face me. "You're not the same person you were last August. And she played a part in that, even if she's not aware of it. Apologies from the heart matter. Making different decisions now is important. And don't hold back. If you love her, tell her. If you want to spend the rest of your life with her, make sure she feels it in her bones. Make sure she knows you will do anything to win her heart back. It will start with forgiveness. If she'll give you the opportunity to explain, she's open to that apology."

I knew all this but struggled to put it into words like she has. She sounds like she's been there and came out the other side, so maybe there's hope for me yet. Tapping the counter, I say, "Thank you." Nodding, I know what I need to do. It's not about stealing Cat's time for me to beg her for forgiveness. I need to prove to her I deserve it. "You've given me lots to think about."

"What are we talking about?" Laird comes in yawning as he crosses through the living room. He goes to Poppy first, cupping her face and kissing her. Then he turns to the babies, planting one on each of their heads. When neither of us speaks, he shrugs. "What?"

Maybe it's the second chance that I've been given . . . or that I forced upon my marriage. Or perhaps it's seeing my cousin and his wife have this life that I wouldn't mind having if I could get my fucking life in order.

I never wanted this life. I never wanted anything until I had it and lost it. Now I can see a whole life ahead of me. Wife. Babies. Rich in love instead of only money.

I don't want a divorce.

I want to save my marriage.

23

Shane

EVERYTHING IS READY, except me.

I'm dressed. The car has gas. The trunk is loaded. It doesn't hold much, but I packed it full of food in coolers along with another for drinks. I bought flowers even though the last time I brought her flowers didn't turn out so well for me.

I can go over every detail for the fifth time, but it's not what I packed or planned that's on my mind. It's that she's not even here.

It's only been fifteen minutes since I arrived, since I checked the time to make sure I got it right, since I showed up at her apartment as we had scheduled through texts. Fifteen minutes, hoping she comes home. Doubts kick in again.

I'm wasting my time.

She'll never forgive me.

I won't get the chance to explain.

For all I know, the paperwork has already been signed,

sealed, and delivered to her attorney, and I planned all this for nothing.

Is she blowing me off?

Busy with patients even though she supposedly was given the extra day off?

Did her car break down running errands and her phone died? She was in an accident? Or she eloped with a boyfriend that I'm not totally sure she doesn't have. Millions of scenarios could keep her from going. She wouldn't hold back from telling me if she had changed her mind. Not Cat.

I shake my hands to loosen the nerves free. This worked in the past. Performing in front of crowds of twenty, thirty, even fifty thousand screaming fans doesn't faze me. A certain audience of one has me pacing her parking lot like the fucking stalker I've become.

"Waited long?" Cat asks.

I look over to find her standing behind her car, looking like sunshine on a rainy day in a yellow sundress and white sneakers. With a bag in one hand and her purse in the other, they swing in her hands as she walks toward me.

I almost open my arms, ready to catch her like I used to —to hug her to me, to kiss her neck and head, those pink lips, and every other part of her. I shove my hands in my pockets instead, but I'm so fucking relieved she's here.

"No. Just got here."

"That's good," she says, stopping in front of me. "I felt bad for being late, but since you weren't here—"

"I arrived fifteen minutes ago."

"Right on time." A smile wriggles the corners of her lips, soothing my nerves and erasing any doubts I had. Staring up at me, she says, "I have my stuff packed inside." Cat's not cold, but she's not receptive either. I definitely have my work cut out for me this weekend. I expected no less.

"I can put it in the car while you finish."

When she opens the door, flashbacks of our argument, of me being out of line, run through my head. Judging by how she pauses in the doorframe with her shoulders tense, I assume Cat feels the same. My heart rate increases, sweat dots my palms, and I can barely meet her eyes when her head turns in my direction. Her smile is gone, too.

"Back to the scene of the crime."

Reminding myself of the strides I've taken to prove to myself and her that I'm a different man, I try for a reassuring smile. "I'm sorry. I'm sorry for leaving that day."

She opens her mouth, then closes it again. Waving me inside, she disappears behind the door. When I enter the apartment, she's unpacking the bag. "I'm sorry I kept you waiting. I stopped at the pharmacy to get my prescription. It wasn't ready, so I had a delay."

I stand in the doorway, trying not to invade her space. Not again. Get in and get out. Give her room. "It's okay. Did you get what you need?"

"Yes. I also got you something."

I hadn't realized I was keeping my eyes glued to the floor until I forced my gaze to her. "You did?"

"Don't get too excited," she says with a little laugh. "It was an upsell at the register." She digs her hands in the bag again, then tosses something silver and small to me.

It's hard and has little buttons. "What is it?"

"It's a beatbox. The switch is on the side. I tested it to make sure it worked."

I roll it around my hand and flip on the switch. Pressing the red button, it kicks into a beat on repeat.

She says, "I know it's dumb, but I—"

"It's not dumb. I like it." I push the blue button. These

beats are the worst. I was hitting better beats in third grade, but what do I expect from a register upsell?

"You do?"

"Yeah. Of course." I hit the green button because why not? "Thank you."

Laughter trails across the room. "Glad you like it. I really thought you wouldn't because the beats are so bad."

"They're the worst."

She laughs even louder. "It's a gag gift, Shane. You don't have to keep it the rest of your life."

"It's from you, so I'm keeping it."

My words seem to give her pause, and a fresh smile grows on her face. That's what stops me in my tracks. She's breathtaking even when she's not trying, maybe more so. Looking around, I ask, "What can I take to the car?"

"Let me get my suitcase." She rushes into the bedroom.

"Suitcase? It's two days."

Pulling a carry-on into the living room, she shrugs. "It's not big, but it was easier to pack the essentials in this. Plus, I could organize by day." I have no doubt she took the extra step. I once threw out the word orderly like it was an insult. Since then, I've worked on getting my life together and have discovered that being organized isn't such a negative concept to me anymore. Clarity came with more sleep over time.

She pulls a tote bag from the kitchen, looping it around the suitcase's handle.

I tuck the toy into my pocket and start for the car with her stuff. Scene of the crime is correct for how it made me feel. Shitty. I left when I should have stayed back then, but that's too much to get to when we're trying to reach Deer Lake before the day gets away from us.

I click open my car, but before I can load her stuff in, Cat runs out. "I'm taking my car."

Stopping, I stand there with her carry-on in my arms, unsure if my confusion is evident to her. This wasn't something I expected. "You want to take both? I assumed we were riding together, but I can load it into your car, if you'd like."

I've given her every out, and she's still moving forward with this wild plan I've thrown at her. She looks at her car, then at mine, and back at hers again, a debate raging inside her. "To be honest, Shane, I worry about being stuck somewhere without transportation to escape."

My hand rises, my forefinger and thumb sliding outward on my brow. I hadn't considered how this would make her feel. I just wanted what I wanted, and it's coming at her expense.

Fuck.

This isn't how it's supposed to be.

"I want to spend time with you, Cat, but I'll be honest. I never worked out the consequences of what this would mean to you. My intentions were good. I was giving you space, time, and whatever else you wanted to make this happen, but the results are not what they should be. Not for you, anyway. I owe you so many apologies. I don't know where to start." My thoughts are shooting like darts in all directions and hoping to land on something solid. I start back for her apartment with her suitcase and bag in hand.

"Hey, Faris?" Just past the stairs that hide her front door from the world, I turn back. Her arms are wide away from her sides, head tilted, the crack of a smile revealing itself. "Where are you going?"

"I don't know anymore." Truth laid bare. I'm lost when it comes to her.

"I packed my bikini for the lake." *She plays dirty.*

I look down, trying to hide the grin that will surely offend if caught on my face. But visions of her in a bikini aren't easily swept from my head. "What are you saying?"

Her expression softens as she lowers her arms and clasps her hands in front of her. "We should get on the road. The day will disappear before we know it. You know how LA traffic is."

Our eyes stay fixed for a few seconds before I return to the back of her Toyota. I don't think we need to have a long-drawn-out conversation. There's no impasse keeping us from moving forward this time. "Pop the trunk."

She walks to my car, parked two over, and says, "I was thinking we could ride together."

"I don't want you to feel uncomfortable."

Shifting on her feet, she moves around me and quirks a smirk. "Maybe we'll leave the keys on the counter."

I look down at the keys in my hand. "The keys to my custom-designed Ferrari? My initials were hand-embroidered on the driver's headrest."

She kicks a tire as if checking for air. I flinch from witnessing the abuse. "These look like an upgrade as well."

"They were," I reply, not liking where this is heading.

"Let me guess, custom?"

"Took two months to make." I look at the car, then at her again. "I'm starting to think you don't understand the gravity of the—"

"Circumstances? I probably understand better than you do as the hostage in this situation."

Unfortunately, I can't argue with her. "I'll leave the keys on the hook by the door. If you want to leave, they'll be there. Or you can hold on to them all weekend if you prefer. Should I add you to my policy?"

"Not totally unwise. I've been in a few little collisions

here and there. Once with a curb at In n' Out Burger that messed up my alignment. Someone dumbly put a concrete pole inside a parking spot at a Target." She raises a finger like a thought just occurred to her. "And then there was the time—"

"Okay. Got your point. I'll make the call." I don't care that much about the car, though I keep her spotless and make sure she's maintained.

She starts to laugh. "I was kind of teasing about the escape."

I flip the front seat forward to put her stuff inside. "What about the accidents?"

"No, those are true."

"*Greaaat*," I say, trying to breathe through the scenario of her wrecking my car that's currently playing through my head like a movie in slow motion.

"What's this?"

I look at the front seat where she's found the itinerary. "I know you like to know what your day looks like, so I printed out a schedule for you." I'm not saying she cries, but she blinks back some water in her eyes.

"It's printed on cardstock. Pink cardstock." I spy her eyes stealing a peek of me before they return to the cardstock.

"Since I was printing it anyway—"

"Thank you." Her hand covers her chest as her gaze runs down the schedule. Glancing back at him between the seats, she says, "I've never felt more seen in my life."

"It's no big deal."

"It is to me." She props it up against the console and shuts the door. I'm adjusting the seat back into place when she comes around the back of the car. I lift to my height, and our eyes meet. It's not a big smile, but it is one that feels genuine and for me. "That was very thoughtful. Thank you."

"You're welcome." Who knew printing an itinerary out would win the day? Wait until she sees what else I have in store for her.

She steps to the side but then stops and asks, "What is the retreat at eight p.m. tomorrow night?"

I lean against the car and debate how much I want to tell her. "I know you want to know all the details, but do you mind going along with a few of them? It will involve trusting me. I haven't earned, but—"

"You'll earn it back by tomorrow night?"

"I intend to." I nod.

She nods. "Okay. Can't wait to see what you have up your sleeve besides that new tattoo you're currently hiding." *Oh shit.* She knows . . .

That tattoo has become such a part of me that I forgot about it being revealed this weekend. That's a conversation I'll ease into, preferably after a few beers.

Walking back to the apartment, she says, "I'm going to lock up. Need anything?"

Her and a second chance. She's giving me both. *What more could I ask for?* "Do you have a bottle of water?" *Except that.* I'm thirsty, and I wasn't planning on stopping.

"I'm surprised we can drink liquids in your custom-designed, hand-embroidered Ferrari." She saunters off before I can reply, and probably best if I don't.

It's a nice view of her ass, but when she walks out, it's that face and the golden-brown eyes that get me every time. I'm the luckiest fucking bastard in the world right now. And I'm going to make sure she knows it.

I open the door for her and help her slip inside. By the time I'm getting behind the wheel, she asks, "So, you got me. The clock starts now."

24

Cate

WE HIT THE HIGHWAY, and I use the opportunity to peek over at him when he merges lanes. It's not that I haven't looked at him since I arrived at the apartment to find him waiting on me. It's that I can't bear to wait any longer to see how he's physically changed since we were together.

I want to look at him, to stare, to analyze every new line, and see if the crinkles around his eyes have deepened. I want to swim in the blues of his eyes for a better vantage point.

Attraction was never the issue with Shane. He's gorgeous, handsome beyond what I thought humanly possible. And looking at him now, not much has changed appearance-wise, but I sense a change that I can't quite put my finger on. *Humility?* The jury is still out on that one.

The Ferrari is why he'll be found guilty. Sure, he offered the keys to me, but it's such a symbol of who he was last August that it's hard to see anything new.

Maybe that's on me, though—holding grudges when I

don't need to. I'm driving my same old car. Using that example, he's being responsible by driving a car he already
owned instead of trading it in for a new one each year.

I roll my eyes, needing to get out of my head so much.
Geez, Cate, relax.

"Why aren't you on tour?" I ask, fidgeting with my seat
belt. "I thought Faris Wheel tours every summer?"

"Things have changed." His eyes stay on the road, but I
notice how his grip tightens around the steering wheel.

It wasn't just the paperwork that demanded I be here. I
wanted to come. Maybe I'm a masochist. I just think what
happened between us can be explained now that we've put
distance to it. Am I just feeding the curiosity beast, or can I
get him to open up to me? "Like what?"

He laughs, though I'm not sure why. Changing lanes
once more, he shrugs. "The band's dynamic."

"That doesn't sound good."

Glancing over at me, he says, "Everything is fine with the
band." I shamelessly watch him, analyzing every detail of
emotion that whisks its way across his face. I don't say
anything before he adds, "It is, but our priorities have
shifted. Laird and Poppy had their twins, and—"

"They have twins?" I lean my head back and smile,
remembering Laird from high school. He and Shane were
practically inseparable and similar in so many ways. They
both had every reason to be jerks—popular, attractive,
charismatic—but they weren't.

"Posey and Mack." As if smiling for himself, he looks
over and says, "They're amazing. Mack is my little buddy. He
wants me to hold him all the time and doesn't need entertaining. He's just happy to be in my arms."

"And Posey?"

"She's so smart. She's got the brightest, bluest eyes and a

giggle that has her dad wrapped around her little finger. She's the sweetest like her mom."

I'm not going to wave the green flag, but I'm ready to pull it out and streak through Griffith Park waving it like mad after listening to this giant of a man talk about his sweet baby cousins. "You close to them?"

He inhales a deep breath and blows out of his mouth slowly. The question seems to be hitting close to home from his reaction. "They've had a big impact on me."

The calm I recognized, the cool confidence instead of cocky arrogance, the way he seems more relaxed in his whole being has me angling toward him. "I'll interrogate you if you let me."

"I don't mind the questions. Not even the hard ones." Briefly looking over, he says, "It's what I wanted for us this weekend."

His voice is steady, no fear to be found. No worries are heard. Everything about him makes me believe he's telling the truth. But it still leaves a lingering question. "Why? Do you need closure? Want the information so you can move on with someone else? Why didn't you just divorce me, Shane?"

Life seems to move faster in a Ferrari. We've reached the edge of LA and keep heading toward the mountains. The view doesn't matter. I look at him, waiting to hear the one thing I could never figure out.

He says, "We were attracted to each other and thought that could save us. We barely knew each other and hadn't built a foundation, much less anything strong enough to keep us together."

His words aren't hurtful, but my chest clenches, making me feel every pressured squeeze of my heart. I now know why my throat has thickened. I asked the question. I've wanted to know because I couldn't answer it myself. He's right. Every word made so much more sense when I realized we were set up to fail from the beginning.

"I didn't expect so much honesty before we reached the city limits."

"We left the city and the county behind us already."

Although there's so much to unpack emotionally, to sort through the dirty laundry of what happened to us, I know I've been going along while not asking many questions. I need to participate and not just react anymore. "Where are we going?"

"Deer Lake. My aunt and uncle own a cabin on the lake." Our eyes meet for the briefest of moments before we both look forward again. "It's about an hour from where we are."

"Where are we? Really, Shane, what do you think will change in the next forty-eight hours?" A part of me wants to get the heavy stuff out in the open, to address our issues, and arrive at our destination with less baggage weighing us down. The other half of me wants a glass of wine, some cheese and crackers, maybe some grapes as well, and to lounge lakeside without worrying about Shane, me, the two of us together, or anything else. To let what's destined to happen, happen like Luna always says.

She has the luxury of money supporting her belief system. I've had to create my life from the ground up all by myself. So leaving things be doesn't come naturally to me.

He replies, "I hope you won't hate me anymore."

"I never hated you. That was part of the problem. I accepted you for who you were."

"I'm different now." The words are fine, though they don't penetrate the skin. I'm not cruel, but I can't believe everything someone tells me until they show me as well.

"This is a chance to start over, to erase what happened like it never did?" The bitterness that rises from a deeper side of my heart, one I had locked out when I closed the door on our relationship, resurfaces. I didn't even realize how much anger I had held onto. Now I hear it through a tremble of my tongue, exposing the pain he caused through my tone.

"You can ask me anything. You can yell or shout at me, Cat, but that doesn't mean I'll give an answer that suits what you need. All I can do is say I'm sorry for hurting you. I'm sorry for dragging you into the world that revolved around me with no place for anyone else. I can't seem to be sorry for what gave me the opportunity to apologize. Forced or not, I want you to know I left your apartment. It wasn't you I rejected. It was my life, the life I called living."

"Did you return the text you got that night? Did you meet up with her? Tell her that you'd broken my heart, but would fuck her like you thought you'd be fucking me?" Tears fill the waterline of my eyes, threatening to pool over. I didn't mean to revisit the hurt of that night, the thoughts that ran rampant in my mind if he left me for someone else or just didn't want me anymore.

"Cat?" His voice is low as he reaches over to rub the back of my neck. "I'm sorry for hurting you."

Despite how good it feels to have him touch and comfort me, I anchor my elbow on the door and stare out the window. A few tears fall, but I grow stronger with each passing minute. Harder on the outside to protect the softness of my heart from being damaged again.

When the warmth disappears from my skin, clarity enters. The lack of an answer is the answer I needed. *Now I know.* I can never trust—

"They were from Laird."

I whip my eyes back to him, narrowing as I try to understand. "The texts?"

"Laird texted me because he took Poppy to the hospital. Twins tend to come early. She'd had contractions, and he wanted to make sure she and the babies were alright."

I've always heard there are two sides to a story. It's so easy to forget when you're caught up in your own emotions. I whisper, "Why didn't you tell me?"

"Because I knew we were already over."

The blade was so slick I barely felt it pierce my heart. And then I felt everything all over again. "I wish I had known."

"I did you a favor. It had already gone too far that night for us to salvage the remains."

The elevation changes. I can feel it in my ears as my stomach twists from the gradual curves. "Can we stop the car?"

"I'll have to find a place to pull over."

I grip the door with one hand and press to the seat with the other. "I'm going to be sick."

Shane pulls off the main road, parking just off the edge of a turnoff. I pop the door and run to the nearest bushes and bend over. The fresh air settles my racing thoughts, the solid ground helping with my stomach. I plant my hands on my hips, standing back up.

In through the nose. Out through my mouth. In. Out. In. Out.

I don't know if it's the confirmation that he didn't care or the change in altitude. Either way, I'll need more time to recover.

After a few more deep breaths, I turn around to find him standing on this side of the Ferrari. He looks at me, and says,

"We were heated. We argued. When I left, I didn't know it would be forever."

I cover my mouth, disappointed that I'm even crying. I hate feeling powerless, but I do with him. "Then why didn't you come back?"

"Because I loved you too much."

"What does that mean, Shane?" I shout across the short distance as anger fills me. "You loved me too much, so you hurt me?"

"I loved you too much, so I saved you from being with me."

I throw my arms in the air, frustrated. "That makes no sense." Walking away from him and the car, from this conversation . . . argument or whatever it is. The gravel crunches under my sneakers, the wind blowing against my dress and pushing my hair behind my shoulders. I keep walking because I need the distance to clear my head.

Forty-eight hours of this.

Damn him.

Staying steady on the one-lane road, I walk until the tears dry and my resentment tempers. I stay close to the line of trees but keep my feet on the edge of concrete.

I stop when my blood pressure has lowered along with my anger. The bear crossing sign also alarms me. I've gone far enough. I turn around to find Shane right there with me all along. *Twenty feet back.* Smart enough to give me distance and enough room to allow me to work through my feelings

He says, "I wanted to make sure you were okay."

"You didn't say anything."

"I was here when you were ready."

I cross my arms over my chest. "What if I'm never ready, Shane?"

"I'll still be here."

Everything he says feels real, and the pain in my heart lessens from hearing the words. But seeing him and not asking anything from me but my presence has me wondering what he needs to close the door on us. *If not that night, then forever.*

Forty-eight hours.

At the rate we're going, I'm about to find out.

25

Shane

WE RODE for the past forty-five minutes in silence.

She had just as much to think about as I did. We ripped off the bandage, but it didn't stop the bleeding like I had wanted. My apology should have been the tourniquet she needed, but it didn't help. *Did I make it worse instead?*

Getting it out in the open seemed the way to go and get through this. It's my fault for assuming it would be easy, all would be forgiven, and we'd be spending the weekend together instead of feeling the distance between us now. Despite having only a foot separating us in the car, where does that leave us?

How have I already fucked this up so royally?

Anger rolls off her in stages, slipping across the leather console. I caused that. I'll take the hit if it will make her feel better. I'm not sure if anything will, but I'm willing to try. There's nothing left to lose when I've already lost her. So I can sit and stew on how to move forward, break the ice, and get us back on the path of a second chance. Or I can make the effort. Fuck it. *Nothing to lose*, I repeat in my head.

I shift my car from manual to automatic and reach over, slipping my hand under hers that's resting on her leg. She yanks it away to her chest. "What are you doing, Shane?"

"I want to hold your hand."

Her blinks are erratic, her brows tugging together, but her mouth and the roundness of her lips when they part capture my attention. I miss those lips so fucking much. She has a stubborn streak that keeps her feisty. I like the fight in her, but I know it doesn't come from nowhere. I ask, "May I hold your hand, Cat?"

"No." From her immediate response, I'm certain she didn't give the idea a chance.

Slow down, Faris. I don't have to rush with her. She likes to take it slow. I can do slow if it's with her. I rest mine between us with my palm facing up—an offer if she wants to take it on her terms instead of mine.

Although I try to keep my eyes ahead, I check on her several times, catching her staring at my hand and shaking her head. She looks out the window but then turns to face me, and asks, "Why do you want to hold my hand?"

"Because I'm not here for a vacation. I'm here to spend time with you." I grip the steering wheel and roll my hand over it and back down again. I'm sweating, so she'll know I was nervous if she holds it now. I don't do vulnerable well, but I'm doing it for her. "I wanted to get to know you in high school. I wanted to keep in touch. I wanted to fuck you the first time I saw you again. And the second. The third and fourth. I'm an asshole because I still do. This time, though, I want to know you as well. I want to learn about you—"

"That's all about you, Shane."

Hearing her disappointment has my heart thumping in

my chest, and everything tells me to stop the pain and pull my hand back to the steering wheel. I fight the retreat, pushing forth and leaving it lying between us. I might be an idiot, but I'm willing to take the chance to find out. "I've thought so much about us and what really went wrong."

Resting her elbow on the window, she sighs and tilts her head onto her hand. "What went wrong in your eyes?"

"We didn't build a foundation. We weren't friends."

"We were attraction," she says as if she knew it all along.

"I want to hold your hand because it's the familiar, the only olive branch I have to give while driving. I just thought if we touched, we had that connection, that we could build from there this time."

Her chest rises and falls with each breath she takes. Her lips are still parted as if she needs the air in her lungs quicker.

"I'm trying for you, babe." The name fell from my tongue before I could stop it, but I won't take it back.

I'll give it a few more seconds. *One. Two. Three. Four—* she slips her hand into mine and pulls the bond to her lap as if she's the guardian of our connection. Without looking at me or our hands, she raises her chin. "You are trying." She takes a deep breath as if she can finally breathe freely again. Looking at me, she says, "And I don't think you make the effort for anyone."

She'd be right, but that's also why I've never been in a real relationship. Cat feels right; she's something steady that I can rely on. I can trust her. Maybe not with my Ferrari, but with my life and that ramshackled organ beating in my chest. So yeah, I'll make the effort for her. She's worth it.

The particles of anger exposed in the sunlight streaming through the windshield dissipate from the air.

"Anything interesting on the agenda?"

"Yoga on a paddleboard. Will you be joining me for that?" She pulls the paper back out and continues, "*Very* adventurous, by the way." Every time her fingers squeeze my hand a little tighter, hope renews, motivating me more than ever. "You surf, so I suspect you have good balance."

"It's great."

She laughs, or maybe it was a scoff. I definitely catch an eye roll, though. "I had no doubt. I look forward to you showing off your skills in the morning." Tapping the paper, she adds, "At eight thirty a.m." She cocks her head to the side, pursing her lips. "Have you ever seen that hour before?"

It feels good to laugh with her. "Glad your humor is still intact." Chuckling, I reply, "Early mornings aren't typically my thing anymore, but for a good set of waves, I'll show up before the sun rises." I tip my head and glance over at her. "As for yoga, I'll stick to paddleboarding while you enjoy doing your routine."

"Disappointing, Faris. And here I thought you were trying to impress me."

I balk, leaning back in my seat, still holding her hand like the lifeline she is for me. "There would be nothing impressive about me doing yoga. Trust me on that."

"I think that's the first time you've ever admitted you can't do something."

Her pretty smile tightens my chest and instantly elicits mine to the surface. Though my lips morph into a smirk. "I'm well aware of my strengths and weaknesses and stick to what I do best."

"According to you, there's not much that doesn't make the best list," she teases, pulling our joined hands to her chest. I'm not sure she notices, but I do. It's fucking amazing to be held like we've moved beyond the bad of the past and are firmly seated in the good of the future. I can even feel her heart beating beneath the surface.

A breath catches her by surprise as if she'd been holding it prior, and she lowers our hands to her lap again. I go out on a limb of the olive branch I offered and bring our hands to my chest so she can feel how hard my heart beats for her.

She doesn't pull back or away. Thank God. She's looking into my eyes when I have a second to look over at her. "Shane?"

"Yes," I reply, matching her quieter tone.

Whispering, she asks, "Do you mind if we go slow?"

I bring our hands to my mouth and kiss the top of hers. I shouldn't savor the feel of her soft skin or inhale the lightly fragrant scent of her hand, but I'd be a fool not to. *Is this moving too fast?* Judging by how my heart beats wildly in my chest, it might be. So I take a breath and look back into her beautiful brown eyes and promise to put her needs before mine. "I'll go slow. I'll do anything for you."

It's not only the physical that she means. It's the issues we need to work through. They don't have to be resolved in this car ride. The little moments we share give me the patience to sort it out in due time, like she needs.

She nods and then appears relieved by the release of a breath. Resting her head back, she says, "It's pretty here. Different from what I expected."

"What did you expect?" I round a bend that always signifies we're close.

"I thought it would be pine trees everywhere and their needles on the ground."

"There are pines, but there are also aspens and sumacs, and some coastal oaks around the lake."

With her gaze directed out her window, she says, "I'm going to like it here."

Every approval feels like a reward. When her guard is down, it's a victory. But it wouldn't be us if I didn't seize the opportunity and give her a wink. "Even though you're here against your will?"

"If I didn't want to be here, I would have signed the papers, not rode along with you or helped you load the car." The admission is dropped, causing my face to split into a ridiculous grin. She's left me speechless, which is an impressive feat unto itself. "Don't act so shocked."

Does she realize the gift she's giving me? The inkling of trust she's put back in my hands? It might be small to her as she laughs softly, but it's huge to me. I give her hand a squeeze, not needing words to do the labor.

She says, "Speaking of divorce."

"Were we?" It's become my least favorite topic over the ten months we were apart.

"Did you ever figure out why we're married?" she asks, launching into it like it's us against the state of California again.

"I didn't, but I once had an idea."

"What's that?"

I feel the little squeeze she gives me. It feels good to be a team again. "I think we should retrace our steps."

She starts smiling, already invested. "How do we do that twelve years after we graduated? Well, thirteen this month." The concept takes her by surprise, causing her to blink hard. "How did time fly so fast?"

"Passed without warning."

She closes her eyes, turning toward the window where the sun shines in. Opening her eyes, she smiles at me as if it's been mine all along. "If only my eighteen-year-old self could see me now. I'm living every girl's dream. Kidnapped by a rock star and taken to his secluded cabin in the mountains." She tries not to laugh but fails. *So do I.* The sound of her melody brings me to life. I've missed this high so much.

"And here I thought we weren't supposed to make that sound so naughty."

With an easy shrug, she says, "I call it like I see it."

"Careful with those confessions, or I might start thinking you're into this fantasy."

She shifts our hands to her lap and laughs again. "I'm okay with that."

Holy shit.

I'm never going to be able to look at her without imagining taking her every which way in this cabin. Just the two of us for forty-eight hours. I thought I was the one in control of this weekend, but I'm damn certain Cat is. I can't fucking wait to see where this goes.

With perfect timing to get this weekend started, I release her hand and make the sharp turnoff to the property. Pulling up to the gate, I shift into park and look over at her. "We're here."

26

Cate

SHANE LIED TO ME.

The cooler bumps into my ass, a not-so-subtle hint. I turn back to see him balancing it on his leg. I move into the living room so he can get by. "That cooler looks heavy. Need help?"

"Nope," he grits. "I've got it."

Wheeling my suitcase with the bag situated on top, I move into the kitchen area of the open concept massive room. "You kept calling it a cabin. I expected logs and wood everything, like cabinets and floors, walls and—"

Dumping the cooler on the floor, he stands back up. "The floors are wood."

"Designer wood floors are not the same thing."

"I don't know what to tell you." He wipes the back of his wrist across his forehead. "We've always called it the cabin. I guess it's more of a lake house." Resting his palms on the edge of the stone counter of the island, he says, "Sorry if you're disappointed."

"Disappointed? This is a dream retreat. I'll take this every day and twice on Sunday over a creepy-crawly cabin. I'm more of a hotel than a camping girl."

He bends down and opens the cooler, but I hear him mumble, "I know what I'd like to take twice on Sunday."

"What was that?" I tease.

Standing, he twists the cap off a bottle of water and downs half. "What were we talking about?"

"You said you would like to do something twice on Sunday. What do you want to do?"

His eyes steer to the window behind me, staring out as if I'll give up if he avoids eye contact long enough. Tapping the bottle to the countertop, he says, "I think I'll finish unloading the car now instead of leaving it for later."

"Yeah," I say, laughing. I turn around and watch him hurry out the door. I watch as he treks across the ground to where he parked the car on a concrete pad. Sitting in the passenger's seat, he keeps one leg propped out and tucks the other inside.

Leaving my suitcase where it is, I walk closer to the window, being nosy. I stand off to the side and watch as he stares ahead.

It took a lot for him to share his feelings with me. I know it's not something he's comfortable doing. That's why I'm here. I see him trying, and it makes me feel special. Shane has a way of making me feel like I matter to him. I'm not sure what caused the change since he left last August, but I can't keep setting off the same dynamite sticks.

He's doing the work. I need to do the same.

I double-time it to the door to open it for him when he starts back with another large cooler. "We're only here two days," I say, trying to lighten his mood.

I close the door behind him and follow him to the

kitchen. He sets the cooler on top of the other. "I tried to be prepared."

When he stands back, he turns to find me waiting for him. Questions populate in his eyes, pulling his brows, but he doesn't say anything. I don't know what I'm doing, but I stand there like I do. I want to touch him, to ease the burden he's trying so hard to hide from me. So I do.

I reach up and run my fingertips over his jaw, then higher along his temples. I lick my lips, watching as he does the same. Holding my wrists with a gentle touch, he leans into my hand and dips his lids closed for a few seconds.

When he opens his eyes, I whisper, "Thank you."

"For what?" I've failed, placing the blame on him all this time. "For extorting you to come on this trip?"

He chuckles. Taking one of my wrists, he lifts and turns the inside toward him to kiss. And then again, with a little dip of his tongue running along my veins.

"Yes," I reply breathily, a surefire sign of how this man affects me. "And torturing me with a beautiful lake and stunning scenery, coolers of food, and—"

"And?" he whispers with his lips running over my wrist once more. He places a final kiss, then smiles at me. It's not a smirk. No sign of arrogance is found in the softer corners. The gesture is reassuring. Comfort at the simplest level. But his expression holds conviction that has me gravitating even closer to him.

His light cologne sweeps through the air. I take a deep breath, wanting to touch all parts of me any way he can. "I'm sorry, what?"

Laughter follows as he releases me, leaving me to drift into the ethos under the aftereffects of his sweet kisses. "You were saying how this will be a total drag of a weekend."

"Right. Just horrible." I laugh, moving away from him. I

must, or I'll end up rotating in his orbit all weekend. As I take hold of my suitcase, it's become obvious that I will never survive this man.

"Let me show you your room." He swipes the case, rolling it right out from under my hand while taking my other hand. I can't lie; his confidence is a major turn-on.

Down the hallway on the left, he opens the only door and moves inside before turning around and pointing out the highlights. "I thought the suite was best for you. There's nice light and a comfortable bed." Inviting blankets and puffy pillows cover the mattress. I'm holding his hand, the callused fingers of a musician, his strong hold protecting me even when I have nothing to fear, and wrapping around my hand so gently but firmly that the idea of sleeping alone just became a lot less appealing. His gaze travels over my shoulder. "There's a bathroom for privacy with a big soaking tub. I remember you like taking baths."

"It's . . ." I look around once again. "It's more than I expected. Are you sure you don't want to stay here?"

"Is that an invitation?" Seemingly catching himself, he leans down and whispers, "I'll be good."

That's the last thing I want him to be. *Behave, Cate.* You're a mess because of this man. "That's too bad." I did, in fact, not behave, giving him every mixed signal known to humankind. It's cruel at this stage. Good thing I came prepared like he did.

I win a smile bordering on seductive, a devilish look in his eyes fixed on mine that has me feeling both to my core. After clearing my throat, I say, "I saw a bath on the schedule. Maybe I can bump that up and take one during the hour allotted for freshening up? Of course, I can wait if it's a strict timeline."

"We're flexible around here. I can draw you a hot bath

now." He walks into the bathroom, still talking, "You can relax while I prepare some snacks to tide us over for the evening."

Drawing baths.

Preparing snacks.

Flexible to my needs.

I fall back on the bed, staring up at the ceiling.

To say I'm not charmed would be an injustice. I'm not even sure he's the same person from last year. So much drew me to him beyond the circumstances back then. *Sexy. Magnetic.* He knew exactly how to make a girl go weak in the knees and her panties disappear.

I'm not that same girl anymore, though.

He's still the most captivating man I've met, absurdly sexy, and affects me like no other man ever has. But the change in him is profound. Set in his eyes like a goal he's striving for, he's not only after my body. He's after my soul.

This is new. And I very much approve.

"The bathtub is filling, but I need to get—"

I lift my head from the bed, my arms still wide and legs dangling over the edge. "Need to get what?"

He scrubs a hand over his face as if he needs to clear some thoughts away. "I brought things you might like."

Propping up on my elbows, I ask, "What kind of things?

"Bath salts. Bubble bath. Wine." He reaches over his shoulder and scratches the back of his neck, so sweet and lost, stepping out of familiar territory and into mine. "The lady at the store said you might like a bath bomb, so I bought ten."

My eyebrows shoot straight up along with my spine. "Ten? We're only here for two days."

"I know, but I couldn't decide," he says, "and they all smelled like something you would like." My eyes water, and

I open my mouth to get more air. I don't want to cry in front of him, but I've never been spoiled like this before in my life.

I push off the bed and go to him, tugging on his shirt at the waist. Shameless, but it's getting harder to stay away. "Shane, you've done too much. Thank you. I'm so grateful, but you didn't have to do all that."

"I know. I wanted to." His eyes dart to my hands on him, and he drags his tongue across his lower lip. "I should go grab the basket."

"Basket?" Is it wrong to feel this happy when we haven't worked through all the issues? I've been softening my stance since he said he was sorry with his heart on his sleeve. He felt it, but he also felt the loss of me. Two things that drive me to forgiveness, even if selfishly. He didn't have to redeem himself, but he's doing it and going all in.

"Check the water to see if it's to your liking. I'll get the basket so you can choose what you want to use." He slips out of my hold and leaves the bedroom.

A part of me thinks it's for his own need to keep things from progressing physically. Emotionally, though, he's never been more in tune with my needs. He's wooing me. God, I can't wait to repay him.

I see him through the window, trekking across the yard again. It's so tempting to spy, to see if he's hiding his emotions from me, so I do. But the smile on his face can't be mistaken. That man knows what I was doing. Not behaving, that's what.

Scooting into the bathroom, I test the water. Am I surprised it's the perfect temperature? No, he's doing everything right and reading me like a book. I wonder which is his favorite chapter.

He returns, slipping in through the open door to the bedroom. When he sees me, his face lights up like it's his birthday. Holding the basket out to me, he says, "It's all yours. Can I bring you a glass of wine? Sparkling water? Soda?"

"Do you have white wine or red?"

"White. The kind I remember you drinking at your apartment."

My heart clenches. Hugging the basket to my chest, I wish it were him. The first step is acknowledging I have a problem. I'm addicted to Shane Faris romancing me. "Is there anything you don't remember?"

"About our time together? No. I remember every second." He reaches down to turn off the water. "Careful, or it will overflow."

My heart is already. "Thank you again for all the bath products."

"You're welcome. I'll go get that wine."

It's too late to add bubbles, so I choose a bath bomb to soften my skin and because it smells so good. After leaving my clothes on the bed, I slip into the tub and sink under the hot water, covering my shoulders but not my feet. Maybe one day I'll get to try out that huge tub he spoke about at his place.

He walks in after a quick rap on the door, too fast to warn him. "Wait."

His feet halt, and he turns sideways. "Sorry. I thought you'd be covered in bubbles."

"Bath bombs don't bubble up," I reply, not feeling the need to cover up. It may have been ten months, but I can't imagine my body has changed much. Or I'll need a refund from the yoga studio.

His eyes aren't closed, but he seems to be solving the great mystery of the pyramids by staring at the shower tiles. "Ah. Okay. I have your wine."

"Do you mind handing it to me?" He comes forward in silence. I take the glass and a sip as he returns to the bedroom. "Thank you." Before he's gone, I ask, "Shane?"

"Yeah?" he replies out of my line of sight.

"Do you want to stay and talk to me?"

"From the bedroom?"

I take another sip and open the possibility for more once again. "No. In here with me."

He appears in the doorway, but his eyes stay locked on mine. "Isn't that how it started last time?"

"We could try a second time?" Even I know I'm asking for more than a bathroom companion to talk about the weather.

"I'll get a drink and be right back, then." Shane doesn't take long, but when he returns, I notice his body seems lighter, his shoulders straighter, the smile on his handsome face wider. He sits beside the tub, leaning against the wall, and says, "Hi."

"Hi." I knew then that this was the beginning we were meant to have.

27

Shane

"WHERE WILL YOU SLEEP TONIGHT?" Cat asks, appearing from the hallway dressed in tight black shorts that show off her tan legs and a Faris Wheel T-shirt that fits her curves in all the perfect ways.

I could fuck her right here against this counter looking that good. Great tits, pert nipples begging for my touch or for me to wrap my mouth around them. Just a little nip between the teeth before going lower and fucking her with my tongue until she comes, screaming my name. "Nice shirt. I didn't know you were a fan?"

"The biggest," she lies. I can tell by the smirk and mischievous eyes.

"My mom and dad could argue that title."

She laughs. "Must be nice." She looks relaxed after the bath, so I won't dig in with deep questions. I've been curious about her parents for a while, and the story that led her to our high school junior year.

"That shirt's a classic from our San Diego days." I eye

her, pretending I'm interested in the design, when I'm still staring at her tits. "That's before we had a record deal. Nikki made those shirts in her bedroom. I sold them after the concert. Did you go to that show?"

"No. I wish I had, though." She pulls it away from her chest and looks down at it. The edges are peeling off, and it hasn't aged well, but it looks damn good on her. "I found it on eBay." Lifting the hem of the shirt, she pulls something from the top of her shorts and slaps it down on the counter between us. "It came with your autograph."

Chuckling, I pull the paper closer and study it. I glance up at her. "I would have given it to you for free."

Strutting around the island, she holds the shirt up by the seams at her shoulders. "But then I wouldn't have this gem."

What am I going to do with her? *I know what I want to . . .*

"Nikki probably has some lying around back at her parents' house." I turn to face her as she leans her elbow on the counter and crosses one ankle over the other. She's not only looking incredibly sexy but sassy as fuck. I thought she only had one glass of wine. I can't wait to find out what happens when she has two.

"I'll let you know if this one falls apart in the wash. It's seen better days, but it's vintage."

"Sure is, and by the way"—I push the paper toward her —"it's a forgery."

Offense fills her muscles as she stares at the autograph. "Really? That sucks."

"I have connections."

She smirks. "So do I."

Chuckling, I ask, "Wine?" *I'm an evil bastard.*

"Absolutely." She stands upright and asks, "What's for dinner? Eating brie and crackers while soaking in the tub was pretty glorious, but I'm hungry again."

I pour the wine, still grinning. "Chicken pesto. Poppy's specialty." I slide the glass to her and then turn to get the dish out of the fridge. "She's a private chef. Retired with the twins but still loves to cook." Setting the foil pan of food on the stovetop, I heat the oven just like the directions say to do.

Cat comes behind me and peeks around. "What didn't you think of? You've taken care of everything."

Condoms. I remembered the wine and the bath products, so much food and drinks, and planning our days down to the hours. But I forgot the condoms. I don't tell her that. I like to be prepared for action, but I'm not expecting us to make that leap this weekend. If all things go well, though, it might be back on the table. But 'go slow' still plays on my mind.

"Ow." I turn to find her grinning like she's up to no good. "Why'd you poke me?"

"Just making sure you're real."

"Oh, I'm real alright." Since she can't seem to keep space between us, I put my arm around her and pull her to my side.

"What's going on, Faris?"

"Just making sure you're real."

Her arm comes around my back, holding my ribs. Leaning her head against my bicep, she whispers, "I'm real alright."

The timer goes off, interrupting the moment. I'm not sure if we'll get it back, so I wait a minute to hold her a little longer. I want to kiss her head like I used to, but that's not slow, and it's not about her. That's about me. I get it. I even understand her request. It's an adjustment, and it's new for me to have boundaries.

That she knows who she is and what works for her is so

fucking sexy. And if I can be that guy for her, I won't fuck it up again.

I put the pan in the oven and start the timer again. Cat retrieves her wine and walks to the window facing the lake. "How cold is it?"

"Freezing all the time, but swimmable." I grab a beer from the fridge and toss the top in the trash on my way to join her. "Want to walk out? We have forty minutes."

As soon as I open the door, she hightails it back to the bedroom. When she returns, she's in a sweatshirt and sheepskin boots. How does she look so damn good in everything she wears?

Seeing her body through the clear water in the tub is a reminder. Although she had her back to me, she didn't try to hide her body or make me look away as she bathed. She even asked me to wash her back. Slow has become the new foreplay for us.

I'm just glad she didn't see my erection bulging against my jeans. It's so uncomfortable and even worse when you know nothing can come of it, and you'll be hitting one off in the shower later.

We walk out to the lake with our drinks in hand. The sun sets on the west side of the lake, reflecting off the water's surface.

She asks, "Where are you sleeping?"

"Across the hall. There are two other rooms. I'm taking the back bedroom. It has a king-sized bed."

"For a king," she says, reminding me of the conversation we once had about her mattress. My memories usually resort to the bigger events where emotion plays the biggest role. So when I recall these moments of ours, I savor each of them.

She walks to the edge of the water and looks back like a

kid in a candy store. "It's so clear." She really doesn't get out much.

"It's clear half a mile out. This lake is a hidden gem here in the mountains. Clean water, good fishing—"

"Privacy from the world always watching?"

It's nice to just exist without a camera on me. "It's a perk."

"Will you take me swimming tomorrow?"

I could crack a joke about yoga on a paddleboard helping that wish come true, but she seems confident and didn't bat an eye at that activity listed on the schedule. "We can do that."

The sun has just about set as we take sips and listen to nature sing its chorus—leaves rustling in the breeze, the lake lapping at the shore, and the birds that have come out to find their dinner singing in the trees above.

I watch strands of her hair blow around her neck and tickle the side of her face. She eventually pulls the long strands into a mess of a knot on her head. "Why didn't we date in high school?" I ask.

Her wine spews. She hops backward in reaction to avoid the spray. When she stops laughing, she wipes her chin with the sleeve of her sweatshirt. "You stand there, a real-life rock god—"

"I'll allow. Continue," I say, rolling two fingers in front of me.

I'm popped on the arm before she can stop herself from laughing too hard to even speak. So one glass makes her sassy, and two leaves her with no inhibitions. Got it.

"You asked that like I have a say in the matter."

"You could have asked me out," I say, tossing it back to her.

"I could barely speak. I'm thrown into the deep end of

the popular kids club simply because of my last name and the alphabet." She stretches her neck. "Imagine being new, and you walk in your first day of school only to be sat next to Nikki, a teen beauty queen and lead singer of a rising beach band. Laird, who had girls scheming to sit next to him, and the prom king, Shane Faris, who had girls ready to hand over their V-cards. Like, how did I survive?"

"Just fine from the looks of it." I take a long pull of beer. "You had guys lined up to date you, Cat."

"Where?" she asks, throwing a hand out to the side. "Because they weren't asking me out."

"They were intimidated like I was. And just to set the record straight. Laird was prom king. I was homecoming king."

She rolls her eyes, being absolutely adorable. "Tomato—"

"Tomahto."

"Comme ci—"

"Comme ça."

That earns me another laugh, and I'll happily drink it in like this beer. She says, "You're stealing my lines, kid." Facing me like I can compete with the lake, she plucks the front of my shirt. "Let's loop back to that part about you being intimidated by me. I'm going to need more details. Please explain."

I recognize someone fishing for a compliment a mile away, but I don't mind getting caught on her line. I'm happy to feed her. "You made me nervous. No girl had before. Why do you think I avoided you during junior year?"

"I thought you hated me for the longest time."

"God . . ." I fill with regret. "Why would I hate you?"

"I don't know. Insecurity from being a new kid because

you were stuck seated next to me instead of Rachel Ferguson."

"What? Why would I want to sit next to Rachel Ferguson?"

"Because she was beautiful and only had eyes for you."

I laugh. Closing in on her, I wrap my arm around her shoulders. "If it matters, I don't remember Rachel Ferguson, but I never forgot you."

"*If* it matters? Yeah, it matters." She leans against my chest with a gorgeous smile on her face. Turning to stand in front of me, she fists her shirt with one hand as she lowers the other with the glass in it. "You say the sweetest things. If you're not careful—" She stops herself and takes a deep breath.

I cup her face, sliding my palm under her jaw and lifting until her eyes meet mine. "I'll be careful with you, but I won't be careful with how I feel. I'm all in, babe."

Our gazes hold as the sun sets beneath the tree line. She nods slightly and then says, "Rachel Ferguson would be so jealous right now."

"And how does Catalina Farin feel?"

Gripping my shirt as if the thin material could keep steady, she whispers, "Like the luckiest woman alive."

I'm close to kissing her, but that's not slow, so I lean down to whisper in her ear, "You make me feel like I did something right in this world."

She raises her hand, sliding it over the rough of my unshaven face, and holds me to her. "I know you're trying to do the right thing, Shane. I see you. I feel the change in you. I never asked for you to do that, but I won't deny that I've never felt more cherished than with you. You make me feel like I'm your world—"

"My world. The universe. The stars. A goddess. My

everything." Closing my eyes, I angle to breathe her in but am met with soft lips that caress mine and a craving that her body can't quite satisfy by how her nails scrape across my scalp and down my neck.

I drop the beer and take her face in my hands. "Are you sure?"

Covering my hands with hers, she says, "Kiss me, babe."

I kiss her so good that I grab her when her knees go weak, our tongues caressing while our bodies find purchase against each other. This is what I dreamed of.

The warmth of her embrace.

The slick of her tongue as it dances with mine.

The bump of teeth doesn't matter.

Only we do.

I bend down and scoop her into my arms. Our lips stay attached as I walk back to the house, backing through the door, and when I set her on the couch. But are ripped apart when I tug her by the ankles lower on the leather couch. Getting on my knees, I slide my body so she feels my full erection between her legs. I kiss her again as I lower down on top of her.

Her arms come around my neck, and her thighs squeeze both sides of my torso. And when our tongues explore each other's mouths, I rock against her. She feels too good, and I know I won't last. It's been too long, holding myself back.

I pull back, our mouths separated against my better judgment. I don't know why I torture myself this way, but I breathe through the ache that would have me fucking her so hard that she wouldn't be able to walk tomorrow, much less do paddleboard yoga.

She searches my eyes. "Why'd you stop?"

"I said it before. It stands true now." I slide my hands

under the bulky sweatshirt to find her nipples sharp and stretching against the fabric. "I only want to be inside you."

"We can. *You* can."

I can't. *Fucking hell.* How could I forget the condoms?

Distract. Distract. Distract from getting myself off by rubbing her raw. I can't use her like that. Lowering down to the other side of the couch, I hook my fingers over the top of her shorts and pull them down, admiring her sweet pussy again. "Damn, I can't wait to taste you again."

And then the timer goes off.

Fuck me.

28

Cate

I LOST my appetite for food and only want Shane to satisfy my cravings. I'm convinced he's the only one I'll ever need for survival. Morning. Noon. And night.

Rubbing my legs together like a damn cricket, I try to assuage the ache left cold by his absence when he jumped over the couch to take the foil off and bake the chicken pesto for another fifteen minutes.

He's very good at following directions. Maybe I should leave a Post-it where my shorts used to be. I lift, pulling them back over my hips, then lie there, trying to catch my breath. So close. We were so close to paradise.

I don't think I'll ever be able to forgive Poppy. Obviously, she's to blame for sending the dish that sidetracked Shane from finishing what he started. I giggle to myself. Letting one arm hang off the couch and leaving my legs stretched out on the leather, I ask, "How's it looking?"'

"Not as good as you."

"It's always been my dream to have a man tell me I'm sexier than chicken and pasta."

He hops over the back of the couch again, landing one knee between my legs, and kisses me on the lips. "Dreams do come true." He looks down to see the shorts back in place. "For some. For others, their dreams are destroyed by black Lycra."

He kisses me again, and I push my head back to look into his eyes. "Fifteen minutes isn't enough time to get the job done."

"Wanna bet?"

I cup his cheeks with a smile splitting mine apart. "I don't think that's the flex you think it is."

"Trust me, sweetheart. It is." He starts pulling my shorts down again.

My head falls back, and my lips part to help me get air from the thought of what he's about to do to me. "Flex away."

It's not the wine. *It's him.* Shane Faris is a walking aphrodisiac. But I need to come to my senses. *If he can wait, so can I.* I stop his hands before my shorts lower any more past my lower abdomen. "Shane?"

"Yeah?" he asks with the most deliciously devilish look in his eyes.

"We should wait and do things differently this time." I bite my bottom lip, hoping I make sense.

His smile lessens, but the happiness never leaves his eyes. He kisses over my shorts where he wanted to be beneath them, and then says, "I understand. Slow. That works for me. I want to know you so much better. I want to know what your favorite color—"

"Blue."

"Your favorite book?"

"Not original, but *Pride and Prejudice.*"

"Movie?" He rests his chin on my leg while he looks up at me with a grin.

"*Gladiator.*"

A quick pop of his eyes makes me smile. "That's unexpected."

I shrug. "What can I say? I like to keep people on their toes."

"Do I want to know who your favorite band is?" He laughs. "My ego can't take a blow right now."

I cup his face and slide farther under him. He lifts, taking me in his arms and balancing above me. "Any band you're in." We kiss. It's gentle and slow, more appreciative in the caressing pressure that I know will lead to more later. Looking into his eyes as he hovers over me, I say, "I don't want to erase our past. I want us defined in the good, the here, and now, and how it feels this time around."

"I want that, too. I'm glad you shared your feelings. I always want that with you."

With his erection still pressed against me, I could look into his eyes for the rest of my life and never tire of them. The color, the lines at the corners, the way they express pure happiness when looking into mine. "We're still married," I add like we're trading one for the other. I know we're not, but it's not bad to need the reminder.

"We are," he says with a smile growing before my eyes. "We never did figure out how, though."

"Well, Roberta blew my theory."

He laughs gently. "Good old Roberta."

I've reviewed it a million times and still can't figure out how our signatures are on that marriage license. "If it wasn't an accident, how are we married? It makes no sense."

The timer goes off again. He pushes up to stand, grumbling, "Fucking hell." Bending down, he places a kiss on my lips. "This spot is mine later."

"Which spot?" I touch my lips, dragging my fingertip across the bottom, then dipping my tongue to slide along the corner. "This spot?" Lowering my hand, I touch my neck. "Or this one?" All the spots populate my thoughts, addicted to watching his eyes darken as he takes me in. Slipping my hand even lower between my breasts, I ask, "Maybe you meant this—?"

"All of you, babe. I want all of you."

"I'm already yours." Along with my heart. I want to tell him I always have been, but nothing about that indicates or respects my own demand of going slow.

The timer goes off again as a reminder, and he throws his arms into the air. "This is why I don't fucking cook."

"Because it gets in the way of sex?"

Turning back, he cocks a brow. "That's exactly why." I sit up, enjoying the view of his ass, when he pulls the dish out of the oven. I like the feel of it even better.

I fall back with my arms above my head. Why am I torturing myself with slow when I want him so much? And then my stomach growls, so I get up and pull plates from the cabinet.

"JUST GONE TEN," he answers my question about the time.

Tightening the blanket around my shoulders, I sit back in the Adirondack chair, loving the view of the moon reflecting off the lake. "Do we stick to the agenda and go to bed early orrrrr . . ."

"Toss it. I'm not ready to go in."

"Me either." I sip my hot tea, feeling more relaxed than I

have in forever. I reach over and slip my hand on top of his, our fingers folding together like we do this all the time. "Thank you for bringing me here." A light laugh rumbles through me. "Legally coerced, or whatever we're calling it. I'm glad I'm here." I lean forward, meeting our bonded hands and kissing his knuckles.

"Legally coerced sounds better than extorted into a getaway with me."

"However we got here, I'm glad we did." Three kisses are placed before I lean back and notice the tattoo on his forearm again. "I can't figure out the design of your tattoo. You didn't have it last year."

He lifts our hands, twisting our arms so he can get a better look as if he needs to see it for proof of existence. A leisurely loll of his head to the side has his eyes locking on mine. A few beers and a long drive today mixed with the emotions and physical intensity we share hang his lids lower and have me reconsidering sleep soon. As if he knew that would be the case when he created the itinerary.

He deserves all the credit. Maybe this place plays a significant role, which he'd already know from growing up here. The fresh air gives a new perspective, and leaving most of our troubles in LA allows room to recuperate from what the universe has thrown our way.

He says, "Do you really want to know?" I'm briefly mesmerized when he scrapes his tongue over the center of his bottom lip.

I catch myself and pull my gaze to his arm again. The design is innocuous enough, but now I'm more curious than ever, especially since I haven't been able to figure it out when I get glimpses. "I wouldn't have asked, silly." I laugh, but then stop, starting to wonder if I don't want to know.

"Why does this sound so mysterious? Do I *not* want to know?"

"I wasn't trying to freak you out. It's just . . . It's personal." Lowering his arm with my hand still held in his, he shifts his elbow so I can see the design.

We only have the moonlight and light drifting from a lamp hanging over the front door, allowing us to see anything. It's enough, but I release his hand and lean closer for a better look.

With his finger, he runs along the gentle line with soft shading that flows like a river down his arm. "It's the curve of a neck, hair captured at the base of the head, and loose strands of hair falling over the back."

Angling my head, I can see it now. A woman, personal to him . . . my heart sinks as I sit back. I nod unable to speak. After all we've been through, after the storms calmed, giving us smooth water to sail—ten months. He fell in love in the ten months we were apart, fell hard enough to memorialize her on his skin.

I feel sick, sitting back and covering my stomach with my arms.

He says, "This is what guided me to a new life." I can only look at it before my eyes dare to look into his again. "A freckle on her back was my North Star. I'd look at it to tide me over until I could return to her again."

Redirecting my gaze to the water, his words sting, my heart barely repaired before broken again.

Shane reaches for my hand, but I slide away from him so he can't reach me from his chair. "Don't be like that, Cat."

"Like what?" I shoot a glare in his direction. "Like you're talking about the love of your life, so much so that she's immortalized in a tattoo that covers your entire forearm while being here with me? Is that what you don't want me to react to?" I sit forward on the edge of the chair and drop my head in my hands. "What am I doing?"

"Look at me." His voice is so even, so smooth that the command feels like it was my idea even though it was his.

I look, but then stand, dropping the blanket in the chair. "And you made me be the one to ask about it." I shake my head, keeping my eyes on the lake and him at my back. Crossing my arms over my chest, I say, "You could have just told me you were in love with her." I look over my shoulder, feeling worse than the first time we broke up. It figures. "And to think, you could be here with her."

"I am." His low voice is unwavering.

His answer has me questioning what I said though. Running the words through my head, think . . . could be . . . here with her. He said I am. I am here with her. I am with her. The full picture comes into focus. I turn around and stare at him. "What are you saying, Shane?"

Taking hold of my hand, he's fast, pulling me into his lap before I can protest. He knows I won't. My legs fly out from under me as I land hard in his lap. His arms wrap me in a vice grip that won't loosen for me to escape.

"I'm saying that this, right here," he replies, tapping the dot on the design. He then runs a warm hand over my sweatshirt and circles a space on my back. "Is this. My North Star, my guide through the hard times when we were apart, a reminder that lives on my skin that nothing is impossible if you love them enough. I needed something of you with me always."

Tears rush the corners of my eyes as I stare at his arm and into his eyes again. "This is me?"

Caressing my cheek, he says, "I stayed away for me, but I came back for you."

There's no way for me to keep the tears at bay. They spill

over, running down my cheeks and over my lips. The salty water reminds me of the beach and how we should have been so much more after that bonfire. I kiss him. Tired of taking things slow, I kiss him in need and desire, in loyalty to this man who has given me everything I could ever ask for—unconditional and everlasting love. "I love you." I kiss his lips. "I love you." Lowering to his chin, I place one there as well. "I love you." Leaning my head against his, I say, "I love you, Shane Faris. I always have."

That's the last time we go slow. Why bother when it feels this good to be in love?

He stands with me scooped in his arms. Our lips melding, our tongues caressing, our body raw with need. I'm set down but held by the comfort of his arms around me. Pressed to the inside of the front door, he says, "I've loved you since that bonfire. I came back from tour to tell you I didn't fuck around on the road. I couldn't stop thinking about you."

"And I was gone . . ." I feel sick all over again. Knowing I could have had a life with him, maybe a family, that I wouldn't have been so alone. It's gutting.

"We weren't meant to be together then."

Through a stifled sniffle, I ask, "We're meant to be this time?"

"I'm never letting go, Cat. Not again." He kisses me so hard that I melt to the wood behind me.

Throwing my arms around him, I kiss him right back, and whisper, "Make love to me, Shane."

29

Shane

"OH NO, THE LAMP!" Her ass bumped into it, tipping it over onto the couch.

We probably should have left some lights on before we went to sit by the lake. I couldn't have predicted we'd go from slow to not-inside-her-soon-enough in point two seconds. But that's where we've ended up.

"Replaceable." Unlike the woman in my arms.

Our teeth clash when her mouth crashes back into mine, and I stumble through the house with her attached to the front of my body. I don't even need to hold her because she's clinging so tight. I do, though, because I love the feel of her around me and in my hands, the weight of her presence and how it consumes me.

"I want you, Shane, so badly." *Who am I to deny her needs?*

I press her against the wall at the opening of the hallway and kiss her good and proper. Deep, so deep that I don't want her to remember any other kiss existed before this one. Toeing off one shoe and then another, I push under her sweatshirt and then under the Faris Wheel T-shirt to find what I want—those great tits that I plan to worship with my mouth. And my cock, if we're up for more fun later.

She moans, her head hitting the wall when I take one good handful of the softest skin, rubbing my thumb over the little bud that perks for me. Such a good girl. Shifting, I carry her down the hall, beyond ready to tease her with my tongue and taste her again.

She squeals, laughter following in the wake of me tossing her on the bed. I'm already tugging my clothes off. "Get naked for me."

Propping up on her elbows, she holds one leg up. "The boots. I need help."

I take her boot by the heel and toe and pull it off with ease, then take off the other, dumping it beside my feet.

The frenzy of discarding clothes becomes the main attraction until the real show begins. I like watching her maneuver around the bed. I just like looking at her, period.

Lifting her ass, she slides off her shorts and flings them in the air, baring her sweet pussy to me again. *Damn, so good.* Wriggling about with her arms and head tangled in the sweatshirt, I grin because that's my girl right there—a beautiful mess.

Reaching down, I help her out by tugging it off, then lean down to kiss her. "How'd I get so lucky?"

She falls back, smiling like the sun is still shining outside. It is for me. "We haven't even done it yet."

"I'm not talking about sex." I slide between her legs in a sweep of my hips against hers, anchoring myself above her. She feels like heaven, her warmth embracing my erection while hooking her leg around my ass and rubbing her socked foot to spur me on with a tap. "I'm talking about you."

"You're charming, but you do realize you've already gotten me naked?" She steals a kiss. "Except this shirt. Can you help me get it off? It's tight."

I know. Perfection. That's what I liked about it—tight around her tits. I sit up, and say, "Lift." She raises her arms above her head and thrusts her pelvis upward—the vixen. I pull the shirt off and toss it behind me.

I've been fortunate to witness her natural beauty several times before, but I'll never take it for granted. Reaching down, I grab her tits and knead, giving each their due care. I savor the feel in my hands—soft, pliable, full—and it's sexy as fuck to watch her get turned on for me.

Rocking against her, I know it would be so easy to slip through her lips and slide inside her sweetness, but I don't. "Can you feel how much I want you? What you do to me?"

She grins and moves her hips, but the mischief in her eyes has me smirking. "Hmm, I'm not sure."

"Little vixen"—I chuckle—"I'm going to savor you."

Swallowing her moans with a kiss, I drag my fingers across her ribs and stomach, pulling back enough to watch as goose bumps trail across her skin.

Cat is stunning, but this feels more than the rampant sexual energy we typically share, like the desire that had us racing back to the house. I feel it in my chest, my throat, that I'd sacrifice my life for hers. I've never felt this before. Not with any other woman. I've never stuck around long enough to find out, another thing that makes Cat an exception to rules I thought I had firmly put in place. I broke all of them for her, wanting anything she's willing to give while searching for ways to get more.

The extortion is working in my favor.

It's not one-sided, though. I see how she looks at me and bites her lip when she wants to say something inappropriate or flirt. I've seen it enough to know how to identify the attraction women have for me, but with her, it's different. Cat looks into my eyes like I'm special beyond the image, the fame, the reputation, the wealth. She asks for nothing but devotion and trust. I'm ready to give it to her.

"Where are you going to start?" She rubs my shoulders, then runs the tips of her fingers over my muscles. I hear a gulp and watch as she closes her eyes, embarrassed. I lean down and let her hide, though I hate that she'd feel anything but incredible when she's with me.

"There are so many great options." Kissing her collarbone and her neck, I slide my tongue higher and higher until I reach her ear, and whisper, "I've waited years to be with you." *Like this.* In a relationship. Finding comfort in each other. *Being myself.* I knew back in high school that she was special. If to no one else, she was to me.

I brush her hair back, pushing enough away to admire her. Our connection runs deep. As it should for a married couple. God, I love that and will take advantage of the fact any chance I get if it means I get her—her smile, wit, her caring nature, and her intelligence. There are so many facets to this woman that I can't name all the reasons I've fallen for her. It's her as a whole person who has me captivated.

Her arms tighten around my neck, her eyes finding mine even in the dark. "Bad timing that we finally got right." When she reaches between us, taking my dick in her hand, I shift to the side to give her better access. Sliding up and then down several times, she varies her pace, watching me and adjusting. "You're big, babe. I'm nervous. It's been . . . longer than I care to admit."

Slipping my fingers into her hair, I'm not above encouraging her to put her mouth on me, but a driving desire keeps me focused on coming inside her, claiming her in ways that seemed impossible even a week ago. "Flattery works." There's a shyness to her smile that draws me in to kiss her. Fisting her hair gently in my fingers, I pull her close, making sure she's looking at me when I say, "You don't need to be nervous. It's just you and me. I'll do whatever feels best to you. Just tell me. Okay, babe?"

"Okay." She takes a breath that seems to calm her tightened expression, softening the corners of her eyes. Her hand never stops jerking me off, not even a break in rhythm.

I shudder, wanting to collapse on the mattress. But she keeps me here, where it feels so good, so close to giving in to her hard work. "Shit."

"What's wrong?"

"I don't have condoms. It's the one thing I forgot. *Fuck*."

"Oh." She stops, making me regret saying anything. Waiting to say anything for two more minutes would have worked out a lot better for me. She lies back with her breath coming heavy. "Oh no," she says, draping her arm over her forehead. "That means . . ." Dropping her arm back to the mattress, she looks at me like I've stolen her favorite toy. Maybe I am that for her. I smirk even though nothing about this situation is funny.

"What does it mean? I mean, I know, but what were you going to say?"

She hesitates. I already know why. We haven't talked about our sex lives. I think she wanted to avoid it as well. We've not exchanged details like how long and test results, so I don't blame her for any reluctancy. I blame myself.

My sex life has been plastered across gossip sites since we became famous. It was shoved in her face without wanting the information. Different women in other states and countries, actresses, models, even a UN Ambassador. Online sites don't get clicks for the truth. That's boring to most. They get paid for the juicy gossip. I don't talk about my history because there's never been anyone worth mentioning. *Until Cat.*

"You're worried about my past?"

"I don't have to worry about mine." She scrapes the tips of her nails over the scruff on my chin. "I'm sorry, but I need to protect myself."

"Not from me. Not ever."

"As a nurse—"

"It's okay." I kiss her head and move beside her, lying flat on the mattress. "My medical portal is online. I can show it to you."

Sucking in a breath, she closes her lids just briefly, seeming to allow her to gather strength. "It's not a fun topic, but it is important." She exhales. "To me."

"It is to me, too." I run my knuckles over the back of her hand, then hold it in the small space between our legs. There's no easy way to have this conversation, but right before fucking adds another layer of complication. I turn to my right to find her already looking at me. "I've not been with anyone since you, and we never—"

"No, we didn't," she says, sadness coating her tongue. I hate that she only remembers the pain instead of the happiness we shared. It took me a long time to get here, and I won't taint that period with what went wrong. But I understand her dealing with it at her own pace.

Sitting up, I grin at her, though, needing the levity. "It's been fucking torture. We were so close to getting the deed done."

"I don't know how you survived the pain?" I'm detecting a note of sarcasm in her tone, and I'm glad to hear it.

"Not going to lie. I took a lot of showers."

She rubs my back to soothe the trauma I experienced.

Smirking, I say, "After taking all the tests, I passed with flying colors . . . passed as in I got a clean bill of health last month. I get my reputation may worry—"

"Was it *just* your reputation," she asks, twisting her lips to the side, "or was it you living the rock star lifestyle to the fullest? Which I have no reason to be mad about. We might have been married, but we weren't committed to each other."

She takes hold of my hand and gives a comforting squeeze as if she understands my struggles because my wife is amazing.

"We've come too far to hide any secrets. They always find their way to the light."

Nothing about her body language or expression changes. She stares at me like I'm still the hero instead of the villain. "You can tell me anything. I'd rather know the truth."

"I came close a couple of times last September on the tour." I shouldn't feel ashamed since I had every right, but there's a first time for everything.

"Why didn't you go through with it?"

Turning to find her eyes on mine, no judgment set inside the golden centers, I lean over and kiss her cheek. "Because they weren't you."

Pressing her palm on my chest, she leverages herself above me. "You're more amazing than you know, Shane Faris." She kisses me and then whispers, "You see yourself through the paparazzi lens instead of who you are in real life. But I see you. I see everything you're doing to change for me. You don't have to." Bouncing her head to the side, she laughs. "The usual still stands. No cheating or hurting each other again, but I fell in love with you, not the rock star persona you embody for others."

A tightening in my chest has me reaching to loosen the knot forming.

She sees me. There's nothing more I could ever want than to have this perfect being love me for who I am on the inside. And that she likes my ass helps.

When she bends down to kiss me, she rolls her hips along my length. The torture feels too good to stop her.

Straddling me, she lifts, pressing her hands to my chest and rising above me. She positions my dick exactly where she wants me and begins a slow descent. "I'm on birth control."

Four of the sweetest words I've ever heard spoken.

30

Shane

MY THOUGHTS SCATTER as untamed desire builds from deep within. Cat's hips are cradled in my hands, her warmth so close to my cock that one move would have her slipping over my length. But her gaze, the deep browns of her eyes, tells me I've earned her.

The reminder to give her what she deserves. Slow, savoring our first time together. The control to restrain myself from slamming her down on top of me.

I look up as her hair falls forward with her head. Sweeping it to one side of her neck, I watch as my girl takes me, all of me, her body embracing me and her mouth falling open. I reach up to touch her cheek, her soft skin under my callused fingers, and say, "It's been so long. I'm . . ."

"It's okay," she says, her tone comforting like I've never had sex before.

Fuck that. She deserves the best, and I'm here reporting

for duty. I should be soothing her after fucking her just right.

I lift her by the hips and help her slide up my hard length. Her eyes meet mine, and she pushes down on her own accord, her mouth shaping into a sexy fucking O making me wish I had started there. Slick heat consumes me as she slides down so slowly on top of me that my patience is threadbare. "You feel," she starts on the edge of a breathy moan. "You feel so good." Her teeth scrape across her lower lip, and she bites, her eyes closing as she savors the feel. "So full. So good."

I cover her hands that she's resting on my chest, and my breathing staggers as her hips undulate, taking me deeper. I catch the hitch in her breathing, too, as she leans forward to rest her forehead against mine. *Close.* So close I lift to connect with her to find that perfect spot.

She's so quiet. I ask, "Are you okay?" I can feel a pulse in my dick inside her. I can't help but smile and want to fist pump in celebration when I feel her lift her head.

"Yes," she replies, the corners of her mouth curling up for me. "You're so much more . . . my heart is tied to you." With a flutter of her eyes, she lifts her chin and sits higher, exhaling as she seats herself deeper on my length. "It's more than physical with you."

"I feel it too," I whisper, sitting up to wrap my arms around her waist. "Do you want to do this? Want me to move in you? Show you everything I've wanted to do to you since the moment you walked back into my life?"

"Yes." She takes another breath. "Please . . ." Words keep escaping her, but she rises to the occasion as if determined to move past the acclimation.

Rocking under her, I soak up the softest of mews she elicits. I nip at her earlobe, pulling it between my teeth before whispering, "I want you to fuck me, Cat. Do you understand?" She nods against my cheek, taking a breath and pushing down again. "That's a good girl. Breathe for me and do it again."

I was on the verge of madness, losing my mind without even being inside her. Now, my senses have returned, my thoughts intact. She feels incredible, but nothing about this will be slow. I can't any longer. Bending to kiss under her jaw, I bite gently, thrusting to purge a moan from her lips. "I'm going to fuck you so good, sweetheart."

When I flip her to the mattress, her hair flies in my face but settles around her like a halo. *My sweet saving grace.* Cat centers herself at an angle, then looks me over once before using her finger to come hither.

I climb on top of her, sliding my hands along her arms she laid above her head. I look at her tits, her nipples rising to greet me. *Fucking beautiful.* As she squirms beneath me, her chest heaves. Dragging my fingers over her mouth, I stick my thumb in from the corner and watch her wrap her lips around it and suck.

Fuck me.

I lose all sensibilities and start fucking her, thrusting so hard that my name comes out in vain. But she holds on, even digging her nails into my shoulders as if to prove a point. Point taken, baby. Game on. When I slow, she begs me to go fast, "Please, faster, babe."

When I go faster, she breathes heavier and wants me to go slower. "What do you need, Catalina? Tell me. Faster. Harder. Slower. Softer. Just tell me, and I'll do it for you."

"I want—so good," she says, licking her lips. "I want it all. I want all of you."

"I'll be everything for you." Planting my hands beside her head, I say, "Remember, I love you."

The rise of her brows and drop of her mouth have her asking, "Why do I need to remember—*Oh God*."

I dive deep and pull out only to thrust inside her, claiming every part of her as mine like a conquering explorer. Her gasps and moans, her body and thrusts, her bucks and wiggles, I take everything she gives and plunge right back into her.

We align in rhythm, our bodies slick with desire, every ounce of my being awake and craving more. More. More of this. More of her and me together. The connection too strong to break even when she turns over and pushes up, wanting me to take her from behind.

I do. I do. I'll take every which way, relishing in the knowledge that I'll be rewarded as well. Holding her hips, I push into her, seated so I'm deep inside her depth. I'm not a selfish bastard. Not all the time that is. Reaching around, I slide two fingers into her wet lower lips and tease and circle before focusing on her swelling clit.

One touch, and she's jerking and using her toes to slide up higher on the bed. I wrangle her still and increase the pressure on the sweet bud I love kissing.

The view of her ass is divine, but I want to see her when we finish, and I'm close. So is she. I stop, taking a breath to slow the pace, and find it ironic that *I'm* the one insistent now. *For a good reason.*

Bending over her, I kiss her back and shoulders, the North Star, and then say, "You look fucking amazing, but I want to look into your eyes when I come inside you."

She drags her fingers over my abs, admiring the hard work I put in, and then lowers to the bed, sliding forward and rolling over for me. With her knees bent, she drags a hand over her inner thigh and lower. Her renewed confidence is a threat to my restraint. "I want that with you, too."

The blankets are a mess underneath her, her hair just as wild, but she's never looked as beautiful as she does now. I move to her, lifting to position myself at her entrance once more. With our gazes locked, I kiss her and push in—slow and steady—pulling back just enough to maintain eye contact.

Each breath comes with the quietest of sighs that lilt at the end, a gentle appreciation of the satisfaction we find in each other. I kiss her cheek and then the other, whispering her name in reverence. "Catalina. Catalina. Catalina." And then travel to her mouth, our lips embracing. I close my eyes and fall deeper in love with her. "I love you, my wife."

Her eyes glisten, and water pools at the far corners. When one tear falls, I dip my tongue to catch it, and like every other thing I've taken from her, I drink her in, enchanted by this woman. *Bewitched by my wife.*

"Ah," she moans, her back arching as her mouth falls open. When her body erupts in ecstasy this time, she takes me with her.

I pump and thrust, losing myself and my rhythm when I reach the edge and descend with her into the darkness and the bliss of us. Her body trembles as my name tumbles from her lips. The urge to fuck through my orgasm has me pushing twice as hard, making sure she feels every inch as her body swallows me whole.

I collapse on top of her, my breath heavy against her neck. When I open my eyes, I catch another tear falling down her cheek, but she's smiling, giving me relief. It was so good to me that I couldn't bear that I hadn't made her feel the same.

Sucking a jagged breath, she wraps her arms so tightly around me, kisses my shoulder, and then says, "You're killing me." A stilted laugh follows, but the smile never leaves.

"You're killing me, too. So fucking amazing, babe."

"No," she gasps, pressing against my arms. "I can't breathe."

"Oh shit!" Rolling off her, I kiss her heaving chest. "Sorry. I didn't realize."

"It's okay. I didn't want you to, but the best sex of my life was flashing before my eyes just before my last breath."

"Okay. Okay," I say, laughing lightly. "Do not lie on top of Cat. Stored in memory forever."

"Let's not get carried away. I liked it for a minute."

"Until the lack of air part. Based on that alone, I'll concede to one minute." *And to loving this woman endlessly.* "As for the best sex of your life—"

"Shane Faris. Hands down."

I pop my imaginary collar. "That's what I like to hear."

"I know, but it's also true." She wiggles her shoulders while turning to look at me. Slipping the back of her hand over my abs, she says, "That wasn't on the schedule."

I chuckle. God, this feels good, too. It's not the same as being inside her, but it's still freeing. "I need to print a new one for tomorrow. My wife is a goddamn goddess, and I'm going to need the remaining thirty-six hours to worship every inch of her."

"I like this plan." She snuggles against my side, propping her leg over mine. "A lot."

"I like you a lot." I hold her in my arms, our hearts still racing against time, and kiss the top of her head. "Extortion was the best idea I ever fucking had."

Her body rattles with laughter. "It seems to have worked out well for you."

"Like you, babe. Best I ever had."

31

Cate

I STARE at the bottom of the empty pharmacy bag, and my gaze pivots to the prescription prenatal vitamins on the counter. "This isn't mine," I whisper as if needing to verify I'm seeing what's right in front of my eyes.

Taking a breath doesn't help calm the anxiety riddling through my brain, though. So I hold the bag to my mouth and breathe in and out. *In and out.* In. Out. But it's not going to solve my problem.

I jump up from the toilet and run into the bedroom, grabbing the tote bag and plopping it on the mattress. It's packed full, so I start to unload it, tossing my purse, the book I had planned to read this weekend, the brush I haven't used once since arriving, and the empty water bottle on the bed.

Hair clip.

Perfume.

Bag of Cheetos to help my monthly cravings that hit out of nowhere.

Gum.

Ah!

I fish my pill container from the bottom of the tote, eagerly opening it in hopes that I imagined destroying the packet two days ago instead of it really happening. Fresh from the shower with slippery hands is not a good combination for a foil packet when you bust multiple pills out accidentally while trying to catch it. Me and hazy pre-coffee mornings don't mix.

The new prescription wasn't just backup.

Clicking it open, I stare at the empty plastic container, my heart instantly sinking to the pit of my stomach.

All I needed was one active pill to bridge the gap until I could retrieve my correct prescription. *Just one . . .* But there are none. Okay, don't freak out, Cate. I took it yesterday, so I'll just get it transferred to Deer Lake, and I'll be fine. A good plan is in place. It'll be okay.

If it's all so fine, why do I sound like I'm trying to convince myself?

In through the nose. Out through the mouth. They're open twenty-four hours, so I can call the pharmacy now and get it going. That way, I can relax and pick it up later.

I brush my teeth while I'm on hold, and rinse right when a human finally answers the call. "Hi, I was there yesterday to pick up my prescription . . ."

Breathing becomes easier by the time I hang up. Deer Lake Pharmacy opens at nine. Shane and I can cruise over and pick it up anytime today. No need to worry him when it's taken care of. All is good.

I tiptoe back across the hall to the other bedroom, where I left Shane sleeping thirty minutes ago. I got up to freshen my breath, brush my hair, which I've forgotten to do again, and take my pill while hydrating from the sex we had last night. Stopping, I press my hands to my heating cheeks, blushing just thinking about it. It was overwhelming with the thoughts in my head racing toward a goal I've craved for so long, an elusive orgasm that I wouldn't be giving myself. My body was full, filled with so much of him—the emotion, his body, the pleasure—devouring me whole and leaving me in awe. Even my heart beats as if it were his, and his were mine.

We were one.

I've never felt more at peace than during our connection, body and soul.

Breathing has become easier this morning. Whatever troubles I had been carrying vanished under his ministrations. I'm making it my mission to do the same for him.

The inner muscles of my thighs and the stretch in my center feel so good, like exercise that pushed me to hit new goals. The ache is there, but Shane is the reward.

I open the door and am greeted by eyes that brighten even in the low light of early morning. "Good morning, my wife." He flips the covers open for me.

I giggle because I'm that far gone for him and happy to play along. "Good morning, my husband." It's not a lie, but it feels bigger in the moment than I expected as if I hadn't tried it on prior, and it doesn't quite fit. I strip off the sweatshirt I had thrown on and climb back into his arms again. My back to his chest.

Pushing my hair away from my neck, he plants a kiss there. "How are you?" he whispers. His breath coats my shoulder, sending shivers down my spine. This is what I want—a slow and easy morning. I don't want to jump into the deep end just yet.

I turn in his arms, lifting on my elbow to get a better view of him. The sexy hair is not disappointing, his eyes like sleep could still pull him back in with lids hanging a little lower. Running a hand over his neck and higher, I tap my fingertips lightly across the lips I'm anxious to kiss. "Can I ask you something?"

"Anything."

"Without judgment?"

"Hm." Concern wrinkles his forehead, and his hand lowers to rest on my hip. "I won't judge, but you have me worried."

"Don't be. Last night . . . this place . . . it's all been magical. I just always imagined my husband would be someone I exchanged vows with. To me, our relationship started over yesterday, so it's hard for my mind to wrap around that we're married."

His fingers brush around the shell of my ear, then grace the side of my face so gently it's barely felt. "I'm not upset, and I'm not judging you. It makes sense. When I say it to you, I'm able to voice what I've felt for a while now. A dream. A wish. My future wrapped in a second chance."

"*Shane.*" My heart squeezes, flooding with even more love than I could possibly explain. I lean forward and kiss him, the emotion so big that I can't reason through being rational right now.

He says, "It will come in time for you. I don't expect you to say it when you don't feel it. Not just because I did."

"I love you. I know that and can say it without any terms or conditions." I grin, feeling closer than I ever thought imaginable to this man, and I imagined a lot. "Unlike how you got me here in a forced proximity situation, hoping to trap me here as a hostage and have your way with me." God, why am I suddenly turned on? "It worked just like in my favorite books."

Narrowing his eyes, he angles his head as he studies the

words coming from my mouth. "I have no clue what you're talking about, Cat."

"Sorry, I got lost in our storyline. Forced proximity is one of my favorite tropes."

"We're still talking about books, right?"

I shrug my free shoulder. "Or in life. Like now."

"Your favorite books are about kidnapping and forced proximity?"

I wave him off. "It's hard to explain." My gaze deviates to the window where the curtains are still open from yesterday, giving me a view of the beginnings of the early morning light. "It's romantic, and the characters fall in love—oh, forget it. Just trust me."

"I'm going to have to on this one." He rolls onto his back, his arm still tucked under my neck. "I don't even know what we were talking about anymore."

"It's okay." I laugh. "It's been worked out."

His hand rubs over my bare hip under the covers. "How are you feeling after last night?"

"So good."

Falling back again, he stares up at the ceiling with a chuckle. "I caught that when all of Deer Lake heard you screaming my name."

I mimic him and lie on my back as well. "Scream might be exaggerating a little." I look over to see him putting his hands up in surrender. The smirk on his face has me rubbing my thighs together. Sooner is better than later for that next hit of bliss.

"I just call it how I hear it," he teases, "and calling me god is a little formal. I'm also good with your highness, your majesty, my king, lord of the stage—"

"Lord of the stage?" My eyebrows shoot to the heavens

above as a fit of laughter catches hold of me. "I know you're not even joking."

"I never joke about sex." Rolling onto his side again, he runs a finger down my chest and between my breasts. "Speaking of . . . I was asking about your body." The joking ends, and the air stills in reaction. I don't make a move, and I'm not sure if I should even take a breath. Shane props up on his elbow, cupping my face when he leans forward. "Are you okay? I wanted to go slow for y—"

I meet him, a breath left between us. "It was perfect. Perfect for us."

His eyes reflect mine, confidence widening his pupils as he takes me in. No words are said. None need to be. We stare into each other's eyes, silently saying everything we feel.

His gaze dips to my mouth, and he licks his lips, still caressing my cheek. His strong hand is gentle when he pulls me to him. Our lips meet in a tender kiss. I tilt to get closer as I part my mouth, enticing him to take anything he wants of me. *Again.*

The slip of his tongue has me welcoming him into the depths he's exploring. It's as if he touches it, it's his forever. I return the favor, wanting to own as much of him as I can.

A push and pull that I find so incredibly sexy, neither of us wanting to win or lose. We just want to be in the arena together.

I slide my hand up his neck and weave my fingers into his hair. Pulling him closer as if our mouths attached isn't enough. *It's not.* "I want you inside me."

"Thought you'd never ask." He has no qualms about pushing me onto my back as he slides through the covers.

"I didn't. It was a command."

"So fucking sexy, baby." He kisses me. It's a formidable embrace as he settles between my legs. The tip of his cock presses against my entrance, and he leans forward, blue eyes alight with anticipation.

My fingertips play over his ribs before I grip his shoulders. "So fucking sexy."

His growl sends a shiver through me for just a moment, and he steals a breath before I have time to release it. "I'll be gentle."

"I'm not sure I want that." I try for confident, but the lightest of chuckles rumbles from his chest as he leans down to kiss my neck, working his cock inside me inch by glorious inch.

A thrust has me shoving the back of my head into the pillow and groaning, a mixture of heaven and hell coming together. I want it all with him, so I embrace the stretch, the burn, and the fullness of his cock as it fills me by wrapping my arms around him and taking what feels so much like mine already. "Yes, babe," I purr, letting my senses take over. Feel. Touch. So good. The scent of him and us coming together is a potent aphrodisiac and driving me for more. "So good."

His hips thrust, and I meet him each time with a push of my own, enveloping him as he engulfs my soul. My thoughts swim in him as he plunders my body on his own accord. His back and shoulders are taut, and the feel of hills and mountains of muscles makes me even wetter for him. The sound of our connection grows louder, intermingling with uncontrollable moans of pleasure. "Lord of the stage, you hurt so good."

His entire body stills. I don't think he's even breathing until he says, "Oh fuck me, you did not go there." His hips slam into mine as he pins my arms above my head. "You like that, baby?"

"I fucking love it."

The word ignites a fire burning in his sky-blue eyes. His jaw ticks as he grinds against me. "*Fuuck*, baby. You feel so fucking good."

Swiveling my hips, I pull back, empty without him all the way in me. I thrust and take, pull and give to him, wanting him to feel how he makes me feel. Amazing.

Balanced on one hand, he squeezes my breast and then lowers to take my nipple into his mouth. Swirling his tongue, he then flicks it, which was already hard for him. The sensation shoots straight to my core, and the coiling begins.

Shifting to the other, he doesn't leave that breast out. But when he slides his hand over my belly and lower, my vagina clenches around him, causing his mouth to open in the slightest of gasps. When his eyes shoot to mine, he says, "Do it again."

I squeeze and slide, taking him in and not releasing. "Again," he demands, slipping his fingers around our connection and then upward to bring the slickness to my clit. He does what he did to my breasts, teasing and then flicking. My nerve endings are live wires under his stroke, every touch shooting through my veins.

It's so hard to embrace him when I want to fall into my own orgasm. His thrusting gets wild and unpredictable, too much of everything dancing between my head and every part of my body.

One pinch of my clit sends me tremoring into a release, triggering him to fall with me. My hips still move, grasping for every inch of him until he's pumping inside me. The unrelenting drive eases, allowing me to disappear into the bliss, happily floating in the aftermath.

My breathing is too harsh, but I reluctantly come to my senses. Seeing him spent and the sweat glistening on his tan skin make me grateful I did. He's beautiful and makes me feel the same.

When he finally opens his eyes, he looks over at me and smiles. "Did I ever tell you how I used to fantasize about fucking you?"

Already grinning, I reply, "No."

"Those fantasies pale compared to the real thing." He closes his eyes again, and his breath is still uneven. "You're fucking incredible, baby."

I reach between us, slip my hand in his, and close my eyes. "So are you, husband."

32

Cate

"UNFORTUNATELY, I'm too sore to make paddleboard yoga this morning," I tease, gently breaking the news to him. "The class will have to go on without me."

With his head stuck in the fridge, Shane starts chuckling. He retrieves a bowl of berries and a container of Greek yogurt, knowing the way to my heart, and sets them on the counter. "That's too bad. For me." He winks and then taps my pouty bottom lip. "I was looking forward to seeing your ass in the air."

"I can save us both the trouble and show it to you now."

"Naked?"

I hate dashing his hopes, especially when he looks so cute from even the thought of me stripping off my clothes right here in the kitchen.

"Ehh." I sidle up to him at the island. "I think I need a few hours to recover. Silver lining, we've burned a lot of calories over the past twelve hours." I run my hand under his shirt and casually count the defined muscles of his abdomen so I can make a proper plan of licking them later, or maybe in a few minutes if he lets me. "So no need to burn more with things that are just a distraction from us having sex."

With a raised eyebrow, he asks, "Have I created a monster?" And then he waggles his brow in the cutest dang way.

I just want to pinch his ass cheek or hump his face. It could go either way with how horny he makes me. "Not a monster per se but an addict."

"It's not like you haven't had sex before. Though there's no fucking way I want to hear about some other guy—*fuck*. Let's not even go there."

I'm leaning toward the face humping when I see the way his jaw ticks. He's just so freaking gorgeous I almost can't stand to look at him. It's like staring into an eclipse—fiery sun rays and darkness shadowing his other half. I'd burn my retinas for him. "The past is the past. Your past is a no-go for me as well just to be clear." Resting my butt against the countertop, I ask, "Is it only us that feels like we were made for each other, our bodies fitting together so perfectly that I'm missing a piece of myself when we're apart?"

His arm comes around my neck, locking it under his chin and bending to kiss it. "I've never felt this way either." Simple and direct, sharing our hearts without worrying about what's next. "As for burning calories together, I'm happy to give you a good workout anytime you want."

Holding his arm, I giggle, but then I remember how he's gone so much. "I need you all the time, but what happens when you're on the road?"

"*Shhh.*" He presses his lips to the top of my head, then rests his chin there instead. "No reality this weekend. I just want this for a few days. Normal. Quiet. Us and no one else.

No screaming fans. No paparazzi. No demands being made of me. Unless it's you, of course, and then I'm here reporting for duty."

I know he's trying to be funny, but he still speaks the truth about his life. And it worries me. I won't ever be someone who loves the spotlight or even shines it. I'm good with my low-key life. How will we balance the two?

A calm has soothed his storms, but I can't help but wonder if it's only temporary. Will the thunder return when we go back to LA?

I agree with him. I don't want the outside world to invade this little piece of heaven-on-earth perfection we've found. "The beauty of this weekend is that we can do whatever we want—stay up late or sleep in, avoid certain topics and talk all night about others." Spinning in his arms, I fist his shirt and lift on my toes, but I can't reach his mouth unless I jump. I pull him to me. "It's glorious really. Now kiss me, you giant."

He does not disappoint, but I knew he wouldn't here in Deer Lake or back in Los Angeles. He's rid his life of a lot of the demons he had, bad habits that were dragging him down, and flipped his mood like a light switch. Open and honest. I love seeing him this free, this happy. I love seeing him in love. And I'm the lucky one who gets to love him.

"This is a good transition to talk about the itinerary."

Releasing me, which makes me feel cold and desolate without him wrapped around me, he opens the container of berries and plops a raspberry in his mouth. "What about it?"

"It's the sweetest that you went to so much trouble for me, *buuuuut* I was thinking we could go into town today. What do you say?"

He feeds me a blueberry, then kisses the tip of my nose.

"I thought we decided to keep the real world at bay for a few days?"

"We did, but I need to pick up something in town."

"Cryptic."

I reach over and grab a berry from the container. "A prescription." I don't know why I suddenly feel weird talking about this. I also don't like that it feels like I'm keeping secrets from him. "I had the prescription transferred up here."

"Should I be worried?"

"No. It's all taken care of."

Running his hand at the curve of my waist, he smiles as if he's been given a secret. Nodding, he replies, "We can go after breakfast."

"Thanks."

We eat breakfast down by the lake. Finding the wineglass and beer bottle left as evidence from last night's prelude to sex makes my typically prudish side smile regarding the spontaneity.

Sitting in the same chairs as last night, I can imagine they'd be the ones we always chose until we're old and gray. I smile just thinking about it.

"What's got you smiling like that?"

I roll my neck to face him. "Nothing. I'm happy to be here."

Bridging the divide, he reaches over to hold my hand. "Me too."

I return my gaze to the lake, soaking in the beautiful scenery and fresh air. My head feels clearer because of this trip, so I need to take advantage of all it has to offer. But there is still a mystery to be solved. "I've been thinking a lot about the marriage."

"Our marriage?"

"No. The cheating scandal rocking the Danish royal family." I laugh because I think I'm pretty funny. "Yes, our marriage."

"Are you going to divorce me when we return?" He chuckles, but no humor is found in its sound.

The question hits me sideways. I've never had the intention of staying married. Dating shouldn't change the plan. But then I look at how far we've come—from our attorney's office to falling in love. We're proof that anything is possible. "I'm not looking to rush and change the status quo. It's something we'll talk about another time. Lay everything out on the table and figure it out from there. But that's not the aspect of marriage I was talking about. I want to solve the mystery of how we got married in the first place."

"It would be good to know." He sits forward, resting his arms on the tops of his legs. "Where do we start?"

"I have a yearbook somewhere in my apartment. I didn't keep much over the years, but I kept that. Maybe it will lead us in the right direction."

"Who said we were going in the wrong one?"

I'm not sure if I detect a hint of annoyance or if it's a genuine question. "You know what I mean."

His gaze redirects to the lake and distances off the choppy waters. "Yeah. I know." Standing, he offers his hand. "You ready to head into town?"

I slip my hand into his, and he pulls me to my feet. "Ready as I'll ever be—No. Scratch that. I need to change first."

"Get ready for an adventure."

I DIDN'T REALLY UNDERSTAND his comment about an adventure, but I do now. Big dually trucks covered in mud, a few with logging trailers, plaid on everyone we've seen, and beards for days. The Deer Lake sign came with a distinctive feature. "I've never seen a statue that big before. Impressive deer."

"It's a stag," Shane says, his eyes glued to the winding road.

"It's a deer, right?"

"A male deer. A buck. A stag."

"It's weird they can't just be called deer. Seems someone was overcompensating when carving that thing."

Reaching over, he covers my leg with his hand. "We're not in LA anymore. It's a way of life for slower, hard-working people. Friendly but also love to gossip."

"So how does a family of celebrities fit in?"

"I hate being called a celebrity." There's no anger or frustration. His tone is altogether indifferent as if he gave up fighting that battle a long time ago, which is worse. "Makes me sound like a talentless hack. Famous for famous sake."

The word "celebrity" is tossed around LA all the time, a part of the culture of being near Hollywood. So I hadn't thought twice about using the word as if it encapsulates him that easily within it.

"I'm sorry—"

"Don't apologize." He glances over and gives me a reassuring smile. "It's just a pet peeve of mine, but I'm used to it."

"No, I agree with you." Covering his hand with mine, I give it a squeeze. "I've never thought twice about it because I never had to. You're more than a celebrity. And you're everything to me."

"Look at you charming me." I playfully shrug like it's no

big deal when it's the opposite. "And to answer your question, we don't, but most of the locals don't care about fame or . . ." He laughs. "Celebrities. Plenty pass through. The tourists in high season are the ones who tend to steal the peace."

A set of stores appears around a bend and just after a dense line of trees. I squint to make out the signs. "There." Just like I saw in an online photo, the word Pharmacy sits solidly in green under a big sign that reads Grocer. "There it is."

He hasn't asked me anything other than if I'm okay, though I'm sure he has questions. His concern for my well-being is his top priority. I've never been someone's top priority before. It feels good, better than good. It feels fulfilling.

He shifts his Ferrari that stands out like a sore thumb into park. Out of the car and coming around before I have a chance to unbuckle my seat belt, he opens the door and offers a hand.

That little awkward turn and the muscles I use to get out of the door's way remind me, and not so gently, of being with Shane. I love you is said with ease, and husband and wife rolls off the tongue. The assumption that everything will be the same as it is now once we return to LA makes my heart flutter. I believe in us.

The groundwork for a solid foundation—trust, honesty, a deep connection, and the physical—makes me feel invincible with him. We're a team we've created to take on the world together.

Entering the store hand in hand, I glance at him, walking with his head down and sunglasses covering his eyes. He is either truly in tune with how the world sees him or has no idea that sunglasses don't disguise him like he thinks they do. It's probably somewhere down the middle.

The cashier stands straight from where she was leaning against the register when she sees us. "Welcome to Grocer." I'm thinking the abrupt change in body language isn't for my benefit.

The store is tiny compared to grocery stores back in LA, so the pharmacy sign pointing to the back of the store is easy to find. "Hey," I say, stopping in front of an aisle containing wildlife feed. "I'm going to run to the back and get what I need. Meet you at the register . . ." I check the time on my watch. "In say, ten minutes?"

"I'm going to look for some healthy juice shots. Do you prefer beets or turmeric?" I love how he thinks he will find that here when the vegetable section is practically nonexistent, and we're literally standing in an aisle of food for wild animals. *Maybe he will.* At least it will keep him busy while I pick up my prescription. "I'm good with either."

Walking backward, he says, "Got to replenish for our afternoon activities."

I thought I was okay letting him walk away from me, but that wink and click of his tongue just made my entire body tighten in anticipation. I'm running back to him, jumping into his arms, and kissing this man simply because I can. He's mine, and I'm his.

He caught me with a thud, one hand protectively on the back of my head and the other under my ass. Our mouths part, and I lower my feet back to the linoleum. Watching him lick me from his lips is an aphrodisiac that has me wanting to detour back out to the parking lot.

I look around. The place is basically empty.

Bending down, he whispers, "What's on your mind, pussycat?"

Who am I? I'm actually considering having sex in public? I sure am glad I left my comfort zone back in LA because this is what he does to me. And I'm not saying no to the possibility.

But I should get my prescription first. Nothing sounds appealing about walking back in here after having fresh sex in a Ferrari. The shame would eat me alive before I could get what I need. *Baby steps, Cate.*

Speaking of babies, get your prescription.

"I'll be quick." I pull away, the tip of our fingers the last contact shared before we're out of reach.

He shoves his hands in his pockets, probably able to read every naughty thought I was having about him. As soon as I round the corner to the nearest aisle, I rush to the back of the store.

I reach the counter and lift to see if I can find anyone working. A man walks from a back room with his eyes on a pill bottle. His eyes spy me over the top of his glasses, and he detours in my direction. "How can I help you?"

"Hi, I had my prescription transferred to this pharmacy this morning."

He starts typing on a keyboard. "Name?"

"Catalina Farin. It was transferred by—"

"Yes, I see it here." He shifts back in front of me, and says, "Unfortunately, we've had to order it. We should get it in with deliveries this Tuesday."

"It's Saturday," I say, like I need the confirmation. "I don't understand. In LA, they'd have it ready in an hour. We're not even three hours away from the city."

"You do have that option."

"Of going to LA to pick it up?"

"I'm sorry. We're a small pharmacy. We can't carry everything, and it's a holiday weekend. I can offer you a different type. We have samples." He opens his drawer and starts rummaging through it. He's offering me birth control shoved in a catchall drawer? This is an adventure indeed, and not the good kind. "Let's just make sure they're not out of date."

"It's hormonal." He knows this already as a pharmacist, so it's an odd suggestion. I glance at the wall to the right of me covered in a hundred varieties of fishing lures, wondering how they can carry so much of the same thing but not one of the most popular brands of birth control in the country. Their different priorities have my thoughts racing to figure out another plan since this one didn't work out. "I can't just switch for a few days."

"I understand, but there's nothing else I can do to speed up the delivery. They only come twice a week, but the good news is that your prescription will be on the next truck." He uses his whole hand to point as if that's less adamant. "If you need something immediate, prophylactics are on aisle four."

And on that note . . . "Thank you."

Me being upset isn't going to get me what I need. I walk down aisle four, grabbing a small box of condoms just in case. I don't mind going old-school, but this will throw my whole month out of whack. I grab a variety of candy bars and a bottle of Gatorade because I can't just show up at the register with condoms. I mean, I could, but yeah . . . no.

When I reach the front of the store, Shane waits for me with a bag of hot 'n' spicy fried pork skins in one hand and a big bottle of orange juice in the other. "That doesn't look like health shots." I laugh, though it's only surface, me smiling for him as I try to sort through this prescription mess in my head.

He's smiling the moment he sees me. The man knows how to make a girl swoon. "I don't think we're surprised they didn't have any." His gaze dips to all the crap I grabbed on my way up here. "Get everything?"

I start for the register, whispering when I pass him, "We need to talk outside."

"That doesn't sound good."

I stop before I feed into the line and turn back. "It's nothing about us. I have a little situation that needs to be handled."

"That sounds worse."

"It's fine. Really." I don't sound convincing even to myself. "We'll just talk outside."

"Are you okay, Cat?" I hate that he's worrying over me. He has enough to worry about from his own life. This is supposed to be a break for him. Not a dose of reality that I would typically handle on my own. But I can't. We're here together, so I reply, "It's okay. For real." I dump all the stuff on the grocery belt. "I'm okay."

He sets his stuff down and pulls his wallet out. "I'm buying." He eyes the stuff I want, and says, "Why do we need condoms?" Alarm bells fire in all directions when I see him pick up the box. Shooting me a glare, he opens his mouth and closes it, then opens it again. "Small?" Offense sews his brows together in irritation. "What the fuck?"

I whip my gaze to the box just as the cashier starts ringing our order. Flustered, I scan the words on the front. "I wasn't looking at the size. I just grabbed it."

"What is going on, Cat?" Shortness clips his tone, and then he tells the cashier, "We won't need these. Thanks."

"We do need those." I try to calm the distress in my voice, but it's not working. "Just get a bigger size."

"You're on the pill."

"I need birth control, Shane," I shout in a panic. *Oh God.* The ringing stops as I close my eyes, hoping the earth opens us and swallows me whole. When I open my eyes to find I'm still stuck here at the Deer Lake Grocer with a gob-smacked cashier and a manager who seems to have nothing better to do than stare at me, I turn to bury my head in his chest. "I don't have any with me."

His arm comes around me as he pulls his wallet out to pay with the other. The cashier asks, "Do you want the condoms or put them back?"

"Put them back, please." The purchase is quick, and he's guiding me out the door by my lower back. We've been trapped in tension since I lost it at the register. I dread what's next. I tried so hard not to worry him, and now I've done it for the entire staff of Grocer to witness. As soon as our feet hit the pavement, he releases me and runs a hand over his head. "You definitely gave them something to gossip about in there."

I cringe. "Sorry about that."

He shakes his head, but looks at me while we hurry to the car. "You told me you're on the pill. That's why we could have sex last night and this morning. Did you lie to me?" I can hear the betrayal in his voice and see the hurt clouding his eyes.

"I'm on the pill. I wouldn't lie to you about that. I picked up my prescription right before I got to the apartment yesterday. But there was a mix-up, and I didn't discover it until I went to open the new pack to take one this morning, and my prescription wasn't in the bag they gave me."

He opens the car and tucks the bag behind my seat before holding the door for me. "You're on the pill, but you're out?"

"Yes. I had the prescription transferred here to pick up. It shouldn't have been a big deal, except they don't have any in stock and don't get their shipment in until Tuesday."

"Tuesday?" I slip into the car, and he closes the door. As soon as he sinks into his seat, he asks, "What do we need to do?"

I reach over to hold his hand, hoping he doesn't hate me for ruining the trip. "We need to go back to LA. Today. It's the only way to keep me on track."

"Okay." He leans over and kisses me once and then twice more. "We'll pack up and head back." He steps in without hesitation to support me and to make sure we get what we need, no matter the inconvenience to him.

Something I was stressing about became a non-issue in a matter of seconds. Another brick cemented to strengthen our foundation.

And just like that, it became us against the world.

33

Shane

CAT SLIPS BACK into the car and tosses a box on my lap. "Happy?"

"Massive Cock Covers?" I pick up the black-and-gold box, turning it over in my hand. "Double extra-large. At least you got the sizing right. Of course, that doesn't save my pride when visiting Deer Lake." I reverse from the spot where I waited for her in the pharmacy parking lot.

"We could do a press release?" She opens the small bag in her lap, the crinkling competing with her voice. "We can stage a setup. You can get caught on camera by the paparazzi with your box of massive cock covers. That will put any rumors to rest." She holds up the bag. "Got my pills."

"That's a relief."

"Yes. We have nothing to worry about. No skipped days."

"That's good." I'm not a baby person, but they take to me like Mack and Posey have. It doesn't mean I want kids of my own. *Do I?*

Having kids isn't something I've been in a situation to

want. I look over at Cat, who has propped her elbow up on the door and is staring out the window. "Oh," she says, looking back at me, "an anonymous tipster can call in a blind item about how they had to get a few stitches after having sex with you?" She's so eagerly hopeful that I almost feel bad letting her down.

"You're a little too good at this, babe."

"I'm a quick study."

I've tried to keep it serious since it usually is when my dick is the topic of conversation, but I chuckle, letting her win this round. She's too cute not to. I pull off to the side before I reach the line of cars exiting the shopping center. Looking at Cat sitting so contentedly beside me, I run my hand over her thigh. "I'm not holding you to the forty-eight hours. We're back in Los Angeles." Glancing at the line of cars lengthening, I add, "We're right around the corner from your apartment. I can drive you home."

"Is that what you want?" she asks, all joy stolen from her eyes.

"No. I want to spend time with you, but I want to do it without the threat of legal proceedings. I want it because you want to be with me. I want it—"

"I want to be with you, Shane." Her voice is steady, her hand resting on mine. Her eyes are set on mine, and there are no doubts hidden anywhere in her body language.

I nod, then pull into the line to exit. Ferraris aren't uncommon in this city, so I don't worry about outsiders catching me, but I do wonder if we should be going to my house versus her apartment. Giving her leg a little squeeze, I lean over and kiss her. And then a car's horn blares, driving my eyes back to the green light ahead. I start driving, heading to her place. At the gate, I look over at her once more. "What do you think about coming to mine? You don't work until Tuesday. You're already packed. You can grab whatever else you need, and we can go over there for a few days."

In her smile, I see what I thought was only a dream—a future with her and the possibilities that come along with it. "I like that idea." After pulling into the complex, I drive us to her building. When I park, she adds, "I only need a few things. I'll run in and be quick."

I watch her hop out and rush to her door. She doesn't need to. I've waited ten months for her. I can wait five minutes. Sitting in the car builds the anticipation for what's to come, a lot like a first date—slightly nervous, more excited.

I don't know that my house offers more than her place does, but it gives us privacy, and that's worth its weight in gold to me. My phone rings. Laird's name appears on the screen on the dashboard. "Hey, what's up?"

"You've gone radio silent," he says. "Thought I should check on you."

"I'm touched," I reply sarcastically. "It's been like two days tops."

A chuckle frequents the other end of the line. "Seems longer. Hey, I have a new riff I've been working on. I think you'll dig it. You have some free time this week? I can come over, and we can mess around your studio."

"Tuesday onward." I'm not going to lie about Cat, but I don't need to blurt out every detail of what's changed in my life practically overnight.

"What do you have going on this weekend?"

This is where I need to decide how I'm going to handle it. Straightforward is always best. "I just got back into the city from an overnight at Deer Lake."

"Oh yeah, Poppy mentioned you were doing that. With a girl or just getting away?"

Wife comes to mind as the correct adjective, but he doesn't know Cat and I are even dating. Hell, I didn't know we were until yesterday. Things move fast. Life even quicker. The pieces came together because it was right, but I should probably ease the family in on the marriage detail. "Yeah, a woman I'm seeing."

"Is it serious? It sounds like it, considering you called her a woman, not a girl or chick."

He knows me well. "It's I-took-her-to-Deer-Lake serious."

"Damn, dude. This came out of nowhere."

"Not so out of nowhere, Laird. You've just been busy with the twins and new music."

"Yeah." I hear crying in the background. He says, "Mack's throwing a fit because he missed his nap."

Staring at the plethora of plants on Cat's patio, I say, "I do the same. How are my favorite cousins?"

"Nikki and I are great." He laughs a little too hard.

I'm laughing too, so it's all good. "Fucker."

"Mack and Posey miss you. So do Poppy and I." Laird wasn't always sentimental. We were one and the same that way. It made it easy to maneuver through the rise in fame with a closed-off heart. Poppy changed all that in him and the twins even more so.

I'm not so opposed to wanting the same these days.

"It's good to be missed sometimes. Let's catch up this week about the riff and so I can see the babies." I see Cat locking her door. "I need to go."

"We'll talk soon."

Cat pulls open the door and slips into the passenger seat next to me. She doesn't feel like a passenger. She doesn't feel like a co-pilot. She feels like a partner—in crime sometimes, but a partner all the same. "Look what I found." She waggles a thick and oversized blue book in front of her. "Our yearbook."

Her excitement is contagious, but mine's not regarding the yearbook. It's because she's in my life. "Oh wow. That's great."

"We can do our research tonight."

"I had other ideas to pass the hours, but maybe we can fit it in."

She laughs, buckling her seat belt. Pleased as punch, she sits back with a huge fucking smile on her face. "This is going to be fun."

"It sure is."

"Oh, and by the way, I took my pill."

More fun indeed.

I SET a glass of wine on the table next to the lounge chair where Cat has taken up residence. "Look how cute you were, Shane." Tapping the page in the yearbook she has spread open in front of her, she looks up at me and grins.

My whole world is wrapped up in that gorgeous smile of hers.

Popularity came easily based on our looks in high school. Some people never change, putting weight on stuff that's not as important as who a person is on the inside.

I peer over her shoulder and smile when I see the girl beside me at eighteen. Leaning down, I tap the photo. "Look at that beauty. Wonder what she's up to these days?" I smirk when Cat giggles.

"No one would believe it."

"Everyone would believe it. You don't see yourself properly."

Rubbing the back of my leg, she angles her head back and puckers, calling me for a kiss. As my lips press against hers, I realize this is one in a million. A million more kisses span our lifetime, and if she lets me, I'll double it. Returning to the page, she says, "It's how I felt on the inside. Invisible to the world."

I move around to the other chair and sit down on the side facing her. I don't know what to say to make this right for her. I don't think it's something I can fix. Resting my hand on her ankle, I watch as she sits there with the sun shining in her eyes. "You were never invisible to me. I wasn't brave enough for you. I wasn't ready to be what you needed."

Sitting forward, she smiles with the sweetest expression embedded into her pretty face. "You don't have to be a knight in shining armor for me. I can save myself. I always have. But at eighteen, you were the perfect crush for me."

I move over to the end of her chair, pushing the year-book closer to her. "What about at thirty-one?"

Her cheeks pinken, and she leans forward to whisper, "At thirty-one, I get to call you husband."

Leaning forward, I push up on my knee, shoving the yearbook aside. The book hits the deck as I kiss my wife like she deserves to be. She fumbles with my shirt, dragging it up my body until I sit up and tug it off over my head. When she starts on the button to my jeans, I still her hands. "We can't. Not out here."

She looks around but then turns back with confusion, stitching her eyebrows together. "The neighbors can't see us. I don't see any houses facing us."

"It's not about the neighbors. It's about the long lenses."

"Oh . . ." She steals a quick but shuddering breath, and then says, "Let's go inside then."

I'm on my feet and scooping her into my arms. Her long hair hangs over my arms, and her giggles are a shot of happiness to my heart. I don't bother closing the door. It's dark enough in here compared to outside to fuck up some shutter speeds. I lay her on the couch, reaching down to help her take off some of those clothes, but she sits up. "No."

"No?" She was giving me every green flag. She's the one who wanted to come inside. *Fuck.* I can't say I'm not disappointed. On the outside of the jeans, I adjust my dick because they're feeling too tight with an erection.

"No. I mean, yes. God yes." Her eyes almost roll back in her head just saying the words. "I want to please you first."

"You always please me, babe."

"I know." She stands, walking me backward until the backs of my legs hit the chair. She lowers, undoing my pants and then dragging them down.

"What do you think you're doing?" She gives a little shove to my chest, causing me to sit in the chair.

Lowering to her knees, she pulls the jeans from my body, then looks up at me. "I'm hungry." Her hand rubs over my cock and goes higher to my waistband to start taking my boxer briefs off.

"Let's get you fed then." My dick springs free as the underwear is tugged down and discarded.

Sitting back on her heels in front of me, she strips her shirt away, then frees her tits from the lace wrapped around her. I reach forward, toying with her pink tips that are already hard for me.

She leans forward, dragging them along my legs as she

slides into place. Her hand takes the base, and her mouth takes the end. Swirling her tongue around, I sink lower as the feeling overwhelms my other thoughts.

Her and me. That's all that matters.

Sliding her mouth over my hard dick, the tip of her tongue teases under the ridge and then swipes over the top again. "You taste so good, like my favorite candy."

"Fuck me, baby." I dig my fingers into her hair and hold her close. When she takes me into her mouth again, I lean back and devour the view before my lids fall, and I give in to the feel, the pressure, the scrape of her teeth up my length, and the intensity of her tongue tracing the vein on her way down again.

I force my eyes open to see her suck me so hard that her cheeks hollow and her breath stalls in her chest. She comes up and gasps for air before the exquisite torture starts again. And again.

Her eyes are closed, but they open and fix on mine. I hold her head steady and start pumping into her mouth. "So fucking beautiful. You take what you need. You take everything, sweetheart."

The pace quickens, her moans becoming louder as she takes every thrust and most of my dick down her throat. When one of her hands slips down between her legs, her eyes close as her breathing jags.

"Come back, pussycat."

She looks up again, her eyes wild with desire. Her grip tightens around me, and she goes back down and up again, focused and determined. When she hums in pleasure, I lose it, fucking her mouth over and over until I'm drained of every drop.

Just when I stop, she lurches forward with her eyes

closed, moaning in her own hedonism as she comes. "Ahh."
Her head falls forward, resting on my leg as her hand rushes
and then stops.

Stroking her hair, I want to kiss her but don't. I stay
where I am while she lies on my lap, recuperating. We both
need the time to catch our breath anyway.

When she angles up, setting her chin on my leg for a few
seconds before sitting back, she then looks at me with a
peaceful grin resting on her face. She's not looking for
approval, though she'd get five times over if I were asked.
She's just happy.

I fucking love it.

"What do we have to snack on?" she asks, that serene
grin becoming a smirk.

WHILE SHE SOAKS in a bubble bath with a glass of wine she
didn't get to enjoy earlier, I go outside to clean up the mess
we left. I squat down to study the yearbook that fell open to
a different page. I had so much fun in high school. Surfing,
partying, playing with the band because it was so fucking
fun to live life without a care in the world.

Some faces are familiar, and some aren't, and then a
photo in the bottom corner catches my eye. *Catalina Farin.*
She hasn't changed much. Neither has the asshole beside
her. I chuckle, seeing a photo of us together back then.
What are the chances?

I know she'll get a kick out of seeing this, so I carry the
yearbook into the bathroom. She says, "You were right. I'm
never leaving this tub." She takes a sip of wine, then sets the
glass down. "It covers my entire body."

"Sadly, that's true." Her laughter bubbles up, reaching her eyes. *Beautiful.* Still holding the book, I say, "Look what I found."

Holding it out for her to see, her smile blooms right before my eyes. "I don't remember that picture."

"Neither do I, but I wasn't one to flip through a yearbook back then."

It's instant—her smile dashed, her eyes staring, and her body pushing to get closer to the book. "That's it, Shane."

"What's it?" I look back at the picture, trying to see what she does, but it's a normal photo. "I don't get it."

Slipping into the tub, she lies back, redirecting her gaze to the ceiling. "That's it," she repeats. Her eyes pivot to mine, and she says, "We did a project together for government class."

"I don't remember." And then I kick my own ass for sounding like I wouldn't remember time with her. It's not that. It was school, in general. *I hated it.*

She rolls her eyes. "Of course, you don't."

"Don't take it like that. I don't even remember graduation. I remember receiving our first Grammy, though."

By her indifferent expression, I'm thinking she's not impressed. "Babe, that's amazing. I don't even know how many you've won—"

"Two."

Smiling for me, she slips through the water to lean on the edge facing me. "That's incredible. I'm so proud of you."

"Thanks. What were you saying about a project in government class?"

Bolting upright, she says, "We went to the library to do research." Was I high? Possible. "It was statistics or something about the state of California."

I jerk my head back. "How the fuck do you remember that?" I shut the yearbook and set it on the counter.

"Well, I loved school, and it was with you." She takes a long drink of her wine and then stands up, soapy and slick. Fucking hell, I'm drawn to take her pink bud into my mouth and lick the bubbles away. I do because she's all mine. And she really likes my mouth on her.

But then she grabs the towel and wraps it around her as if I wasn't just seducing her. "Um . . ."

She laughs as she steps out of the tub. "I'm sorry, babe." She kisses my chin, which is all she can reach barefoot, and then starts drying off. "But we're on to something here."

"I'm still lost. Want to fill me in?"

"It's that project." Cat rushes into the bedroom, still talking. "That's the clue we needed. We need to find out what we were researching." I follow her and sit in the chair in the corner. She's doing great, so I decide to stay quiet and let the expert do her thing. She pulls on some tight pants, then flips her hair up in the towel. Standing with those fantastic tits as an utter distraction to what she's been saying, she asks, "Shane?"

My eyes dart to her. "What?"

Planting her fists on her hands, she says, "I'm going to need you to focus."

"I'm going to need you to get dressed then." At least I can still elicit a grin. Even if it is ripe with exasperation, I'll take it.

She doesn't cover up because she loves me. Coming to settle onto my lap, she kisses my cheek and takes a breath. "Whatever that project was will lead us to the answer. We need to figure out what we were assigned to do because it wasn't getting married."

"Let's ask the teacher."

"You make it sound so easy. What if we can't find him online?" Adjusting her arms around my neck, she says, "My number isn't listed out there. Yours isn't. I know the school won't give it to us."

"Don't worry." He kisses my temple. "I have my ways. I found you, didn't I?"

34

Cate

SHANE KISSES the inside of my wrist, then holds it to his chest. "I should warn you."

"I'm too comfortable to be worried. Warn away." Making a sheet angel with my free arm and leg, I ask, "How is this the most comfortable bed that ever existed? What count are these sheets?"

He chuckles. "I have no idea. I didn't buy them."

I still, looking at him on the next pillow over from me. "Who did?"

"I don't know."

Rolling onto my side, I snuggle against him and prop my leg over the top of his. If I could climb inside this man, I would. The closer, the better. "I want a bed fairy when I grow up."

"You can have mine."

Doodling across his chest with my fingertips, I ask, "Do I even want to know how many women have enjoyed this bedding and mattress?"

"We said no pasts." His tone is tempered, but he's right.

"Ah, yes, we agreed," I admit begrudgingly because my mind is already spinning, imagining a high number being pulled from a bingo basket.

"One."

Okay . . . I don't love it, but it beats two or ninety-nine. "She must have been special to be the only one before me."

"She wasn't before you, Cat. She *is* you. You're the one." He drapes his arm over his head. "Now I sound like an asshole feeding you lines."

"There can never be too much romance, Shane."

"Good." He pulls me on top of him, running his hands over my hips. "Because you're the only one I want in my bed."

"Yeah, that's too much." When his eyes widen, I laugh. "I'm kidding. I'm kidding." I lean down and kiss him, lingering against his lips. "Tell me again. I'll be serious this time."

"I'm not falling for your tricks. I can tell you're delirious."

"How can I not be? I reunited with my high school crush, who happens to be an amazing musician, though he never plays for me." He laughs, the sound rumbling around the abs I'm currently straddling, causing me to wiggle because it feels so good.

"Drums aren't usually the woo-a-girl instrument, but I'll play for you. I also play bass guitar. I clearly chose the wrong instruments to get the girls or the glory."

"It was never about your talent, babe. You got the girl anyway."

Running his hands up my back, he pulls me down and kisses my neck. He tilts to catch my eyes, and says, "I did indeed."

"Correction. It was never about your musical talent. As for your tongue—Ah!" He flips me to the bed and crashes his lips into mine. Reaching between us, I position myself at his tip, rocking to inspire him.

With our mouths attached, caressing tongues, and our hands roaming each other's bodies, he starts a slow back and forth. This time, we don't just have sex. We make love.

ONE A.M. ISN'T the hour I expected to have a private concert with Shane drumming to tracks of guitars of their recent songs. Since the studio is across the hall from his bedroom, the commute was easy at this hour.

Concert posters for Faris Wheel hang on the walls, but there are no frames, only padding to keep it soundproof from the rest of the house. The two Grammys are in a case directly in front of him. Inspiration? Motivation? Maybe both, but it makes me proud as hell as I sit for a personal drum solo.

Wrapped up in one of his long-sleeved T-shirts that has me drowning in cotton fabric, I sit in a black velvet chair in the corner with my legs tucked under me, mesmerized by his talent.

Closing his eyes, Shane loses himself in the music, letting the rhythm take over. When he opens them, the drums are loud and hit with a passion that seems to come from deep inside him, like there is no other option for him. But the way he weaves the melody in with the ear-catching beats has me astounded.

I could never deny my sexual attraction to him, and seeing him shirtless with sweat running down his forehead, the muscles in his arms and abs flexing, is making it even harder at this moment.

He puts all of himself into the song—body and soul. I can imagine he does this and more during a live performance. The sticks are dropped into a pocket hanging from what I learned is a snare drum earlier when he taught me a few paradiddles. "Are you tired?" he asks, rubbing his shoulder.

"I'm getting there, but I'm good to hang out a little longer if you want to play some more."

Spinning off his stool, he stands. "No," he replies, heading for the door. "I'm going to shower and then crash." His mood has shifted in the past hour or so since we came into his studio. It's late, and I'm sure he's exhausted, especially after that workout on the drum kit. I could barely keep my eyes open when he was inspired to play.

"Oh." I stand, coming toward him. "Alright. You can crash after playing like that?"

"Yep." He hits the switch behind me and closes the door to the room. "I had to learn that trick years ago if I wanted to sleep while on tour. I could fall asleep in the middle of an arena. Tours are loud and chaotic. We had to get sleep when and where we could the first couple of years we toured. One of us was stuck driving while the others hunkered in the back of a Suburban." We enter the bedroom, and he chuckles to himself. "I used to sleep in a sleeping bag wedged between the bass drum and a bag of cables."

"Now look at you with this glorious bed to sleep in."

Wrapping his right arm around my waist, he pulls me to him. "It's not the bed I look forward to sleeping in. It's having you here." He takes a breath that appears to sober him. "I'm going to take a shower."

Craving the closeness, I hold him to me. His heat is

intense after that workout, yet the sweat doesn't bother me, not when I'm living my very whirlwind romance. "I'll wait up for you."

"You don't have to." He kisses the corner of my eye. "You look sleepy. Go to bed. I'll be out shortly."

I step back, but he pulls me in again, cradling my head. With his lips pressed to the top of it, he whispers, "I love you."

His tone borders on a goodbye more than a good night. I look up, needing to see his eyes and hoping for insight into his feelings. I could ask a thousand questions, but I'm learning that doesn't always get me the answers with him. I don't want to read too much into something that can most likely be explained by the late hour.

He's probably just tired. The past two days have been exhilarating and exhausting. It's caught up with me, so I'm sure he's feeling the weight of it as well. "I love you, too."

We kiss before he retreats into the bathroom. When he shuts the door, a bar of light at the bottom is all that connects the two rooms. Though my chest feels empty without him as if he took that into the other room with him.

I sit on the edge of the bed, listening to the faintest sounds of the shower running. Not a peep from him, no singing while washing up. Silence. There's no sleeping when I feel like something might be wrong.

I pad across the floor and crack open the door. It's already steamy in the room from the hot water running, but not so much that I can't see him through the clear glass of the shower. With one hand pressed high to the stone wall, Shane's eyes are closed, and his head lowered.

There's very little movement, really only the water pouring over him, pounding his neck and covering his shoulders. There's such peace found in the moment, but also sadness. I want to go to him, but does he want me to?

I take the chance and strip off the T-shirt. I open the door, the sound alerting him to my presence. Opening his eyes, he lowers his arm when he sees me. And then, he offers me his hand. I slip mine in his and am pulled straight into his ardent embrace. My head is kissed, and then my cheek, the water soaking me as he douses me with sweet affection.

Reaching up, I caress his face. "Talk to me. Tell me what's going on."

He searches my eyes for a moment before he says, "I'm having trouble with my left shoulder."

The image of him leaning against the shower wall comes back, him rubbing his shoulder when he brusquely stopped playing, even the arm he held me in the bedroom. I turn to his left and kiss the arm that's holding me like I'm precious cargo despite the pain. "For how long?"

"A while." A grimace sits squarely on his face, telling me more than he has. Men and their pride. *Geez.*

"The past few months, the past year?"

"About five years on and off."

"Oh, Shane." Five years with pain? He's stronger than he needs to be and too stubborn to ask for help. I run my fingers gently over the culprit shoulder. "This is not my area of expertise, but tomorrow, I can do an assessment of sorts so we can get you in to see the right specialist. Do you think it's your rotator cuff or muscular?"

"I don't know. Both probably."

"Why haven't you had it looked at?"

He releases a sigh, then looks down as shame weighs down his brow. "I'm the third member in a band. Number one spot goes to Nikki. Two is her twin. There's no slacking.

There are no off days allowed. I have to earn my spot every time I walk onto that stage."

"I thought you guys were close."

"We are. Laird's my best friend, and I love Nikki like my own sister. But they're moving on with their lives. Tours are scheduled around what's best for them while I'm given scraps. It's not their fault. They'd never get rid of me. I can't show weakness, though. They have families now. Music is all I have."

There's so much to unpack, but he's been silently suffering, making the injury worse because he believes he's replaceable. I hug him. I don't know how to fix this, but I do recognize that he's trusted me. Over his cousins and managing team, he told me. I hold him tighter. "You have me. We'll get it looked at, and we don't need to tell anyone." When he lifts my chin and our eyes connect, I'm glad he can't tell my tears from the water raining down on us. He doesn't need to worry about me. I'll be there however he needs. "Tonight, though, let's get some rest. I'll make some calls after the holiday weekend."

"I'D HAVE a big garden with flowers overflowing the beds in the front and back of the house. Fruit trees to pick our own lemons and limes, oranges, and figs. Avocados, of course."

Standing at the edge of the pool, looking over the property, he turns back and smiles. "Of course." His mood has shifted this morning. A spark resides in his eyes as if a weight has been lifted. I'm glad he's allowing me to take on some of his burdens. That's what partners do. Though the sex this morning could have played a part in improving his mood as well. It was amazing.

"Lots of vegetables in raised beds." His beautiful back-yard has a stunning view, but there's not much space to do what I'd like to accomplish with my home. I sip my coffee, knowing I'm getting ahead of myself. "And lots of kittens."

"Kittens turn into cats."

"That's why I want them. I could never have a pet growing up. We moved around too much."

He returns to sit in the chair next to me. "Why is that?"

I shrug, something I generally do when people ask about my parents. It usually works to distract them, but he's still staring at me like he's genuinely interested. "Why did we move so much?" I repeat, giving myself time to determine whether I want to talk about this.

"Yeah, you never talk about them. All I know is you moved to La Jolla to live with your grandmother."

"I was close to her. She had a lot of health problems that she didn't take care of and passed away before she saw me graduate. That was hard because she encouraged me to go to college and inspired me to go into gerontology. If she would have had the support of a nurse or doctor, I know she would have lived longer."

His attention doesn't divert from me even when a bird starts singing from the roofline above us. "She'd be proud of you. I am."

"You are?" My heart clenches. Swoons. I'm tripping over myself in love with this man, determined to protect what we have at all costs.

"Absolutely. You're incredible and giving. You care about others and save lives."

I reach over and cover his hand resting on the table. "I appreciate that, but you do the same in a different way. You may not realize it, but you do. You make people happy by creating music that touches hearts and helps people through hard times. Your songs are played at weddings and baby showers. Music is universal. It's an art form for a reason. It evokes emotion."

He covers my hand with his other. "I love you, Cat. It means a lot when people relate to the music, but I want to tell you something. It doesn't always have to be even, fair, or tit for tat. It's okay for you to shine your brightest without me needing the spotlight. You don't need to take the credit away from you by giving it to someone else. You're amazing. That's a full sentence. Full stop."

Don't cry. Don't cry. Don't cry. A tear slips free despite my objections. I tip my head and wipe it away. His words are healing, a balm I didn't know I needed.

He trusted me with his secret. I can trust him, not only with my heart but with the past that shaped who I am.

"My dad walked out of my life when I was nine and never looked back. It's like I never existed. Last I heard, he had a new family—two daughters and the son he always wanted—with a woman out in Yuma, Arizona. It's been a few years, though, so I don't know if they're still there."

The sympathy clouding his eyes is the last thing I wanted. "This is why I don't like talking about my parents." I attempt to pull my hand back, but he doesn't let me. "It makes others feel bad for me, and I feel worse."

"It wasn't you, babe."

"What wasn't?"

"He left because he's an asshole. You don't need to keep dragging his weight around like it's yours to carry. That's on him. He's an asshole, but someone else's problem."

"I understand I'm not to blame. I was nine, though. That doesn't change the hurt I carry. He walked away because I didn't matter." I hate the shame that rushes my veins. Logic doesn't lessen the pain. "I wouldn't make a sound when he was home to avoid his temper. I had to be perfect because I understood the consequences."

I take a breath to prevent the mix of anger and frustration from rearing their ugly heads. It doesn't help. I say, "I'm not carrying that pain around because I want to, but it's instilled and embedded into who I am. So I don't talk about it. I don't think about him or his family in Yuma, my half-siblings. I think about my grandmother who loved . . ." I choke on the grief as it comes rushing back. Struggling to swallow, I lower my head, needing out of his concerned gaze.

The feet of his chair grind against the concrete as he slides it back from the table. He wraps around me from behind, resting his head in the crook of my neck. "He fucking missed out on someone extraordinary. His loss."

My throat loosens, and a breath finally enters my lungs. No reasoning ever helped heal the pain. It never did, but Shane does. I kiss the arm he's tucked under my chin and then turn to look up at him. "Thank you."

His nod is enough as he comes to sit down again, staying on the end of the seat and still holding my hand. Might as well get it all off my chest. "My mom got a job modeling in Paris when I was seventeen. She lied about having a kid and said she was twenty-five. She could pull it off since she had me at sixteen and looked young for her age."

"How long did that last?"

"Until she met a rich man to marry. They live in Bordeaux. I've never been because I've never been invited. I'm the dirty secret she carried into her marriage."

"Shit, Cat. Fucking awful. You don't talk to her?"

"I get a birthday card some years, if she remembers. She somehow managed to take credit for my hard work in college, saying I got my brains and looks from her. No money. No present. She has millions in the bank and lives the life of luxury in France. I struggled to pay my tuition. My grandmother paid for my room and board. So yeah. That's what you're getting into with me."

"Sometimes people can have it all but don't realize until they lose it." Kissing my hand, he says, "I'm not afraid of your past or fears. I can handle orderly, neat, and predictable because I know where that need now comes from." He brings me to my feet and into his arms. "I can handle you. It's a privilege, and we can handle anything as long as we're together."

I love you doesn't seem enough for how Shane makes me feel. *Safe, for the first time in my life.*

And then my leg vibrates. We look between us. I'm already holding my breath while he digs the phone from his pocket. A grin springs to his cheeks as soon as he sees the screen.

Holding it up for me, he says, "It's Mr. Waldrip."

"Who's Mr.—*Oh my God*! Our government teacher? How in the world." I bounce, gripping his arm. "Answer it. Answer it."

"Hello? Yeah, this is Shane." He plugs his other ear and walks inside the house. "Thanks for calling me back . . ."

When Shane says he has his ways, I'll never doubt him again. The man worked miracles in a matter of hours and helped heal a part of me just by being here for me. I love you is definitely not enough for how I feel about him. He's amazing. *Full stop.*

35

Shane

TIME IS TICKING like a bomb in my mind. Yet I still steal a few minutes to work through everything I've learned.

Cat likes things neat from what I remember of her apartment.

Orderly is a way of life for her.

Beige. *Fucking beige.* That motherfucking father of hers taught her to be invisible. *Or else.* I'll spend my life making her feel the opposite.

I need more time after hanging up with Waldrip to process the damage her parents willingly did to her. Pacing the bedroom, I try to collect my thoughts on her parents. She's so fucking strong and fiercely independent. It all fucking makes sense now, and I want to rage with anger. To make them pay for hurting her.

Stopping at the glass door to the outside, I stand with my arms crossed over my chest and stare into the hills and skyline of the city. She's better than me, but she's had years to deal with it. That's the thing—I can't rage in front of her. I don't want to upset her. I want her to retain the power she's created from within, not regress into the pain. So I can't make this about them. It's about her. *Only her.*

A knock on the door draws my attention. I try to adjust my face, demeanor, anything to be supportive of Cat now. I smile, seeing her cross the room. "Hey, so the call went well."

Taking her hand, I lead her into the living room. Her hair is pulled back in a ponytail, but I tuck some escaping strands behind her ear and kiss her on the cheek.

"That's good. What happened?"

"Water? I'm going to get some water." I move into the kitchen. "He said that he needs to do some research on what the curriculum was back then. It's been updated each since, so he doesn't know."

"Did you tell him it was the month of April?"

"I did." I pour from the pitcher, filling the glass. "I told him everything we knew." Sliding it across the counter to her, I add, "Except I didn't tell him we were married, or that we're dating."

"I agree." She takes the glass and is about to drink but stops and lowers it to the counter. "We have to be careful, don't we?"

This is the part that I hate, and now I've dragged her into it. "We do, or we become fodder for public consumption."

She nods, turning the glass between her fingers. "So what happens next?"

"We wait." I take a drink of water, watching her do the same, and then tap the screen of my phone to see the time. I wasted this morning sleeping in when I could have been guaranteed more time with her. Fuck it. I put it out there. "We're at forty-seven hours and thirty-six minutes."

The words hit her hard, judging by how she flinches. She lowers her glass, and a small smile appears, then grows wider. "Is that why you're so nervous?"

"I'm not nervous."

Her eyes go wide. She licks her lips, unable to stop her grin from returning. "Did you really think I was with you against my will, waiting for the hour to strike so I could run out of here?"

"Yes . . . *No*. I know you love me, babe, but I feel shitty for forcing you to spend time with me." Moving around the counter, she stands with our knees touching and looped fingers hanging from my waistband. So casual, like this is a normal Sunday for us. I want it to be. So badly.

"Truth?"

"Truth." I run my hands along her shoulders, needing to touch her and always be close to her.

"I would have answered the door if you had come back. I would have taken your call. I would have gone to Deer Lake if you asked. That's the thing, Shane. You gave up on us, but I never did." She leans against me, so I dip my hands down her back, keeping her close. "I didn't date. Although I was mad at you and hurt, I was no good for anyone else."

"You're perfect to me." Holding her in my arms, I stroke the back of her head, so fucking grateful to have her here. "So you're taking off in . . ." I tap the phone again. "Thirty-one minutes?"

Lifting, she kisses my chin. "You're not getting rid of me that easily."

I dip her down to kiss her neck, slowly working higher under her musical laughter. I kiss her lips, then look into her eyes. "It won't be easy being my wife, but if we can get through the toughest days, I'll give you a beautiful life."

Bringing her upright, I cup her face and kiss her again,

never tiring of this second chance I've been given. And then my phone buzzes. Fuck.

Every time it does that, dread fills my gut. I never want to see her upset or jealous over another woman again. She doesn't deserve that.

Cat reluctantly backs away, resting her hip against the counter. I turn to look at my phone beside me. "Mr. Waldrip," I announce with relief washing through me.

Her reaction matches mine. "What does the text say?"

Hovering over it, I rest against the cold stone and read, "It was a state government statistics project. We were researching . . . oh, uh." I glance over at her. "Marriage and death certificates in California."

She takes off running and flops on the couch, pulling her laptop onto her legs. She types faster than me, so I sit beside her as she pulls up the information for the state of California. While she scans, I point at a link about obtaining marriage licenses. "There."

Clicking the link takes us to a new page. "No to courthouse ceremonies. It wasn't at a venue. No to church." She glances at me and smirks.

"I'd burn in the pews for all my sins."

She nudges me with her elbow. "I still love you, though."

Wrapping my arm around her back, I say, "That's all that matters."

Dragging her finger in front of the screen, she pauses again and shoots me a nervous look. "This one? Online?"

"I think so. It's the only possibility that works for us."

When she clicks, it takes us to another page of information. We both take a few minutes to read, and then I sit back, giving her room to finish. "I didn't know you could get married online. Did you?"

"No." She huffs, sounding defeated. "This doesn't give us any helpful information. Where do we go from here?"

"This happened thirteen years ago last month—"

"Online licenses seem really advanced for that time period." She switches to a new search bar and enters online marriages in California to see what pops up. "It's been around for fourteen years."

"That's a little coincidental."

"But even if we did it online, we would have been required to appear in person to make it official. That's changed since." She falls back on the couch cushion and sighs. "We're never getting this solved."

"I have an idea."

Angling her head, she asks, "What?"

"We need to talk to Roberta."

My phone vibrates against my leg, and hers by the glare I'm shot. "Jesus, Shane. You're going to kill me with the texts."

I'd chuckle, but I think she's serious. Pulling it from my pocket, I see a message from Tommy:

> The car will pick you up at ten a.m. on Wednesday. Enjoy the day off tomorrow.

I look at her. And though she's feigning complete disinterest, I know she's on edge from it. "It was Tommy, my manager. We have two shows next weekend."

"When do you leave?"

"Wednesday."

"The county offices open on Tuesday. I can't go this week, though. My schedule is booked full." She sets her laptop on the coffee table, then slides onto my lap.

I slip my hands up the back of her T-shirt, and say, "What if I go?"

"It might work better for us. She loves you." Wrapping her arms around my neck, she says, "In the meantime, it looks like we have another thirty-six hours. How should we spend them?"

Squeezing her fine ass, I stare into her playful eyes, reading a whole book of naughty ideas populating the irises. "I have a few ideas."

"I thought you might."

I kiss her, then rise to carry her into the bedroom. We've fucked all over this house, but this time, I want to savor our time together.

TUESDAY 8 A.M. sharp

"YOU'RE HERE BRIGHT AND EARLY," Roberta says, hoisting herself up on the stool that's too tall for her legs. "My first account of the day."

"Wanted to make sure I got in to see you."

"You're seeing me. How can I assist you today, Mr. Faris? Are you still Scooby Doo-ing the mystery marriage?"

"Sure are." I rest on my elbow, leaning in. "I wanted to get a little more information, and I'm hoping you can help me with that."

Poised with her fingers over the keyboard, she says, "What am I searching for?"

"How was the marriage license sent? Was it an online form back then, through email, fax, or . . .?"

She types, stares at the screen, and then types again. "*Ah.* Submitted online." Tapping the screen, she says, "Did I tell you that you and Mrs. Faris were part of our original beta program?" My mind is still stuck on the Mrs. Faris part of that question and how much I like the sound of that.

"No, you didn't mention it, Roberta. What does that mean exactly?"

"We've had so many people come in over the years to finalize the marriage."

My gut twists. My chest tightens. I start rubbing the knot forming near my heart to loosen it while the worst flashes through my head. Is she saying— "What does finalize mean?"

"There was a glitch in the system. Some people got their emails, and some didn't." Spinning on her stool, she leans on the counter in front of her. "We were testing an online system to move from hard copies . . ." Her hands roll into the air above her head. "And put everything into the clouds. It was also being tested in case of emergencies. Natural disasters, pandemics, the ocean swallowing up California like they've predicted forever. That kind of thing."

I'm still staring at her when she sits back like she's wanting to chat all day while my life is falling apart. When I don't say anything, she continues, "Anyway, you were part of the program. The license was filed as if it was complete, but now I see you never got the follow-up email. I wasn't looking at the file as a whole. I was looking at the license since that's what you were both verifying. The license is correct. The marriage . . . "

Please don't say it. Please don't say it. Please— "Mystery solved. You're not married, after all." She's smiling like she's done me a favor. "All that upset for nothing."

It's for something alright. I've not only had my life ripped out from under me, but I no longer have my wife. Now I realize they were one and the same.

I can't lose Cat. *I can't.* "How do we finalize it?"

"Easy. In the beta cases, the license is being honored. Complete the second step, and you're good to go."

"What's the second step?"

"Getting married."

36

Shane

GET MARRIED.

Roberta makes it sound so easy. *She even said it. "Easy. Get married."*

What the fuck am I going to do? Cat's not going to want to get married. Not when we've been trying to get divorced this whole time.

Fuck.

I pull into the parking lot of Parkdale Retirement Home and lock up her Toyota. Though it's tempting to let thieves steal it. The air-conditioning is shit, the check engine light is on half the time, and the steering wheel is tight on the turns.

Spying my Ferrari parked away from other cars, I smile, knowing she'd taken good care of it this morning on her drive in.

The buzzer sounds, alerting me before the doors slide open. I nod at the camera in thanks before stepping inside and catching Cat's eyes. She waves, my pretty girl, my gorgeous wife. *Mine.*

I'm a fucking caveman, but I have no shame. I'm not losing her, not again.

Holding her finger in the air, she nods. I catch her drift and detour to a table by the window to wait for her to finish with her patient. Staring out the window, I think about how I'll tell Cat about us not being married. Or if I just let it go and pretend I never heard different than we did before.

"Mr. Big and Strong is back."

I turn to find the little lady from last time standing behind the chair next to me. "Mrs. Winston, right?"

"You can call me Maggie." She eases into a chair like she was invited. I don't mind. She was entertaining last time. She looks over her shoulder like she's making sure no one's eavesdropping, and then asks, "You're here to see Nurse Cate?"

"I am." I glance across the room at her, sitting beside the patient and holding her hand. She's the kindest soul I've ever known.

"Love runs deep like a river through your veins. No matter how long you're apart, the other person is always with you."

I'm feeling seen in ways that make me shift in the chair, but I push past that and reply, "It does for me."

"It does for her, too. She doesn't talk about you because she's always so uptight." I smile along with her, appreciating those qualities about Cat now that I know where they stem from—strength. "But I also see the change. She's a pretty girl, but she carried sadness in her eyes that even a smile couldn't hide."

"I don't remember sadness. I only remember sunshine."

Touching me gently on the wrist, she says, "That's because she shines for you. That's how love works when you find your person." I have a feeling she knows this for a fact. She checks her watch. "Want to watch *Wheel of Fortune* with me?"

Cat looks like she's going to be caught up for a while. "I'd love to, Maggie." I stand and then assist her getting up.

She quickly latches onto my arm, leading me straight for the ugly beige couch in the middle of the room. "Invite me to the wedding."

"What wedding is that?"

She looks back at Cat. When she turns back to me, she smiles. "I'm not going to live forever, so hurry up and make her your wife."

"I intend to."

THIRTY-FIVE MINUTES LATER...

MAGGIE HAS SLEPT through the show more than she's watched it. But every time her eyes opened, she looked to make sure I was still here. So I stay until I get a tap on my shoulder. "Hi," Cat whispers. "Want to go outside?"

Maggie perks up and looks in my direction. "It was good to see you again."

"You, too."

"Maggie, do you think Shane's still my Marty?" I have no idea what Cat means, but she's smiling like it's a good thing.

Maggie rests her arm on the back of the couch and angles toward her. "No."

"No?" Cat asks, surprised. "I thought—"

"No. This is your Henry, Nurse Cate." Maggie reaches

her hand out, and Cat takes hold of it between both of hers. "It's not about one kiss. It's about a lifetime, an eternity together, creating a family, and loving each other through the years." Maggie says, "Martys are fun. Henrys are forever."

Turning back to me, Maggie taps her watch. "Seal the deal, Mr. Big and Strong. Time is a tickin'.."

I wink, and she winks right back. Cate takes my hand when I come around the couch, and says, "She's a spitfire."

"She sure is."

We walk into the sunshine and down to the corner. Holding my fob for me, she says, "No dings."

It's funny how that car used to be my pride and joy. Now it's the cargo inside. "Good to hear." I hand her the Toyota keys as we stroll to the Ferrari. "It was good to see you in action."

"It's good to see you, too," she says. "I have to say if I weren't already charmed by you . . ." She signals back to the building. "Seeing you in there with Maggie would have done it."

"She's a nice lady and thinks highly of you."

Humility creases her cheeks into a smile. My sweet girl. "Before I forget, I got you a diagnostic assessment with Dr. Lazlo in Beverly Hills. Unfortunately, he's so booked, he can't see you for six weeks."

Always thinking of me. "Thank you. I appreciate you doing that for me."

"I'll help however I can. I'll send you the details so you can check the tour schedule for any conflicts." She starts to lean in for a kiss but stops herself and looks back at the building. Taking my hand, she pulls me to the other side of the car. "Dragging me into the shadows to have your way with me?"

"I wish." She throws her arms around my neck and kisses me instead. It's a solid substitute. Pulling back, she sinks back on her heels, but since she's standing on a curb, she's closer to eye level. "So what happened this morning? Did you talk to Roberta?"

"I talked to Roberta." Why does doing the right thing feel so fucking wrong?

"And? What did she say?"

I run my fingers through my hair and glance toward the intersection. It's not the light that has my attention. It's a long lens. *Fuck!* "Get down."

"What the hell?" She's lying in the dirt, pushing herself up and then dusting her hands off. "You got my white coat dirty."

"Sorry, babe." I peek up, still spying the lens just above the bushes at the corner.

She huffs. "I like the way you get to lie low on the cement while I'm tossed in the flower bed. What the hell?"

"There's paparazzi taking photos of us."

She whips her head back to look, her hair flying over her shoulders. "Where?" she asks.

"Down at the corner. They're not great at hiding. Most of the time, they don't bother. They want that picture, the face front photo. It sells better for them." She scoots to the curb next to me and sits with her head lowered. "A photo of us kissing . . ." I scrub a hand over my face. "Fuck."

"What do we do?"

"I'll call Rochelle. She'll take care of it."

Wrapping her arms around her legs, she asks, "Who's Rochelle?"

"She's the one who handles these situations for the bands at Outlaw Records."

"Does she also happen to be the one who gets you

phone numbers not listed and addresses of places of business?"

Chuckling, I sit beside her. "I'm not one to give away my sources."

She nudges me and then laughs. "So tell me, rock star, how long do we need to hide out?"

"Well, that's where it gets tricky. We need a plan."

Her eyes light up like Christmas morning has come early. "I love a plan."

Two hours . . . I managed to distract the paparazzi long enough to get her inside so she could work, but I ended up driving around half of LA to keep them busy.

Five Weeks Later . . .

THE PHOTOS NEVER CAME OUT. Neither did the truth about the marriage.

I never claimed to be the hero of her story. I was always meant to be the villain. So I left the truth out by omission. She even lost her house because of this mess. I don't want to be the one who breaks her heart over it twice. *Kill the messenger . . . yeah, no thanks.*

I've wanted to tell her but we've both been busy, and I don't want to waste the time I do get with her on frivolous details like, *"You know how we thought we were married for the past year? We're not. Want to head down to the courthouse and get the deed finalized?"* Yeah, that doesn't roll off the tongue. You know what does? Her sweet cli—

"Yes. Yes. Yes, lord of the stage." *She gets me every time with it.*

"Fuck yes!" I hit my peak just as she reaches hers. Our bodies align in a release of ecstasy. But it's when we're lying in the aftermath, Cat cuddled to my side, that I finally get the nerve to say, "Move in with me."

Her breathing had been steady, but it stops altogether. Lifting onto an elbow, she finds my eyes through the moonlight in her bedroom. Before she has time to overthink it, I caress her cheeks and ask, "Will you move in with me, babe?"

Resting her hand over my heart, she replies, "I want to live with you, but you live so far from my assignments. I leave by six to make it to work by eight when I stay over there."

"There's nothing reasonable about my request. I stay here when we're together because I don't have a morning job to report to. So I get it. But I want us together. I want to come home from the road and have you there. I want your stuff and your books around my living room, your mugs in my cabinet. I want you lying on the chaise at the end of a long day like you love to do. Cat, I want you."

She lies back down, her head on my chest and her leg over mine like I hadn't said anything at all. "Babe?" I whisper.

"I want all those things with you, too." Tilting her head up again, she says, "It's a really long commute two times a day, upward of two hours in either direction."

"I'll buy you a house. Anywhere you want it. You can have your garden and flowers filling the beds. Kittens. I'll buy you as many kittens as you want even though they become cats. Anything you want."

Sliding up higher, she strokes her fingers through my hair and smiles. "Let's start with what we have and grow from there. For you, I'll commute. When you're touring, I can stay at the apartment."

"Or you can come with me. Not give up your career. I know how much you love it. Just to the show in Albuquerque. I can fly you out Friday after work. We'll come back Sunday. What do you think?"

"I'd love to see you play live, lord of the stage." She can't even say it with a straight face. It surprises me she can climax to it. That makes two of us.

"I still can't get over the fact you were the secret woman Shane was dating." Nikki hugs Cat again when we run into each other backstage.

"It's been a whirlwind," Cat replies.

"All the best romances are," she says. "Hey, can I ask you a favor? This dress has a hook that's come undone . . ."

While they work on the wardrobe malfunction, Laird says, "Poppy approves." He laughs. "Not that you need our approval by any means, but we're more than a band. You know that, right?"

"I know that." We bring it in for a back clap and push apart again. "Where is this coming from? Need a babysitter and buttering me up?"

"The twins do miss you. Where have you been hiding?"

"We're moving in together."

"That's a big step." If he only knew all the other steps we've been through. "If you're happy, I am. You and Cat should come around when we're back in town."

I look toward the sunlight when a garage is opened nearby. Crossing my arms over my chest, I say, "I want to. I want her to meet Poppy and the twins. We'll make plans when we return."

Tommy whistles. "Get your asses over here. You're being announced."

I slip to Cat's side as she turns to look for me. "Hey," she says, "break a leg. Just not yours." She never fails to make me smile.

"You know where to go?"

"Tommy said he'll help me find my seat."

"Good." I wrap my arm around her shoulders as we walk toward the stairs that lead to the stage. "Stay close to him. Crowds can be finicky."

"Don't worry about me, babe. Just have fun. I will be."

I kiss her quick as my sticks are handed to me. Watching her walk away is fucking painful. At least I have the memory of what she did to me in the dressing room to keep me company while we're apart.

The lights go out, and I run up the stairs first to settle onto the stool. A roadie hands Laird his guitar stage right, and Nikki waits just off stage left, ready to run out and kick into the first song. Standard operating procedure.

I'm not looking for them. I'm looking for Cat. With the stage lights out, I can't see jack shit, though I can hear the noise of the crowd grow louder with the two of us out here.

I count us in and slam down on drums. The lights come up and kick into the song Laird and I worked on. It has a sick opening beat and was made to kick off the set. Nikki runs out, waving to the crowd before putting her own guitar on and taking center stage at the mic.

Left of her foot, I see my wife. So goddamn beautiful dancing to our music.

It doesn't take but half a song for our eyes to connect. I play the rest for her.

Four songs end, and Tommy changes places with her. I keep playing, and my hands know where to go all on their own. My shoulder is already giving me trouble, though. Next week is the appointment.

A scream, a fight, and beer flying in the air has Nikki pointing at where security is needed. When I see where she's pointing, I stand at attention, noticing the scuffle. I hit the notes but don't see Cat.

Sitting again, I try to get a better view, but security is in the way. I lean left, then right. There's no good angle to check on my wife. And then I see her being shoved into Tommy from a fucking asshole in the audience.

I throw my sticks and run before thinking about what to do otherwise. Jumping off stage, I head to the railing and lunge into the crowd with my fist meeting the fucker's face.

"YOUR SHOULDER IS BROKEN. You're going to need surgery," the medic says, "and you might have a broken rib or two. We'll need x-rays to determine what you didn't mess up out there."

"You should see the other guy," I reply, eyeing Cat next to me.

"I did. He's not faring better."

"I hope he's faring worse."

The medic doesn't laugh, which is probably the appropriate response. "Your knuckles are swelling. Keep the ice pack on them and decide whether the ambulance will take you to the hospital to get your shoulder set or you're riding in the private SUV."

"I'm not riding in an ambulance." I smirk, giving Cat a

wink. "The SUV works. Anyway, I have my personal nurse with me."

The medic starts scribbling something and then stands to dig through his bag.

Cat whispers, "That's one way to handle a bad rotator cuff. In a blaze of glory."

"Worked out, didn't it?"

"Not for the other guy."

"Damn right. That's what he gets for shoving a woman." I lower my voice so only she can hear me. "That's what he gets for shoving my wife." I can make myself feel bad. Who shoves a woman? Even more so, mine?

She has been summing me up with every once-over she gives. Kicking into nurse mode, she asks, "Are you in pain?"

"Not a bit. Whatever they gave me is working, baby."

Shaking her head, she laughs. "Good to know."

The medic returns to the catering table, where we were propped up when we were rushed backstage. The guy sits in front of her, and asks, "How's your arm?"

"It's bruised. It's definitely not broken. See?" She winces when she moves it, but she's right. It doesn't look broken, according to my uneducated opinion.

He takes her temperature, then checks her blood pressure. "All normal, which is good under the circumstances. Are you currently pregnant or might be without prior knowledge?" Cat hesitates, so he says, "It's standard to ask. You can just say no if you're not."

"I'm thinking." *She's thinking?* What kind of answer is— oh shit.

"Are you pregnant, babe?"

Her eyes dart to mine as panic rises inside them. "I don't know."

What the fuck?

I take her hand in mine, fighting through the pain in my shoulder. Tears well in her eyes when she says, "I might be."

Turning back to the medic, she says, "I'm a week late, but I was under a lot of stress recently, so I didn't feel it was necessary to take a test just yet."

"Would you like to take a test now?" he asks, keeping his voice down.

"I probably should."

37

Cate

I'M PREGNANT.

As soon as we arrived at the hospital, I was sent one way, and Shane was rushed off in the other direction. If he had his shoulder taken care of years ago, I wouldn't be standing in this unfamiliar city in a hospital I've never been in before all by myself dealing with this life-altering information. *Damn.*

I'm not leaving the hospital until he does, but worst-case scenario, how long could that be? Hours? Days? I press my hand gently over my stomach and walk down the hall toward the waiting room. Shane is in surgery. Luna's in New York at a premiere. I'm stuck in Albuquerque. *Alone.*

Sort of . . . I shift my crossbody bag around to my back so I can wrap my arms around my belly. I know it's too early, but I steal one moment to feel the blooming of love for the new little life in my tummy.

Shane's not here to share the news. I wish I could tell my

grandmother. She'd be thrilled. She once told me I would break my parents' pattern and be a wonderful mother one day. It was like she could see what I'm struggling to process.

I'm going to be a mother.

I can't wait to tell Shane.

Being single for so long, I didn't dare let my heart hope for something this amazing. Kittens were easier to imagine than me meeting the man of my dreams and having a baby. But somehow that dream found me anyway, just like Shane.

Spying the nurses' station ahead, I make my way over. "Hi, I'd like to check the status of a patient."

Without looking up from the monitor, she asks, "Patient's name?"

"Shane Faris. We arrived together, and he was taken into surgery."

Her eyes slide to me. "Are you related? I can only release that information to relatives." She's not unkind and only following the rules, but the rules suck when it comes to wanting details about the man I love, and he's being gatekept from me. *And then it occurs to me . . .*

I don't have the energy or time to make up an elaborate story to trick her into looking the other way while I sneak into his room to wait. The truth should be enough in this case. "I'm his wife."

Her eyes narrow in the slightest, but she turns to the computer and starts typing. "Name?"

"Cate, although he calls me Cat, which is cute and only something he does, but my real name is Catalina Far—"

"It's right here on the approved list, Mrs. Faris." She smiles at me like I've broken through her tough exterior. "Your husband listed you on the form before he went in. I see there's a typo, though. Someone entered Farin instead of Faris. I'll get it corrected."

"One letter apart." It's funny how little things like the letters of our last name brought us together in homeroom junior year. All these years later, I'm having his baby while he's getting his rotator cuff fixed.

"What?" she asks, looking at me again.

"Nothing. Thank you."

"You're welcome. The status shows prep. Your husband is still being prepped for surgery. The doctor doing the surgery hasn't yet arrived. It will be a while before you'll get the first update." She uses her hand to guide me. "The waiting room is ahead, and although the cafeteria is closed, vending machines in the public lounge on the second floor have coffee and snacks. It's just one elevator ride up."

"Thank you again."

I start down the hall under sterile light that's not flattering on anyone while searching for any recognizable faces. I don't find anyone else waiting on him after a quick sweep of the room we've all been relegated to, which feels sad to me. *Alone again.*

I sit down, my mind still reeling with concern for Shane. Though I know this isn't a life-threatening surgery, it's still going to take time to recover. If I had to guess, he's not the best patient, though I'll be happy to take care of him.

Having the best news of my life and no one to share it with has tears welling in my eyes.

I'm pregnant.

I'm going to have a baby.

With Shane.

"Cate?"

I look up, and the quick action causes a tear to fall down my cheek. Tommy is standing in front of me. "Are you okay?" he asks. The concern wrenching his eyes down on the outside corners seems like it would be reserved for his family, the bands he works with, or his friends. *Not for me—* a woman Tommy met a few hours ago and the person responsible for Shane getting injured. But there it is, comforting and earnest.

A nod is managed, but I'm too choked up and afraid I'll start sobbing if I speak. He's kind enough not to force me. "Would you like to wait with me and the others?"

"Yes." I stand, and he waits until I'm ready to walk. He starts down a different hall than the one I came down.

"They put us in a private room to lessen any disturbances the band would cause."

"With fans?"

"Yes. Can you imagine Nikki hanging around, worrying about her cousin while being mobbed by fans? Not a good scenario." He knocks and then opens the door. "It's me."

Laird stands when he sees me. Nikki's on her phone beside her brother but quick to hang up. Tommy shuts the door behind us and then takes a seat on the rolling stool in the corner, leaving the couch for me and Nikki.

Nikki comes toward me first with her hands out. Taking mine in hers, she asks, "How are you doing? Are you okay? Hurt?" Pulling me into her arms, she's warm and welcoming, hugging me like I'm an old friend and not a high school acquaintance she barely knew. Leaning back, she looks me over. "I heard you were hurt."

"I'm fine. There's a little bruising on my hip but no swelling. I'm a bit sore, but nothing is broken."

Laird remains standing by her side, and I've never seen such a big guy look shy. "Am I that intimidating?" I tease, hoping to break the ice.

He smiles, and I can see so much of Shane in it that I feel close to him simply because of the resemblance. I also know he's someone I can joke with. He chuckles, light and not from the heart, but we're all in the same circumstance—waiting to hear an update about Shane.

Rubbing a hand over his head, he replies, "Kind of." As a group, we laugh. It feels good and like I'm a part of their club. "It's going to be a long night. Do you want to take the couch?"

"Please sit," I say to Nikki and move to sit on the other end from her.

Laird stands at the window, but with no view and it being too dark to see anything, he makes his way to a chair at a table in the corner. Tommy's sitting in the other chair.

There's silence for a moment, and then Laird starts talking about Mack sitting up on his own. The superstar lead singer of one of the biggest bands in the world melts. "Ah, my little Mackie. That's good."

They talk about a lot of everything to nothing and then sitting peacefully in silence and playing on their phones. I join in here and there, but so much is on my mind that I struggle to focus.

Nikki shows me a photo of her daughter, and Laird shares pics of his twins. My heart swells in happiness thinking about the secret I'm literally carrying. When the guys leave for coffee, Nikki says, "I heard the medic ask you about being pregnant." She allows space for a response, but my throat is tightening as tears spring to my eyes again. "You don't have to tell me anything, but if you need a friend . . ." *She knows.* Reaching across the couch, she gives my hand a little squeeze, and it's enough for me to know she'd listen and be there for me.

I swallow the lump in my throat but don't speak. The effort will be raw, and I'm too close to the edge of breaking down—happiness over a baby and worry why this surgery is taking so long. I turn my hand and squeeze her hand back.

The door opens and we step apart. A nurse comes in and I'm on my feet and then Nikki follows. The nurse says, "Surgery is going well. They'll be wrapping up soon, and then the doctor will come speak to you, Mrs. Faris."

Nikki steps forward as if she were answering roll call. "It's Crow actually."

Laird and Tommy approach her from behind, carrying steaming cups of coffee.

Smiling awkwardly between us, I realize what is about to happen too late to stop it. The nurse says, "I was referring to Mrs. Faris, the patient's wife."

Pins dropping come to mind when everyone turns to stare at me. "Thank you," I say, my tone trembling.

The awkward tension couldn't be thicker. She slips out of the room like she's escaping. As soon as the door closes, nothing changes. We stand there in silence.

Laird comes to stand behind Nikki, fortifying their twin powers together. Although I want to laugh at my inside joke, I can't. They aren't doing a *them-against-me* thing. They also couldn't be nicer, more supportive, or more welcoming. But standing here, I understand how Shane could feel like a third wheel.

Tommy sets his coffee down on the table and pulls his phone out like he's ready to call the police. "Are you and Shane married?"

The question doesn't throw me into a panic, and I'm not made to feel intimidated in any way. I also know this probably wasn't how Shane wanted them to find out either. I won't lie, and I can't avoid a direct question. "We are married."

The words feel strange, not in a bad way, but in a

getting-to-know-you way. I'm sure one day they'll roll off my tongue without a second thought.

I'm smiling to myself when I look up to find their mouths open. Nikki asks, "Do his parents know? Do yours?"

The question doesn't sting as much as it would have not too long ago. Because of Shane, I'm healing. "No. No one does, except the people in this room."

"And you shared the news with us first?"

"Shane loves you, but he also trusts you."

I'm not sure what tips her over, but red blotches cover her chest and throat when tears fill her eyes. "Cate, oh my God." She throws her arms around, hugging me so tight. "Welcome to the family."

Maybe it's the words or the sentiment, the baby news, or that I've just admitted I'm married to Shane Faris—not because of a mistake but because I love him and want to be. I finally let myself cry all the joy I've been holding inside since I got the test results back. Dropping my head to her shoulder, I embrace her. Now that they know one of our secrets, I can't wait to share the other news.

Laird nudges Nikki, and says, "Welcome to the family, Cate." It's a hug fest all around. I hug him and then Tommy because I can see the sincerity in their demeanors. Shane would want them to know, and the support has replaced any awkward tension.

"Oops, I lied. Accidentally," I say, realizing someone outside the room knows. "My best friend Luna knows because I told her when I found out Shane and I were married." My head wobbles as I explain, "This was before Shane knew, though, and before we were dating. It was when we still thought it was a mistake. Not for real, like it is now."

I spoke too soon or said too much because their eyes

have widened as they stare at me rambling. Laird asks, "How did Shane not know you were married?"

"Well—"

"Hello, folks." The doctor walks in and looks around the room. "I have to say it's quite the honor to meet you." The comment doesn't seem to faze them as much as mine did. "And to operate on the great Shane Faris."

"How is he?" I ask, my feet glued to the spot where I stand, too nervous to crowd the family out.

"Great. He did well and is in recovery." Turning to me, he says, "When you get back to Los Angeles, he'll need to get in with a local doctor regarding follow-ups, physical therapy, and recuperation."

"We have someone we're working with," I say. The others redirect their attention to me. "He already has an appointment set up for next week."

"Great. Get with the nurses, and we can get the files sent over." He rocks back on his heels, smiling and looking relaxed. That's a good thing. That means the surgery was a success, so I'll take that reaction. "This isn't a surgery we normally require an overnight stay for unless you think it might be best. Otherwise, he'll be ready for discharge in the next two hours."

Tommy says, "Thanks, Doc." His eyes go to the twins. "If we can leave by three a.m., we'll have a better chance of getting out undetected and can have him in his own bed by seven. I'll call to get the plane ready."

Nikki says, "Thank you, Doctor. We appreciate you taking care of him."

"My pleasure." He holds out a clipboard. "Do you mind signing an autograph for my daughter? She's a huge fan of yours."

"Not at all. What's her name?"

They go about signing and talk a minute about his daughter. Before he leaves, I ask, "When can I, we, see him?"

He replies, "Shortly. The nurse will be in to take you over to see him."

A collective sigh of relief fills the room, and we chat until we are taken down the hall to see him. My heart skips with every step I take, little nerves kicking in, excited to tell him the news.

Stopping outside the door, the nurse says, "Preferably one person at a time. Once he's fully alert, though, you can all go in."

Tommy says, "You're family."

"Oh, right." I step aside for Nikki and Laird.

Laird smiles. "That's you, Cate. You're family."

"Go on in," Nikki says. "He'll be happy to see you."

I'm trying my best, but they're making it really hard not to cry. "Thank you."

Nikki rubs my back as I press my hand to the door and open it ever so gently. The room is dim with only a small lamp putting out light. A tray beside the bed has a pitcher and a cup next to it. But hearing his steady heartbeat on the monitor has mine beating faster.

It's not until I close the door that my eyes fully adjust, and I see him. I walk to the bed and stand at the railing. His eyes are closed, his breath even, and his hair still stupidly sexy. There's no pretense in his build, no ego to check. He's not a rock star but the love of my life.

I slip my hand under his and stand, studying the bandage and how they wrapped him. Would I have done it differently to make sure he's had the best care? It looks like they did a good job. So I take off my nurse's cap and stand by my husband.

His lids slowly open, the smallest of urges tugging the

corners of his mouth up when he sees me. "Did I survive, or did I weasel my way into heaven?"

I cover his hand with my other as well. "You're right here with me, babe." I start to debate whether I should wait to tell him until we're home and he's fully awake and aware. *Home?* I don't even call my apartment home.

"That's the only place I want to be."

"The surgery went well."

Shane nods but doesn't seem as interested in that topic. He takes a breath and wraps his hand around mine. "I've been meaning to talk to you."

I laugh. "And this is the right time?"

"On the edge of good pain meds and reality . . . yeah, feels like the right time."

Sliding the railing down, I lean down to kiss his head, and whisper, "What do you want to talk about?"

"Let's get married."

"Those must be good drugs." I slide my finger down his nose, grinning. "Did you forget? We're already married."

"No, Cat," he says, his tone dropping and taking a turn. "Will you marry me? Forget about the school project. I want my life to be tied to yours in every way possible. I want the vows exchanged, the kiss at the altar. The honeymoon. All of it." I'm shocked he can waggle his brows in this condition. "I want you and to raise a family together."

"Shane," I say, but it's softer and has my heart burrowed in it. "I want that, too. Everything. The life, the family, the love, the vows." I smile. "I want a family with you and to create our own home together."

Home. It's not about the house. It's about us. I found my home in him. He's found his in me.

He asks, "So that's a yes?"

"That's a yes."

We're about to kiss, but he stops and pushes back into the pillow to see my eyes. "Hey," he says, rubbing his thumb over my cheek. "Why the tears?"

"I'm happy." I lean over and kiss him. His arm comes around as our mouths embrace. When our tongues touch, the slow dance begins. "We can't do this here."

"Sure we can." A drowsy smile hangs on his face, reminding me of the meds he's on, which appear to be doing a solid job. "We're getting married." His lids dip closed for a few seconds before he opens them again, and asks, "How'd the test turn out?"

The debate ended the moment he asked. I lean in and kiss him again, and with my lips still pressed to his, I whisper, "You're going to be a daddy."

His right arm comes around my waist to hold me closer. "Really?"

The tears I kept restraining now freely flow down my cheeks. "Yes. I'm pregnant."

He lifts but then winces in pain. "I love you so much, Cat." I stay closer, so he doesn't have to move at all. "More than anything."

"I love you, too, babe. More than anything."

"I want you to hear this straight from my heart." I wait with bated breath, and then he says, "I'm going to be the best damn husband and dad I can be for you and our babies. I promise you that."

We haven't been together all that long even when counting the last time and that kiss at the bonfire, but this feels right for us, and I know he'll keep his promise to give us a beautiful life.

We kiss once more before my feet land back on the tiles. "So we're going to bust you out of this place and get you home so I can take care of you. How are you feeling?" I press my hand to his forehead.

"I'm getting married and having a baby. I'd say life is pretty fucking grand."

Even on meds, he's a handful and all mine. "I think you're going to live."

38

Shane

"A little to the right. The table is blocking my view."

Cat picks up her mat and shuffles closer to the pool. "Here?"

"Perfect."

She bends away from me in the downward dog pose, causing me to shift my—*fuck*. Okay, that fucking hurt. I use my right arm this time and tuck it behind my head to watch my wi—fiancée do yoga on the deck this fine morning.

The good life.

And then the meds kick in, and my eyelids grow heavy again.

I wake up to see Cat asleep next to me, curled on her side with her hand on my stomach. I reach over and stroke her head, not meaning to wake her but in appreciation of her being here. She canceled her week to stay and take care of me and take me to the doctor.

She lifts her head, worry gripping her gaze. "Is everything okay?"

I touch her again, letting her silky hair flow through my fingers. "It's perfect."

Her grin widens as she sits up, shifting to lean against the headboard. "You have a broken shoulder, and life is perfect?"

"Yes." I start to adjust, so she helps arrange the pillows to support my back when I sit up. "I'll heal in no time. You heard the doctor. And he called me a star—"

"Yes, yes. He called you a superstar patient."

"And he wasn't referring to my fame."

"You sure about that?" she teases, her laughter shaking her shoulders. "I kid. I kid." She taps my nose. "You've actually been a really good patient. I expected a lot more whining."

Leaning over to the point I know I can before it hurts, I wait. "Sorry to disappoint." She meets me halfway. Partners.

"Not a disappointment. I thought you'd need me more."

I rub her leg and look at her face, not liking the sadness that has permeated her features. "You know I need you. As a matter of fact, I could use some special attention right now under the covers, Nurse Cate." I lift the blanket to show her that I haven't lost my desire for her.

"You're incorrigible, Shane Faris." She climbs out of bed, padding toward the bathroom.

Still holding the covers, I ask, "That's a no, right?"

"Yes."

"It's a yes?"

"No." And then I hear her vomit. "Ugh. It's the second time today."

I drop the covers because I realize we're entering a new relationship era.

"WHAT IS THIS?" Cat walks around the back of the vehicle, taking it in.

"It's your new car. An SUV technically."

"I have a car." She points across the driveway. "The Toyota."

"Now you have a new one." I present with both hands out. "A Volvo."

Her gaze bounces between me and the SUV. I can tell she likes it because her eyes have brightened, but she doesn't like that she likes it so much. "You can't give me this gift, babe. It's too expensive."

Confused, I ask, "What do you mean?"

Her eyes find mine across the top of the hood, and she laughs. "I know money is no object—"

"Money's an object that I like to spend on you. But it's not like I'm buying a two-hundred-million-dollar yacht."

She walks to the front, sliding her finger along the emblem. "I've always wanted to go on a yacht."

Tipping my head, I smirk. "Random but noted. As for the vehicle, it's a Volvo, babe. Safest in its class. The inventor of the seat belt. Airbags all around to protect the kids and you." I catch her smiling. She's warming up to the idea. "I got a car that I thought you would like and fits what you would look for in value and reliability. But if you'd like something else, choose whatever you want sensible or impractical. I want you to have what you want."

"I do like it. It's pretty in this blue. Reminds me of your eyes." If she'd let me spoil her rotten, I would.

"I thought you'd like it." I open the driver's door. "Get in. I want to show you the best part."

She doesn't bother coming around to the driver's seat. She opens the passenger door and slips onto the leather.

"The interior color is called camel, not beige." *No beige for my babe.* I ease in carefully, not to irritate my shoulder, and ask, "Notice anything?"

The smile splits her cheeks as soon as she sees it and a giggle bursts free. Reaching toward the headrest, she runs her fingertips over the design. "You did not."

"I did."

Angling for a better look, she says, "Why do I like it so much?"

"I know, right?" She pulls her phone out and takes a photo of her initials embroidered on the seat. I kept it classy for her, so the thread is camel-colored as well. "CMF," I say, "Catalina Marie Faris. Or Farin if you prefer. Works both ways."

She replies, "Tomato."

"Tamahto."

"I love it, Shane. It's beautiful and it will make the commute a lot easier and more comfortable. Thank you." Checking the back seat, she adds, "And it fits two car seats."

I'm about to move to surprise number two when my brain catches up. "Wait . . . what?"

"Just in case." She shrugs. "Twins do run in the family."

"Talk about expensive."

She leans over to give me a kiss. "It's only money. I need you to remember that."

"Now it's no object," I reply sarcastically.

She laughs.

Suddenly, I'm nervous. I shouldn't be. We're together. We're happy. We're having a baby together. "I should have given you this a long time ago."

"The car? You didn't need to worry about—"

"Not the car." *Why is this so nerve-wracking?* "There's something for you in the glove box."

She pushes against it with her fingertips, and it begins slowly openly. It's the reveal I was hoping for. "What is . . ." She's staring at the velvet ring box, dragging her palms down the front of her jeans.

I shouldn't but she seems to need the help. I reach over with my right arm and retrieve it. Opening the box, I say, "You deserve the universe, but I hope this ring will be a good substitute."

Tears fill her eyes as she reaches for it but hesitates. "It's too beautiful, Shane."

"I thought of you the moment I saw it. Luna helped. So if you don't—"

"Luna was in on this?" She wipes her eyes and rests her hand on her chest.

I'm prepared, so I pull tissues from the console. "I had it picked out, but this should be forever, so I didn't want to fuck it up. I showed it to her to get her opinion. She approved."

"I can imagine. I'm speechless." She clasps her hands together at her chest. "I really am."

"Four carats in total. Nothing too flashy."

She shoots a glare in my direction with an arched eyebrow in a pointed gesture. "Not flashy, huh?"

I shrug. "Luna told me to go for six."

Laughing, she says, "That sounds like Luna."

The diamond is a brilliant cushion cut situated on a platinum band. "Can I try it on you to see if you like it?"

"I like it in the box. I can't imagine it's going to be worse." I take it from the box and slip it on the ring finger of the hand she's holding out. Pulling back, she admires it in the sunlight drifting in through the open door.

I think she likes it, but I ask, "What do you think?"

"What do I think? God, Shane, it's the most beautiful ring I've ever seen." She lunges over the console, wrapping her arms gently around my neck as her mouth collides with mine when she kisses me. "I love it so much." Waggling her fingers to watch it sparkle, she adds, "When should we get married?"

SIX MONTHS LATER . . .

SHE JINXED US.

Although I'm probably a lot responsible for making twins with her.

"The babies want a burrito from El Fuego's Burrito Shack," she says, sending me out at nine at night to pick up food for a snack. I used to not even go out before midnight. Now I'm ready to stay in by seven. Life changes fast, and our priorities have shifted even quicker.

I should have bought stock in El Fuego's last July based on how much I now frequent it. I have a standing order ready to go. I'm not sure that's normal. But the babies get what the babies want.

Tossing the keys on the kitchen counter, I notice Cat asleep on the green couch that made it over from her place when the lease was up. The painting she did hangs proudly as the centerpiece of the living room. She brought more than color to my life. She brought meaning.

And soon two babies. I sit on the coffee table with the bag of food beside me. I always hate waking her up because she's tired when she gets home from work. But if I don't, she'll sleep until morning, and she needs to eat.

I lean down, kiss her temple, and whisper, "I love you."

Her eyes open, and a slow smile graces her face. "I love you, too." She sees the bag of food next to me, and asks, "For me?"

"Yep, for you and the babies." I stroke her cheek before standing. "Can I get you anything to drink?"

"Water is good. Shane?" I turn back to see her holding her hand out. "Can you help sit me up?"

"Of course," I say. Sitting down, I wrap my arm around her to help her shift and find a comfortable spot.

"Thanks. Have I mentioned today that I miss my waist?"

Chuckling, I reply, "Not today."

"I love these babies dearly, but I did not foresee this," she says, widening her arms, "situation happening." She clicks on the remote. "Of course twins weren't on my radar either, so there is that."

I'm not sure if she's looking for an apology or someone to listen. I do both because it's not about me. This gorgeous woman is having my babies. The least I can do is lend an ear. "The Faris genes are strong." Not quite an apology, but she gets me.

I set a glass of water next to her and hand her the bag. "I'm going to the studio to play for a while. I'm working out a new rhythm I want to bring to the next album."

"I'll be fine. Don't worry."

"Text me if you need anything. Soundproof room. I won't hear you otherwise."

Sweating and exhausting my muscles, I hit as hard as I can on this new custom drum kit. Ergonomic and fucking loud. It's fantastic. I can play longer and intend to be in the best shape of my life for the tour next fall.

The door catches my eyes when it opens, so I park my sticks on top of the rim. Cat peeks in and then enters, belly first, my beautiful girl. "It's after midnight."

"Did I keep you up?"

"No. I just miss you. I fell asleep but woke up, and you hadn't come to bed."

Picking up my sticks, I tap lightly, then spin them between my fingers. "I've been hitting the shit out of these drums. I like them. They're tight and loud. They remind me of you."

"I'm going to take that as the compliment it was intended to be." She crosses her arms over her chest and leans against the doorframe. "Talk to me. What's on your mind?"

"What's the plan after the babies come?"

"Plan sounds monumental right now."

I drop the sticks in the pouch and call it a night. Getting up, I cross the room and lean against the door in front of her. "What's your plan?"

We've talked about this a few times, keeping things light and skirting the real issues. I'm not generally one to make a lot of "plans," but I think we need to. She's rubbing off on me.

She takes my hand and leads me into our bathroom, knowing me well enough to know that's what's next for me. "I love my job."

"I know. I want to support you however I can, but we have two babies coming soon. We need to have people in place if we're hiring one or two someones." I reach in and start the shower.

Sitting on a chair in front of the mirror, she says, "I love my job, but I want to be home with them. If I were to spend money, I'd spend it on time raising the babies."

I go to her, kneeling in front of my goddess. "When I'm not on tour, I'll be here with you, or you can work part-time. We can do anything that you want. I just think we need to plan for that."

"I'll think about it, okay?" Kissing her forehead, I then rise to my full height. "I'm going to take a shower, and then I'm going to make you feel so good that you'll—"

"Scream your name?"

"It's an excellent start."

She crinkles her nose. "It's more of an ending, but I'll give you credit where it's due. Your talents extend way beyond the stage. You should probably come with a warning."

"I thought everyone already knew what they say about drummers?"

She's already smiling. No one else would put up with my shit like she does. "What do they say?" She humors me.

"Drummers hit it harder."

Rubbing her stomach, she says, "I have the evidence to prove it."

"Guilty as charged."

Why am I staying up late when I have this beauty to go to bed with every night?

I'm a lucky fucking bastard.

39

Cate

THREE MONTHS LATER...

"I CAN'T BELIEVE the babies are almost here." Maggie sits beside me, handing me another baby shower gift and then rubbing my belly like a genie in a bottle.

"I know. The pregnancy has flown by." I glance at Shane, my love and greatest support, watching a few feet behind the circle of retirees surrounding me. I'm sure he could argue this has been the longest nine months of his life. He smiles, evoking mine. Of course, he's been having me smile pretty much since the day we met, so it's nothing new. I still never take this life for granted.

If I know one thing, these babies were meant to be just like me and Shane.

And I can now find the humor in how we rushed around from the mountains to LA to make sure I got my pill only to end up in the one percent fail rate. We see it as a win.

Laird keeps Shane company since Poppy catered the food and assigned him setup duties. It's been entertaining to watch those two famous musicians taking on the jobs needed to be accomplished so I could celebrate with my favorite patients.

They've done everything without complaint. I think Shane likes the normalcy of it. Here, he's not Shane Faris, drummer of Faris Wheel. Not the sexiest man alive, though he is to me. Here at Parkdale, he's Nurse Cate's special beau. He once told me it was his favorite role until we became husband and wife.

Luna waves at me, then returns to a conversation Maggie's grandson struck up with her. He happens to be in town from Germany, where he's stationed. He's handsome like Maggie's Henry. She showed us a photo. Both have dark hair and striking brown eyes. Edward is coming in tall at six-three, and as Luna puts it, "Fills out a uniform nicely."

She'll eat him alive, and it will be the best time of his life.

Poppy bends down next to me. "You look stunning in that dress. Emerald green is your color."

"Thank you. I'm huge now so I went with silky drape-like material."

"It's fantastic." Looking at the cup in my hand. "Do you need a refill?"

Checking my cup of water, I reply, "No, I'm good." I catch her before she runs off again. "Thank you for doing all this."

She hugs me. "I'm happy to use my skills as a chef here and there."

Shifting in the chair, I whisper, "Can I ask you something about your job and the twins?"

"Sure." She runs her hand along the sides of her hair,

feeling for strays that have loosened in the bun. "What would you like to know?"

"I love working. I love my job." I glance around as if it's obvious since this is where I wanted to have an extra party to celebrate with my retirees. "Did you quit or put things on hold while they're babies?"

"Oh, um." I catch the shared look exchanged between her and Laird. He looks at her like she is his world. And she smiles just looking at him. "I wanted to raise the babies. I liked my job, but I was barely back into my career after an accident when I met Laird. Again, you've heard the story. Amnesia. Night in Austin."

"It's unique."

"So is yours with Shane." I've been smiling so much lately that my cheeks hurt, but she manages to make me do it again. "Listen, Cate, you can work if you want to. We live very exceptional lives. We're given an opportunity to do what feeds our hearts, our souls, and our ambitions. My best friend, Marina, didn't give up her acting career. She's an amazing mother. I chose to stay home. Having twins helped with that decision." She stands, rubbing my shoulder.

She's become a great friend because we have a lot in common. That we get to spend time together because of the family and band only makes it sweeter. "I've never been in a position where money wasn't at the forefront of my decisions."

"When it's removed from the equation, you'll know what you want to do when you have the babies. There is no losing scenario here. A happy mother is all they want. A happy and fulfilled wife is all Shane wants for you. He's very special, but you are, too."

"Thank you, Poppy." I have a lot to think about, but she made good points. The privilege of not having to decide right now is not lost on me. "Oh, and Luna knows Marina Westcott. We should all get together . . ." I rub my belly like I'm wishing for luck. "Long after the babies are here."

"We'll have a girls' night."

Daphne, Maggie's arch enemy by how she practically growls anytime she sees her, stands. "It's time to play pin the diaper on the baby. Everyone line up for their turn." She points at a poster stuck on the wall. It's very sweet that they went to all this trouble for me.

"She is such an attention whore."

"Maggie, that's not nice. And don't tell me you gave up on being nice. I see how helpful you are to the others."

"Well, don't let the secret out," she snaps, getting up to play the game.

I start to stand, but when a pain shoots through me, I sit down again. A deep breath is cut short when my stomach tightens. I angle to my left to take pressure off my side, but it doesn't relieve it.

Glancing at Shane, I find his eyes are already on mine as he comes toward me. "Hey there, Kitty Cat." He sits next to me, taking both my hands in his. "What's going on?"

"I—ow!" I grit my teeth and tighten my mouth. Angling away from the pain, I finally breathe through it. "I think I need to go to the hospital."

"Is something wrong?" he asks, helping me to my feet.

"No." I look at him. The comfort I need is found in his eyes as we take the next step into the unknown. "We're having the babies."

Shane

"I can't, Shane. I'm so tired."

Her hair is stuck to her forehead, her makeup worn off hours ago. Her cheeks are rosy from the hard labor she's been doing for the past five hours.

Holding her hand, I lean in and kiss her forehead, lingering to hide the tears threatening my eyes from seeing my love, my soul, my whole fucking heart breaking apart from the pain and exhaustion. "I know you're tired, but you can do this. Clara will join her big brother in this great world with two more pushes." I look back to see our son. An overwhelming need to take care of him keeps me determined to help Cat get through this.

Turning to see Luna holding Kick in her arms, Cat takes a breath, and says, "Okay." When they tell her to push, she squeezes my hand so tight and pushes with all her might while staring into my eyes. Two pushes, and our baby girl is new to the world.

Cat breaks down crying when she hears Clara's little cries. I tuck my head into the crook of her neck and kiss her. Again, and higher. Whispering in her ear, I say, "You did good, little Mama." I kiss her again. "You are so amazing."

Her hand comes around my neck, holding me to her. She turns, her lips brushing across mine, and through quiet sobs, she says, "You're a dad, babe."

The staff bustles around, and after they work with Cat on the next stage, I take a seat in the bedside recliner to hold my babies for the first time. One in each arm just feels natural, and it feels right.

"They're so perfect and so small." I kiss my daughter on the head and then my son. I don't think I can fully comprehend that those tiny humans are mine and Cat's to care for.

Scary and exciting, like the first time you get back on the stage in front of a live audience after being away for some time. The fear subsides, and I find my rhythm in the situation.

Cat looks over and smiles. It's weary but no less beautiful than she always is. "Luna, will you take a photo of them? I never want to forget this moment."

Luna steps in as her best friend and support. She was all these before I took the job from her. "Say cheesy," she says, snapping the photo before I can.

Carefully, I get up and move to the bed. "You ready, babe?"

"Yes," she says, reaching up with tears already slipping down her face. I settle Clara into one of her arms and her brother, Kick, into the other.

A nurse comes after me and fixes my errors. "How did you come up with the names?" she asks Cat. Cat glances at me and smiles. "I was named after Catalina Island, so I looked up something similar. Santa Clara popped up, and I fell in love with the name."

"It's pretty. And Kick? That's more unusual."

"A kick drum is part of the kit." I stroke Kick's head over his little cap. "I'm a professional drummer."

"That's exciting. Would I have heard of you?"

"No," I lie, not sure if she would have, but not wanting to get into it. Cat's the star of this show.

Cat says, "He was in the Sexiest Man Alive issue the past two years." She laughs, knowing I'm cringing inside.

"Oh." The nurse perks up. "I can see why." Touching Cat's hand, she says, "I need to check on other patients. Congrats on the babies." Looking at me, she adds, "And the sexiest man title." I level a look at Cat, but she knows I can't stay mad at her.

When the nurse leaves, I look at my wife. Fiancée just doesn't fit despite being the correct terminology. "She's going to think that's all I'm known for."

"I'm okay with that." She starts swaying her arms gently. *A natural.*

"We won Band of the Year, and you're prouder of something I technically had no part in creating—my looks."

"Your looks are really impressive." She laughs but then rests her hand on my chest. "So is your heart, and how you work so hard, how big you love, how great you kiss, how you'd do anything for me to see me smile."

My heart swells like a balloon in my chest. She says, "I'm not prouder that you're sexy. I'm proud of all your accomplishments. But the sexy part *is* a perk of the job."

"That job being your husband?" *I'm so ready to be married again.*

"Yes, I'm a very lucky girl." With her arms full, she whispers, "I've been thinking September for our ceremony."

I'd take her down to the courthouse tomorrow if she'd let me, but she deserves all the things we were robbed of the first time around. Even if it was technically not official, we've created a life as if it were. But I owe her the traditions she dreamed of as a little girl. "You sure you want to wait that long?"

"Four months will fly by." She lifts her head with puckered lips. I'll oblige her every want and desire. It's not like I don't benefit. "I promise."

40

Shane

I LET HER GO ONCE. *I won't make that mistake twice.*

This part of the beach was as close as I could remember to where we had the graduation bonfire years ago. We were fresh from the graduation ceremony and drinking beers. I don't remember anything about that night other than I kissed Cat Farin. And now, fourteen years later, I'm marrying her. *For real this time.*

With Luna holding Clara on the left and Laird holding Kick on the right, I walk up the aisle, stopping to kiss my mom and shake my dad's hand before he brings me in for a hug. "Proud of you, son."

I don't get to see them much, but it feels good they made the trip and got to meet their grandkids. "Thanks, Dad."

Kissing Kick's head and then Clara's, I stand beside Laird and wait for my bride to arrive. He says, "Hope you're prepared."

Prepared for what?

The music starts, drawing my eyes up the aisle to see

Tommy with my bride on his arm. "Fuck." I dip my head and squeeze my lids tight. I don't know why they're watering all of a sudden.

"Yep," Laird says, handing me a tissue. "It happens to the best of us. And you're the worst." He laughs under his breath.

"Fucker." I drop my head again and wipe my eyes before balling it up and shoving it in my pocket. Holding my head high, I don't want to miss a second of this beauty walking down the aisle to marry me.

I may be the king of the stage, but Catalina was always the queen of my heart.

Stepping forward, I take her hands and lean in to kiss her on the cheek. I've had children with this woman, but for some reason, we were told to keep it clean at the altar. We'll see.

She checks on each baby before taking my hands and standing before me as I stand before her.

The rules are followed. I make sure I do for Cat's sake.

I slip the platinum band around her finger. I didn't write vows. I wanted to speak from the heart, so I say, "We were meant for each other. I knew that the moment I laid eyes on you. But I was no good for you at eighteen. We would have broken up and never looked back. So I can't regret the time lost, the years I didn't get to love you. I can only make up for them. Every day. Every hour. Every minute. I promise to be the man who's earned his place in your life."

My gaze travels to her mouth and the lips I can't wait to kiss—this time as my wife. Officially. Looking into her eyes, I see the beginnings of her tears. I don't want her to cry, not over me. Not even if they're happy tears. I only want to see her smile. "I swear to love you with intention, fiercely protect you and our family, and to be there, to be present in our lives as we change and grow, and bloom in new directions. I will always be your biggest cheerleader and shine the spotlight on you whenever I have the chance. I've said it before, but I'm well aware that I'm the most fortunate man alive because I get to be called Nurse Cate's husband and the father of her kids." She sniffles, blinking away tears. "I love you from the depths of my soul, babe. Marrying you is the honor of my life. And it's just fucking sexy that I get to call you my wife."

She laughs, wiping under her eyes, but Kick starts to cry. I get it; no kid wants to hear his dad calling his mom sexy. Laird peels off to calm Kick back to sleep.

Cat slips the band on my finger. It's not confining like I expected. Holding my hands, she says, "I didn't dream of a better life. I had already created that on my own. I dreamed about having a family and being loved so completely that I wouldn't remember my life prior. And then destiny brought you into my life and already had us married." She takes a breath. "I could say I'm married to Shane Faris, and everyone would know who I'm talking about. Or I could say I married the love of my life, the man who held my hair through the early stages of pregnancy and my hand when I was upset. A man who went out of his way to make a plan because I adore them, made a weekend schedule of activities that I love, but also pushed me to be brave in new experiences. He looks at me like I saved him when I'm convinced he saved me. He's generous to a fault and . . ." She comes closer, and whispers, "Magical with his tongue."

Luna hoots, startling Clara, who starts crying. She also walks to the side to entertain the baby.

Cat continues, "He's a man who loves so big that he used to misplace it to unburden himself. That's not who he is with me. He's my heart, the father of my children, and my other half. But he's also my soulmate. Here's to the present, future, and eternity loving you."

I kiss her because I can't wait any longer. Sliding my hands over her shoulders and higher onto her neck, I kiss her because we don't have to be announced to know that were always meant to be. And then I dip her because it's what I read in her romance novels, and I want her to have that moment.

"HAVING EL FUEGO'S Burrito Shack cater the reception was a stroke of genius." Laird takes a big bite. "I have to admit, I never took you for the traditional type, cousin."

"They're traditions for a reason." I take a gulp of my beer and scan the deck of the restaurant we rented out. It was only a short walk from the ceremony, so it kept the wedding plan simple.

After we sat with the twins to feed them, my aunt and uncle took them home to put them to bed. They're great sleepers. Everyone calls us blessed. It's such an odd thing to say. We're blessed, even if they didn't. We have each other. Everything else is gravy.

Receptions are for other people to celebrate—cutting cake, first dance, and whatever else is required of me, I'll do for Cat. I just want my wife.

"Have you seen Cat?"

"She was with Luna and Maggie at the food truck last I saw them." He scowls, looking personally offended. "Damn, I'd forgotten how bad music had gotten. This is Top 100 shit."

I chuckle. "It's not an issue when we're on top." We both turn to see the DJ in the corner, rocking like he's listening to real music, like ours. *He's not.* This singer's balls haven't even dropped. "That's why we make our own music."

He tosses the trash in a bin nearby. "I'm off to find Poppy." Grabbing my shoulder, he says, "Congrats, man." He drags me in like the sap he is and pats my back. I humor him and knock my shoulder against his and pat him right back.

The crowd shifts as trays of desserts are brought out, giving me a view of Cat—stunning in a white dress with no straps, her hair pulled back since the ceremony because of the wind that's picked up, and wearing shoes with no heel because she intends to dance the night away. Other than when the twins were born, I've never seen her happier.

My chest tightens, so I scrub my palm over it. It doesn't ease it. It never does. Because it's not about pain but the beauty of living this life with her.

Come to think of it, she was really fucking happy the first time I showed up to her work. And she found some sick joy when we were leaving the divorce meeting. I've seen her happy more than anything else. The Grammys don't matter. That woman, our two kids . . . their happiness will be my greatest success.

I leave my beer on a table and cross the deck, ready to pull her into my arms once again and give her the fairy-tale ending. But then I look to her left. *Fuck.*

Rushing past guests, I slide my arm around her waist. "Hey, what are you guys talking about?"

She's barely five foot, if that. My gaze dips to Roberta when she says, "I was just telling her about the funny mixup..."

I shamelessly kiss my wife by sliding my hands over her ears and attacking her mouth. She swats me away. I don't blame her. "What are you doing, babe?"

"Kissing you."

I receive a pointed stare and then a smile contradicting it. "Did you forget we're in public?"

"Nope."

She starts laughing, running her hand down the front of my jacket. "Okay, I'm not sure what to do with that, but I guess it's something we need to discuss privately and not during our reception." Great, that went sideways. Now she thinks I'm into that when there's no fucking way anyone will ever see my wife naked.

I take my jacket off and wrap it around her shoulders. Pulling her against my side, I tuck her under my arm. "How long do you want to stay?"

Her hand covers mine, and she looks up at me. "Not long, I promise, and then I'll be ready."

Kissing her head, I say, "We can stay as long as you want."

She turns back to Roberta. "She was just telling me the most interesting story about their online beta program. Apparently, we were part of it. That's what caused the marriage mess."

"Is it a mess?" I ask, lowering my hand to get a good grasp of her fine ass. "I see it more as divine intervention."

Angling against me, she rubs her hand over my stomach, but she's not sneaky. I know she's copping a feel of my abs. She glances up at me. "You knew about the beta program?"

Fuck me.

My eyes dart to Roberta, who is cringing for me. Yeah, not the way I wanted to start my real marriage. Roberta shrugs. "I thought she knew."

"Knew what?" *My sweet girl.*

"There's really not much to tell. Does it matter now?"

"No, but I'd like to be in on the secret."

Roberta's joy gets the better of her. "It's so good to be here to witness you guys finally coming together. I knew you two were meant for each other, and now you're legally married."

I see the thoughts running through Cat's expression when she asks, "I thought we already were?"

"Officially married," Roberta says so cheerfully, and then backtracks when she sees Cat's face. "I must be confused." She turns. "Brownies." And then she's gone, leaving me stuck in this trap of lies all by myself.

My eyes dart to Cat, who appears to be muddling through this information to make it make sense. Facing me straight on, she asks, "Were we ever married?"

Best intentions or not, I kept it from her. But it was always going to come out.

"We are now. That's what matters." I move in to kiss her again because I can tell she's not mad and even holds me close by fisting my shirt. She is quiet, though. And that's unsettling. The last thing I want to do is upset her. That's what got me here, though.

"It's hard to be upset when it all worked out better than I could have dreamed. We have two beautiful babies, and we're married." When she looks up at me, she asks, "Do you have any other secrets? Now would be a great time to share."

"I bought the house."

"You bought what house?" She's not generally shocked anymore when I make big purchases. We consult each other anyway, but I know this one is different.

Pulling the key from my pocket, I hold it in my palm. "You deserved that house you lost."

Her head jerks back, surprise taking over. "Shane . . ."

"I took a chance."

Tears well in her eyes. Taking the key from me, she looks

back up just as a tear falls. "Why would you do that? It's too small for our family."

"It felt like the right thing to do. You worked hard to have something of your own. Now you do. Paid in full." She rests her forehead against me, staring at the key in her hand. "Make it an art studio where you can paint. You're so talented." I stroke her back several times, then hold her. "Fill the yard with gardens and those overflowing flower beds. Take a nap when you need a break from the house. Rent it out to make money on it. You can do whatever you want with it because it's yours."

"Is it mine when we didn't sign a prenup? I mean," she says, wrapping her arms around my middle and smiling up at me. "What's mine is yours, and what's yours is mine."

"What's mine is yours, but that house is in your name alone."

She rattles the keys in her hand again. "Thank you."

"You're welcome." I kiss her head.

Looking up at me again, she says, "We always call the marriage debacle a mess, but I don't see it that way anymore. I see it as destiny course correcting."

"I like that." When I lift her chin, those soulful eyes I fell in love with so long ago still make my heart beat hard in my chest, steadier and stronger than any drums ever could.

She says, "I think I'm ready."

"Yeah? What are you ready for?"

"To start this beautiful life. Let's go home."

Looking around the party, we'd be stuck for two hours saying goodbye if we made rounds. When I glance down at my wife by my side, I can tell she realizes the same. She asks, "Want to sneak out?"

I laugh, loving how much I've rubbed off on her. "That wasn't part of the plan."

"Sometimes life has other plans for us. Come on. I scoped out our escape path earlier in the day." Pulling me by the hand, she leads me to the steps that flow to the sand.

"So this was the plan all along?"

Shrugging, she laughs. "Tomato."

"Yeah, yeah, yeah."

We make it out without anyone noticing, and even into the Ferrari the valet pulled around. Hopping in, I'm tempted to squeal the tires in a fast getaway, but that would draw too much attention, so I drive the speed limit instead.

We make it a few lights down, cruising toward the highway entrance. Sitting at a stoplight, I rest my hand on her leg. "I love you." I feel so fucking happy. I didn't know life could be this good until Catalina Farin, now Faris, showed me by loving me.

"I love you, too." There's a pause, causing me to look over at her. "You know what I've been thinking about lately?"

The light turns green, so I start driving again. I bring her hand to my mouth and kiss it, then hold it to my chest. "What have you been thinking about lately?"

"What are the chances of having twins again?"

Slamming on my brakes in the middle of a busy street was not my best reaction. "I'm going to need you to hold that thought." I pull into the nearest shopping center, grateful we weren't hit. Parked between a grocery store and under the glowing sign of an In-N-Out Burger, I turn to her. "Are you pregnant?"

She takes my hand and pulls it to her stomach. "The babies are craving french fries."

The words hit quick, sinking into my thoughts. Pregnant. *Twins.* We haven't even had a honeymoon. Dropping my head forward, I scrub the inner corners of my eyes as they begin to water, too happy to give a shit about a fancy vacation.

I swallow down the emotions threatening to stick in my throat, then look at her, my stunning wife, the mother of my children, waiting so patiently for my reaction. I rest my palm on her stomach and rub gently. Leaning over the console, I kiss her, her lips the sweetest thing I ever tasted. Loving her is my greatest pleasure.

I nod, too overcome to say anything. I kiss her again and then along her jaw because I find comfort in our connection. Bending down, I kiss her stomach twice for the twins.

When I finally sit back, our fingers are woven together, our hold on each other solid. Looking at this incredible woman beside me, I say, "We should get the babies those french fries then."

Eliciting her smile is everything, the heavy sigh she releases as if she'd been holding her breath also gives me relief. She nods, her shoulders relaxing, and then asks, "And maybe a strawberry shake?"

I chuckle, shifting the car into drive. "We're definitely getting a strawberry shake."

Pulling her hand to my chest again, I smile like a fool pulling into the drive-through lane. When I glance over at her, she's smiling the same. *Partners in crime.* Forever. Eternity. Always.

What a wild ride we've been on. "And to think, we started with a glitch."

She laughs, but then it settles into a sweet smile. "No, babe. We started with a kiss."

EPILOGUE 1

Cate

Eighteen months later . . .

The envelope sat on the counter for three days. But it wasn't addressed to me, so I left it for Shane to open when he returned from Atlanta.

From the bathroom, I hear my name being called. "Babe?"

Speak of the devil.

I spit out the mouthwash and then run down the hall. Shane drops his bag on the floor when he sees me and opens his arms just as I spring into the air. When he catches me, his hold is tight, but his hands are quick to lower to my ass to give it a good squeeze as I attack his lips.

He pulls his mouth from mine, and asks, "Where are the kids?"

"Your parents, aunt, and uncle are watching them over at Poppy's for a few hours."

"How many hours?"

"Just enough time to reunite properly."

He's already moving us toward the kitchen. "That means I can fuck you anywhere I please." He sets me on the cold stone counter, the chill causing me to react and goose bumps to cover my legs. My nipples harden, but they're always on alert with him. *The little hussies.* I lean back on my hands, making them obvious.

Taking the bait, he teases me by pinching and then caressing them between his fingertips. Resting his hands on either side of me, he leans forward, nudging my chin with the bridge of his nose, then sliding it under my jaw as he takes a deep breath. He whispers, "Is that what you were waiting for, kitty Cat?"

He leans back to catch my eyes, and his gaze dips to the shirt I'm wearing, the one I stole from his closet. Seeing me in his clothes is one of his kinks. His discovery that I'm not wearing anything underneath is one of mine.

"I've waited hours for you."

"The plane was late taking off." Pulling my shirt over my head, he kisses my neck. He kneads my breasts within seconds of being revealed. "Did I tell you how much I missed you and these incredible tits?"

My breathing shallows, my body catching fire for him. Like it always does. Our passion burns deep. I hold his head to my chest as he teases with his tongue. My breath staggers, but I manage to say, "We hadn't gotten that far into the greeting." I tilt my head to the side, needing him to take me in ways that would make the angels blush. "How about you show me how much you missed me instead?"

He does, two times, leaving me lying across our counter, arms wide, wishing the stone was still cold enough to cool my heated body. Leaning over me once more, he kisses my mouth and then bends down to pull his jeans up. His clothes didn't fully come off before we were fucking like single people after drinks at the bar. We don't have the freedom to christen every surface like we used to, but we just made up for it.

His gaze slides to my right. "What's that?"

I know what he sees—the return address. The same envelope has plagued me for days. I never doubt our relationship, and I know when Shane said forever and eternity, he meant it. But what's in the damn envelope? "It's addressed to you, not me."

He doesn't bother with his shirt, leaving it where I tossed it, but he helps me to my feet and gives me a quick kiss, distracted by the envelope next to my head.

Ripping it open, he walks to the couch and sits down. It's a few seconds, but man, it feels like hours.

"What is it?" I ask, pulling the T-shirt down over my hips.

His eyes find mine above the legal letter in his hands. "This is the condition you requested at the divorce proceedings."

I pause at the counter, gripping the edge. "I forgot about that."

"Obviously, they did too. Until now." His eyes return to the letterhead of my attorney, the ones who originally typed it up to be kept on file at his lawyer's office. Every word is seemingly scrutinized by how he studies it.

It was a simple request, but I'm not oblivious to how it would have affected us and changed the course of our relationship back then. That is, if we had not reunited. Thank God, we did. I say, "I couldn't have predicted how things would turn out."

Running his hand over his hair, he shakes his head and sighs. "No." His eyes find mine, "How could we?" He glances at the letter once more, and asks, "Why didn't you just ask me?"

"We weren't together, so I thought you'd say no."

"Have you met me? I could never say no to you, babe." He stands, returning to me. "Legally, I'm required to do this since you completed the forty-eight hours."

"You make it sound like a sentence that made me serve time."

Slipping his arm around my waist, he pushes his hips against my middle. "You're serving time, alright. A life sentence stuck with me."

"That's no punishment. That's getting away with the crime." I run my fingers over the growing bulge in his jeans. "What do you say? Are you going to grant me my request, or do I need to contact the attorneys?"

"Trust me, sweetheart, sex in my Ferrari isn't a punishment. I'm just surprised we haven't done it in there already."

I giggle when he throws me over his shoulder and races toward the garage. And for the next two hours, he thoroughly defiles his most prized possession. *And it wasn't the Ferrari.*

EPILOGUE 2

Shane

"Hey, babe?" I stop in the doorway when I find her on the bed with all the kids asleep around her. She holds a finger to her mouth. I walk to the bed and whisper, "You need help out?"

She laughs, but it's quiet, making her shoulders rattle instead of hearing the beautiful sound. Reaching her hand out, she takes mine, and I lift her by the waist when she gets to her knees.

I don't put her down. I hold her to me like we used to do all the time. Her legs come around my middle, arms around my neck. She drops her head to my shoulder as I carry her out of the room.

We don't go far. The kids can't be left unsupervised, but I've wanted to do this for so long that it seems now was a good time. Now or never.

"We wrapped the album," I whisper, pressing her back to the wall just outside our bedroom.

"That's amazing," she murmurs against my lips. "I'm so proud of you."

My pride for her extends well above what I could ever do for the family. Though she doesn't see it this way. She believes this is her opportunity to give our kids what she never had in her own life. But I know what she gave up to be here for us—not just for the kids but also for me to chase my goals. So I'll make sure her wildest dreams come true.

"I wanted to give you something."

"Ooh, a gift?" She reaches below my belt. "Is it—"

"No," I reply with a low chuckle. I've created a monster. Catching her hand, I want this to be about her, not me. I reach into my back pocket and pull out a piece of paper. "Here, this is for you."

When I set her on her feet, she unfolds the paper. I didn't expect a gasp or a glare. "Tell me you did not buy a yacht, Shane Faris."

"Did you just use my full name like I'm in trouble?" I try to stifle the laugh that wants to erupt. Running my finger along her bottom lip, I ask, "Why is that so sexy coming from your mouth?"

She rolls her eyes. "Please tell me you didn't buy a yacht."

"I didn't buy a yacht, but I did book one for our honeymoon."

"A honeymoon?" Her whole tone changes, the gold of her eyes shining even in the dim hallway light. "What about the kids?"

"They'll be taken care of. It's only a few days. I didn't think we'd want to be gone long. My parents will watch them for two nights here, then my aunt and uncle are coming to stay at Laird's. They're going to be there with them. A big cousin sleepover." Our fingers fold together. "What do you say?"

"I always wanted to go on a yacht."

"I know. We'll have four nights just the two of us cruising the Hawaiian Islands."

Wrapping her arms around me again, she smiles, lighting up my life like she always does. "The kids will have the best time, but I can't wait to honeymoon with you."

This time, our kiss is gentle and slow. We take our time to savor the quiet moment alone.

"Daddy?"

With my arms around Cat, I turn to see Clara holding hands with Berkeley. "She peed."

Glancing at my wife, I say, "I'll take over. You mentioned wanting to finish a painting. Why don't you head over to your studio?"

"You sure?"

"Yep." I kiss her cheek, then go to my girls to kneel in front of them. "Did you go potty, Berkeley?"

She has dark hair like her mother's that lightens when she spends time outside in the sun, and her eyes are so much like Cat's it's like looking at her mini twin. But she giggles, and I know that devious look in her eyes is all mine. "Let's get you cleaned up." I pick her up under the arms and hold her out in front of me.

Just as I get Berkeley cleaned up and in fresh clothes, Kick comes to find me. "Arrow hit me in the head with the drumstick, Daddy."

I knew giving that little hellion a weapon was a mistake, but he's the only one who's taken to playing drums. And at two, he hits an impressive paradiddle. I snap Berkeley into my arms and rush into their playroom, converted from my old studio.

I remove the drumstick from Arrow's hand just before he lands another on Kick. Those blues fill with a fire, and he starts crying. I scratch the back of my neck and then get an idea. One loud clap gets all their attention. "Okay, guys, let's go to the park."

Rock star status. Fame. Millions in the bank. All my fuckups and sins. None of it matters to them. I'm a hero to my kids. I can't imagine anything better.

I march them down the hall just as Cat is about to slip into the garage. I keep them focused forward so we don't get tears because Mommy's leaving. The kids are digging through the fridge for juice boxes when I hear, "Hey, Faris?" I turn back to see the hero of my story put her hand over her heart, and say, "I love you."

Our eyes stay locked for a few seconds, exchanging everything we feel inside. "I know."

She's quick with the eye roll and smirk twisted to the side.

But before she leaves, I say, "Hey, Faris?" She smiles, genuine and so much like the girl from the bonfire that made me fall in love at eighteen.

Old enough to know that wasn't love. That was a crush. This is love. Real. Enduring, Soul deep. My chemistry changes to match hers in every stage of life. I say, "It's always been you, babe."

Want More?

You got it!
Flip the page for a Bonus Scene. *Happy Reading!*

BONUS SCENE

Shane – 18 Years Old

"I NEED TO PACK." Nikki looks around, making sure she won't miss any fun potentially springing from the sand and the gathering post-graduation crowd.

"It's a van. One suitcase, Nik," Laird cautions.

"Yeah. Yeah," she says, already walking off.

I laugh. "You know she's bringing more than one suitcase, right?"

He sighs. "I know."

"For every additional suitcase she brings, you lose more of your space. I'm not sacrificing mine for your sister."

"Such a traitor, Shane." He laughs and then drinks from the red Solo cup. "I'm going for a refill from the keg. Need another?"

"Yep."

Just as he turns, I hear him say, "Ladies, can I get you a drink?"

Giggles and more girls drooling over my cousin always happen when he's around.

"Hey, Shane," says a familiar lilt of a female voice.

I turn around to find Rachel Ferguson standing with a bottle of Crown Royale and cups in her hands. "Hey, Rach."

"We graduated. Yay!" She throws her arms around.

"Oh." I pat her back. "Yeah. Yay," I say with a nod. "We did. Congrats."

"I hear you're heading off on tour tomorrow?" She sways back and forth.

The girl's had a crush on me forever. I didn't act on it for the past four years. I'm not looking to start anything with her now. Pretty girl, but not that interesting. "It's a low-budget kind of thing. Some stops are booked, and some aren't. We'll just see how things go."

"I'm sure they'll go well. Faris Wheel is amazing. You're so good on the drums, too." Holding her hands up, she says, "Do you want a shot?"

Glancing at both chicks giggling and hanging on Laird's every breath at the keg, I think it's safe to assume he's not returning anytime soon. "Sure."

I hold the cups while she pours. She then taps her cup against mine, and says, "To greater things."

"To greater things." Just as I tip the cup back, I catch sight of a last chance I won't let pass me by. Not this time. Unlike Rachel, Catalina Farin was an anomaly who captivated me the moment she walked into homeroom last year. Now, with a few classes under our belts and some one-on-one time working on a project for our civics class, I might finally have the fucking nerve to tell her how I feel. The night before I'm leaving . . . yeah, our timing may be off, but life happens for a reason. "Hey, thanks for the shot, Rach. Catch you around."

"Yes, for sure." I'm already two steps away when she says,

"Do you want my number?" I keep walking. "Okay, next time. See you, Shane."

Mike Dodson jumps at the chance, hopping over to talk to her. Cat's polite enough to entertain his antics, but he won't keep her attention for long. He's an idiot who hits on every girl. It's a numbers game for him, and he'll eventually score. We all know the game he plays, though, and Cat, for sure, won't give him any leeway past casual conversation.

Not that she will for me either, but at least I have something that ties us together. Her eyes find mine over Mike's shoulder, and I swear the moonbeams shine inside for me. The smallest of smiles she fails to restrain crosses those pretty lips of hers just before she looks down.

She looks up again when I approach, coming around the obstacle Mike is and wrapping my arm around her shoulders. I look right at him, and say, "If you'll excuse us, my wife and I have business to discuss."

"Your *wife*?" he asks, his nose scrunched in disgust.

"Yes." I look at Cat and into her gorgeous eyes, cup her jaw to angle up, and then whisper, "My wife."

Her plush lips part as she stares into my eyes, her hand finding purchase against my side and then fisting my T-shirt to hold me close. "My husband," releases like a purr from her tongue.

Leaning down, I kiss her, savoring the taste of her sweetness against the bourbon lingering on my lips. A hurricane of thoughts and emotions that don't feel familiar spin deep inside me, my chest tightening as I hold her even closer until we're pressed together, and the rest of the world disappears.

The warmth of her body, the caress of her tongue when it meets mine . . . I feel protective over this girl as if she's mine. She's not, but maybe—

"Fuck, Faris. You can't leave me one girl? Between you and your cousin . . ." Our mouths part, but I hold her like she belongs tucked under my arm. Mike kicks up sand as he walks away, still mumbling. "I can't wait for you guys to hit the road and give the rest of us a chance."

Catching my breath, I turn back to Cat when a heavy breath escapes. She brushes her hair back, but the wind whips it between us. She releases me, which I fucking hate, and uses her hands to capture the long dark strands and wrap a small band around them. Looking back at me, she asks, "My wife?"

"We're married, aren't we?" I tease, reluctantly releasing her.

"I guess we'll always have our government class marriage tying us together." She laughs. "I hear you're leaving in the morning?"

Running a hand over my head, I catch a glimpse of Nikki finally working her way toward the parking lot. "Yeah." I return my gaze back to Cat, not wanting to lose this moment to what happens next. "We're rolling with the summer with no set timeframe. If we keep getting gigs, we'll keep going. You?"

"I'll be here working and helping my grandmother—"

"Shane?" I look up to see Laird waving me over. "Let's go."

Cat looks back from Laird, her shoulders dropping and the smile that felt like it shined only for me fading. "Guess you need to go."

"Yeah." I reach across the small divide and take hold of her fingers. Running my thumb over her soft skin, I say, "Fuck, I wish I didn't have to leave . . ." I'm not ready, not when I've finally kissed my dream girl. "We'll reconnect. I promise you that."

"One day." She smiles again. Visions of taking her out on a date come to mind. She looks down, but then her eyes find mine again, and she asks, "Do you always keep your promises, Shane Faris?"

Leaning down again, I close my eyes as I kiss her cheek, wanting to remember how she feels at this moment. I take in a deep inhale of her scented skin—sweet vanilla with a hint of orange—and whisper, "Always."

The gentlest nod is felt against my cheek.

I back away, her fingers slipping from mine, and take a sobering breath. "Another time—"

"Another place."

Stealing one last look at her, I memorize everything about her face—the sweet bow at the top of her lips, the way her chest rises for deeper breaths, her golden-brown eyes taking me in like it's the last time she'll see me.

Maybe it is.

Who knows what lies ahead for us.

But on that beach, next to a bonfire, I felt alive, all of life's possibilities, hope . . . I felt everything with Cat Farin.

I give her a wave and a smile before turning and catching up with Laird. "You're an asshole, you know that, cousin?"

He chuckles. "No point getting mixed up with someone you're leaving behind." Grabbing my shoulder, he squeezes. "Think of all the chicks we have ahead of us to meet."

"Yeah . . ." I stop, my feet digging deep in the sand.

Laird stops a few feet ahead of me and turns back. "What?"

"I'll meet you at the car."

I turn and start running. I don't care about girls on the road, groupies, or chicks I've yet to meet. *I care about Cat.* That's a first, so I refuse to ignore my feelings and let them slip into oblivion. But my feet slow and then I come to a stop.

Looking around, I can't find her—not by the bonfire, the water, or even hanging out with the random people scattered through the sand.

"Fuck," I groan. Maybe it's a sign. That's what Nikki would say.

What would I have said to her anyway? Hey, I'm the asshole who was too scared to shoot his shot before tonight, but here I am with my heart on my fucking sleeve hoping you'd take a chance on me.

So fucking ridiculous.

She'd be a fool to fall for that, even if it's true.

No . . . it's not our time, or she'd still be here. *Take the clue, Shane.* I'll look her up when I get back into La Jolla in a few months. If it's meant to be, it's meant to be.

I jog to the car where Laird's waiting behind the wheel. When I get in, he asks, "You ready to hit the road?"

I look back at the bonfire, our friends, and the graduating class with no sign of Cat anywhere to be seen. Life is changing and moving fast, but it's time to embrace it. Drumming on my legs, I give him a grin as we're off on our next adventure. "I'm ready."

Want Even More?

Subscribe to my newsletter and score bonus scenes from this book and others. Or use the QR code below.

When you receive the email, click the Bonus Scene button.

Happy Reading!

TURN *the page for a sneak into Never Have I Ever (Laird's story).*

FARIS WHEEL

If you enjoyed this book, you can read more of these rock stars' dreamy books, which bring the heat and heart to your reading experience.

Faris Wheel - the band:

Laird's book is called Never Have I Ever and is available on Amazon, Audible and in ebook, audio, hero paperback, special edition paperback and hardback. *Turn the page for a sneak peek.*

Nikki's book is called Tulsa (The Crow Brothers Series) and is available on Amazon, Audible and in ebook, audio, hero paperback.

NEVER HAVE I EVER

New York Times *Bestselling Author*
S.L. SCOTT

*There are no trigger warnings for this story. Visit my website for additional information. Please note this page contains spoilers.

PROLOGUE

"I'M IN LOVE."

Him, a famous rock star.

Me, a mere mortal witnessing greatness.

Hard abs and broad shoulders.

A guitar god in the flesh.

I've never been a groupie, but I'll be one for him.

Across a sea of people, his eyes meet mine.

Kismet.

Destiny.

Whatever we call it, it's real with him.

"What?" My best friend says, "The music is so loud."

She's got earplugs in and is still complaining. I laugh when leaning closer to her and yell, "Look at the guitarist on stage." Of course the song ends, and everyone is now staring at me, including her boyfriend. I hope the shade of red I'm turning is at least flattering. Just going with the mortification, I throw my arms out and shrug. "What? Like he's not perfect?"

A lady pressed to the railing in the front row yells, "Marry me, Laird!"

Laird.

I've never seen a more beautiful man in my life. That he's shirtless, a rock star, and plays amazing music just adds to his perfection. While the lead singer of Faris Wheel talks about the sweltering heat and all of us being here together in Austin, I'm still distracted by the guitarist.

Tall. Dark. So good looking it's hard to believe men who look like that even exist. I wish I had freshened up, but there was no time before the concert. So I sweat, beads rolling down my temples, and enjoy the view . . . I mean, the music.

Marina says, "He's just your type."

I take a sip of beer and then giggle. "He is." Before I let my imagination run wild, I turn to watch this glorious man perform. His gaze latches onto mine, I swear. He singles me out, mesmerizing me under his spell. Stunned to the spot, I'm unable to look away, my heart thundering in my chest and my throat going dry.

Bumping my side, Marina asks, "Is he staring at you?"

"God, I hope so."

When the song ends, he steps up to the microphone. Our eyes meet across the crowd filling the sold-out concert. With a killer smile that about knocks me on my ass, he points at me and says, "We've got a date with destiny, baby."

And then the drums kick in.

CHAPTER 1

Poppy Stanfield

"What are you craving?" Laird Faris runs the pad of his thumb over my bottom lip, his eyes trained on my mouth as if he's imagining what he can do with it. "I'll give you anything you want, baby."

Three o'clock in the morning is not the best time to make life-altering decisions. Fortunately, I know the answer. "You."

"I'm yours." *At least for tonight.*

Closing my eyes, I breathe him in and savor this moment deep in my lungs. It's not something I'll get to do tomorrow, so I take full advantage of the situation. I'm kissed, the sweet pressure turning firmer with each stroke of his tongue.

If I only get one night with this rock star, I'll deal with the consequences of my choices come morning.

He pulls away, his piercing blue eyes that could give the sky a run for its money meeting mine. A grin punctuated with the slightest of dimples digging into his cheeks holds pure amusement. "You look like you're concocting a plan I want to be a part of," he says, running the back of his hand along the side of my neck and leaving a wave of goose bumps in its path.

I squirm under the intensity of his stare as he allows his gaze to drift over my body, drinking me in like a man fresh from the desert despite already having me bare in bed for hours. My heart beats faster, and my breath quickens. I almost hate how easy it is for him to incite a reaction from me, but I love it as well.

"How much mine?" I enjoy teasing him, maybe too much, but that lady-killer smile gets me every time.

"I'm all in." The laughter I expect doesn't follow from him, but he situates himself between my legs, which feels like a win.

One small shift and we're back together again. It's tempting to dare myself to take the plunge, but I haven't lost all my senses . . . yet. "We need another condom."

Darkness flares in his eyes, widening his pupils. He shifts, exhaling a deep breath as he hops off the bed to locate the box we bought on the way to the Capitol Hotel. That trip was a blur of whims, from the matching tattoos we got earlier to stopping at a convenience store for condoms, bottles of water, and more beer. The necessities for a good time.

Our attraction was instant, our chemistry undeniable, and the freedom to do as we please recklessly exhilarating. I'd forgotten what unadulterated happiness felt like until I met the famous guitarist from the band Faris Wheel. *And smelled him.* I don't know what this man bathes in, but he's intoxicating.

My impatience gets the better of me, the need to feel him inside me again becoming too much. I kick the sheets to the foot of the bed and prop up on my elbows to inspire him, "I want you."

"Fuck it." He grabs the box and returns to me. I admire the perfection of his body—eight hard abs, shoulders that rival his reputation in grandeur, and muscular arms with colorful tattoos covering sections of both. I can't wait to touch him, to feel every hard hill of muscle, and get lost in the valleys of sensations this man creates. *Again.*

But it's his striking blue eyes that capture me most. The strong jaw covered in a few days' scruff and the lips that beckon mine to his have me foolishly imagining what it might be like if we could last more than one night.

He climbs onto the bed, taking center stage, ready for me. "Come here."

I move to straddle him, locking our gazes and pressing my palms to his chest before I lift all the way. He wastes no time positioning himself at my entrance. The frenzy from earlier is gone, but the heat between us remains. He reaches up to squeeze my breasts and tease my nipples with gentle flicks, bringing them to life, awakening my entire body. It's so tempting to slam down, take what I need, and chase the fireworks.

I don't because this feels too good to rush toward the ending. I go slow, lowering myself over him inch by glorious inch. The stretch, the burn, the overwhelming sensation of him filling me so completely.

"That's fucking perfect," he says, groaning as I rock on top of him.

Our bodies move together and against each other. I take, and I give. I lift and fall while he thrusts so hard I'm not sure I can last much longer. "*Laird.*" His name falls out of my mouth, wistful among the sounds of our bodies coming together and apart, and together again. I drag my nails over his chest, hitting the edge of the plastic covering his new permanent art, causing me to open my eyes and admire what we did earlier.

He breathes against my shoulder, then kisses me there. "That feel good, baby?"

"Don't stop. Please."

An untethered emotion dominates his expression as he shifts, meeting me with a thrust so hard that I gasp. His grasp tightens on my hip as I track his other hand between my breasts and down to my stomach. My breath quickens when the tips of his fingers land between my legs, but I hold it all together in anticipation.

He sits up, holding me close as I continue to rock, the ache for more consuming me. His fingers tease, coaxing me toward the edge while the bridge of his nose runs along the crest of my jaw as he inhales my very soul, swallowing me whole. "Breathe, Poppy." It's only a breeze across my heated skin, but it does wonders in bringing me back to him. "Breathe for me."

As if I needed permission. I exhale and then catch my breath as he pushes in again. "Oh God, yes." But my head spins, and the torturous pleasure between my legs over-powers my will to hold on any longer. "Oh God, Laird."

His mouth steals my next breath, his tongue finding refuge tangled with mine.

We kiss.

We thrust.

We fuck.

The push. The pull. The chase and the inevitable fall. Ripped from reality, I plunge into ecstasy, the bright lights rippling through every nerve ending until the tremoring ends.

Left unraveled, I become jelly in his arms.

But he's not finished yet...

A growl rumbles through his chest while hot breath coats the side of my neck. "You feel so good, baby. Too good," he groans, anchoring his body around mine as I grind to help him find his completion.

"*Laird.*"

"I'm sorry," he says before fucking me so hard a moan is pushed right through me.

I cling to him, my hands pressed to hot skin and taut muscle as I'm pummeled and then caught in the undertow of his orgasm. "So good," I spill through jagged breaths. I'm chasing the reward I crave, which hits quick this time.

Falling with me, he moans through gritted teeth, "Oh fuck."

Everything.

Everything.

He's everything.

My body trembles while wrapped around him in the blissful aftermath. Another breath is stolen as he punctuates his own finish, another "*Fucking perfection,*" following, making me grin this time.

Looking up at me, he smiles, and it matches the beautiful admiration reaching his eyes. "You're incredible, Poppy." He cups my face and kisses me once more before falling to the side with his arms going wide.

As if he hadn't just made me orgasm twice.

As if he didn't make me feel like the sexiest woman alive.

As if he can say my name like it's the only one to ever touch his lips and expect me to survive without him after that.

Tonight's been fun, incredible as he said, but I'd be a fool to fall for a rock star. I've been a fool before, but with Laird, I thought I knew what this was, and one night seemed to be understood. But something's changed over the course of the past hour . . .

I'm falling for him.

I can't let my emotions get twisted. I hate that this is one night, and then we go back to our regularly scheduled lives, but I know what we are. Laird is with me on a tour stop in Austin, but I'll be back in New York tomorrow, and he'll be in another city surrounded by other women.

Why does he have to be so talented? Making me feel like I'm not just another groupie seems to be his MO, yet I still fell for him. But I know the truth and can't let that get skewed.

"I love your tattoos," he whispers. "These were little surprises hidden for me to discover."

I smile, digging my fingers into his hair. "Sometimes I forget about them, and they're a surprise for me, too."

He chuckles. "I forget what half of mine are for."

"No great meaning behind them?"

"Some," he says, tapping his ribs. "The guitar on my side. It was my first. It's a rendering of the first guitar I ever had." He bends, kissing over the plastic of my new artwork that he designed. "This is my favorite on you."

I don't need to see it to know how I feel about the new tattoo. "That's my favorite, too."

"You didn't flinch once while he inked you."

I laugh, rubbing over the three others on my hip bone. "The knives hurt more."

He reaches over to trace the small tattoos usually hidden under my clothes, fully exposed to the man who now owns all of me. My breathing stumbles as if my last breath hangs in the balance. "Bold choice."

"What can I say? I earned every one of them."

"I have no idea what that means. But . . ." He lies back

and pulls me to him like I weigh nothing. "I want to learn everything about you and your bold choices."

Talking about being a personal chef for the wealthy isn't a turn-on for me, so I'm sure it won't be that impressive to him. "You have to leave."

Shock rattles his chiseled face, pulling his brows together. "You're kicking me out?"

"What? No." I push up on my elbow, confused by the accusation. "*Oh wait.* I meant you need to leave for your tour."

"Right." He exhales a laden breath. Draping his arm across his forehead, he looks at me out of the corner of his eye. "The plane leaves at ten in the morning."

The idea of not seeing him pierces my heart. Knowing the magic of being with Laird will be gone by daylight is unbearable. And I'll be alone in this hotel room.

I take a long, steadying breath, trying to ease the panic I'm feeling inside. "Is this where you let me down easy?" I thought I had more time before being faced with the consequences of my whims. *Guess not.* "It's okay." I reach over and rest my hand on his arm as if the contact will comfort me. "You don't have to worry about me. I won't give you trouble."

Propping up on his arm, he angles toward me. His eyes are missing the levity of the night. In its place is a somberness I feel in my bones. "What if I want the trouble? What if I want to worry about you?" I don't know what to say, but he does. "What if I already do?"

My heart clenches from the concern I spy in his eyes, but I force myself to stay strong. Lying to myself and pretending this isn't goodbye won't help in the long run. "You don't need to, Laird. Time will heal, and I'll get over it."

He runs the tips of his fingers over the plastic stuck to

my skin, careful to skirt the area. "Get over me? That's too bad."

"You know that's not what I meant." I can't allow hope to grow where it doesn't belong.

"Try as you like to forget this night ever happened, this tattoo will be a daily reminder that we once existed at the same time and place." A smile splits his cheek while a hint of gratification drifts across his face. "Do you ever play games, Poppy?"

My thoughts are still spiraling when the change of topic blindsides me.

"It's an easy one. I promise," he adds while caressing my cheek.

I'm conflicted about what to think or even believe, but I play along to see where he's going with this. "I'll bite." That elicits a dulcet hum in response. "What game?"

"Never have I ever."

"That's a drinking game."

"I'll go first." He appears so serious, and that makes me nervous. "Never have I ever been wholly captivated by a woman before."

Okay . . . he's in it to win it, shooting an arrow straight to my heart.

Laird's not playing for fun. *He's playing for keeps.*

Bending to kiss my ribs, he says, "Your turn."

I'm still distracted by his admission. What do I say to that? "Never have I ever been more attracted to someone than I am right now." The words tumble from my mouth as if they've been there all along. *Traitorous tongue.*

"Mmm," he hums, savoring my declaration, then hovering above the three tattoos before kissing each of them. "I like that."

"The tattoos or the confession?"

He smirks. "Both."

I smirk right back. "Your turn."

He slides against me until he reaches the corner of my mouth and kisses me again. "Never have I ever gotten a matching tattoo with anyone else."

He has so many tattoos, from lyrics scrawled over his shoulder to several guitars and other symbols I assume are from his life, but the one we share seems to matter so much to him.

I'm emboldened. "Never have I ever fallen so hard for someone." I lower my voice as if it makes a difference and add, "Before."

Lying back, he puts his head next to mine on the pillow and stares at the ceiling.

Oh no, did I take it too far?

The lengthening pause thickens the air with expectation. Our connection has been wild and beautiful, unparalleled to any I've experienced. *But am I on the verge of losing it all?*

"Never have I ever," he says, scrubbing a hand over his face as I wait with bated breath, "believed in destiny before now.'

It's easy to believe in such things as kismet with him. "Never have I ever either."

"I've got another one. Never have I ever asked a woman to go on tour with me."

The words are filled with hesitation . . . *and hope*. It's the latter that I cling to.

"You could fix that, you know." My heart thumps so loudly he might not hear me.

He grins cautiously. "You think?"

"It's worth a shot." What am I saying? *If he asks, will I go?*

I'm swallowed in his arms as he kisses the top of my head. "What would you say if I did?"

"Yes." Without a doubt in my head or heart.

He pulls me even closer, burying his face in my hair. "Poppy?" The charm of hearing him say my name is lost in the sound of regret.

I brace myself, my heart flip-flopping in my chest. "Yes?"

"I don't want you on tour with me."

Pushing away enough to see his face, I search his handsome features for any trace of what he's not telling me. "What do you want, Laird?"

Squeezing his eyes closed, he opens them, and the blue strikes like lightning. "You. I've never met anyone like you, never felt like this before—"

"Like what?" Would it be so wrong to believe we can make something from nothing? That one night could lead to something more meaningful?

Oh God, did I just fall in love with this man?

"I don't want to lose you."

Resting my hand on his cheek, I lean forward to kiss him. "I'm right here. I'm not going anywhere."

"Until morning. Then we're going to who knows where. I don't know where you live. I don't know where the tour is headed next. I just know I want to be with you wherever I end up."

And there it is. His heart on display.

Too happy to waste time with words, I kiss him. But I'm too giddy to contain myself. "First, tattoos, and now this. Next, you'll be hitting me with a marriage proposal." I laugh, and then indulge in another kiss.

But his lips don't move, the buzz I thought we were riding tempered. Did I misread him? "What's wrong?"

"Would it be so far-fetched? People have done crazier things," he says as if that makes this idea less ludicrous.

My jaw slacks, but then I ask, "Are you being for real right now? I know we've said a lot of things. We've been under the influence of beer and even each other in the past few hours, so if you misspoke or let that slip out—"

"I didn't know how to say it before, but it's how I feel." The conviction in his tone has me believing he's telling the truth. There's no way. *He can't be.*

"We just met." I laugh, trying to pretend I'm in on the joke, but it sounds as fake as they come. He doesn't even try to hide behind a lie. "You're not joking, are you? Give me something, Laird. Some clarification. Repeat what you said. Are you feeling alright?" I reach out to check the temperature of his forehead.

His chest rattles with laughter, though the sound doesn't escape him. He takes my hand between his, and the smile gives him away. "I don't have a fever, babe. I'm not drunk. I'm not even tired. I just know what I want."

"And that's me?" Still staring at him, I ask, "For eternity?"

"If you believe in that kind of thing, then I do too."

Dragging my other hand from his shoulder and down lower, I'm gentle when I place it over the new tattoo and smile when I feel his heart beating with the same conviction as his tone. Suddenly, the what-ifs infiltrate my thoughts . . .

What if he's right?

What if we're meant for more?

What if we're supposed to be together?

What if we're soulmates?

His hold on my hand makes me think I might never get it back. That it's my left supports the thought. "We have a few hours to sleep," he says. "I get on a plane in less than seven, though. I need to pack and clear out of my hotel room. Add in traffic, and that doesn't leave much time to get to the airport, but I want you with me, Poppy. I want you there as my fiancée. We can get married in Nashville or anywhere on the tour—even Paris. Just the two of us."

He exhales as if freed from the burden he was carrying and gives me the smile that got us here in the first place. Sincere and full of charisma. "I won't pressure you," he adds. "Just think about it, okay?"

The word fiancée floats around in my head, keeping me from formulating a reasonable answer. "Think about *marrying you*? Laird, it's so fast—"

"I know," he says without shame. "But I know what I feel. If you feel the same, meet me before I get on that plane. Tell me you'll consider my proposal."

He's been nothing but confidence and sexual prowess, going after what he wants without apology. I should expect nothing less when it comes to getting married, but he nods, allowing a rare shyness to come over his expression. The corners of his eyes soften, and his smile barely shapes his mouth. He's attractive no matter what, especially on stage, but I might prefer the man before me—the quieter one who wears his heart on his sleeve only for me.

"We'll get those pancakes you've been talking about since we left the tattoo shop," he says.

"Gingerbread?"

"Yeah. Magnolia Café." His breath deepens as sleep tries to control him, but he wraps his arm around me, holding me tight. "Meet me there at seven o'clock."

It would be irresponsible for me to even consider marrying him on a whim.

A tattoo is one thing.

Marriage is quite another.

We haven't even exchanged I love yous, though I could say it in all honesty.

"Be right back," he whispers and places a kiss on my shoulder. Slipping out of bed, he disappears into the bathroom, leaving me enough space in thought to wrap my head around what's happening.

Pros: My heart feels too big for my chest, and I've never felt safer than when held by him. I've not regretted one decision I've made since we met—not eating too much barbecue and getting drunk on beers, not having sex with him on the first date, not even the tattoo.

Cons: We barely know each other.

A responsible person could probably list a thousand more, but nothing else comes to mind at the moment. I care about him. I know that for a fact. *Enough to marry him?* If we were in Vegas, I would have already walked down the aisle.

Through the dark, I watch him when he returns but stops at the nightstand. He scribbles something on a piece of paper and then rips it from the pad. Crossing the room, he slips it into my bag.

I don't ask him about it, thinking we've said all we need to tonight. We have tomorrow to fill with more questions and details.

When he returns to bed, he silently wraps himself around me as I feign sleep. I memorize everything about him—his breath against my shoulder and the feel of his hard to my soft. I don't want to miss anything when faced with such a monumental decision.

I'll either win his heart or break it altogether.

I can't be rash. I need to be careful and think this through, but my heart wars with my head, leaving me more confused than ever. I close my eyes, hoping sleep gives the answers I need and a clearer head because I don't know what tomorrow will bring. But I know where to find him when I do.

CHAPTER 2

Laird Faris

"MORE COFFEE?"

I cover the mug with my hand and look up, spying the server's nametag—Emmie. "No, I'm good. Thanks." The pity in her eyes is easily seen in the sunshine flooding the diner. I really believed Poppy would show up.

I feel stupid for leaving a note telling her I love you. L.

Humiliated for putting myself out there in the first place. What was I thinking? *I wasn't.*

She's drop-dead gorgeous, witty, could hold her own against my bad reputation, and unpredictable. So fucking unpredictable that I read her all wrong.

Fuck.

I'm an idiot.

Not again, though. I'll never leave myself open to being humiliated again. Feelings are for fools. I knew better than to trust someone I barely knew. *Never again.*

Just as the server begins to walk away, I stupidly hold on

to one last thread of hope and ask, "Do you have another location?"

She shakes her head. "We used to have several around Austin, but only the original still stands." Her gaze drops briefly, and she adds, "I like your tattoos."

I glance down at my arms as if I could forget I had them. I can't, just like the new one I'm sporting on my chest will now haunt me for-fucking-ever. It's already a part of who I am, ready to torture me further. "Thanks."

The bell above the door chimes, directing me to look up like Pavlov's dog. Sitting here for over two hours has me well-trained. But like every other time, it's not who I want it to be.

Poppy could have told me if she changed her mind or needed more time to think things through. I would have waited even longer than I already have. We would date long distance or when the tour ended. I'd have waited however long she needed me to. *But to not show . . .*

I push away the plate of pancakes I ordered for her, leaving them untouched as the realization finally sinks in. *She's not coming.*

CONTINUE READING *Never Have I Ever on Amazon or in audio.*

YOU MIGHT ALSO ENJOY

Recommendations - Four books you'll enjoy reading after *Speak of the Devil* and *Never Have I Ever* and in addition to The Crow Brothers Series. These interconnected stand-alones will grab your heart and have you falling in love along with the characters.

**Turn the page to read a sample of When I Had You & Swear on My Life

Read in Kindle Unlimited and Listen in Audio

Swear on My Life - You met Harbor in Forgot to Say Goodbye. Now read the captivating and emotional journey that will break and heal your heart. Free in Kindle Unlimited.

Read in Kindle Unlimited and Listen in Audio

Never Saw You Coming - You met Loch in Forgot to Say Goodbye. Now is the time to jump into this unexpected amnesia journey that will have them discovering who they want to while figuring out the mysteries that surround them. Free in Kindle Unlimited.

Read in Kindle Unlimited and Listen in Audio

Forgot to Say Goodbye - You met Marina's brother Noah in When I Had You. Now you get to follow his journey from playboy to the journey that leads him where he never expected - right into being a dad. *Surprise!* And how the life you thought you needed isn't the one you're destined for. Free in Kindle Unlimited.

Read in Kindle Unlimited and Listen in Audio

When I Had You - You met Marina, the youngest Westcott sibling and only sister to those devilish brothers of hers, in all the previous books. Now it's her time to shine as an actress trying to stand out of the shadow of her family and their achievements while also dealing with the paparazzi buzzing about her personal life. She's on a collision course with a famous race car driver that has built his own bad reputation. This single dad is on a mission to redeem his legacy, but he never expected to meet the girl of his dreams . . . especially after their initial hate-cute. Free in Kindle Unlimited.

ACKNOWLEDGMENTS

Thank you so much to this incredible team:

Kenna Rey, Content Editor
Jenny Sims, Copy Editing, Editing4Indies
Kristen Johnson, Proofreader
Andrea Johnston, Beta Reading
Cover Design: RBA Designs
Photographer: Ren Saliba,
Back Image: Depositphotos
Audio Producer: Erin Spencer, One Night Stand Studios.
Narrators: Erin Mallon & Chris Brinkley
Candi Kane PR
Thank you to my amazing Super Stars and my awesome SL Scott Books Facebook members. To those who are not only peers but also friends. I adore you! Adriana, Andrea, Kerri, and Lynsey.

To my husband & sons, I love you more than the universe! Thank you for your forever support and love. Love you always. XOXOX

ABOUT THE AUTHOR

Suzie loves a great view of the ocean, spicy margaritas, and spending her free time with her family and sweet dog, Ollie.

New York Times and *USA Today* Bestselling Author, S.L. Scott, writes character driven, heart-racing suspense, and swoony romances that will leave you glued to the page. With stories ranging from witty beach reads to heart wrenching and heart healing, her stories are highly regarded as emotional, relatable, and captivating.

Her books are more than escapes for the voracious readers of today. They are journeys of the heart that always come with a happily ever after reward at the end.

Find her at: www.slscottauthor.com

Made in the USA
Columbia, SC
19 November 2024

46462958R00276